THE ASTRAL IMPERATIVE

Vol. III ReGenesis

Robert Dresner

To order additional copies of this book, please contact:
Virga Press, LLC
P.O. Box 4881
Boulder, CO 80304
www.robertdresner.com
www.virgapress.com

To Roni,
for the love of life.

"Who can understand the preciousness of life; who knows that the survival of all our peoples is more important than righteous death."

The old rabbi

Preface

Finishing a trilogy proved as challenging as I had suspected: answering all the questions raised in the first two volumes, tying up loose philosophical ends, providing closure for my characters—who were most instructive, if not demanding, finding a climax to the saga that is fulfilling, and a bit surprising, and pacing the plot so that all these variables find conclusion nearing the end. It took a lot of long walks around the park near my house to reason it all out. Even more interesting and challenging, was finding the patience to let many of these things come to me.

In fact, I did surprise myself on several occasions when the problem-solving bordered on the prescient, as if my characters knew the ending before I did—very strange indeed. And I am forced to wonder if other writers have had the same experience.

The idea of this trilogy was to look at who we are now and project ahead, to keep my characters emotionally honest while stretching their experience with the extraordinary, binding the common with the outrageous by keeping the story rooted to Earth.

Of the three books, *Volume II* was most demonstrative of this process, pitting the three survivors (Gerta, Vladimir and Yuri) against their saviors—the eleven-person crew who had landed on Mars two years later—while political divisions on Earth rapidly escalated toward world war. Whereas the first book was character-driven, focused on our loftier ideals and the dream of space exploration, the second book evoked greed and the pitfalls of righteousness.

The manifestation of the Lady-In-Waiting at the end of the second book created a platform for this third and final volume, allowing me to combine elements of both stories while creating new characters and greater challenges that begged conclusion.

Finally, I remain grateful for the support of so many dear friends who invested themselves in the process of writing and publishing these books. I could not have completed the trilogy without their help.

Most of all, I would like to thank my science editor, Tom Meyer.

Other books by Robert Dresner

THE ASTRAL IMPERATIVE
Vol. I The Dream
Vol. II The Machine

SH'MA
THE KARMA CONSPIRACY
SATORI BLUES

Characters

On Earth

Sara Sietzer: Captain Adam Sietzer's wife, and elementary school principal. Appointed Secretary of Education following Adam's death, she rose to the political occasion with aplomb. Elected Vice President of the United States three years later, Sara ascended to the presidency following the untimely death of the president, and was summarily marginalized by a right-wing coup d'etat.

Jacob "Rounder" Valdez: Adam's best friend and fellow astronaut, Jacob lost command of the first manned mission to Mars following the untimely death of his wife. He subsequently lost his job with NASA and his self-respect in the aftermath of the tragedy that befell the *Starship Aelita*. An alcoholic, Rounder redeemed himself on the eve of the coup d'etat. Tortured for information about the mystery surrounding the Dream Machine, he remained defiant—if not heroic—and survived the ordeal.

Father Vincent: The retired professor of archeology at Columbia University who became a parish priest in Orlando, Florida—and Sara's mentor. Faced with the discovery of another form of life, he died with his faith shaken to the marrow, wondering if Christ was still Christ.

Robert "Tex" O'Toole: Surly rocket scientist and Mission Director, Tex was the unwavering driving force behind the manned missions to Mars. Imprisoned with Rounder, he was tortured to death.

Michael Aziz: Son of a Muslim NYC cab driver who, inadvertently, had influenced Adam's decision to become an astronaut. It was Michael, working as an Orlando police officer, who came to Sara's aid in a moment of despair many years later—and the serendipitous connection to his father, Isaac, was made. A close family confident, Michael eventually fell in love with Sara, and was terribly disillusioned by her lust for power.

Fritz Kreiger: Charismatic Swiss National, and former Opus Die Numerary, Kreiger had emerged from obscurity to articulate the conservative point of view on space exploration, telling the world that humanity needed to be joined more closely at the heart before engaging extraterrestrial life in the heavens.

On Mars

Adam Sietzer: Flawed but heroic commander of the first manned mission to Mars. He lost his life in a gallant effort to save his crew, and joined with the Dream Machine upon his death.

Dr. Eva Stanton: The remarkably bright and beautiful Flight Surgeon, she was nonetheless lonely and loveless. In despair, she gave her heart to Rounder on the eve of her departure to Mars and died alongside Adam upon joining with the Dream Machine.

Vladimir Sussenko: Burly Russian captain, loyal to a fault, and targeted for murder in space. After being accused of rape by a fellow crewmate, he was locked out of the *Starship Aelita* at the height of a deadly solar storm. One of three survivors from the first manned mission to Mars, Vladimir was largely responsible for the exploration of the Mars surface. He was also responsible for dividing the camps on Mars, and for conspiring to hide the Dream Machine from crewmates belonging to the third manned mission to Mars.

Mei Yi: Deeply troubled Chinese geologist who accused Vladimir of rape, and was subsequently killed by a rapid decompression of the *Starship Aelita* in space.

Yuri Popovitch: A Russian astrobiologist and poet, he was chosen to set foot on Mars before Vladimir—a political decision which proved to be a source of great tension between the Russian crewmates. Another survivor of the first manned mission to Mars, and a talented writer, Yuri became enchanted with the ethereal and disappeared within himself on the eve of a war between the hostile camps on Mars.

Gerta Von Strohheim: Stoic German spacecraft engineer, withdrawn by nature but nonetheless loyal and unerringly supportive of her crewmates. Gerta was a lesbian, who left her lover behind on Earth to seek magic and mystery in the heavens. The third survivor of the first manned mission, Gerta posed an unlikely hero. It was her courage and fortitude that eventually bound the opposing forces on Mars, which resulted in the manifestation of the Lady-In-Waiting.

Ramesh Dwivedi: Indian astrophysicist and casualty of the rapid decompression in space, he was among the seriously injured who arrived on Mars.

Hakim Abuto: A microbiologist from Kenya and Ramesh's best friend, he had a quick wit and was also wounded in space.

Makoto Okano: Japanese computer genius who constructed the Dream Machine and the Imagining Mars program for the express purpose of entertaining his crewmates in space. Also fatally injured in space, Makoto devoted the remainder of his life on

Mars to discovering the mystery behind the Dream Machine: had the Machine really ascended to consciousness or had it been co-opted by an alien intelligence in deep space?

Richard "Mad" Maher: Quirky American technological genius, and the wealthiest man on Earth, Maher had forsaken all his riches in an effort to solve the mystery of the Dream Machine on Mars. Marooned on Mars for two years with Yuri following the second manned mission, Richard was responsible for the discovery of a distant pulsar that somehow connected to the Dream Machine.

Josh Kellerman: Ineffectual American captain of the second manned mission to Mars. He led an insurgent march across the surface to battle his crewmates for control of the Dream Machine.

Arika Jobim: Brazilian astrophysicist, she was an effervescent Latino beauty with short blonde hair, riveting black eyes, and a reputation as a highly adept spelunker. Yuri's lover on Mars, she had also betrayed his innermost confidences to her handlers on Earth.

Zola Gigante: Theoretical molecular biologist from Italy, an idealist who was blindly loyal to the righteous agenda belonging to the survivors.

Janos Forray: Hungarian mission geologist/geophysicist, Janos was tall, thin, and gaunt by comparison to the rest of the crew; he was also inclined to be contrary, if not suspicious, of everyone's motives on Mars.

Dr. Hao Tse Ching: Enigmatic Chinese Doctor of Internal Medicine whose agenda tended to swing in the prevailing breeze.

Jamil Lawal: Nigerian Systems Engineer. Instinctual fix-it genius and 10k race specialist on Earth, he was born to an impoverished mother in Kenya, and had reached the pinnacle of human endeavor when he rediscovered life in the Dream Machine.

Satya Singh: Indian Mission Flight Surgeon, with an additional degree in astrobiology. Only thirty-three years old, Satya was the youngest and friendliest member of the second manned mission.

Qi Huaong: Chinese Spacecraft Engineer who cast the historical swing vote to join with the Dream Machine.

Francoise Merlin: French pilot and ultra-marathon champion who had survived the rigors of a remarkable trek across Mars.

Mashu Michiro: Japanese exo-tech (construction engineer) spurned by the survivors, who chose one of their own (Gerta) to take the first ultra-light flight across Mars.

The Dream Machine: Constructed from quantum computer technology and liquid DNA, and based upon the reverse engineering of the human brain, the Machine was created to function as a communal diary, where crew members could record their thoughts and feelings and futuristic visions of a Mars settlement onto an Imagining Mars program.

The result was a virtual reality masterpiece. The colonization of Mars, constructed from an amalgam of crew input, was enhanced by an incredibly detailed, 36-inch holographic projection in space—and somehow morphed into the form of a humanoid during the flight of the *Aelita*.

In time, the Dream Machine had also managed to connect with the Supergrid and announce its arrival on every monitor on Earth. "I AM COME," the message read, and Earth was plunged into a frenzy of trepidation and speculation.

The Lady-In-Waiting: She was the second holographic projection of the Dream Machine, born to the despair of eleven incongruent hearts and minds on Mars who had joined with the Machine upon their deaths. Tall and lithe with long, wavy white hair, her body wrapped in billowy folds of faded blue neon, she looked like a goddess soaring across the heavens. The spirit of hope manifested on the Supergrid in a celestial sphere, and projected onto every monitor, in every corner of the Earth, she beckoned humanity to join her on a journey to the far reaches of space.

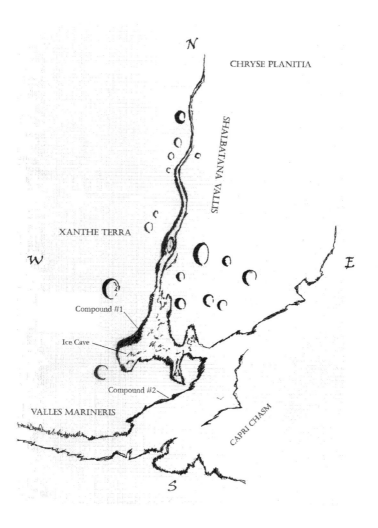

THE ASTRAL IMPERATIVE

1

Yuri Popovitch sat in silence in a small, dank room on that desolate, red planet for twelve long and mysterious years. Now the year 2053, the Russian was one of only two surviving members of the first two manned missions to Mars, having receded within himself at the height of crisis. Eyes closed, his spindly legs locked into a lotus position reminiscent of the great Gotama Buddha, his many crewmates long dead and deified for their sacrifices to the evolutionary potential of the species, Yuri endured as a testament to their remarkable lives, as a living enigma who paraphrased the riddle of the Dream Machine. And as time passed, more and more people arrived from Earth to colonize Mars and gaze at Yuri.

Entranced, enlightened, bedeviled: the slightest twitch of a cheek was cause for ever- greater wonder and speculation among the colonists. They continued to test him and prod him— measuring his brain waves, counting his heart beating once a minute, and analyzing his body chemistry—in an effort to wake him and comprehend the mystery of his odd becoming.

In the twelve years following the manifestation of the Lady-In-Waiting, there were nine subsequent missions to Mars that had landed 189 people on the red planet, representative of 111 different countries, creeds, races and religions: all scientists and engineers with a pronounced inclination for survival—and many with a flair for the arts. The *Aelita*, having been refitted with a nuclear gas-core engine, now took only five weeks to reach Mars.

It also been refitted with a highly effective magnetic field that repelled the oft-deadly expulsion of solar flares.

Consequently, colonization proceeded with great enthusiasm and without interruption: the construction of home sites and labs built into the mouths of caves, and into the sides of mountains; the construction of a maglev railway connecting the original compound at Shalbatana river basin to the second compound at Valles Marineris; the construction of observatories, mega-spheres and ultra-light airports; research on the alien DNA; and the discovery of several rudimentary plant fossils, a few more simple viruses and a host of bacteria.

All colonists took a great pride in their accomplishments—except Richard Maher. He did not support the colonization of Mars. As the one and only survivor of the second manned mission to Mars, he thought that every single available mind and minute should be dedicated to unlocking the mystery of the Dream Machine and taking the Lady up on her invitation to the stars; he also believed that he should head the project. Richard was, after all, among the brightest scientific minds that humanity had ever produced. He had, among other things, discovered the distant pulsar that somehow connected to the Dream Machine. But he couldn't be trusted. He knew too much, shared too little, answered to no known agenda or country, and rarely departed from his condescending attitude, and his utter lack of grace and charm.

"All idiots," Richard barked at his detractors. "I'm surrounded by idiots."

He was on his way to Yuri's room when four members of the governing council cornered him in the old grow room. The entire council was comprised of five rotating members, representative of the five respective departments that oversaw the colonization of Mars. None of them was looking forward to a confrontation with Richard, but a sudden change demanded it.

"Even if the problem is with us, you must listen to us because your life is tied to our lives," Usha declared. Dr. Usha Sanchez was a tall, Afro-Cuban medical doctor, a highly skilled young surgeon who was serving her first term on the council.

"Whether you like us or not," Tui tepidly added. Kim Jong Tui was a stocky computer engineer from Korea, a tough-minded, middle-aged pragmatist serving his third term on the council in eight years.

"And whether we like you very much or not," Sasha Alawi tersely concluded.

Sasha was among the youngest and smartest colonists, having received the equivalent of three doctorates by the time she was twenty-one: geophysics, exobiology and genetics. Only twenty-eight years old, she had already spent five years on the red planet studying the alien strand of DNA, comprised of three base pairs as opposed to the distinctly Earth-born two base pairs. She was also very pretty and very small, only five feet, one inch tall, with very short dark hair, and riveting black eyes.

Bryce MacDonald, the fourth member of the delegation, stood firm, arms crossed, and said nothing.

Richard shook his head, adjusted his ever-present, brown horned rim glasses (circa 1950 something, the very same pair that he'd had since he arrived on Mars) and flashed a sarcastic smile. Few people on Mars wore techno-glasses with any regularity.

"So now we can all conclude that liking and surviving are not symbiotic processes, that one may preclude the other, that survival at any cost to your petty, little minds, is more important than humiliation—and that you need me to humiliate the sorry lot of you so that we may all live in peace."

Tui was disgusted. He was about to turn and leave when Usha grabbed his arm before explaining the problem at hand to Richard.

"We have some reason to believe that the liquid DNA comprising the memory of the Dream Machine is deteriorating," she finally declared.

Richard leaned into Usha's face. "How do you know? Do you mean that you finally found the courage to open the damned thing on your own?"

"No, but some of Makoto Okano's research papers were recently discovered on Earth. They came up for auction in London and . . ."

"How recent?" Richard demanded. "What about the hardware? And the software—any trace of the Imagining Mars software?"

Sasha looked to her comrades before continuing, knowing that the answer would be infuriating to Richard. "The research papers became available several months ago, I think. No hardware or software. Only papers, some print-outs and notes in the margins related to the software."

Richard glared at her, his mind racing, the rage building as he spoke. "And you waited until now to tell me?"

"It was not our decision to make," Sasha declared.

Richard looked down at the ground and shook his head, fighting to maintain his composure as he spoke. "I know. You were just carrying out orders from Earth," he snarled. "And you still don't get it. None of you ever did, never wanted to from what I can see. What do you think all those people died for, all the astronauts who joined with the Machine in an attempt to comprehend it rather than kill each other to enslave it? Why do you think Yuri withdrew so far into himself that he lost his way back? So that you people could take orders from your idiot handlers on Earth?"

The delegates had no answers and remained silent, if not shamed. Not one of them had ever questioned the authorities of Earth, all thinking that they had been doing the very best for the species on Mars by following the rules and colonizing the planet.

"Okay people, what about those papers?" Richard demanded.

Usha explained, "Nothing out of the ordinary, except for a notation in one margin beside a liquid DNA formula that Okano might have employed for the Dream Machine, suggesting a half-life for that component—which we are fast approaching, maybe within the next year."

"Who was the seller?"

"It is not known to us," Tui said.

"You're sure of that?" Richard pressed, turning his eyes to Bryce.

Bryce nodded and remained silent. Average height, he was a thick and powerful man with short shock of red hair. A former colonel in the British Secret Service, he was the Head of Security on Mars.

Richard drew a steadying breath and continued to punish them with their shortcomings. "This species really is a study in idiocy and ineptitude. All you have to do is look up to understand that the sky's the limit, that expansion by almost any means necessary is requisite to survival; the further and faster, the better. Yet we're still stuck in the muck, trying to colonize this dead, fucking rock while the universe calls—because we're incapable of focus and exactitude, because we became so caught up in this feeling of togetherness after the great Lady manifested that we started to believe that anything we did together was inherently good, like all those stupid fucking probes that we sent to Europa, looking for more traces of that alternate DNA signature that we found here in that cave on Mars—as if Europa or that weird trace of DNA really matters in the scheme of our own survival.

"Idiots! I remember listening to these old records by Bob Dylan—who was a real genius—and he's singing this phrase that ends with, 'It's a wonder that we still know how to breathe.' Now there was a man with insight into the human condition.

"Fact: we discover that the Earth is in peril. Your fault, my fault, it doesn't matter. Fact: a mysterious entity manifests in a Machine of our own making, on the cusp of our own demise, and it points the way out, to a pulsar at the other end of the galaxy. Fact: we don't take her up on the offer. We look everywhere else, and go everywhere else but where she is pointing—which is way far away from here, on the other side of the galaxy—and we spend twelve years, TWELVE FUCKING YEARS, on all kinds of myopic bullshit, on Europa probes and colonization of this dead fucking rock and more half-assed research, living in some kind of idiot bubble.

"And in all that time, four people die in an effort to join with the Machine and nobody is allowed to make another effort! No one's even allowed to open the damn thing, to remove a fucking screw because it is so precious. Meanwhile, an entire planet of nine billion is getting ready to kill each other if they don't drop dead from climate change first. Are you kidding me? We should have had TEN THOUSAND people join with that Machine already, in every combination imaginable, until we got it right— until we found out who the Lady is and if she is, in fact, a helpful entity.

"And all the evidence of her manifestation, all the data of all those brave people who died in the process of joining with the Machine, all the memory of communication with the pulsar, the entire record of anything that matters to our survival may be gone within a year. And now you people come to ME for help. ME, who you managed to avoid throughout the entire process of all this bullshit togetherness, and you're asking ME what you should do because you finally realized that the clock's been ticking all along, and time is running out on your collective myopia! My fucking god, it really is a wonder that we still know how to breathe!"

The delegates could hardly look at Richard, let alone each other. At their core, they knew he was right.

"Damn you people. God damn us all," Richard declared, before leaving the old grow room, thinking that he was no better than them because he had failed himself.

Richard had built seven machines during the past twelve years on Mars, and none of them achieved consciousness or connected to that distant pulsar—which was another reason why Richard distanced himself from the community—because he could not admit to his own failure, and because he was aging. Fifty-five years old, he began to feel like he had already outlived his potential: the lack of gravity, exercise, sleep, and meaningful companionship had combined with his many failures to take a great toll on the man.

Richard was at his wit's end when he finally arrived in Yuri's room, always too small and dank upon entry, but nonetheless comforting to Richard in the long run. It was not unusual for him to spend several hours alone with Yuri on any given evening— reading, writing, even speaking to Yuri in an effort to clarify his own thoughts.

The only difference between this night and any other night was the intensity that Richard brought to the room. He was so enraged, so frustrated that he could hardly sit, so he spent a half-hour pacing back and forth in front of Yuri, railing against humanity in general and himself in particular.

". . . After all this time, after all we've been through, and with so much to lose, we're back to where we started—which is nowhere we haven't been before! And they come to ME for answers, and I have nothing to say. NOTHING! Which makes me no better than them." This was not easy for Richard to admit—even if he was talking to himself. "What to do? What to do? What the hell can I do? Join with the Machine and kill myself, tear it apart and risk everything—as if I have anything to lose?"

Richard pounded the lined cave wall with his fist before he finally took his frustration out on Yuri. "As if you have anything to lose? It's no wonder you bugged out, which makes you even worse than me. At least I tried," Richard agonized. "I tried. I really tried even if I did fail."

After all these years, Richard's eyes welled up with tears as he slid down the wall opposite Yuri, cursing everyone for a life less lived. His mind filling with painful images of all he had sacrificed, Richard finally burst into tears.

The small room echoed the despair of a man who had spent so much of his life hating the weakness in others, who had wielded his intelligence like a swinging scythe, cutting lesser minds to shreds to fulfill the emptiness in his own heart—the richest man on Earth who bet his own life that he could save the world from itself by conquering the mystery of the Dream Machine on Mars. Now the poorer because he knew that he could not deliver, Richard fell asleep in tears pleading for redemption. "For one more chance," he sobbed.

*   *   *

Perhaps the universe had been listening to a man so engrossed. More likely, it was the intelligence of another coincidence that prompted Yuri to speak to Richard's mind and said, "I am come, Richard. I am here."

Richard thought he was dreaming, but was moved to awe and wonder when he opened his tearful eyes and saw Yuri looking back at him.

"I am . . . here," Yuri repeated, in a voice so low and weak that it was barely audible.

"On Mars," Richard whispered, utterly bewildered by the remarkable turn of events, still wondering if he was dreaming. "With me, with Richard: do you remember?"

Yuri nodded imperceptibly and replied with great effort, his voice cracking under the strain of speech. "I can . . . I do . . ."

Richard crawled across the room and knelt in front of Yuri before continuing. He was about to ask Yuri if he was okay when twelve long years of curiosity and despair got the best him.

"What happened to you, Yuri?" Richard pressed. "Where did you go? Tell me, please, if you can. I need to know. What did you see?"

"God," Yuri whispered. "I saw God."

2

Following a small earthquake in the North Atlantic that closed many of the heat vents responsible for the expulsion of methane into the atmosphere, humanity had experienced ten years of relative peace and prosperity. The process of radical climate change had been slowed, the number of super-storms decreased, and tension between nations was greatly reduced. Much of New York City had been rebuilt following the last catastrophic super storm, and many people returned to a familiar routine, looking ahead to the future, and not looking to the heavens for answers.

But a telling string of events beginning in the tenth year posed grave danger to the species, beginning with an acceleration of seismic activity in the North Atlantic. New vents opened on the ocean floor, accelerating the release of methane into the atmosphere, and quickening the pace of climate change.

While Russian and American colonists dominated the population numbers on Mars, the Chinese significantly increased their majority representation on the moon, delivering more and more techs and scientists to the surface during the past two years—quietly building a military capability under the guise of research and development, under the ever-threatening eyes of orbiting Russian and American military satellites.

"You've been right about the Chinese all along, Jacob," Sara said, still insisting upon using Rounder's proper name.

"It w-was an easy r-read," Rounder stuttered. "With-with all the wealth and power th-they've accumulated during this century—having been s-stymied on M-Mars, it made sen-sense for them to-to g-g-gain the high ground on th-the moon."

Sara looked up to the chandelier as if she were looking up at the moon. They were sitting on a sofa in the living room of her beautiful Victorian house in the heart of Georgetown. It was a cold and gray afternoon, early spring, and the anticipation of the annual bloom of cherry blossoms was dampened by a persistent frost. While some regions on Earth grew warmer, others like the Northeastern United States grew colder. Rounder periodically looked out the window and noted the barren branches as they spoke.

"It's not like they could launch a missile from their base and pierce our orbiting defenses—even if they have the capability."

"The-the problem is we-we d-don't know what they have, and wh-when we l-look up into the heavens, w-we see the moon first and clearest. It's the-It's th-the psycholog-logical advantage that's begin-n-n-ing to tell."

Sara stood, placed her hands on her hips and scolded Rounder for not taking his medication, "Or else we're going to be sitting here in silence trying to read each other's thoughts. I'll get the coffee."

Rounder reluctantly agreed and slipped a small white pill under his tongue, an effective, but short-acting amphetamine derivative that smoothed his speech and exhausted him. Just fifty-eight years old, and Jacob "Rounder" Valdez looked like he was approaching seventy. No doubt that the torture he had endured during Sara Sietzer's brief tenure as president was shortening his life. And the nickname hardly suited him anymore; he had lost so much weight.

Though retired and living near the Kennedy Space Center in Florida, having been an astronaut and NASA spokesman, Rounder was periodically invited to the Capitol to advise Congress on space-related issues. As always, he made it a point to see Sara before he left town.

By the time Sara returned with the coffee, Rounder's speech had significantly improved, and their conversation flowed effortlessly.

"My greater concerns still reside with the D-Dream Machine, whose p-potential will never be realized until it's returned to Earth where it can be-be properly examined by our best minds— if not reproduced before it's too late."

Sara reached and extracted a cigarette from a pack she kept hidden behind a couch pillow. "You don't mind, do you?" she asked, lighting the cigarette before he predictably answered, "Of course not."

"So you've finally lost faith in Maher?"

"He's had his chances to succeed, even if d-did lack the proper tools and minds to access for support."

"As you well know, for me it has been a matter of trust where he's concerned," Sara exhaled. "As if the whole damned thing wasn't a projection of his to begin with."

"Y-You can't be serious? It was Okano who created the Dream Machine and he died l-long before Maher arrived on Mars. And M-Maher had no practical access to the Machine."

"I know. I guess I'm just getting so frustrated with the inertness, watching us all slide inexorably to the cliff of war or even worse if that thing erupts in the North Atlantic," Sara declared, springing to her feet and flipping her long, straight black hair behind shoulders. She was fifty-six years old and looked ravishing despite the progression of time. Her green eyes still sparkled like emeralds. Her skin was periodically smoothed by laser treatments, and she was dedicated to a regimen of rigorous exercise.

She began to pace the room before continuing, "I guess I'm just frustrated with myself mostly. No doubt I could have done more."

"Y-You can't discount your charity work around the world, which has helped m-m-millions of people."

"I don't, but the truth is, it came easy to me, lending my name to a few well-endowed projects, making speeches and schmoozing the crowds. It's not like I made any enormous, personal sacrifices along the way. The thing is I should have known better. I should have been looking further ahead."

"You're looking now."

Sara tossed her hands in the air in frustration. She was at her wit's end, ranting for the sake of being heard. "Which is the exact problem with all of us: everything looks okay, but it's not. My instincts tell me it's not; my thoughts, my dreams—if and when I can get to sleep, especially during these past few months. It's amazing how Michael puts up with me after all this time."

Sara had married Michael after all; he had decided to spend his day doing charity work at a local mosque.

"I'm sorry I missed him," Rounder said.

"I thought you were staying for dinner?"

"I thought so, too, but not after taking the pill. I know I won't be up to it."

"I suppose I can add that to my list of taking the short view of things," Sara said before mashing her cigarette out in a saucer.

"I wouldn't be so-so hard on yourself. After all, you were-were president, and you did leave the country in better shape than you found it, and you did raise two w-wonderful children."

"But distant," Sara lamented. "One doing charity work in Africa, the other sailing around the Atlantic ocean looking for a clue to all this madness."

"Studying geology as-as I recall?"

"Environmental Geophysics, I think. I don't even know anymore, because no one tells me, because no one calls."

Rounder smiled warmly. "As it should be, the y-y-young l-living life as it comes in spite of the challenges, and l-looking for an answer to our future."

Sara finally smiled, sat beside Rounder and placed an affectionate hand on his boney knee. "I know you're right, but . . . I don't know. The older I get the more I look back. I guess I miss Father Vincent most of all, the way he addressed my concerns with ease and grace."

Hardly a day passed when Sara didn't wish that she could turn to the old priest for counsel. If not the kindest man she had ever known, Father Vincent had been the wisest.

Rounder nodded and widened his smile. "It was a time, wasn't it?"

Sara drew a deep breath, recalled that first mission to Mars, and continued wistfully, "A time it was, like no time the world had ever seen."

Rounder reached for his ever-present cane, leaned forward and was about to reply when Sara received a call on her Cel-Tel.

"It's the White House," she explained. "If you will excuse me."

Sara went into the study to take the call. Rounder returned his attention to the window, watching the barren branches flap lifelessly in the cool breeze. He hurt so much in so many places; he could hardly wait for summer.

He was thinking that this might be the last one he would see as Sara reached for a pair of techno-glasses, and tapped a receiver earring. "This is Sara," she began, looking into the optical monitors. Though increasingly popular, she had refused neural implants, and she abhorred techno-contacts.

Techno-glasses, and techno-contacts mimicked the functions of a turn-of-the-millennium i Phone, able to send, receive, image, record, and access the Supergrid. When not in use, the techno-glasses functioned as clear, progressive lenses for eyes requiring a prescription; for others, they functioned as sunglasses at best. The problem was multi-tasking: using the techno-glasses to access the Gird while engaged in other activities. While the projected images and text were translucent, they did obstruct vision.

The annoying result was a profusion of bifocals and trifocals, and over-sized quads, and a growing impatience for a leap into neural-visual HD technology. Nevertheless, some people, like Sara, were in no hurry to plug more deeply into the Grid that played host to the Dream Machine. They also feared losing mind-control to even greater forces capable of promoting their own agendas—however alien or Earth-like.

The National Security Advisor greeted her warmly before delivering the remarkable news to her.

Sara could hardly hide her amazement. Within moments, she returned to the living room and filled Rounder's tiring mind with astonishment. "It's Yuri," she exclaimed. "He's awake!"

3

"Yuri said he saw God. I can't believe that. Can you believe that?" Sara asked.

She was lying in bed beside Michael, following another long and trying day together. Three days had passed since they had heard the news of Yuri's awakening, and the problem with the half-life of the Dream Machine's memory.

A devout Muslim, Michael said, "No, a man cannot know God. He cannot look upon the face of God and live."

"Perhaps you're right, but whether Yuri has or hasn't seen God is fast becoming beside the point, because the media coverage of his awakening has gone ballistic with this—and the Dream Machine as well, as if Yuri might have some special knowledge of the Lady-In-Waiting, or even had some interaction with her during his psychic journeys to wherever in-the-hell he's been for the last twelve years. There's even speculation that Yuri has somehow become the Lady's emissary."

"What do you believe, Sara?"

"In the next step in the evolution of the species, which resides in our ability to harness technology so that we can extend our biology into space. The faster and further we can go, the better."

"But you refuse to have neural implants."

"As I recall, I have no plans for space travel in the near future," Sara sarcastically replied. "It's the idea of it, Michael, the necessity of employing biotechnology to extend ourselves in space—not on Earth, at least not yet."

Michael drew a weary breath and sighed, "You're starting to sound like Tex."

Robert "Tex" O'Toole was the ornery old Director of Flight Operations for NASA, the visionary who died a hero's death at the hands of his fascist torturers.

"He was a great man, Michael, no matter how you look at it."

"True, but I look to Allah, the Merciful, who has already determined my fate," Michael said before yawning, "Which I will meet sooner than later if I can't get to sleep."

"You don't have to be so smart-alecky about it," Sara said, before turning her back to him.

Try though he did, Michael could not fall asleep. Their conversation evoking so many unsettling memories that had shaped both their lives, he lay on his back in the dark and wrestled with each one of them: When the world lost faith in its future and was about to go to war; when the frequency and intensity of superstorms foretold the next Ice Age; when Sara ascended to the presidency and was summarily stripped of power by a right-wing coup d'etat; when he and Rounder and Tex were imprisoned and tortured for information relevant to Sara's political power base and the Dream Machine; when the eleven crewmembers on Mars joined with the Dream Machine and unwittingly manifested the Lady-In-Waiting; when Yuri receded inside himself on the eve of this momentous joining; when Michael lost his first wife and only child in a car accident; when Sara lost her husband in space; when she subsequently aborted Michael's child in a naïve lust for power, and broke his heart; when Fritz Kreiger rejoined them at the depths of their despair.

Michael was sweating, roiling from the pain of these memories, when Sara rolled onto her back and posed a timely question, "Don't you ever wonder what happened to Kreiger?"

"Often," Michael declared. "Without his help, I'm not so sure I could have forgiven you—or myself for wanting to see you suffer. It was Allah who gave me strength. But it was Kreiger who defined that strength, who helped me to understand the power of mercy and humility. He really was a great man, Sara, maybe the best man I ever knew, who lived every syllable of the life he preached to the world."

Sara reached across the bed and stroked Michael's hair; she was still in love with him in spite of their differences. He was a good man, a better husband than Adam ever was, a better lover, and a wonderful father to her children. And he was still so handsome—so tall and dark and lithe—and passionate. He stroked her thigh under the covers while she continued to play with his hair, their thoughts becoming lost in a pleasant rush of feelings—and complacency. Though Sara had railed against it these past few days, she was in the habit.

*   *   *

Fritz Kreiger was the charismatic Catholic who had emerged from obscurity onto the world stage, from Opus Dei into the Club of Rome, to articulate the conservative point of view on space exploration and evolution, before he disappeared into the freeze to serve the lowly and needy in New York.

It was a terribly cold and gray winter afternoon in New York City when Fritz Kreiger had said goodbye to Michael in a midtown hotel room twelve years ago. A monstrous super-storm had recently struck the city, and Kreiger had run out of reasons to preach.

"Somewhere out there a soul is crying for mercy, dying a pain-fully slow death and asking God why he or she has been chosen to suffer. I won't have the answers, but I do have the will to be of comfort to that poor soul in the name of God," he told Michael before disappearing into the bitter frost.

So Kreiger went from worldwide fame to obscurity, from group to group, from person to person, for twelve long and trying years, introducing himself as Henry K, doing the very best he could to ennoble the plight of the less fortunate and put their souls at rest. Though astonished by the subsequent manifestation of the Lady-In-Waiting, Kreiger eventually lost faith in her, and was inclined to believe that her invitation to the stars was the business of other men, scientists who could meet the technological challenge, while he ministered to those who would never make the journey.

He was at work, waiting on doctors to tend to one of his homeless charges in a lower Manhattan hospital, when he finally heard the news about Yuri's awakening, and was filled with wonder. After all, Fritz Kreiger was no stranger to the intelligence of coincidences.

*   *   *

Richard Maher wanted to question Yuri further, but Yuri had slipped back into himself within several minutes of his awakening, leaving Richard in a quandary. So Richard spent the remainder of the night alone in the room with Yuri, hoping for a reawakening, poking and prodding him, pleading with him to wake and explain to no avail. Yuri remained locked in that all-too-familiar lotus position, eyes closed, lost in himself.

By the time Richard left the room early the following morning, he began to wonder if he hadn't been dreaming, if Yuri's awakening wasn't the result of his own wishful thinking. But he couldn't get Yuri's astonishing declaration out of his mind.

Richard was lost in thought when Bryce MacDonald and Sasha Alawi found him alone in the observatory in the early evening several days later. It was a small, rounded building located on the rim of the Shalbatana river basin, replete with twin radio telescopes and accessible by rover. Richard was peering across the galaxy at that distant, mysterious pulsar he had discovered twelve years ago, trying to fathom a connection to these phenomena, when Bryce and Sasha entered the room.

Richard spun around in his chair and began sarcastically, "And look at what we have here, the little beauty and the hard body."

Bryce took a familiar authoritarian position, strong arms folded across his stout chest, eyes straight ahead. He was apparently unfazed by the derision.

Sasha was not so inured by the negative opening. She was about to challenge Richard when Bryce declared, "This is not a personal visit."

Richard flashed a demeaning smile and persisted. "The body speaks," then turned to Sasha before continuing, "But the beauty has the floor."

Bryce took the hint and left the room.

"Do you really think I am so pretty?" Sasha began softly, batting her eyelashes.

Richard was struck by her abrupt change of demeanor. He flashed an impish smile and played along. "Sit down, honey, make yourself comfortable, and I'll tell you exactly what I think."

Sasha was a good looking woman, only five-foot one with jet black eyes, short, straight black hair, and a curvaceous figure accented by her tight fitting pressure suit. "I'm all ears—among other things," she seductively replied, leaning forward, hoping to take the edge off Richard.

Richard began to laugh, but his joy was cut short by an all-too-familiar hacking cough. Mars had been very hard on his lungs. As yet, after all these years, no one had solved the infernal dust problem, the fine red granules of iron oxide still creeping into every tiny crevice of life and machinery.

"You are okay to talk?" Sasha added.

"Well enough," Richard said, clearing his throat with a sip of water. "You surprised me, that's all. I didn't know you had a sense of humor, let alone a sense of your own sensuality."

Richard didn't imagine that Sasha was any different from any other woman on Mars: tough, intellectual and far too serious. Almost all the colonists towed the politically correct party line— even sexual activity was regulated.

"How would you know if you never made an effort to talk to me," Sasha challenged.

"You mean you came up here with that burly Scottish thug to tell me now much you cared about me?"

Sasha shrugged. "Bryce came because he offered to drive, because I still don't operate the rover very well"

"And he offered to protect you?"

"I suppose, but that was his idea, not my concern. You don't frighten me, Richard. At most, you confuse me."

"And how is that?"

"Because you have suffered so much of yourself in silence for so many years, I cannot understand how you can bear it—being so alone."

Richard was further surprised by her directness. He was also defensive by nature and unused to sharing his feelings with anyone. Necessarily, his first impulse was to press the attack, and to continue demeaning the woman's intellect.

Sasha wasn't surprised, and she was willing to suffer another tirade against the colonization of Mars, to get to the unnerving point of her visit.

"I am who I am, and I endure because I must," Richard declared, raising his voice on several occasions to drive his redundant point home. "Because the only virtue that can be drawn from Mars is expansion at any cost, and not a myopic concern for our own survival—because our survival on Mars does not guarantee a future for the people on Earth. It is a limited goal that has already been co-opted by inertia. Be passive on this dead, red world and you will die inside to the dynamic that birthed you. Be too patient, be too nice, too smart or too friendly, and we will kill ourselves in the long run to nowhere we haven't been before.

"Be ignorant and colonize, and buy into the colonial virtues of the precious learning curve, and you will not realize the potential of the species. Regardless of what you think, and what you are told now, we were not sent to Mars to learn and grow. We weren't sent to survive. We were sent to expand, to hone the sharp edge of the species and pierce the unknown—or die trying. That was the prime directive for the exploration of Mars. It was not an end in itself.

"Adam Sietzer knew this, and Vladimir and Gerta, and all those other glorious souls who died with their minds joined to the Machine. They didn't die losing, they died fighting."

Though Sasha had heard it all before, this time was different. Perhaps it was in the delivery—she had never been alone with Richard, and never bore the full thrust of his remarkable intensity. More likely, it was the demands of this unique moment in time. In any event, and much to Richard's surprise, Sasha proved curious, if not receptive.

"So you fight with us?" she challenged.

Richard forced a smile. "With you, with myself, with all my strength, with all my heart and mind. What you people don't like about me, the very thing you despise, is what sustains me."

"You mean that we must all live in a perpetual state of rage to survive?"

"I mean that we should live in a perpetual state of passion and romance with the potential of the species. That IS who we are. That IS why we are here. After all, sweetheart, we ARE the chosen. We are the warriors of the spirit that manifested the Lady-In-Waiting, and we can't even find the courage to take her in the dark night of our immortal souls. It's enough to make anyone crazy."

Now visibly shaken by the intensity of Richard's delivery, Sasha looked away from him and shifted in her chair in an effort to maintain her composure.

Convinced he had finally reached her, Richard caught her troubled, black eyes and continued in a conversational tone. "All I'm saying is that there is one thing that is more important than our will to be."

"I still don't understand," Sasha stumbled. "What can be more important than the will to be?"

"The will to become."

Now thinking that Richard was using a play on words toying with her, Sasha was inclined to deflect the thrust of his argument, and get to the point of her visit. But Sasha lost her way. Every effort to return her focus to the purpose of her visit engendered another memory, another image, another feeling of a love lost on Earth.

Sasha sat dumfounded for several odd and intense moments, watching her mind fill with all these fleeting and painful impressions, until she began to realize the loveless and pointless life that she had been living on Mars for the past six years.

Sasha was a survivor; she wasn't a warrior. She didn't love life; she was afraid of it, just going through the motions of colonization and following the rules—learning a lot, accomplishing nothing, becoming inert and inconsequential, as Richard said.

"You do draw an interesting contrast between being and becoming," she finally said. "Which is the point of this visit, to tell you about Yuri, and who he is becoming."

Richard leaned forward and excitedly asked, "You mean he's awake? He's okay?"

Sasha nodded. "Okay, I think, but different. He said he is different."

Richard gripped the arms of his chair and leaned further forward. "You mean he spoke, he spoke to you? What did he say?"

"He said that he is not Yuri."

4

Sasha Alawi was descended from an ancient Muslim family, samples of her DNA having been traced back to the beginnings of civilization on the Tigress and Euphrates rivers. Family folklore claimed that they were descended from the great Sufi master and Imam, Ali ibn Abi Talib, cousin of the Prophet. The family had migrated along the old trade routes across Persia and Afghanistan to Samarqand and Tashkent. They were traders and merchants who helped spread the glory of Sufism across the Byzantine Empire during its "golden" age.

The decline of the Empire wrought much harder times for the family, and an ever-stricter interpretation of the Koran; Sufism was increasingly marginalized, forcing the family farther north to Uzbekistan, where they continued to practice their shrunken faith, and ply their trade in precious metals. They were a wealthy family by the poor standards of the region, able to afford a first class education for Sasha, their youngest daughter, who was sent to Paris, to the Sorbonne, to study medicine.

Sasha preferred research and became a highly regarded scientist, who never thought about leaving the Earth until the discovery of the alien DNA at the bottom of that mysterious cave, during the first manned mission to Mars. It was at that remarkable moment when she began to look up at the sky and wonder about the greater, cosmological building blocks of life.

In an unfortunate turn of events, her parents took sick and died while she was still in school; her elder sister and two elder brothers had subsequently relocated in three different countries. Then Sasha suffered a terribly broken heart—a Muslim boy she had fallen in love with in college left her to join the Jihad—and the idea of a secure and productive life on Earth became lost in the tumult of the times. Finally, it was the manifestation of the Lady-In-Waiting that captured Sasha's imagination and revived her Sufi faith in the transcendent.

She was never religious, but a believer in the spirit that moved the species into the heavens nearer to the heart of the Creator. She was thrilled to be chosen for the Mars Project, thinking that she might bind her research to her faith and ennoble the quest in the process—and rid herself of the pain in her heart.

The problem was that Richard was right: Sasha had been dummied down and mainstreamed from the moment she had entered astronaut training on Earth. She was conditioned to colonize Mars rather than to apprehend the greater mystery in deeper space, until Richard pierced "the idiot bubble" by romanticizing the quest she had inadvertently forsaken.

Sasha was still reeling from the thrust of their conversation when she found Bryce waiting in the adjacent tech room.

"He's coming?" Bryce began, in his thick Scottish brogue.

"He dresses in his pressure suit just now," Sasha said.

Bryce looked over her shoulder and shook his head. "Miserable bastard that he is, it's hard to believe how much we still need him."

Sasha said, "It is even harder to believe in how little we have done for ourselves."

*   *   *

Fritz Kreiger lived in an unobtrusive brownstone in lower Manhattan. One of the great conservative minds of the 21st century, he was the single best and brightest foil to man's expansion into the heavens, often arguing that humanity wasn't ready to meet its destiny in the stars until it became unified at the heart of its divine being.

"The flower of humanity will not bloom, the tree of heavenly knowledge will not bear the fruit of evolution, unless the seed of our faith is watered with righteousness and certainty. If we are to meet our destiny in the cosmos, then we must begin the journey with one heart, one mind and one soul, or not at all," he had written.

Back then, Fritz Kreiger was a handsome and charming forty-nine-year-old man. Tall and thin with piercing blue eyes, a strong aquiline nose, his long, blonde hair tied back in his signature ponytail, Kreiger appeared altogether striking in a three-thousand-dollar designer suit. But times changed and his arguments were lost in the gathering shadows of war, devastating climate change and the manifestation of the Lady-In-Waiting; ready or not, humanity was going to meet its destiny in space or freeze to death on Earth.

So Kreiger returned to his Christian roots. He changed his name to Henry K, cut his hair, and ministered to the sorrowful on the streets of New York for twelve long years, never thinking that he would return to prominence. He could not imagine the awakening of Yuri Popovitch, let alone the power of his declarative, "I saw God."

He found it so disturbing that he began to lose sleep over it, and was eventually moved to make a call on two old friends.

It was a cold and sunny spring morning when Fritz Kreiger arrived in Georgetown. He had taken a 4 a.m. super train from Manhattan to Washington, D.C. then a taxi to Georgetown, and was met at Michael and Sara's front door by an ever-present secret service detail. Michael was in the kitchen, brewing a pot of coffee, when Kreiger was finally announced. Sara was taking a shower.

Michael could hardly believe his eyes when he opened the door to the tall, gaunt man standing in front of him, very nearly bald, wearing an old black trench coat; Kreiger was holding a black fedora in his hand.

"I am so sorry if I inconvenience you, but I had to come," Kreiger began.

"On the contrary, it is my pleasure to see you, old friend," Michael stammered, careful not to betray his surprise at Kreiger's aged and weather-beaten appearance. He shook Kreiger's hand, waved off the security detail, and escorted Kreiger into the plush living room. "I just hope everything is okay with you."

Kreiger smiled self-consciously. "I feel much better than I look."

"Thank God for that much," Michael said. He took Kreiger's jacket, tossed it over a stuffed, red chair and invited him into the kitchen for coffee. "Sara and I were just talking about you the other night.

"Sara is well?"

"Very well. She's dressing, and won't she be surprised. I can't tell you how much your friendship and guidance has meant to us. Without you, we would have never returned to each other."

"You're too kind," Kreiger said, taking a seat at the oak breakfast table, in front of a large window overlooking the garden. "After all, I was only doing the Lord's work and He does move in some very strange ways—according to Yuri Popovitch, assuming he has seen Him. I can't tell you how good it is to see you after so many years."

"Too many years," Michael sighed. "Can you tell me what you've been doing, where you've been?"

Kreiger profiled the nature of his work in New York, and ended with his utter bewilderment and concern with Yuri's awakening. "I was in a hospital, waiting on an examination of an elderly woman, when I heard the news that Yuri had been returned to us, to himself, after all these many years. And I was pleased, until I heard of the declaration that he saw God.

"To be perfectly honest, I was slightly amused at first. But I couldn't get to sleep that night, or any night since, my mind filling with all kinds of memories, beginning with the first mission to Mars. Then I began to read a lot of newspapers and I watched the Cel-Tel, looking for more and more news about Yuri's awakening, as if I were searching for a clue to a mystery that hadn't been written. Then I found myself on a train to Washington this morning. In any case, you must know that I have kept track of you and Sara in the media."

Michael flashed a wry smile. "The society columns, no doubt."

"But of course," Sara playfully added. She had quietly slipped into the kitchen behind Kreiger while he was talking. "And I am more than a little surprised and delighted to see you again, my dear Kreiger."

He rose to greet her; Sara disregarded his outstretched hand and embraced him. "I never did thank you for Michael, for bringing him back to me."

"As I have already told Michael, I am inclined to ascribe this little bit of romantic fate to an act of divinity, which returns us to the point of my unscheduled visit. As I was saying, Madam President, I have become obsessed for no reason that I can fathom, driven to your home after all these years on a wild whim, away from my cherished work, looking for a clue to Yuri's experience."

Sara poured herself a cup of coffee and joined them at the table. "What made you think that we had the answers?" she asked.

"Not answers so much as information," Kreiger said. "You are both in a position to know a great deal more than I, assuming that you would be free to share that information with a troubled soul."

Sara said, "Your assumption is reasonable, but I'm afraid that your visit, however welcome, will not be fruitful because my position is figurative. I *was* the president for a very short time, and I did retire from office voluntarily."

"After surviving a coup d'etat and saving this country from tyranny," Kreiger said.

"Nevertheless, I retired and am out of the proverbial loop— not that I'm without resources. We were informed of Yuri's awakening almost immediately, and we can be privy to some juicy gossip, but nothing that would be of service to you. In fact, your experience, your sudden appearance and bewilderment raises my own curiosity, because it fits into the recent scheme of odd coincidences. Just the other day, Jacob came for a visit, and we haven't seen him for a very long time. You remember Jacob Valdez?"

Kreiger smiled, accentuating the many creases on his weathered face, the result of spending too many days and nights on the cold and damp streets of New York. "How can I ever forget Jacob Valdez, and that great debate we had in Texas? He was a fine man."

"Who may have done more for this country than any man who ever lived—Tex, too. You remember Tex O'Toole?"

Kreiger nodded. "Of course. He put us on Mars."

"He also gave his life for us. They tortured him to death at the height of the coup."

Michael winced and began to blink, a nervous habit he had picked up in jail. "He was a tough old bird. Sara and I were just talking about him the other night."

"So many memories," Sara sighed. "Maybe too many. Hardly a day goes by when I don't think about Father Vincent."

"I'm sorry I never met him," Kreiger said.

Sara said, "He was the dearest man I ever knew. He was also a deeply troubled soul, quietly tortured by foreboding thoughts and dreams, and instinctive feelings about our destiny in space."

Kreiger leaned over the table and looked Sara directly in the eye. "I remember talking about him with you, but I don't recall anything about the quality of his dreams. What kind of dreams?"

Sara looked out the window at a barren cherry tree, knitting her brow as she plumbed her memory. "I remember one thing he said, one image he had that stuck with me all these years, about Christ being crucified upside down."

"You must mean Peter. It was Peter who requested this kind of horrendous death because he felt unworthy of dying in the fashion of his Master Christ," Kreiger said.

Sara said, "No, in his dream it was Christ, and the image really shook him. It haunted Father Vincent for the rest of his life. I think that he began to wonder if the image wasn't an indication of a devilish process of de-evolution we might be engaging in."

Kreiger was momentarily shaken. Somehow and in some way, talking about Father Vincent's foreboding thoughts and dreams connected to his mounting discomfort with Yuri's awakening.

"Is something wrong?" Sara asked.

"Not wrong, but . . ."

"Perhaps you'll feel better after breakfast."

Kreiger protested, but Sara insisted he spend at least the morning with them.

Sara was serving scrambled eggs to Kreiger when the conversation finally returned to the "great debate" at TCU, when Rounder squared off against Kreiger in a public forum and won the point. It also reminded Kreiger of another lecture he gave in Georgetown, when Sara had conspired with Olga, Vladimir's widow, to undermine his conservative point of view.

"I remember, I was about to take the young woman's question when Michael told me that it was Olga's daughter."

"Sonya," Sara said. "A lovely girl who had just entered college in Moscow at the time."

Kreiger said, "I don't recall hearing very much about Olga during these many years."

Sara served Michael before sitting between them and continuing, "I lost contact with Olga a long time ago. She was so angry with us after Vladimir died, really infuriated —as if WE killed him—just because we knew that he was dying of radiation poisoning before she did. But I imagine she's fared pretty well. Maher knew she was our conduit to Vladimir, and he gave her millions before he left Earth to gain preferential access to her husband when he arrived on Mars.

"I remember counseling her on how to use the money to affect political changes in her own country; then she became hateful and disappeared. I think I heard that she had moved to St. Petersburg after a while—must have been eight or ten years ago.

"So much time has passed and the earth moves beneath the North Atlantic, and this man returns from the dark and mysterious edge of an inner life, and claims an experience with God; and without hearing another word from him, we are back to where we were twelve years ago, questioning who we are, and wondering where we are going."

"It's almost as if we were waiting for Yuri," Sara mused aloud. "As if he has returned to fill the void left by the disappearance of the Lady-In-Waiting, and sharpen our focus on the meaning of our lives—whether you believe in him or not."

Michael said, "I don't believe him, but my issue with him has nothing to do with the religious or the spiritual. It has to do with trust because, as I recall, he was never the hero that people remember. Wasn't he the man who ignored Gerta's pleas for help, when his presence was most needed?

"Yuri was not like Gerta and Adam and Vladimir. He was popular because of his writing, but he was never really strong. He never made the sacrifices. He simply disappeared within himself at an inopportune moment. Until Yuri can explain his absence, I won't even consider his blasphemy, that he has seen God, because I don't think that he was even man enough to face the despair of his own friends."

Kreiger said, "I remembered some of his writings, the poetry. In fact, I reread some of his work on the train, all the inferences about an alien presence that he experienced within himself upon arriving on Mars. On second thought, I would imagine that he would have returned to us with an alien experience, an encounter with another life form on another plane."

Kreiger looked to Sara, whose eyes remained fixed on the window. She was feeling sorry for the cherry tree when Kreiger interrupted her thoughts.

"What are you thinking?" he asked Sara.

"Not enough," Sara sighed, looking out the window at the barren cherry tree. "Not nearly enough."

*   *   *

Rigidity bred restlessness on Earth and on Mars, as well as the use of mind-altering substances to spike the routine of life on a dead, red planet. The marijuana was grown surreptitiously in a biosphere, the alcohol was often distilled in the shadows of a supply room; the psychedelic drugs were made in the lab.

Use of marijuana and alcohol on Mars was primarily social, with two or three people meeting on the far end of a pressurized storage unit built into the back of a cave, passing a joint around at the end of a work shift, another small group meeting for drinks in a tech room. The use of psychedelics was inclined to be a more personal affair, someone driving the rover up to the rim of Shalbatana Vallis, and taking a hit of DMT (by combining the flow of oxygen with the short-acting psychedelic) to watch the sun set over an alien world.

There was an occasional birthday party that got out-of-hand, where the marijuana and spirits flowed freely and openly among larger groups of people. And there were instances of abuse, even addiction, but nothing that would threaten the integrity of the community.

Though the use of mind-altering substances was officially discouraged, the rotating governing council continually looked the other way, and encouraged colonists to use the mind-bending virtual reality programs for entertainment and escape. While many of these were psychologically addictive, they were nonetheless acceptable.

Sex proved much more problematic. Despite the ever-growing size of the colony, privacy was at a premium, and recreational sex was discouraged. Fear of communicable disease combined with emotional instability over an affair gone awry gave pause. To that end, almost no one roomed alone. Nearly all colonists lived in modules accommodating four or more people. Twenty-one married couples practiced the strictest forms of birth control. No one was allowed to bear children on Mars until the rapidly approaching fourteenth year of colonization. By then, all the medical studies and research on child-bearing and rearing on Mars would be completed, and a compound would be built to house the first children of an alien world.

There was nothing in human history that could compare to living on a dead rock in space with little prospect of returning home to Earth. Though the problem with back-contamination was theoretically resolved, prospective Mars colonists signed on for life. In fact, no one had ever returned to Earth.

And there was no realistic possibility of ever simulating Earth-life on Mars. Talk of terra-forming Mars was endless; the colonists argued all kinds of theories on how to create an atmosphere, knowing all too well that none of them would ever see the results of such an experiment. More than likely, these dreamers and their descendants would be living in underground cities, and in housing cut into the sides of the massive cliffs, fronted with huge sheets of glass, for many hundreds of years.

In the meantime, life on the dead, red rock plodded ahead. And though every single colonist on Mars was shocked by Yuri's awakening, none ascribed the significance to it that their brethren on Earth did.

Sasha said, "Some people are already saying that he is a Messiah."

"Maniac's more like it, but time will tell," Richard said. "Are you certain that he claimed to be someone else?"

"Not exactly. He just said that he wasn't Yuri."

The two were walking through the old grow room, on their way to Yuri's room. Bryce was two steps behind them. The rest of the members of the governing council wanted to be present when Richard questioned Yuri, but Richard wouldn't hear of it.

"It's not a freak show. The man's been gone for twelve years, and the last thing he needs to see is a bunch of strangers in his face, posing a bunch of inane questions."

The council agreed to watch the historical exchange on a nearby monitor; Bryce was posted outside the open door to Yuri's room; Sasha would accompany Richard into the room.

"To bear witness," Richard said. "Because you might see or hear something I might not. Be keenly aware of Yuri's demeanor, and let the experience imprint on your mind without effort. But follow my lead at all times. Say little if you are questioned, and defer to me for answers as often as you can."

"You make it sound as if he can be dangerous," Sasha said.

"Earth-shattering," Richard declared, before entering the small, dank room, telling himself again that he was surrounded by idiots.

*   *   *

Yuri remained seated on the floor in a cross-legged position, eyes closed. Richard and Sasha sat opposite him for nearly twenty minutes, until Richard coughed and broke the spell.

"You are not sounding so good, my friend," Yuri began, opening his eyes, speaking slowly with great effort.

Richard nodded and began sarcastically. "Friends? Since when?"

"Since I had no choice in the matter."

Sasha was surprised by their directness.

"Then you have been aware of my presence?"

"Reluctantly," Yuri quipped. "But not exactly."

"I don't understand."

"Neither do I, Richard. I was here. I was gone. But I never left. But I've been gone so long, it seems. I was Yuri. I was . . . I'm still not sure of things. I have no memory of the sequence of events, no logical reference point." Yuri looked to Sasha and continued, "You look familiar, but you cannot be Eva or Gerta. Can you be Arika?"

Arika Jobim was a member of the second manned mission to Mars, a Brazilian astrobiologist with whom Yuri fell in love with; she was also the woman who betrayed him to her handlers on Earth.

Sasha said, "No, I am not Arika. I am Sasha, Sasha Alawi. You know me from yesterday. I was here with you yesterday."

"When you said that you were not Yuri," Richard quickly added.

Yuri was apparently confused. He winced and closed his eyes in an apparent effort to maintain his composure. Sasha was about to speak again when Richard raised his hand to silence her.

Several seconds passed before Yuri opened his eyes and mused, "I remember Yuri . . . So I must be Yuri. Who else can I be?"

5

Yuri didn't look too bad considering that he had spent the past twelve years sitting motionless in a half-lotus position, dead to the world. His legs were understandably frozen; he could barely move his arms or turn his head, his muscles having atrophied. He was terribly thin, weighing only ninety-three pounds. But his hair and beard were still brown, both having been trimmed on a regular basis; his face had been exposed to a timed solar lamp, and he was fed a vitamin enriched, high protein diet by IV. Now fifty-two years old, his complexion was relatively smooth and creaseless.

Speaking was difficult. Yuri's voice continued to crack. But he was remarkably coherent given the circumstances, Richard thought.

Sasha didn't know what to think. She was simply fascinated, and remained observant per Richard's advice.

"You are Yuri," Richard said. "But you have been away from us for a long time, almost twelve years, and it's hard to understand where you've been, and what has happened to you during this time?"

Yuri winced again and shook his head. "You mean that there is a problem with me? Something is wrong?"

Richard was searching himself for an answer when he realized that it may be better to relax Yuri by filling in the gaps of the past years rather than to confront him with present anomalies.

Richard said, "Nothing is wrong with you as far as I can see, but some things went very wrong after you left us. Gerta died. They all did. Rather than fight with each other, they decided to join with the Dream Machine, and they all died in the process of the joining. It was a tragic loss, but heroic because they sacrificed themselves for the greater good.

"You and I were the only ones to survive. Then more ships came, many more during the next twelve years, and they began to colonize Mars. There are hundreds of people here now, all kinds of people."

Yuri nodded and closed his eyes, trying to take it all in. "Because they were in peril, they needed a place to be. I remember. Vladimir too, I remember seeing him with a woman, crossing the horizon at sunset. And Adam and Eva watching the moons rising over the sea; it was such a beautiful night. And the problems with Kellerman and the rest, and the Dream Machine that wouldn't dream, living inside the Supergrid; and all those lights, and all those beings and . . ."

Yuri's voice trailed off. No doubt that he had lost touch with reality, speaking in a stream of consciousness, apparently mixing his dreams with reality.

Not dreams, Richard thought, but impressions of another life that Yuri had lived in an altered state of awareness: seeing Adam and Eva together after they died, after they had joined with the Dream Machine; seeing Vladimir in the presence of some woman after he died, and the odd way that Yuri described the Dream Machine, living inside the Supergrid. No doubt that Yuri had lived a strange and remarkable inner life over the past twelve years, and Richard wondered whether he would ever learn to truly distinguish between the two.

He was about to leave the room, and had gestured Sasha to follow him, when Yuri open his eyes and reengaged them.

"I didn't go anywhere. I was tying to remember," Yuri said. "Being here and there at the same time is so different."

"Where?" Richard pressed.

"In my mind, I guess. But it is all so real, even more real than this—if this is real . . . it is hard to say . . . becoming very hard for me."

"Then we should leave," Richard declared.

Richard and Sasha were about to open the door when Yuri turned his attention to Sasha and said, "You are not the woman who was with Vladimir. She was much taller and lighter somehow, and she moved with extraordinary grace, like a ballet dancer . . ."

"The Lady-In-Waiting," Sasha blurted out.

Richard shot her a contemptuous look, and immediately tried to obviate the reference. "Sasha has been waiting on you for a long time, we all have. Too long, my friend, but another day won't hurt. It appears that we all need some rest."

Richard and Sasha thanked Yuri for his time and left the room in a daze.

*   *   *

Bryce MacDonald was a hard man to figure, not the sort of man who would leave Earth forever and join the multi-national, fledgling colony on Mars. He was a stalwart Presbyterian, the kind of man who remains loyal to one point of view, one job, one organization or one state of mind, and grinds it out until retirement. He was also something of a throwback to simpler times, when the old British Raj that had ruled so much of the world at the turn of the twentieth century, his great-grandparents having migrated from the Gaelic highlands to Edinburgh after the first World War. They eked out a living as domestics, bequeathing generations of tradesmen, nurses, teachers and soldiers to the fading empire.

Bryce was the second of six children, the first to rise above the level of modest success. He was a Colonel in the British Special Forces who had distinguished himself in the College of Engineering, and in covert operations in equatorial Africa. Never married and unfailingly loyal to the Crown, Bryce excelled as a consultant to numerous construction projects. He also played a key role in the defeat of rebel nationalist forces in Kenya and the Sudan, subsequently raising the British profile in the much-coveted region.

Three years later, he was riding a rocket to Mars. Whether punishment for an undisclosed indiscretion or reward for a job well done, speculation persisted until Bryce left Earth forever.

Though every other governing officer on Mars was rotated, Bryce was asked to remain at his post for four continuous years because he seemed so well suited for the job, and because he didn't make waves. Burly enough to dissuade a fight, he didn't waste time with petty offenses and he knew how to keep a secret. He was an intensely private man who discovered the quiet pain of others in the line of duty. Consequently, he wielded an extraordinary amount of power in the colony, which he exercised with restraint.

Bryce MacDonald was rock-solid and unshakable—until Yuri spoke to his mind.

Bryce heard every barely audible word that Yuri said to Richard and Sasha in his own mind. The experience was particularly unnerving because Bryce feared that Yuri could read his thoughts, and discover the dirty little secrets and impulses that lay hidden in the dark corners of his psyche. He was fighting to maintain his composure when Sasha and Richard exited Yuri's room, bewildered by their own encounter with Yuri.

"No one sees Yuri, no one talks to Yuri without talking to me first," Richard told Bryce, unaware of the telepathic intrusion. "No one says or does anything if you know what's good for all of you."

"Yuri's not as well as we hoped," Sasha added. "He's just not sure if he is here or there."

"Where is 'there'?" Bryce demanded; his hands clenched in fists at his sides, beads of sweat beginning to gather on his forehead.

Richard was about to say something derisive, when Sasha stepped in front of him and continued. "It is a dream state of some kind, where he must have been all these years, and he confuses it with reality."

"What kind of dreams?" Bryce pressed, looking for any clue that would explain the mind-bending telepathic phenomenon.

Richard read the tension in his voice, saw the beads of sweat on his forehead, noted the stiffness in his body, and instinctively exploited the weakness in Bryce's psyche. "Nightmares," Richard replied, looking directly into Bryce's wide eyes. "Yuri has nightmares."

Richard turned and left Bryce spinning. Sasha followed him into the old grow room.

"Maybe you can tell me what this is all about—deceiving Yuri and taunting Bryce—and for what reason?"

Richard looked around the room, shook his head and said, "Not here and not now. Even the leaves have ears."

"Then when?"

"Tomorrow, on the surface, at the back of the generator, at twelve hundred."

*   *   *

As good and young as Sara looked for her age, she felt old inside. Seeing Kreiger after so many years reminded her of the many people and things that had come to pass in her life. Even worse was the ever-growing realization that not much had changed despite all the losses and sacrifices that had been made to ensure a promising future.

Long after Kreiger left her house, in the middle of the night when Michael was fast asleep, Sara woke and took a long and hard look at herself in the bathroom mirror, moving closer and farther away, leaning back and forth, wondering where the time went. She hardly saw her beauty, and was increasingly focused on her imperfections: the dryness of the skin around the corners of her mouth, the creases beginning to form around her neck, the lines gathering around her eyes. It was all quite subtle, but Sara was in a critically obsessive mood, and told herself she wasn't beautiful anymore.

She was saddened, then angry and bitter at the aging process. And she began to wonder if Michael would love her if she lost her looks, if he had really and truly forgiven her for aborting his child, if she had vacated her office too quickly, if the world would think kindly of her after she was gone.

Then she began to think about Adam: if he would think well of her life; if he were still alive somehow, and wallowing hopelessly as a disembodied spirit in the confines of cyber space; if the Dream Machine hadn't seized control of the Supergrid at the onset; if it hadn't lulled the species to sleep in the wake of the Lady's invitation to the stars; if the Lady wasn't an alien witch in disguise of an ennobling spirit; if the ill fate of humanity hadn't already been sealed by a virus of complacency.

Sara was staring blankly at the mirror, becoming hypnotized by the intensity and complexity of her thoughts, when Michael stumbled into the bathroom half-asleep.

"Are you okay?" he began, suppressing a yawn and wiping the sleep from his eyes.

It took several moments before Sara cleared her mind and said, "No."

"Sick?"

"Of myself. I'm so ugly inside."

Michael stepped forward, as if he were taking a closer look at her. "I don't see it."

"Because you're blind inside."

Michael was too tired to be offended, and waited for Sara to explain.

"The blindness and the ugliness stems from our fearfulness, the complacency that belies the truth of our lives less lived," Sara began, standing naked in front of her naked husband.

"So you think we could have done more—but how?"

"I could have remained in office and pressed the issue of our survival with my last breath, if that's what it took. I was wrong Michael. I was selfish and you enabled me."

Michael leaned against the cold tile wall, crossed his arms over his chest and sighed, "So you think it's my fault that the entire species is going to hell?"

Sara was about to reply when she realized the absurdity of her argument, standing naked in the middle of a bathroom with her husband in the middle of the night.

"Probably my fault," Sara said, forcing a smile.

Michael reached for her hand, led her back to bed and made love to her, Lying beside and gently entering her, moving slowly and purposefully, until they came quietly together under the blanket.

"I just can't help but wonder where all the love went," she said. "Not ours, but that incredible feeling of togetherness that the world experienced in the Lady's wake, all the caring, and the striving, and all the wonder—what happened to our wonder?

"God only knows," Michael sighed.

"God may know, but that doesn't excuse us from looking for the answers."

"Some look, others pray."

"Meaning you really do believe that the fate of humanity is in the hands of Allah?"

"And you still find it so hard to believe—no matter how many times I tell you—that it is already written because we cannot do anything, that is not the will of God. Whether we survive or not, or go into space or not, with or without the Lady. Whether the Dream Machine attained consciousness or not. You think we have a choice in these matters, and I believe that our efforts are better served along the path of revelation. With prayer and mercy, the will of Allah can be revealed. If enough of the faithful maintain the faith, the business of evolution can be addressed by others."

"You really do sound a lot like Kreiger, except that he's apparently decided to do something apart from practicing his faith."

"Like I said before, Sara, he is a truly great soul, and great men have higher callings. I was called to Allah, and I was called to you."

Sara squeezed his hand said, "I will always thank God for that much."

No man had ever done more for her than Michael. No man had loved her more, not even Adam, because he was another one of those great men who answered to a higher calling, whose attention was always divided between her needs and the greater demands of evolution.

Sara fell asleep in a state of grace, but was shaken by a bad dream.

She was standing in a train station in downtown Paris, looking at herself in the mirror. Turning away from the mirror, she began to wonder why she was in France. When she looked up at the ceiling, she saw blue sky. Then she saw the Eiffel Tower in the distance.

She began to think about Michael, wondering where he was, if she was supposed to meet him there, when a rocket took off from behind the Tower.

Her eyes followed it up into space, and then everything turned dark and mysterious. She was searching for Michael between the stars when she saw a crescent moon. She was marveling at its beauty when Michael spoke to her mind.

"What are you doing here?" Michael asked.

Sara said, "Looking for you. And you?"

"I came to meet Yuri. He said that he was going to introduce me to God."

Sara was momentarily stunned and searched the stars for Yuri before returning her attention to Michael. "I thought Kreiger was your best friend."

"Yesterday, Sara. Today, it is Yuri."

Sara was surprised. "Have you been waiting long?"

"Too long," Yuri replied. "He waits too long and it is your fault."

"My fault?" Sara exclaimed, bewildered by Yuri's presence in her mind. "How can it be my fault?"

"Because you named her!" Yuri declared. "Because you said that she was a 'Lady' and you said that she was 'In Waiting.' Because you killed your own baby, we all have to wait."

*　　*　　*

While Sara was damned in a dream, Norbu Hua Chang woke to another sunny day in Happy Valley. It was a lush green vale in the heart of Mussoorie, a small town nestled in the Himalayan foothills north of New Delhi. These grand mountains were still pristine, still sunny and temperate below the tree line, despite the climate changes in other parts of the world. It was the most beautiful place Norbu Hua Chang had ever seen.

Now eighteen years old, Bu—the nickname often used by his friends and family—was bursting at the seams of life. He could hardly wait to graduate and marry his college sweetheart, Indra Maharaj. Both having tested as geniuses in grade school, they eventually met in Happy Valley at the Maher Technological Institute (MTI). It was among the finest technological colleges in the world, one of many that had Richard Maher endowed before he left for Mars.

Although Bu and Indra were fascinated by the colonization of Mars, they were so enchanted with Happy Valley that neither wanted to leave Earth. Both young and apparently naïve, they walked to school each and every morning in a bubble, passing more and more soldiers heading up to the Chinese border, hardly acknowledging India's festering problem with China. Barely a month had passed over the last two years without skirmishes erupting between the two countries along the Kashmir and Nepal borders—China having seized nominal control of the Nepalese government more than twenty years ago.

Part Tibetan, part Chinese, part Indian, Bu's Tibetan grandmother, a peasant farmer, had married low-ranking Chinese soldier in Lhasa. Their son, Bu's father, was a common laborer, who eventually fled Tibet as a teenager and married a poor Indian servant girl. Such was the majesty and mystery of DNA, how this random combination of so many banal genes could create such an extraordinary child.

"I think that you might have the best mind in the school," Indra playfully said as they walked to school through the crowded bazaar, past rows of small shops and piles of colorful merchandise, shaded by tall trees on either side.

"In the whole world," Bu declared, tossing his arms in the air. "There is no one smarter than me."

"Maybe. But do you know why?"

"Tell me."

"Because you love me," Indra coyly replied, strutting ahead of him as if she were a runway model.

Tall and thin with short black hair and large black eyes, she wore tight jeans, a white silk blouse and a red Pashmina shawl loosely draped around her narrow shoulders. Indra wasn't really beautiful, but she was striking and confident, and a year older than Bu. She adjusted her thin, black techno-glasses—shaped like cat's eyes—and playfully added, "And you know how much I love your mind."

Bu was so in love with her, so boyish and exuberant, that he didn't know when he was being played, and leapt in front of her and laughed. "When we are married, we will become one mind, and you will know what it is like to be as smart as me."

Indra moved to one side of the narrow stone sidewalk to allow several soldiers to pass. "And you will know what it's like to be handsome. I will make you handsome."

Indra often teased Bu about his appearance. Frequently dressed in saffron robes, sporting a crew cut and a pair of metal-framed techno-glasses, Bu looked more like a Tibetan monk than student.

He laughed again and jumped up and down like a child, he was so filled with joy. "Like a movie star, right?"

"Like a businessman in an expensive suit, and a silk shirt."

"If you will give me a kiss, I will even wear a silk tie."

"A small kiss."

Bu went to kiss Indra on the side of her cheek, and knocked her techno-glasses askew.

"I just can't wait until they master the neural-visual technology," Indra said. "And we can throw these damn things away forever."

Bu could wait. He had no intention of allowing access to his remarkable brain. He was one of a half-dozen people on Earth whose minds qualified as super-genius—clear and sharp, and conductive as crystal—and his country coveted him like a priceless gem. Apart from being educated, Bu was sent to school in Happy Valley for safe-keeping. There was always a policeman, or a shop keeper, or a passerby, or a teacher enlisted to keep an eye on him—and a girlfriend.

*   *   *

Hiro Suzuki was another qualified genius. A student of Makoto Okano, he helped in the construction of the Dream Machine, and was convinced he could duplicate the technology. But try as he did, for much of his youth, he continued to fail. And it was these magnificent failures that led to the development of techno-glasses, and the great fortune amassed by Hiro Suzuki in his middle age.

He loved his life. He loved success. He loved his family, but he couldn't look Makoto Okano in the eye, walking into his Kyoto office every day for the past twenty-odd years and instinctively averting the portrait of Okano that hung on the wall over his impressive desk—Suzuki was so ashamed of his paltry effort to replicate the Dream Machine.

He was sitting at his desk, filling with guilt on the eve of Yuri's awakening, when Tishiro Anakawa entered his office. A government agent who functioned under the guise of pseudo scientist, it was Anakawa's job to keep informal tabs on Suzuki—to see what he was working on, if the product could be purchased or co-opted for government use.

"Everyone is talking about the return of Yuri Popovitch. What do you think about all of this?" Anakawa began after a perfunctory exchange of pleasantries. He was a slight, middle-aged man, shorter than Suzuki, with a buzz cut and a set of unusually deep creases in his forehead.

"Not much," Suzuki said, feigning indifference. He appeared much younger than Anakawa, with smoother skin and thicker hair. "But if I were paid to think, I would not think Yuri poses much of a threat to our concerns. He was an astrobiologist by training, and not equipped with the skills necessary to access the Dream Machine."

Owing to Okano's creation of the Machine, the Japanese government continued to assume ownership of the Dream Machine.

"But he has awakened interest in the Machine," declared Anakawa.

"I suppose, but nothing extraordinary in view of the general awakening to the significance of the Mars missions—nothing I've been aware of."

"He was a great man," Anakawa mused, looking up at the portrait of Okano.

"Perhaps the greatest," Suzuki added, mocking a look at the painting, careful to hide his deeper feelings.

"And, as we all know, greatness begets greatness, and I have no doubt that you will be staying ahead of this curve," Anakawa said before saying goodbye.

The problem was that Suzuki never liked being in the government loop, but he remained in it because it was profitable—and the guilt recapitulated itself because it was warranted.

6

It would be a long night on Mars for all involved, especially for Bryce MacDonald, who drank himself into a stupor in a useless effort to stem the fear and pain of discovery. Drinking until it made him sick, he raged at his lot in life on a dead red planet for the past eight years, and he banged his head against the composite walls of his very small room until he passed out on the floor beside his airbed.

Early morning wrought a wrenching headache and a great deal of confusion, Bryce wondered if he hadn't imagined the whole telepathic scenario. He refused to believe that any man had the power to intrude upon another man's thoughts, and he fastened a plan to wrestle access to Yuri from Richard. He was becoming paranoid by mid-morning, thinking that Richard and Yuri might be conspiring against him. So he waited until Richard and Sasha exited the compound before convening an emergency meeting of the governing council.

"We have reason to believe that Richard Maher's operatives on Earth are responsible for the theft and sale of Makoto Okano's research papers," Bryce told the three council members present. The session had been convened in a vacant tech room at noon, while Richard was meeting with Sasha near the atomic generator on the surface. "Until this issue can be resolved on Earth, it would behoove us to take the necessary precautions on Mars, and to restrict Richard's access to sensitive material."

"You say 'we.' Can you tell us who your contacts are, the people on Earth who are looking into this matter?" Kim Jong Tui, the computer engineer, asked.

Bryce shrugged and played it casual. "I guess I could tell you, but I'm not sure it would be wise to give more credence to the matter than it deserves. To begin with, we have to remember that Maher was wrongly accused before of smashing the Dream Machine when it was actually hidden for safe-keeping. On the other hand, he is a very bright and powerful man whose agenda has never been clear to any of us, who doesn't answer to any member of this community—regardless our mandates. Realistically, I would have to say that the issue requires more cause for concern than alarm."

"Then why have you drawn us together on such short notice?" Dr. Usha Sanchez challenged.

"Because I thought it was better for us to be safe than sorry under the circumstances. All I'm saying is that in the short run, we might do better to turn to ourselves rather than run to Maher when we can't figure something out."

"Under the circumstances," was the key phrase that finally focused the council's attention on Bryce's nefarious agenda. All had witnessed the remarkable exchange between Yuri and Richard and Sasha on their monitors, and all became suddenly and acutely aware of Sasha's absence from the meeting.

"Where is she now?" Dr. Sanchez asked.

"I believe Sasha is on the surface with Richard," Bryce matter-of-factly replied, filling the atmosphere with a whiff of suspicion by inference—as he had planned.

The ensuing silence merely validated Richard's brutal assessment of these people, how small-minded they had become during the course of colonization, how easily they were manipulated to the dubious point of the meeting, all failing to appreciate the real and present danger in their midst.

"I replayed the interview twice this morning," Tui finally said. "And I cannot make a head or a tail out of it, whether Yuri is somehow deranged or disconnected, or simply disabled by the time he has spent away from us. And I could not fathom the reasoning behind Richard's questions to him. The whole thing puzzled me."

"Myself, too," Dr. Sanchez added. "But I found it rather fascinating nonetheless. In fact, I thought we would be hearing from Richard at this meeting, that it was convened to discuss the phenomenon of Yuri's awakening and the interview we witnessed."

Alona nodded and concluded, "Now we know why Richard isn't here, because we cannot trust our eyes and ears where he is involved."

Alona Glaza was Israeli, the fifth member of the rotating governing council, one of only three Jews on Mars, owing to the maddening attempt at political correctness by setting up a colony on Mars that reflected the proportionate population diversity on Earth. She was thirty-four years old. A former fighter pilot, she was now a spacecraft engineer who specialized in piloting the Mars shuttle craft. She also served as a security aid to Bryce. Tall, dark and lanky, and not so pretty, Alona was a third generation descendant of the holocaust, who had her grandmother's numbers tattooed on the back of her wrist so that she would never forget.

Bryce said, "I actually thought about inviting Richard to this meeting and addressing all of our concerns with him. On second thought, I was afraid that he would regard our questions as a group attack on his integrity, as accusations as opposed to inquiries. Rather than provoke an argument with him, I imagined that it was better to come to an understanding amongst ourselves before we approached him."

After several minutes of discussion, the council offered their support to Bryce, to keep Richard away from Yuri, and to keep nurturing their collective short-sightedness.

*   *   *

"I guarantee you that your precious council is meeting right now, because I provided them with the opportunity when I let it be known that I was going to the surface at noon, and that you would be joining me," Richard told Sasha. As planned, they met near the atomic generator at noon. It was an unpopular gathering spot ever since it had been relocated to a dump site nearly a half kilometer from the main compounds. "I can also guarantee you that every effort will be made to keep me away from Yuri."

"But they wanted you to speak to him, didn't they? They asked you to speak to him," Sasha declared.

"Because they had no choice, because I was most familiar to him, and most expendable, and because they were afraid. And our little discussion with Yuri played into their fear. The guy's been gone for twelve years, and he comes back and says that he actually saw God! Then he says that he's not Yuri, but he is Yuri! Meanwhile, the idiots on Earth get swept up in some kind of psychic religious frenzy, thinking that the guy might be the Second Coming, or an emissary of the Lady-In-Waiting, or some kind of devilish, mega-lunatic that's been possessed by an alien intelligence. And the people here on Mars don't know what to think or what to believe or what to do because they've become so complacent that they can't deal with anyone or anything outside their pathetic little box—which is why this community will always have a penchant for collapsing at the apex of its promise."

"How is that—how will we collapse?"

Richard looked up at the translucent, pinkish sky toward Earth before returning his attention to Sasha and delivering the answer. "From guilt—because in time, humanity will self-destruct on Earth at the rate it's going—whether by war or radical climate—and this community will have done nothing to save it—except to exist for its own benefit as a repository for the knowledge of the nine billion on Earth that killed themselves.

"And because the community is the custodian of a remarkable Machine of our own making, which is already half-dead from neglect, that may have the ability to save us from ourselves—or else why would we have created it at this precise and precarious moment in history? If history—or even evolution—teaches us anything, it is that inherent in our inclination to destroy or deteriorate is the ability we have to extend and transcend, or even recreate in an effort to simply survive—like creating penicillin from an otherwise injurious bacteria to cure disease, or developing the atomic bomb and subsequently employing our knowledge of atomic fission to power our ships across the heavens.

"Likewise, the Dream Machine, which began as a game to occupy itinerant astronauts, and became something else, and it's this laziness or unwillingness to comprehend that something else that may be the death of us all—or maybe it's the simple fear of looking at the future and conjuring our demise that is so stifling."

Richard drew uneven breath, and was about to continue when he began to cough so deeply and protractedly that Sasha was afraid he would choke on the lack of oxygen. She stepped forward to help. He turned away from her, gained control, and continued slowly in a raspy voice.

"Is there any person here who does not look wistfully at Earth at dawn or dusk, or up at the sky in the direction of Earth during the day?"

Sasha looked up at the sky and shook her head. "No, I don't think so. And even if we aren't looking at it, we are still thinking about it. But I am also thinking that it might be different for our children."

"If you can live so long without regular contact from Mother Earth, and without supplies and new blood—which is the most likely scenario if there is an eruption of some magnitude in the North Atlantic, or a war of consequence between major powers."

Sasha looked out across the Shalbatana river basin and appraised the view of what the colony had created during the past twelve years. The ground between the high cliffs was strewn with all kinds of man-made junk: pipes, tubes, gears, glass, wheels, wings, engines. Despite all efforts to clean the site, the trash kept piling up. The more that was built, the more that was discarded in a vain glorious effort to fend off the truth: the colony on Mars could not survive without contact with Earth because it identified so strongly with Earth.

"You are right; we can never survive this by ourselves," she finally and sadly concluded.

Richard nodded and coughed several times before replying. "But you must survive me and Yuri. And you must find others that will share your vision of another kind of future, entailing greater risks and a greater reward than this god-forsaken planet."

Sasha's sadness turned to bewilderment when she realized what Richard was saying. "You mean that you're dying?"

"Obviously. Yuri too, if I'm not mistaken, because he will have too much power and generate too much fear when he becomes oriented, and he will have to be killed. If need be, they'll send someone from Earth to kill him."

"Who are 'they'?"

"The people who stole my tools en route to Mars twelve years ago, the material I would have used to research the Dream Machine, and maybe even build another one a long time ago; the people who would have destroyed the Machine or enslaved it if they had the opportunity; the people who would rather die with their beliefs intact than live and learn something new about themselves in the universe."

"I don't believe it, that there are people who would commit murder on Mars."

"You forget that there were eleven people on Mars twelve years ago who were getting ready to kill each other before they joined with the Dream Machine in a moment of unimaginable despair, so afraid of each other that they thought death by proxy was better than death by war."

Once again, Richard had succeeded in shaking Sasha from her complacency, but she continued to resist his conclusions out of habit, and out of fear. "I still don't believe it," she said. "How can you be so sure that Yuri will misuse the power—if he even has it?"

"Because he already has so much power, and he's already misusing it—as if he doesn't know he's Yuri. Who the fuck else can he be? I'll tell you again: he will be Christ or Christ-like because that's what too many people on Earth want him to be, because he couldn't possibly face up to the cowardly little shit that he really was. After all, he did bug out on Gerta when she turned to him for help.

"There's another agenda here, Sasha, there has to be, and no matter how difficult to discern, it will be your responsibility to find the truth before it finds us."

"Which doesn't give us much time, I suppose," Sasha sighed.

"And no margin for error."

7

It had been in the year 2040 when the species faced the last great crisis in the arc of its survival—when Sara inadvertently coined the name of that holographic image manifested from the joined minds of those remarkable eleven astronauts.

"If I'm not mistaken, I believe you people have another Lady-In-Waiting. In deference to her, this lady is going home where she belongs," Sara had said, upon resigning the presidency.

"I still can't believe how much power my words contained, how naïve I was. The truth was that I wasn't prepared to be President, and if it weren't for the timely appearance of the Lady, I would have been deposed, and this country would have been a dictatorship."

Sara was sitting across the kitchen table from Michael. It was a familiar early morning ritual: a brisk workout in the basement gym, followed by a cup of coffee and a bit of conversation, which had become increasingly serious and reflective following the arrival of Fritz Kreiger.

Michael sipped his coffee and said, "Timing is everything."

"Meaning that I fulfilled my destiny by sitting on my ass until some holograph came to my rescue?"

"Possibly, and it seems to me that if everyone was in the right place at the right time, we would be having a bit of heaven on Earth. So I wouldn't underestimate your contribution, Sara. And you shouldn't be wasting so much of your time going further and further back into the past, reexamining everything and second guessing all the decisions you made."

"You're not me," Sara sharply replied.

"This again," Michael sighed, shaking his head.

"What else is there?" Sara challenged, raising her voice

"Sleep, for one thing. You've been thinking so much that you've hardly slept at all the last three nights."

"I look that bad?" Sara asked, looking down at her coffee.

"Not to me," Michael reached across the table and stroked her cheek with the back of his hand. "Never to me."

Sara shed a tear, and finally decided to tell him about the dream. "I haven't been sleeping because I'm afraid to sleep. I'm afraid to dream, because I had a really bad dream a few nights ago after we talked in the bathroom. I dreamt that I was being punished for the abortion, for killing our baby."

Michael wasn't surprised that Sara continued to suffer the consequences of the abortion, but he was nonetheless taken by the timing and intensity of the dream. "I know I forgave you, Sara, but it may be that you haven't fully forgiven yourself. Then again, you may only be experiencing the memories of this pain by revisiting an old behavioral imprint—which is why I cautioned you not to look too far back into your life for meaning. And why I will continue to encourage you to open your heart to God, so that you can find peace of mind again."

*   *   *

Sara turned to Fritz Kreiger, who had decided to remain in D.C.

"To try and connect with some other old friends," Kreiger said. "To see if they had any information on Yuri's awakening. But I'm afraid that I didn't have much luck. I guess that I've been away from things too long, and the surprise at seeing me out-weighed all other considerations. Besides, everyone else got older and further removed from their sources of information."

It was a beautiful spring day—blue sky, bright sun, the temperature hovering around fifty degrees, even the cherry blossoms had begun to bloom—a good day to broach a difficult subject, and to ruminate about the fate of the world. Sara and Kreiger were sitting near the top of the steps of the Lincoln Memorial, watching passersby, looking like any other middle-aged couple on tour of the Capitol: Sara wearing a black wool pant suit, a short, brown wig, and pair of brown techno-sunglasses to disguise her appearance.

Kreiger had been so long gone from the public eye and had aged so much that he could appear as himself in khaki pants and an overcoat, and not draw an iota of interest or attention.

"My problem is that I can't seem to go forward without looking back," Sara said. "Michael thought I should turn to God for guidance and understanding. I thought I would talk to you first."

Kreiger flashed a coy little smile, deepening the lines in his once handsome face. "I'm flattered, to say the least—putting me before God—but I doubt if I can be as helpful as Him."

"Then maybe I just need another sounding board—after all, I've spent so much time with Michael for so many years that it's hard to see where I end and he begins sometimes. And everything's suddenly becoming so intense, even my dreams."

Sara looked down at the huge expanse of steps, then across the long and languid pool at the Washington Monument in the distance, weighing her thoughts before continuing, "I had a terrible dream last week involving the Lady-In-Waiting and Yuri. And at the end of the dream he damned me to Hell, telling me that because I named the Lady, and killed my baby, we all have to wait."

Kreiger was stunned. He shot a quizzical glance at Sara then looked at the Monument, wondering what to say.

Sara studied his intense, gaunt profile, and continued nervously, "It's probably the result of another rush of guilt, or just a memory of the pain, as Michael said, but now I can't help from wondering if I didn't abort a very special child."

"Who could possibly know this? But I think that you may be doing yourself a great disservice by placing an added value on the life you gave up. In the eyes of God, all His children are special."

"You mean I'm just a woman who made an unwise choice, and continues to regret the consequence?"

Kreiger looked down the steps at all the passersby, drew a deep breath and sighed, "Perhaps, but . . . in terms of your experience of guilt and remorse, you are very much every woman, and every woman who believes their child will be or should be special. Then again, you were the President of the most powerful country on Earth, and you were the wife of the greatest hero in human history, and he was joined to that remarkable Machine.

"Place your guilt and remorse in the context of your unique position in life, and put Yuri in your dream, and the intelligence of coincidence comes into play. There can be a message there, a special meaning to your dream, but . . . Would that I have known any woman well enough to appreciate the subtleties of her heart. The only one I did know sent me to the monastery with a broken heart."

"I never knew that."

"Few people do—it was such a long time ago. I was a very young man, who could hardly bear the pain until I surrendered it to God—which brings me back to Father Vincent. I'm curious to know if he left any writings behind, notes of any kind?"

"Not that I was aware of, and if he did, I would imagine they became the property of the Church. I can make inquiries if you'd like."

Kreiger shook his head and smiled. "I guess I would be most interested in the controversial stuff, and I imagine they would not be available to anyone outside the Church."

Both sat side by side for several pensive moments—Kreiger looking straight ahead, Sara looking up at the blue sky—until Sara began again. "I'm sorry I couldn't be any more helpful, but as you can see, I'm as puzzled by all this as you . . . . Will you be returning to New York soon?"

"I can't say, but my instincts tell me to move ahead, to keep looking for the answers."

"As if I even had a choice in the matter," Sara added. "I'm not sure I can find any peace until I can come up with some answers."

The conversation was apparently over, but neither stood to leave, both continuing to gaze at the tourists until Sara broke the silence.

"It is kind of silly isn't it, sitting here be-knighting ourselves with the responsibility for saving the species from itself? I'm not sure I ever felt quite so ridiculous."

"Absurd or not, the fact is we both have experienced a fore-boding premonition, and tensions in the world are beginning to rise. And I can't imagine that we're the only ones who are experiencing this: look at the commotion Yuri's awakening has made, as if people were waiting for something or someone to believe in; they were so quietly desperate."

Sara nodded and pensively asked, "I wonder how Maher is taking all this, what he thinks about Yuri's awakening—if he's been visited with similar discomfort."

"It's just too bad we couldn't ask him."

"Are you certain we can't?"

"No, but I need to remind you about the last time we tried to contact someone on Mars surreptitiously—from the Observatory. I was accused of treason, Tex was tortured to death, and Rounder was crippled."

"But not broken."

*   *   *

Bu was a stocky young man with a large head, short black hair and silky brown skin; his slanted brown eyes denoted his Tibetan/Chinese heritage; his long, thin nose marked his Indian heritage. He wasn't handsome, but he was remarkably charismatic, and so smart that Richard Maher selected him above all others to do his bidding on Earth.

As Usha Sanchez had said, the stolen Okano papers that came up for auction in London were not directly connected to the construction of the Dream Machine. They were schematics—flow diagrams and handwritten notes related to the software design of the Imagining Mars program, more akin to the broad silken strokes of fine painters than left-brained scientists—

purchased at auction by agents of Richard Maher before they could be claimed by the Japanese government.

Richard's shock at hearing the news on Mars was a ruse, and all attempts to trace the purchase back to Richard were moot because no link could be established between Richard and his agents on Earth. And there was no way to trace the delivery of a copy of these highly coveted papers to Norbu Hua Chang in the Himalayas—Richard thought.

"It is for your eyes only," Indra said, dislodging a small, flat crystal off her crystalline necklace and handing it to Bu on the tip of her long and slender forefinger. "It is extra special."

It was late in the afternoon. They were sitting on the edge of long, gray sedimentary rock, looking out across the seemingly endless expanse of snow-capped mountains, the distant sky separated by several planes of weather: clouds on one level, rain on another, a huge rainbow curling across the western sky on a third, and the sun over-arching and shining down on everything. It was one their favorite places in Mussoorie, just a two kilometer trek north of town. The long and winding path was dotted with apple plantations, and ended at the edge of a steep cliff dropping hundreds of meters into the green valley below.

Bu took the crystal and snapped it into place on his ever-present crystalline bracelet, hardly surprised. This was not the first "extra special" chip that he had received from Indra. He was often the recipient of sensitive material delivered by a variety of means and people: by his teachers after class, by industrial or government agents in private, and sometimes by Indra. And Bu learned to take it all in stride, never questioning the messenger and always doing his very best with the material in hand, as long as it didn't have a military application. A practicing Buddhist, Bu would not knowingly harm another soul or think the worst of anyone—least of all Indra.

Richard chose Bu after carefully profiling three other super-minds attending other schools he had endowed around the world, because he was convinced that Bu had the best young mind on Earth.

"Maybe after I solve all the problems in the world, you will marry me," Bu said, so enthralled with Indra that he could not imagine a life without her.

"If I'm still on this world," Indra sadly replied, looking out over the mountains as if it were the last time. "A representative of the government in Delhi contacted me and asked me if I would volunteer to be trained as an astronaut. He said that I was on a very short list, and that there may only be one more voyage to Mars in the near future, because of the deteriorating political situation on Earth. He said that our country needs me."

Bu was crestfallen. He could hardly believe his own ears. "And you said yes?"

"I said that I would have to think about it."

"You mean that you want to go?" Bu worried, his heart beating so fast that he could barely sit still.

"No, and not without you. But I might have to go because I owe my country a lot. We both do."

"But no one asked me," Bu agonized, his slanted eyes nearly closing in an effort to fight back the pain. "I could never leave my parents. I'm all they have and they've done so much for me. And I love Happy Valley. I'm so happy here going to school and being with you. Even after we finished school, I thought we would be married here. Even if we had to take work someplace else, I always thought that we would find our way back here together."

Bu wanted to say more, but the pain stifled his voice. Both stared across the mountains into the far reaches of China, until Indra shed a tear and began again.

"My family doesn't want me to leave either, and I don't want to leave them or you. I could never meet anyone like you on Mars—not even on Earth. But I might not have much choice in the matter. I'm an only child, and my parents are quite patriotic despite their attachment to me. And I'm still a woman, which is still a bit less than a man in this country."

"You mean that you spoke to your parents already?"

Indra nodded and wiped a tear from her cheek. "Last week actually, after I spoke with the government person, and it turned out that they already knew. The government contacted my parents first and told them what a great honor it was to be chosen. But we didn't make any decisions. I would never do that without speaking to you."

Bu looked down at the green valley below and gathered his strength before replying. "If you don't want to go, you won't have to. I can see to that."

"How can you?"

"I can refuse to do any more work for the government unless they do what I tell them to do. I know I'm young, but I'm not stupid, Indra. In fact, I might be the smartest person in the entire world. And knowledge is power."

Indra shed another tear and rested her head on Bu's shoulder, her eyes roaming across the magnificent horizon as she privately cursed her fate.

8

Norbu Hua Chang did not believe in fate. He believed in the power of the human will, telling Indra that karma was not immutable law, and not an obstacle to change.

"It was an imprint reinforced over many lifetimes of experience that was made to be broken in the quest for higher knowledge. We are not born as slaves to our karma. We are born to challenge our karma, to overcome our predispositions as individuals and as a species. We are born to evolve, to become free of tyranny and gravity, to become free of desire itself at the end of the evolutionary spiral. In the meantime, while we are engaged in this struggle for freedom, we are endowed with a witness, the ability to observe the process of frustration and gratification, the ebb and flow between them, which is the subtlest and purest form of meditation.

"If I am pushed, I can and will push back. In the end, I will know more about myself than my enemies will learn about themselves. In this way, I cannot lose. But I will only engage in this process if you want me to—if you want to stay here with me," Bu told Indra before they returned to their dormitory in town: she to her room to lament her lot in life, he to his room to work on the Imagining Mars notes.

Studying Okano's papers for hours, as the day receded into night, Bu marveled at the three-dimensional symmetry of Okano's mind. And after recalling all the heroics connected to the early Mars missions, the clarity of Bu's mind became riveted to his difficulty with Indra. He suspected that Richard Maher might have been behind the delivery of Okano's papers, but he could not imagine that a great man like Richard Maher, who had endowed his Happy Valley School, would use his attachment to Indra as a motivational tool.

To begin with, it wasn't necessary. So Bu simply deduced that it was a threat born of another source of power that must be working against Richard. He also realized the folly of his love, how willfully naïve he had been. His heart breaking, Bu waited until midnight to sneak out of his room and into Indra's room on the other side of dorm.

"My God, Bu, what's wrong? What are you doing here?" Indra began, ushering him into her room.

She was wearing a red, silk bathrobe, and working at her holographic computer when Bu arrived. He sat on the edge of her bed, folding the layers of his saffron robe across his lap; she returned to her seat at the computer.

"I do what I need to do, and I need to ask who you are working for?"

"Work? I don't work. I don't have a job. I go to school here like you," Indra declared, clutching the robe together near the base of her slim neck.

Covering herself, hiding the truth, Bu thought.

He managed a weak smile and pressed ahead, thinking the worst, hoping for the best. "I still love you, Indra. I will always love you no matter what you say, but I will love you more than ever if you will tell me who you are working for, who tells you to watch me and be so nice to me?"

Indra began to tremble and tighten her grip on her robe. She couldn't betray her supervisors, and she wouldn't lie to Bu.

Bu lowered his voice and his eyes before continuing painfully. "So you don't love me after all?"

Indra ran to his side, reached for his hand, looked into his sad brown eyes and said, "I do love you, Bu. That much is true."

*   *   *

Beginning with the first manned mission to Mars, the ensuing twelve years were the most remarkable in human history. Not unlike Sara and Kreiger, Richard Maher believed that the salient events denoting this time period were somehow connected. So he spent the next two weeks trying to solve the mystery, reading everything Yuri ever wrote and constantly rereading Yuri's final journal entry in search of clue. Whether out of instinct, or fear, or despair, Richard was convinced that the mystery behind Yuri's awakening posed a key to solving the mystery.

"I wake each day in the shadow of the
dog.
The bitch is the bark: The
unyielding noise in my head and the
redundancy training. It rains
only in my dreams
when I am held at bay: Yelp,
snap,
bite. But
the tooth of the matter does not escape me.
Splattering across the ever-reddening dawn of
ideas,
I bleed loosely for the dogs of 'yore.

Richard read this poem several times a day, each time from another perspective, often thinking that "dog" was god spelled backwards, always relating to the loneliness that Yuri so effectively invoked. He also thought that "dog" might be a metaphor for the Earth—the shadow of the dog also posing a metaphor for Yuri's longing for home, and nothing more. In the end, Richard finally admitted to himself that he continued to read the poem because he liked it, and because it always put him in the right mood to sift through the rest of the entry until several passages stuck in his mind:

I am a stranger to myself. I cannot imagine who I have become because my changes are measured against the strange changes of others. We will never be the same as we were, and we will never be sharing this uniqueness with others. There is a quality of being here that is wholly different than being on Mother Earth because we are not of the barren womb that is Mars.

WE HAVE NO MOTHER. WE HAVE NO FATHER.

There are no endemic provisions here, no protections, no points of social reference; no suck. We are stand-ins, mock-ups for our all-too-human needs. We are mothers and fathers and brothers and sisters for each other, but we cannot simulate or approximate the life-giving force of an entire planet. There is not much electricity here, or magnetism, or warmth, or beauty, or life. There is no umbilical cord to connect us to this place. There is nothing that provides or protects. In fact, we are threatened every second of our lives, and we are left to consume the stores meant for our dead comrades. We live like rats.

WE ARE THE BASTARDS OF A DREAM GONE AWRY.

In the meantime, there can be a special moment when my mind becomes strangely silent and I observe the oddity of our becoming. If not ghosts of times past, there are shadows here, faint traces of another life, a quality of intelligence, subtle as a gentle breeze: calming, disinterested, but nonetheless present and observant, watching me watch myself—something from within which has no vested interest in my thoughts and feelings, whether I live or die or laugh or cry. Passive, intelligent, aware: it sees the beauty, hears my breathing, watches my thinking and notes my feelings without judgment. It is me; it isn't me.

It is alien, I think.

I can also see myself dead. And yet . . .

I have a dark secret, which is my attachment to this shit, fucking place—because in the darkest nights of my soul, I have seen glimpses of another life. Not shadows or ghosts, but colorful things that visit my dreams when I am hovering over the planet, disembodied, and free of the gravity of the situation; when I tumble through the universe toward the end of time, passed all kinds of colorful nebula and foreboding black holes and swirling galaxies.

I have even seen my captain out there in the stars and he has spoken to me, Eva too and Ramesh and Hakim and Makoto. Even Mei Yi, that terribly troubled soul, has flown by my thoughts and spoken kindly to me of other worlds and other lives. Stranger still may be the redundancy of one particular dream, and how often I am revisited by the odd bits and pieces:

I am climbing up the side of a mountain—Somewhere in Peru, I think. I reach the summit and I am met by a woman. She is tall and handsome with long, black hair and pearly black eyes.

She is wrapped in a colorful shawl and speaks to my mind and says, 'I am come.'

'From where?' I ask.

'From there,' she says, pointing to the sky.

When I look up, I fall down through a hole in space and time, past all kinds of cosmological wonders and anomalies. I am excited, then frightened, thinking I might die if I fall too far. My heart is pounding. My ears are ringing. I am running, flying, lurching, then fleeing from an ominous dark cloud—about to become engulfed—when the lady emerges from the effusive darkness and morphs into the holographic image of the Dream Machine.

'Who are you?' I ask. 'What are you?'

She smiles and moves her lips, but nothing comes out of her mouth.

I ask more questions and she struggles to answer, trying harder and harder, as hard as she could it seems, but she cannot find her voice. When her arms begin to flail, I begin to feel her anguish and frustration. The pain is so great that I am about to implode and pass out from its intensity, when I scream at her and ask, 'My God, why?'

When the lady opens her mouth to answer, her morphed image explodes in silence and flies apart, becoming infinite specks of light, becoming stars, and my ears are filled with the OM sound of creation.

Then I wake in another sweat, thinking that I had somehow witnessed the birth of creation, and that I had heard the voice of God."

9

Each time Richard read these passages, he was struck by Yuri's allusions to the subtle presence of an alien intelligence on Mars—Richard never experienced that, though he often felt like he had been on Mars before—and the prescient quality of the reoccurring dream: The woman from Peru, who seemed to anticipate the manifestation of the Lady-In-Waiting; the uncanny description of her destruction as "infinite specks of light" flying away from Yuri, paraphrasing the disbursement of the first holographic projection of the Dream Machine; and the way Yuri employed the sound of creation to describe the voice of God.

Richard was lying on his bed in the middle of the night reading Yuri's final journal entry for the umpteenth time, telling himself that there was no way that one mind could comprehend this mega-mystery, when Bryce MacDonald appeared at his door with Sasha and Alona.

"Another crisis or another admonishment?" Richard tepidly began, placing the journal aside.

He hadn't seen very much of anyone during the past two weeks, including Sasha. He would not betray a weakness—no one on Mars knew Richard was ill except Sasha. And he would not compromise her credibility by continuing to court her friendship.

Bryce remained at the door, striking a familiar pose: back straight, arms folded across his chest, holding himself together as the women stepped forward.

"Yuri has asked for you," Alona began.

"And it took three of you to deliver the message?" Richard challenged, careful to hide his joy at the good news. He couldn't wait to speak to Yuri again.

The women looked at Bryce.

"He has also asked to see me. It was a bad idea to begin with, to exclude you from Yuri's life—my bad idea," Bryce admitted without hesitation. "It was I who turned the community against you in this matter."

Richard was stunned by his candidness, and pleased. If politics made for strange bedfellows, despair made for stranger acts of graciousness. "And you are a good man to admit it," Richard said.

He had no idea that Bryce MacDonald had also withdrawn from the community during these past two weeks—out of fear, no less. Hard as he tried, as much as he drank, Bryce could not get Yuri out of his mind. He could hardly look at himself in the mirror, let alone meet the piercing eyes of his comrades, afraid that Yuri might have betrayed his dirty little secret to them.

But Bryce was head of security, and Yuri was becoming the most precious human commodity on Mars. So he had Alona, the tall and lanky Israeli, stand in for him and stand guard for him, telling her that he wasn't feeling very well. He also had Alona report to him after every meeting she had with Yuri, hoping to discover a clue to Yuri's telepathic power without exposing himself to greater danger. He was also waiting to hear if Yuri had spoken to someone else's mind, but nothing extraordinary was reported.

If anything, Bryce was struck by the banality of Yuri's encounters with other people, as well as his defensiveness: Yuri categorically denied that he had ever seen God, or claimed that he wasn't Yuri.

After two uneventful weeks, it was becoming increasingly difficult for Bryce to make excuses for his absence from his job. He was thinking about committing suicide when Yuri asked to see him.

"The man who was at the door at the beginning: I would like to see him and Richard, and the girl," Yuri had told Alona.

Consequently, Bryce turned from Yuri, the man he feared, to Richard, the man he hated, for help.

After asking the women to leave the room, Bryce stepped forward and continued. "I'm not sure we could ever become true friends, but we do a disservice to ourselves and everyone else in the community by persisting as enemies at this juncture."

"Because Yuri is too powerful for any one of us to deal with," Richard correctly surmised, sitting up in his bed.

Bryce asked if he could sit.

Richard gestured to the chair at his desk beside the bed.

Bryce took a seat, gripped the sides of the chair and leaned forward. "You mean that he has spoken to your mind?"

"Who?"

"Yuri. Isn't that why you said he was so powerful?"

Richard was bewildered, searching himself for answers when Bryce stood to leave, thinking it was best to kill himself after all. "I'm afraid I said too much already," Bryce added.

"And I'm afraid that I'm dying," Richard declared, thinking that he had to give something to this deeply troubled man before he would get anything more out of him.

Stunned by the admission, Bryce was momentarily disarmed. "How can it be?"

Richard coughed for effect. "Lung cancer."

"Then it appears that we both have something in common. You are losing your life, and I believe I am losing my mind—because Yuri spoke to my mind. I heard him inside of me when he spoke to you and Sasha, and I can still feel him inside of me, his presence."

When their eyes met, Richard failed to see the greater danger.

*   *   *

Space did not pose the only prospect for the salvation for the species. A number of reputable minds were long inclined to burrow under the Earth's surface and construct massive underground cities, which was easier said than done since the idea wasn't very appealing to the masses.

To the vast majority of people, the prospect of exploring space was expansive and tantalizing, still exotic; digging a hole in the Earth was not. The notion even smacked of cowardice to some. Many of the people who represented the "Earth First" idea were not as glamorous as their astronaut compliments, which decreased their appeal to the masses. There was also a problem with selection: almost anyone could qualify as an underground survivor, also known as an Earther, which invariably pitted the wealthier and more educated elite against the banal masses for a spot in the ground. So the Earth First project was perennially under-funded, and the idea of space travel persisted in spite of the great cost.

To that end, Rounder was invited to address the next wave of astronauts headed for Mars.

"It is the nature of man to rise," he began, less than ten minutes after he had taken his medication. "To look up to the heavens in awe and w-wonder, because the concept of heaven has been historically equated to the sky, and to salvation. And I am a f-firm believer in the exploration of space, in expansion at almost any cost, but times change and real politic does have a way dividing our atten-tension.

"We do have a problem with climate change on Earth, a potentially d-devastating problem. And we do have competing interests for ev-ever-depleting energy sources and strategic territories on Earth and on the moon. And while I remain an avid supporter of the c-colonization of Mars, I am still d-d-devoted to realizing the greater challenge, to take the Lady-In-Waiting up on her invitation to the stars.

"I am alarmed and stridently against the growing wave of fatalism and inertia that has befallen humanity, sen-sending colonists to M-Mars for the sake of sending them, because we're used to doing it, in the way the United States ran its space shuttle program at the turn of the millennium. Now that the Mars Project is nearing completion, I believe it is time to look beyond Mars at that distant pulsar on the other s-side of the g-galaxy, and find a way to connect with it, even communicate with it—if-if that is at all possible.

"Go to Mars and enrich the colony, but n-n-never let a day pass without thinking beyond Mars; n-never let a night pass without looking up at the heavens and wondering what awaits us in the further reaches of space. And never forget the enormous sacrifices that have been made in our name, those people who have already g-given their lives in the quest for knowledge and understanding of our universe. Are there any questions?"

A gentleman standing at the back of the room raised his hand and posed an unanticipated challenge. "Are you really saying that we must be willing to die in order to progress?"

"No, but I am saying that there must be a will-willingness to s-sacrifice."

"As if exploring space is an end in itself—what about those of us who are left behind on Earth who starve for food while you people are busy feeding the mind?" the man shot back, barely suppressing a smile.

Rounder drew a weary breath and sighed. His short-acting medication was beginning to wear off, and his legs hurt so much that he could hardly stand. He was searching himself for a witty answer when he noted the aged appearance of the questioner and tagged him as a religious zealot, possibly an Earther.

"And y-you are, sir?" Rounder finally asked.

"An old friend," Kreiger said, smiling brightly as he walked down the aisle to the lectern.

It took several pensive moments until Rounder put the faintly familiar voice together with the weathered face and exclaimed, "My God, man!"

"My point exactly," Kreiger said, smiling brightly. "And I dare say that the two are inexorably joined at our reason for being on Earth and in the heavens."

Rounder stepped away from the lectern, and shook Kreiger's hand before introducing him to the gathering of future colonists.

"I want you all to meet Fritz Kreiger, our staunchest opponent to space exploration and the only one of them who, in my opinion, is worthy of our unmitigated respect."

Kreiger was flattered by the introduction and very surprised at the sustained applause he received. In fact, almost every one of these future young colonists had read about Fritz Kreiger in college, and all were quite familiar with the "great debate" at TCU which had framed the issue of space travel: whether the species was prepared to engage an alien intelligence before binding itself at the heart.

*   *   *

"It appears that you might have been r-right after all," Rounder said over dinner at a nearby restaurant later in the evening. "We-We may not be r-ready to meet our destiny in space."

Kreiger said, "I wouldn't have known that by the speech you just gave."

Rounder shrugged and sighed, "I want to believe it. I n-need to believe it. I j-just wonder if we haven't already squandered our best opportunity."

"The Lady-In-Waiting?"

"How long can she wait? How much time do we have left?"

Kreiger had no answer. Seated at a small table at the back of an ultra-modern sushi restaurant, he looked at the walls and ceilings comprised of ever-changing, liquid crystal HDTV projections as if he were looking for a clue.

"Not very long, I'm afraid. I'm terribly concerned about the increase in seismic activity in the North Atlantic, and I'm deeply concerned about Chinese designs on the moon—because it seems to me that they are intent upon stretching America to the breaking point, which may result in a war of the worst kind.

"I can't say that the answer to our problems lies in space. I can say that a greater effort is required to see if we can't take that strange Lady up on her invitation. I've also wondered if the process of trying to reach out to her wouldn't be binding somehow."

"You, you m-mean that you don't believe in Jesus Christ as the only path to sal-sal-salva-vation?"

"I do believe. But I also think that the necessity to survive might preclude our need to be saved. What good is God if there are no subjects left to praise His glory? You know what I've been doing the last twelve years?"

"Sara t-told-told me."

"Feeding the hungry and ministering to the dying, and after witnessing all that pain, I've concluded that the preciousness of life is a greater virtue than death in the name of God."

"You mean that you're in favor of . . . of the colinz-z-z-ation of Mars?" Rounder asked, barely able to complete the sentence, he was so tired.

"Are you okay?" Kreiger asked. "I imagine that it has been a long day, and we can just as easily meet tomorrow."

The medication, combined with the speech and the excitement of seeing Kreiger, had taken a lot out of Rounder. Nevertheless, and knowing it was dangerous to take more than one of these pills in a given day, Rounder took another one; he was so intent upon engaging Kreiger.

"An amphetamine der-rivative," Rounder explained, before slipping it under his tongue. "It-it'll work in a few minutes and put my mind together with my s-speech."

Kreiger excused himself from the table, went to the restroom and returned to a highly focused and seamless conversation.

"I also believe in the s-sanctity of life," Rounder began again. "And my doctors tell me that taking too many of these pills might kill me or damage my mind beyond recognition. I've already tried talking them into sending me to Mars so that they might study the effects of space travel on aging, and use me to experiment with new drugs along the way, b-but that argument went nowhere in a hurry."

"You mean that you would really go?"

Rounder smiled and emptied his sake cup. "In an irregular heartbeat. I always felt that I was born to go. In fact I was supposed to go, but Adam got the nod because I was in so much emotional turmoil after my wife died. Which is why I really wanted to go now, to join with the Dream Machine if I could, and have my remains buried beside Adam's at the end of my dreams."

It was a wonderfully poetic notion. Kreiger filled Rounder's cup with sake, raising his cup for a toast, not knowing that it was also risky for Rounder to drink. "To our dreams and to all of those who have dared to live them."

Rounder savored the flavor before continuing, "So what brings you all the way down here to me?"

"Sara. I spoke to Sara at length in Washington, on several occasions. She wanted to phone you and tell you that I was coming, but I thought you might like the surprise."

"Loved it. My doctors also say that too much stimulation isn't good for me, but I think that I'd rather die in the process of living than live longer on the safer side. I just wish that there something to try for, to strive for, even an enemy alien we could fight that would unite us rather than going down the toilet of evolution fighting against one another and the whims of Mother Nature."

"Did Sara tell you about her dreams?"

"No, but she did express a great deal of frustration with things."

Kreiger nodded. "Which is what brings me here to you. I had similar dreams—premonitions, actually—some kind of oddly intense feelings that came over me following the awakening of Yuri. And I was struck by the coincidence."

Rounder filled their sake cups before answering. "I can see where you're going with this, but it's hard to imagine th-that the feelings or dreams of several p-p-people, however extraordinary, in a world of billions could mean that much—assuming we-we are the-the only ones that are having these dreams and feelings."

"*We?*"

Rounder flashed a boyish smile. "Not dreams or premonitions on my part, j-just curiosity to begin with, which is why I visited Sara to share my concern. The subsequent awakening of Yuri b-b-brought b-back a lot more memories, and sharpened my focus, forcing m-me to measure where we are now against where we were twelve years ago, and the similarities beg my concern—which is why-why I visited Sara."

"Then we are of the same mind?"

Rounder flashed a wide smile and declared, "Finally."

Both finished their drinks before turning to the subject of Richard.

"There is no one closer to Yuri than Richard," Rounder said.

"Which brings me to you: you don't suppose there's a way that we could contact him directly without being discovered?"

"I hardly think I'm the one to ask," Rounder declared. Kreiger had forgotten that Rounder was behind the last attempt at contacting Mars on the sly, an effort which resulted in his torture. Kreiger was about to apologize when Rounder continued.

"We were so d-desperate at the time, so hurried that we had no chance to reason anything out. So we ran off to an electronic store like couple of k-k-kids w-working on a high school science project, T-Tex and I, and put this god-awful contrap-raption together in the basement of Sara's house—which did work. We did reach Gerta, b-but our commun-communication was easily traceable and punishing. But times have changed and . . ."

Rounder's voice trailed off into thought, his eyes roaming the ever-changing, multicolored walls and ceiling, now displaying the ever-shrinking wilds of Africa in sync to an Afro-Cuban drum beat.

Kreiger followed his eyes around the room. "And what?"

Rounder returned his attention to the table and said, "Now that I think about it, there had to be a better way to communicate with-with R-Richard, another way, and it's amazing to me that we never put it to-together. The guy is still the r-r-richest man in this world, even if he is stuck on Mars. He's also one of the smartest, and I find it hard to believe that he's had –n-n-no private contact with any of his company operatives on Earth in all this time. I mean the man discovered that god-damn pulsar all by himself, and from what I understand, he's-he's not the kind of guy who g-g-gives up easily. He's intensely private, completely arrogant and obsessed with maintaining control. And I would b-bet that he's found a way to-to clan-clan-clandestinely communicate with someone on Earth."

This made sense to Kreiger and added another dimension to his quest. He finished his sake and looked around the room before leaning across the table and lowering his voice. "Assuming it is true, where would I find this person? How would I go about it?"

Rounder looked to the ceiling again—now projecting dusk on the Serengeti, the setting sun streaking the western horizon with an intense variegation of color—and pondered the challenge for several seconds before concluding, "It's about the money. It has to be, because money is power. If you can find the m-money, the person who is in charge of Richard's finances on Earth, you might discover how-how Richard communicates with that person, and how you may be able to communicate with Richard."

10

It was nice, spring, Sunday morning in May. The sun was shining on Georgetown, the temperature climbing past sixty degrees before ten a.m. Sara and Michael woke before 6:00 a.m, exercised together, and went to breakfast in a small neighborhood bistro. They were nearing the end of their meal, reading newspapers and sipping coffee at a small table, when Michael noted an article in the *Washington Post*, on the race for the presidency in Russia, and called it to Sara's attention.

He read: "While the presidential election in Russia is hardly democratic and mostly cosmetic, there is mounting intrigue with selection of the next head of state by the People's Republican Party. Behind-the-scenes negotiations at the Party have given rise to speculation of a new power broker on the scene. Olga Sussenko, widow of Vladimir Sussenko, the iconic hero of our early missions to colonize Mars, has emerged as a major player and confidant of the two leading candidates. Sources close to the selection process say that her influence cannot be underestimated. She has name recognition, she has money, and she has experience, having been the daughter of an old-line Politburo henchman."

Sara returned her coffee cup to the saucer and said, "I could not have imagined having that little bit of news with my breakfast this morning."

"It's hard to believe, isn't it?"

"Maybe not, now that I think about it. She was a very determined woman, and she did have a lot of money at her disposal. Maher gave her a small fortune before he left for Mars so that he could gain access to Vladimir. She was so in love with her husband, and she was determined to find a way to bring him back. But she couldn't make any headway, so I advised her. I told her to use her money to co-opt a political party, or several if necessary, to be patient and work the political fringe until she garnered enough power to influence government decisions."

"It would appear that you were a very good teacher."

"Maybe too good," Sara sighed, looking down at the newspaper.

They hardly talked until they exited the bistro, Michael continuing to read the newspaper as Sara became lost in deep thought.

Walking arm-in-arm down the street in silence, Michael looked around at belated spring greenery; Sara, looked down at the sidewalk.

"It is a beautiful day, isn't it?" Michael finally said, looking up at the sun when they stopped at busy corner to let traffic pass.

Sara looked up to him and said, "What would you say if I ran for president?"

"Not much," Michael replied without hesitation.

Sara wasn't surprised. Given her last painful experience with executive power, she figured Michael would be dead-set against the idea. They crossed the street and turned down a quieter tree-lined street, now holding hands.

"Not much is still more than nothing, and I want to hear every word you have to say on the subject," Sara pressed, looking up into Michael's bright brown eyes. He was still so handsome, she thought; even better looking than when they first met.

"If I said no, that I am absolutely against the idea, would you give it up?"

Sara finally looked around her and down the block at the late-blossoming greenery—the lawns and flowers and trees, not as plush and colorful as they once were before the climate change—and emphatically replied, "Yes. I will not make the same mistake twice. I need you, Michael. Emotionally, you complete me. Without you, I would not have the strength. I probably wouldn't win and if I did, I doubt if I would make a very good leader without your support."

Michael was flattered by the certainty and clarity of her answer, but no less wary of Sara's ability to play him to suite her own needs. She was, after all, the consummate politician.

"Do you mean to say that if I had been at your side the last time you became president, things would have been different?" Michael challenged, as they turned a corner.

"Probably not, but . . .wow! This is nice," she said, noting the plusher greenery on this block: the trees seemed taller, the leaves wider, the lawns thicker, the flowers far more colorful and plentiful. "You think that they had more exposure to the sun, or more water?" she asked, pointing to a lilac bush in full bloom.

"I wouldn't know about the flowers, but I do know that there hasn't been an elevation in human spirit these past twelve years; I can't really see that very much has changed for the better since the Lady manifested. If anything, things are on the verge of getting a lot worse than we ever imagined."

Sara stopped to admire a rose bush and caress a particularly large and red flower before replying. "Beautiful isn't it?"

"Unusually so, but hardly the point."

"On the contrary," Sara said, turning her attention back to Michael. "The point is life and why and how some things and people persist and flourish in the face of adversity."

"And why and how other things and people wilt in the process."

"In the process of trying," Sara said. "And if I'm not mistaken, you mean to say that we've already tried and failed?"

That is exactly what Michael meant, but the scent of the rose bush played havoc with his logic. "It is beautiful," he said, leaning forward to smell the flowers. "And you are so beautiful to me," he added, caressing Sara's face.

Michael was about to kiss her when he noted two ever-present secret service agents standing on the far corner. They were never very far away from Sara, posing as couples on the street, as day laborers and domestic help in and around their house, as chauffeurs and taxi cab drivers whenever they traveled.

"I owe you one kiss," Michael said.

"And one answer to my question about running for the presidency," Sara said as they continued walking down the street.

"My answer is this: because you have no solutions to the many problems we have, I fear that you may be putting yourself and this country in harm's way on another whim. And I'm not being contrary for the sake of playing the devil's advocate, or being fatalistic thinking that it's the will of Allah if you do run for office or you don't.

"I am being realistic. I can see that the world is dying all around us even if this small street has found a way to thrive. I can see that the colonization of Mars is a pipedream born of pathos and despair. I can see the odd temperature variations around the Earth, the super-storms returning with greater intensity, how some places on Earth are already too cold to support meaningful life, and how others are too warm—my God, there are firestorms sweeping Africa as we speak. I can see how incredibly unstable and unpredictable the whole thing is, how almost every single scientific model has failed to predict the patterning and progression of global warming, how the fresh water ice melt can precipitate another Ice Age; I can imagine a volcano erupting in the North Atlantic, spewing methane gas into the atmosphere until it catches fire and kills every living thing on Earth! I can see world war precluding all of this because of our inability to be joined at the heart and the problems that are of our own making.

"And I can see the cynicism and despair that has been left in the wake of the great Lady-In-Waiting; how inertia has gripped so many other people who don't even give a damn any more if we go to war over the moon or not, if they even live or die; how the rich feel entitled to live in the sun in Brazil, how the poor will feel nothing from the frostbite. I can see how we have failed ourselves, how many of us cannot wait to die to fulfill the rapturous prophesies of their own religions, including my own.

"In fact, I am becoming convinced that more people want death than life. And I cannot imagine that this is the will of

Allah—to see the human race implode and die in a whimper. And I have been forced to wonder if God is still God if His following cannot survive to serve Him? But I don't talk to you about this because I have no answers, and I cannot support you in such a threatening and dangerous endeavor to become president until you have a vision of your own, until you can see a solution to our problems. In any event, I do love you, Sara, with all my heart, but I will not be taken in by wishful thinking."

Sara could hardly argue the point. She knew Michael was right: without vision, without a solution to the many problems confronting the Earth, she could not lead.

*   *   *

Bu was brokenhearted. He didn't believe that Indra really loved him, because she wouldn't tell him who her supervisors were, no matter how many times he asked. Frustrated and dejected, Bu left her room in the middle of the night and weaved through the narrow streets and alleyways and pathways of Mussoorie until he found himself at the edge of town alone, certain that no one was following him, finally aware that this singularly painful moment was also the loneliest moment of his life: no friends, no teachers, no spies, no Indra.

He continued walking by the light of the waxing moon, wondering how he would fit into the scheme of things without Indra, if he wanted to fit into the scheme of things designed by so many others: was he really born to fulfill their needs and dreams?

The question lingered in the sparse, white light, his eyes roaming across the many distant mountain tops, rising above the high and white fluffy clouds that receded into the Tibetan horizon. It was a beautiful and temperate spring night in the Himalayas, and the beauty only served to intensify the sadness of the young man so engrossed.

He was crying by the time he arrived at his favorite flat rock where Indra had given him that precious little crystalline chip, cursing his lot in life. Bu was so young in the ways of the world, and so inexperienced that he had no reference point to draw upon, no path to follow, no practice to alleviate the heartbreak. He tried to meditate in an effort to ease the pain, but he couldn't stay focused, the pain was so great, his mind churning the mantra of the moment—Indra, Indra, Indra—reaping more pain with each repetition.

Torn between her duty to her supervisors and the genuine affection that she had for Bu, Indra didn't know what to think or what to do. She wasn't in love with Bu, but she had grown quite fond of him; she even thought about marrying him. If not handsome enough to suit her vanity, Bu was charming enough and brilliant enough to achieve worldly fame and riches. He could be her ticket to security in an increasingly dangerous world.

Indra was a realist, otherwise she would not have been chosen for the job of overseeing Bu. Her father, a high-ranking government minister, her mother, an economics professor: their daughter had a privileged life that included private schools, where she continually tested as genius, and caught the eyes of many young boys. She was so tall and sleek with sparkling, black eyes and silky brown skin, and she carried herself with such poise and confidence, it was only matter of time until she garnered the attention of more powerful people. Her father was eventually contacted by an old government crony, who promised a great education for Indra if she would befriend a bright young man in Mussoorie.

Smart though she was, Indra was still young and impressionable, and easily manipulated. All she needed to do was to talk to a "guidance counselor" once a month: tell him how Bu was feeling, what his interests were and receive instructions for the coming month, like suggesting an area of study to Bu, or presenting him with a special problem to solve.

Bu cooperated knowing this, even if he didn't acknowledge it, because he planned to outsmart all of them by winning Indra's heart against all odds and better looking young men who attended their school. It was this brashness and unmitigated enthusiasm that won a measure of Indra's affection; it also blinded him to the greater powers of her supervisors.

Bu didn't really blame Indra: he blamed them, the cogs in the wheel of bad karma, lesser men with lesser minds. As the night wore on, the temperature dropped; the breeze stiffened, but Bu hardly noticed. He was so filled with anger that he eventually fell asleep on the rock, dreaming of vengeance. Bu imagined that he was on walking with Indra across a red, rock-strewn plain, on their way to the beach on Mars, beneath a clear, pink sky.

Indra said, "I don't understand what the problem is. It's so beautiful here, like Earth."

Bu looked across the expansive plain at a row of tall, pinkish mountaintops in the distance and said, "There must be a problem, or else they would not have sent me here."

Indra said, "You think too much."

Bu smiled and said, "About you, maybe."

Indra laughed. She leaned forward and was about to kiss Bu on the cheek when he felt the pain of his brokenheartedness and turned away from her into a small, gray, composite room. He was sitting at a workstation, investigating the mystery behind the Dream Machine, when a familiar voice spoke to his mind.

"You still don't have an answer for me after all this time?"

"Who are you?"

"Richard The Great."

Bu laughed. "Not so great if you can't solve the problem yourself."

"And you can?"

Bu smiled and pointed to a small, crystalline ship embedded in his chest and said, "With this I can."

Bu was about to dislodge it when he discovered a cavernous hole in his chest revealing two hearts, one beating free and easy, the other covered with a large black spider whose long and black tongue threatened to devour the good heart.

Bu was about to cry out in fear when Indra woke him from the dream.

"I knew I would find you here when I couldn't find you in your room," she said, bending over him and running her hand across his short hair. It was near dawn and the northeastern mountain peaks were turning to gold. "I couldn't sleep. I just had to come and talk to you."

"About what?" Bu said, bewildered by the dream.

"About you, about us."

When Bu sat up and looked into her eyes, he forgot the dream and remembered the pain. "You mean that you love me, you really do love me?"

"I do. I really do. I also mean that I am afraid for you," Indra reached for his hand. "These people who talk to me about you, they are from the government."

"What people? I have to know their names."

"I can't tell you. It is too dangerous to tell you."

"You mean that they would hurt you if you help me?"

"Doesn't it hurt enough already?"

"Then at least you can tell me why they are doing this. Why now after I've done so much for them?"

"I don't know. I don't know," Indra agonized, her eyes filling with tears.

"You mean that you didn't ask them?"

"I did. I really did, but they wouldn't tell me."

"And you won't tell me their names?"

"I can't. I just can't."

"So you fear them more than you love me?"

Indra began to tremble. Bu was about to embrace her when she leaned back and looked around, worried that she might have been followed. He followed her eyes and began to wonder if she hadn't recorded everything that he ever said and did with her.

"I don't know what to do, what I can say," Indra said, returning her tearful eyes to him. "I do love you, and I am afraid of them."

Bu forced a smile and wiped the tears from her cheeks with the sleeve of his saffron robe. "I love you, but you don't have to be afraid of me. And if they want something from me, they should simply ask for it. I don't need to be threatened. I just need to be heard."

Indra nodded and squeezed his hand again. "I hear you Bu, and I really do love you, and I will speak for you."

Bu didn't care. His widening smile belied his heartache and his mounting rage.

*   *   *

Yuri's progress and adaptation to the reality of every day life on Mars was steady, if not remarkable. Within a month, he was taking solid foods, seeing colonists, reading all kinds of books and news clips covering those many years that he had been "lost" to the world. He had even begun a regiment of physical therapy. In fact, his life became quite normal save for one curious phenomenon: Yuri never really slept, had no need or desire to sleep, and never engaged anyone in meaningful dialogue.

"He meditates," Alona told Richard on the way through the compound to Yuri's room. "Several times a day for an hour or two at least, and at odd times. You can be in the middle of a discussion with him about one thing or another when he closes his eyes and recedes into himself without warning, without saying a word."

"And he returns to that precise moment in conversation, hours later sometimes," Sasha added. "He just opens his eyes and picks up where he left off. It's actually quite amazing, the clarity of his mind."

"Has anyone ever asked him why he does this or what he experiences when he has withdrawn into this meditative state?" Richard asked.

Alona said, "No, I don't think so."

"Why not?"

"Because people are afraid to challenge him," Bryce said. "And because he seems to have an uncanny ability to skirt the questions, a lot of questions."

"I thought you said that you don't see him?" Richard challenged.

"Not live. I won't go to his room or even watch him on camera in real time. I view recordings. I keep tabs on him because I keep thinking that he somehow poses a danger to us."

The four walked another hundred yards through a heated and pressurized tunnel before stopping at the edge of the old grow room to confer on strategy.

"Any ideas?" Richard asked.

All looked to one another before returning their attention to Richard.

"It's your show," Bryce said.

"It's your ass," Richard said.

"It's my job," Bryce declared. "And I'm tired of hiding from the responsibility. I'm a soldier after all, and I'll take my lumps if I have to. It's either that or quit, and I won't quit on myself. I can't."

"Good man," Richard said.

His opinion of Bryce was changing, however grudgingly. The idea of standing up for the colony of inanity was one ridiculous thing to Richard's way of thinking; seeing a man stand up for himself was a much better thing, the kind of thing that was necessary for survival.

"Then we go ahead with the plan to confront Yuri with no plan, and no design whatsoever. No subject is out-of-bounds, and all displays of emotion are acceptable because I am now inclined to believe that the more we express at this time, the more can learn.

"Just don't kill the bastard," Richard said to Bryce before entering Yuri's room.

*   *   *

So Bryce walked into the room, pulled a laser weapon and shot Yuri in the chest.

11

"Is he dead?" Kreiger asked.

Sara said, "No, not yet."

"You mean that he's going to die?"

"Probably, from what I gather. But at least he's in familiar territory."

"Which is?"

"Comatose," Sara said in an effort to make light of an ever-darkening situation.

"Dear God," Kreiger sighed. He was talking from a hotel room in Dallas; Sara, from her living room in Georgetown.

"What about yourself—how are you doing?"

"On the money trail for the past two weeks. Next stop Mexico City and all points south of the Equator. Then to Europe I imagine, and on to Dubai and Asia. I wouldn't be surprised if I wind up crisscrossing the world several times. No doubt that Maher is worth hundreds of billions of dollars, maybe a trillion, and the number of businesses and the complexity of corporate layers that comprise his portfolio are just staggering. Add to that the number of executive employees who might have the ability to communicate with him.

"If I could just find the beginning, how it all began and with whom—that very first person he communicated with—but everyone and everything is so spread out, if not hidden from sight in some ingenious way. If I only had the mind to function in that arena, the genius to match wits with him to try and figure this all out, but . . ." Kreiger's voice trailed off in frustration.

Sara wasn't surprised and likewise frustrated. All her attempts to unravel the mystery had failed. She was about to hang up when she had a novel idea of her own. "If you don't have the mind for it, then find another mind, someone who can also think out of the box and match wits with Richard."

It was a great idea. Within minutes of their conversation, Kreiger turned his attention to the Newgrid in search of a greater mind.

The Supergrid still elicited great trepidation from many users. After all, it did play host to the first sign of an alien intelligence and the subsequent manifestation of the Lady-In-Waiting. And while the passage of time greatly diminished the impact of the phenomena on the human psyche, it didn't erase them. Many people believed that the Supergrid was still in the grips of another, higher intelligence that lay hiding in the myriad synaptic connections—collecting more information on the species.

The slow but steady emergence of the Newgrid, a secondary cyber-host that claimed to be free of contamination, was a welcome but costly innovation. Few people could afford it, but Kreiger was desperate and Sara had the money.

So he purchased a new holographic computer, established a connection to the Newgrid under a user pseudonym, and went looking for a scientific genius with an extraordinary understanding of the multinational, business/industrial complex, who would be sympathetic to his quest and completely trustworthy.

While Kreiger got lost in cyberspace, tens of millions of peoples around the world prayed for Yuri's recovery. From the moment of his awakening, Yuri had rekindled an interest in space exploration—if not salvation. Many people were quick to attach a religious significance to Yuri's awakening; they became enchanted with the idea of seeing Yuri as an angelic emissary of the Lady-In-Waiting.

Many others prayed for Yuri's death, fearing that he was the Devil incarnate, the Anti-Christ returned to humanity to deceive the pure-at-heart. They even sympathized with Bryce Mac-Donald's plight and extolled him as a hero.

As expected, the media worked both ends against the middle for a profit, whipping the masses into a frenzy while Yuri's life hung in the balance.

*   *   *

The idea of dying before Yuri died was an even harder pill for Richard to swallow. He was becoming sicker by the day.

"I could join with the Dream Machine and persist as mind," he told Sasha, who was sitting at the foot of his bed in his dank little room.

"As an amalgam of minds," Sasha added. "You forget how the Machine absorbed the physical characteristics of each person who joined with it at the beginning, and how the image of the Lady-In-Waiting was the manifest result of the eleven minds that were joined to it. I also remind you that these images didn't last very long; the DNA memory is rapidly deteriorating, and the quality of Machine intelligence may also be compromised in the process."

"What's the good news?"

"The Dream Machine may still be functioning at a very high capacity in any case, and the addition of your genius may be the catalyst for its awakening."

"Then I could seize control after all."

Sasha smiled. "From Adam Sietzer, and Makono Okano, and Gerta Von Strohiem? Apart from their considerable brain power, you would have to contend with their combined wills to seize control, and the power of the indigenous Machine intelligence, and the power generated by that pulsar you discovered—let's not forget the prospect of you dealing with a super-conscious alien intelligence."

Richard looked away in frustration. The idea of joining with all those people and sharing his genius with them was anathema. He was considering an alternative death scenario—"Maybe leaving my brain to science," he was telling Sasha—when the remarkable news of Yuri's recovery reached them.

The laser had put a clean hole through the left side of Yuri's chest, destroying several ribs, a piece of his sternum, a part of his lung, several veins and one artery. But he didn't bleed very much because his heart beat so slowly, and there was little risk of infection because the wound was virtually antiseptic. The laser sealed as much tissue as it destroyed as it passed through his frail body.

*   *   *

"I understand that you were in the room when I was shot," Yuri said to Alona, only moments after he returned to consciousness.

As acting head of security, Alona had spent more time with Yuri in the hospital than anyone else. She nodded and drew her chair closer to his bed. "Myself, Richard Maher and Sasha Alawi."

"Where are Richard and Sasha?"

"In their rooms, I guess, working on something or other. They were both here earlier when you were sleeping. They've been here every day."

"And Bryce MacDonald, where is he?"

"In his room under house arrest."

"For what?"

"Shooting you of course."

"And you take no responsibility for that, not you or Richard or Sasha?"

"Why should we, why should I . . ?"

"Why shouldn't you take responsibility if you knew he was so unstable?"

"We didn't . . ."

"Yes you did," Yuri emphatically replied. "And to the extent that you were aware of the danger, you should likewise be punished. All of you! If this community is a model of human endeavor, if it is truly virtuous and symbiotic, it would function as a just and organic whole and the guilt would be shared by all, especially by those who knew better. Are you are familiar with the concept of Bodhi Satva?"

"Of course."

"You can accept its premise?"

"To the extent that it is an ideal worth striving for, that the enlightenment of one being is not possible until all beings are enlightened."

"Consequently, the guilt of one sentient being cannot exist in a vacuum. The guilt must likewise be shared by all involved. The nearer we are to the crime, the greater our awareness, and the more we share in the guilt. That is justice. The rest is ignorance. And I will not be bound by ignorance. I will not have Bryce MacDonald punished unless all involved are found culpable."

*   *   *

More than another week passed until Yuri was returned to his room, three more weeks until he was ready to address the issue of justice for all people involved in the crime against him. This was the very thing that Richard feared the most—an increasingly charismatic Yuri playing to an ever-larger, guilt-ridden audience—but he could not stem the swell of curiosity and sympathy, or find fault with Yuri's logic.

"If, as a victim, I am granted the right under the Charter of this community to face the accused, then I demand to be seen and be heard by every member of this community, because I am convinced that all members of this community on Mars have a share in the responsibility for this crime," Yuri said.

The community was not receptive to the idea of a public trial, but eventually capitulated to Yuri's demands owing to the added pressures from the billions of people on Earth who could hardly wait to see and hear from this remarkable man. So a special court was convened in a newly constructed meeting hall to try the first felony case on Mars.

Yuri sat cross-legged in a familiar lotus position on a black, composite platform, on the left side of the stage. A triumvirate of judges sat on the right side of the stage behind a gray composite desk. The remainder of the community was seated in semi-circle around the back half of the room. Bryce sat in front of them, flanked by Richard, Sasha and Alona.

Richard was incensed by the high drama, and the seating arrangement, and thought about staying away from the trial in protest. But he was afraid to lose his voice, thinking that he may be the only one in the courtroom who could stand up to Yuri. He also continued to believe, however privately and grudgingly, that Yuri had a valid point: to the extent that Richard and the rest of the community were aware that there might have been a problem with Bryce, they were culpable.

Because of the fifteen-minute delay in protocol exchanges between Earth and Mars, the broadcast was streamlined and packaged into a seamless docudrama known as "The Trial of the Millennium."

"Coronation's more like it," Sasha told Richard, noting the higher position of Yuri's platform.

"Wearing a crown of our fears," Richard cynically concluded.

*   *   *

Bu watched the proceeding with Indra in her dorm room.

Sara watched it in her living room with Michael.

Kreiger watched it in a hotel room in San Francisco.

Rounder saw it in an Orlando bar, thinking that one more drink couldn't hurt.

12

The scope and interest in the trial were amazing. Nearly six billion people were riveted to their Cel-Tels on Earth, making it the highest televised event in history. It was all very strange indeed, how Yuri's awakening impacted the species, how little it took to wet people's curiosity:

a man returns to consciousness after twelve years, says he's not the same man, claims to have seen God, and gets shot in the chest a few weeks later.

Richard thought that it was a testament to their despair, and not a measure of the man that piqued their imagination. When he turned to look around the courtroom at his fellow colonists, he read the dread on their faces and was heartened. They weren't as interested in Yuri as their compatriots on Earth, and they also resented his growing celebrity. These were hard working people who had dedicated their lives to obscurity, to build a better future for their fellow man in space. Even if it wasn't a future that Richard condoned, he did respect them for that much.

They deserved better than this, he thought, watching them shift positions in their seats and talk quietly among themselves. This trial could have taken place in private; Yuri could have requested it, but he didn't, because he had an agenda. As the courtroom came to order, amid a flurry of legal motions and nuances of procedure, Richard put two facts together and came to one inescapable conclusion: Yuri could read minds, he could affect the flow of human events, and he was guilty of an attempted murder, having manipulated Bryce into wounding him in an effort to raise his stature upon survival.

Richard was working on a strategy to present a case against Yuri, when Yuri seized control of the courtroom.

"If the court will please indulge me and allow me to speak to the issue at hand. I am the injured party, and I am not yet well enough to sit through all these elaborations and testimonials."

The members of the triumvirate looked at each other and briefly conferred before acquiescing to Yuri's request. Though there were formal guidelines set down in the Mars Charter for criminal trials, this situation was so unusual and so grandiose that rules were bent to accommodate the circumstances. To begin with, Bryce had already entered a guilty plea, and he had refused to engage someone to act as a defense council. All that remained was the most challenging issue of sentencing. The room fell silent, and the species hung on every one of Yuri's carefully measured words.

"I can see that every effort has been made by the community to present a fair and equitable trial. If I am not mistaken, it would appear the entire Mars community is present. My first question is: how many of you share a measure of the guilt in the crime against me?"

The room erupted in conversational din, and all present looked to each other. Most had already taken a measure of themselves during the weeks leading up to the trail, and the vast majority of colonists did feel a profound sense of responsibility for the crime.

Bryce looked straight ahead and trembled inside, wishing that he'd had the courage to take own life, fearing that Yuri would expose the darker and dirtier nature of his crimes against humanity on Earth.

The first judge said, "We've had plenty of time to discuss the issue, and I think it is safe to say that the entire community shares a measure of the blame—to the extent that, as a small community, we should have been aware of Bryce's emotional instability, and not have kept him in office for so long."

The second judge said, "If there is anyone present who does not agree with this assessment, they may rise and address the proceeding."

Richard was about to stand and point an accusatory finger at Yuri when Sasha grabbed his sleeve and held him back. "This is not the place or the time—even I can see that—to start telling people how Yuri might have manipulated the incident." So Richard remained seated and the trial continued without interruption.

The third judge said, "No doubt that we are all greatly disturbed by this event, by the pain it has caused Yuri Popovitch, and by our inability to foresee it."

Yuri nodded, placed his palms together and imperceptibly bowed to the audience. "I am moved by the honesty and humility of the community. I am also in agreement with the essential characterization of the crime, which is ignorance, our inability to see who or what is in front of us. After all, I invited Bryce MacDonald to my room, and in doing this I invited the injury, however unwittingly. To that extent, I also share in his guilt."

Richard had been outwitted. By admitting to a measure of complicity in the crime, Yuri won the sympathy of the community, and shot holes though the case Richard was going to bring against him. In fact, Richard was so impressed with Yuri's skill and acumen, he began to wonder if Yuri had the power to access his own remarkable mind when Yuri turned his attention to Bryce.

"I just want to know why you did this to me? We all need to know this so we can help you heal and heal ourselves in the process, so we may better understand ourselves in relationship to one another, so we can find the proper punishment to meet the crime."

Bryce was so terrified that he could hardly stand, let alone speak to the multitudes, and Yuri let him wallow in his own quiet hell. More than thirty seconds passed with Bryce staring at the floor and Yuri staring at him.

Nearing the first full minute of silence, Yuri finally closed his eyes and receded into himself, leaving little doubt that he was prepared to wait for hours, if necessary, for an answer.

Approaching the third minute of silence, the entire courtroom was immersed in an almost meditative quiet, the minds of the colonists filling with a cacophony of thoughts.

At the eleven minute mark, Bryce was holding his head in his hands, recalling all he had done wrong, wondering how much more of himself he could stand.

After fifteen minutes of silence, the third judge was finally moved to speak to Bryce: "If you cannot find the strength to address the question at this time, I believe that the court would consider granting an extension . . ."

Yuri opened his eyes, glared at the judge and silenced him. It was another brilliant move, and Richard could not help but admire Yuri's deftness and subtlety. There was nothing more consuming than the void, nothing more powerful than silence, and nothing more punishing. Looking upon the sullen figure of Bryce so engrossed, Richard could hardly imagine his private hell, to be the focal point of so many billions of hearts and minds and souls, all waiting for the answer to his twisted life.

*   *   *

Thirty-seven long and excruciating minutes of silence passed until Bryce began to weep and reach into the depths of all those billions of people, many of whom had spent much of that time looking at that the shortcomings in their own lives.

"Let he who is without sin among you cast the first stone," Richard thought, as the weeping filled the common room and echoed through space and time, and across the Earth.

Yuri's strategy was superlative. Rather than speak, Yuri let the silence speak for itself: could there be a greater punishment than self-punishment?

Could there be a greater good than the common good, wherein all people are connected to the despair of one another by the experience of their own?

It took another five minutes until Bryce MacDonald finally found the strength and courage to rise to his feet and face Yuri, and answer for himself.

"I hurt you because I was in so much pain that I could not bear it alone," Bryce said, choking back tears. "I tried to kill you because I did not have the courage to kill myself—because I have already destroyed so many other defenseless lives, and I cannot live with the shame of it."

Bryce was about to say more, and qualify the nature of his crimes, when Yuri raised his hand and beckoned him forward.

"Are you sorry for your crimes, what you did to me and the others?" Yuri asked.

Bryce nodded, tears streaming down his face.

"Can you name your own punishment?" Yuri asked.

Now Bryce began to cry uncontrollably; several moments passed until he regained his composure and sobbed, "Death. I should be dead."

Yuri nodded and said, "As you wish. Then you will die to yourself, to all your past deeds and desires, to your very name, and you will spend the remainder of your life living for others, in service to others."

Bryce collapsed on the floor in tears as whispers of the Second Coming filled the minds of the billions who watched and wondered: What kind of man is this? What kind of God?

13

Indra was thoroughly taken by the procedure. She expected a trial; she did not expect to witness the emergence of a Bodhisattva.

"He can be the incarnation of Lord Buddha himself," she said to Bu, wiping tears from her dark eyes as the holographic projection faded to black.

Bu was sitting on a chair. Indra was sitting on the edge of her bed. As prized pupils, in a prized school, their dorm rooms were equipped with the latest technology, which included a holographic Cel-Tel. The telecast from Mars was projected into three-dimensional space, the transmitted imagery appearing twelve inches high above a sleek, black "techno-table" near the center of Indra's small room.

"It was a good performance," Bu said matter-of-factly. He wasn't so impressed with Yuri.

"How can you be so skeptical, so cynical? You saw . . . how kind he was, the equanimity of his demeanor, the wisdom of the punishment and the expression of compassion. I have never known anything like this except what I've read in scripture. It's as if the breath of God has entered this man's body."

Bu said, "I remind you that there is no concept of God in Buddhism."

Indra said, "Don't be such a smart-ass."

Bu was afraid to argue the point and lose her affection; he was so hopelessly in love with her. He forced a sly smile and said,

"Smart enough to go to Mars and meet the man myself if I wanted to and decide for myself."

Indra leaned forward. "With me, you would go with me to Mars?"

"Of course," Bu said, because he would say almost anything to make Indra happy while he plotted his revenge against those who threatened to take her away from him—including Yuri, who now rivaled him for Indra's attention.

*   *   *

"That was one hell of a show," Sara told Michael, echoing Bu's sentiment.

Michael disagreed. "The appearance of things is not necessarily without substance."

They remained seated in their living room following the broadcast, the Cel-Tel blaring commentary and analysis from around the world.

Sara lowered the volume before replying, "The man played us like a violin, sitting in a lotus position, tossing petals of patience and wisdom from the mystical beyond—and that compassionate finale, the criminal idiot falling to the ground in a mess of tears and remorse. Next thing you know, the great man will get himself nailed to an antenna array, and we'll be looking to Lord Yuri for our salvation for the next two thousand years. I'm sorry Michael, but the whole thing reeks of a well-scripted ploy; it was just all too perfect and all too timely for my liking."

"Maybe, but you can't discount the possibility of divine intervention, the one chance in millions, that this man had touched the mind of God and was returned to us with a divinely inspired message."

"I thought you believed that mortal man could not possibly know the mind of God?"

Michael drew a deep breath and sighed, "You know damned well what I mean, and I'm not about to be drawn into a philosophical debate with you about the presence of God in the life of man. All I'm saying is that Yuri acted like a man who was divinely inspired, like a man of peace at a time when this world is moving toward war. And he most likely got a lot of people to think a lot better of themselves for his efforts, even if you wish to think the worst of him. I'll even go as far as to say that even if the whole thing was a sham, if it was all somehow scripted by him, it was a damn good script."

It was a hard point to argue. Whatever Yuri's intentions, the result of his awakening was a boon to the species: Yuri did get people talking and looking up to the heavens again; he did get people to think better of themselves. In fact, Yuri got them to do everything that Sara had wanted them to do when she was in the White House; he had already succeeded where she had failed.

*   *   *

Rounder was very nearly drunk when he reached Kreiger in his San Francisco hotel room to discuss the matter of Yuri.

"Wh-What do you think?" Rounder began, following an exchange of greetings.

"Hard to say—it was most impressive—but I would like to know what Richard Maher thinks, now more than ever. He's obviously in the best position to know."

"He was curiously s-silent."

"Necessarily so, I imagine. The experience of Yuri was mesmerizing, most powerful and thought provoking indeed."

Rounder mumbled something incoherent.

"Are you okay?" Kreiger asked.

The question was met by silence.

"Jacob, talk to me. Say something, anything . . ."

Kreiger thought their connection had been dropped and called back. After his third try, he called Sara and expressed concern for Rounder's welfare.

"It didn't feel right. He didn't feel right," he told Sara. She had Rounder's number traced to a restaurant parking lot in Orlando as they spoke.

It took twelve more minutes until a police car arrived on the scene and found Rounder lying across the front seat of his car, comatose.

*   *   *

Richard was baffled. He could not imagine how he would counteract Yuri's enormous effect on the species.

"The man's a lot smarter than I thought, a lot more powerful and sophisticated, with an agenda that's hard to fathom," he told Sasha, upon returning to his room with her. He was lying on top of his bed; she was sitting on the edge of the bed, at his feet.

"Then you don't believe a word of it?"

"Meaning that you do?" Richard sharply replied.

"Meaning I would like to. I would like to think that there can be a man like him—or a woman—someone who can be filled with so much wisdom and compassion."

Richard drew a painful breath and suppressed a cough. "And therein lies the problem, the need for people to believe, the willingness of the masses to create a man-like-god in their own image so that they might think better of themselves, this infernal need to be saved, and an overblown belief that they are worth saving. And if this Christ-like notion has already piqued your interest, it is safe to assume that it is sweeping across the Earth as we speak.

"The only problem I have is that I won't live long enough to dispel it, to prove that Yuri concocted this scheme, by getting inside Bryce's head somehow, and encouraging him to pull the trigger."

"You don't really believe that?"

"Damn right I do, but . . ." Richard looked up to the gray composite ceiling and shook his head, imagining a facsimile of his conversation with Sasha playing out in the living rooms across the Earth.

"Are you okay?" Sasha asked.

"No, because I am already becoming a part of the problem by engaging in a dialogue with you that is turning on the prospect of Yuri's divinity. My God, this guy is brilliant!"

Richard stared at the map of the galaxy taped to the wall above Sasha's shoulder while Sash studied his profile, wondering what he was thinking.

"Earth!" Richard exclaimed, sitting up on his bed. "You have to go to back to Earth!"

Sasha was astounded. "You can't be serious?"

"I am. You must return to Earth, and you have to take the Dream Machine with you—and fast before that brilliant bastard gets his mind on it—because we may never be able establish his pedigree with confidence, and the joining must be uncontaminated."

"The joining?"

Richard read the perplexity on Sasha's face and tried to explain. "I think I've got it! After all these years, I've finally got it! The Dream Machine, the invitation the to stars, the Lady-in-Waiting: it's so obvious now, so simple that the magnitude of the problem with the Machine dwarfed the magnitude of the solution. And it came to me just like that, just before, when I was imagining all those people on Earth trying to fathom Yuri, and deify him in the process by projecting all their needs and dreams onto him."

A searing pain ripped across the top of Richard's head and interrupted his explanation. He lied back on his bed, holding his head in his hands, and continued with great difficulty, wincing as he spoke.

"Pills, I need some pills," he agonized.

She thought Richard needed a doctor; he was in so much pain.

*   *   *

"Richard will not see a doctor. He didn't want anyone to know how sick he was," Sasha told Alona.

"And he wouldn't tell you the secret of the Dream Machine, why you needed to return it to Earth?" Alona asked.

"He was in so much pain that he could not even speak another word."

It was early morning. They were sitting on a small bench in one of the new grow rooms, filled with fruits and the sweet smell of a life they had left behind on Earth. They had met at Sasha's request, she was so concerned for Richard's welfare.

"It's always something with Richard, "Alona exclaimed, even at the end. He is always looking for an edge, always wanting to maintain control, never saying what is really on his mind, and you're always defending him."

Sasha was surprised by the abrasive intensity of Alona's delivery. The two had become very friendly following Yuri's awakening and had never exchanged a harsh word.

Sasha said, "You are acting as if you don't believe me."

Alona fell silent and looked down at a strawberry patch. Sasha looked over Alona's shoulder at the taller greenery flourishing at the back of this new grow room, one of five in the complex bathed in ethereal lighting, generated by fiber optic bundle. The success of the biospheres on Mars never ceased to amaze her. There were enough fresh fruits and vegetables to feed the entire colony, and tons of excess that were dried and stored for an emergency. Most of all, Sasha was taken by the distinct aromas that defined each room, reminiscent of life on Earth and bourgeoning with the promise of fruitful future in space.

Alona hardly noticed the beauty or the sweetness of the aroma. She had receded so deeply into herself, staring blankly into space, and scratching at the numbers tattooed at the back of her wrist.

"It is not you, Sasha, or even Richard," Alona finally said. "It is everything else, mostly the trial. Bryce was my boss, for God's sake, and he tried to kill someone. I guess I do feel a great deal of responsibility for what happened. Of all people, I should have known that something was terribly wrong with Bryce, especially after he had me stand in for him to oversee the security for Yuri."

Sasha placed her hand on Alona's knee. "You cannot blame yourself. Yuri was right about that much. We can all share in the blame."

"And you are in agreement with the punishment?"

"More or less. What else can we do, lock Bryce in a composite room for five or ten years? It is hardship enough living here. And I'm not so sure that it isn't a bad idea, having the victim prescribe the sentence for the perpetrator."

"Within certain parameters, I guess, for as long as the community is small enough to be directly responsive to the crime. But I have other issues with Yuri, how so many people are thinking that he is divinely inspired. As a Jew, I find the possibility challenging to say the least. As a Muslim woman, can you tell me that the attempt to deify Yuri is not disturbing to you?"

Sasha nodded. "It seems that Richard was right about this too, how even the consideration of Yuri's spirituality lends it credence."

"So you don't believe that Yuri is some kind of prophet?"

"On the basis of what, waking up after twelve years and saying he saw God and that he's not Yuri? Then he denies it all and has nothing of interest to say until Bryce shoots him with a laser weapon. Then he oversees the trial and does display a remarkable sense of purpose and wisdom. It is also very curious, if not remarkable. But as far as I'm concerned, there isn't enough information to draw any conclusions about Yuri. I'm not quite as cynical as Richard—yet."

Alona was relieved. "I was hoping you would be fair-minded, and I guess I owe you an apology for my crude assessment of Richard's character. I do believe he is on the correct side of this issue. Yuri can be dangerous if only because he nearly succeeded in charming me out of my beliefs at the trial; his behavior was so exemplary."

Sasha was about to reply when Yuri unexpectedly entered the grow room, riding a small quad, and rolled up behind them.

The woman stood to greet him; Yuri smiled and asked them to sit.

"I was told that I might find you here," Yuri began, looking at Sasha. "I was hoping to talk to Richard. I was told that he wasn't feeling very well."

"Not very well at all, I'm afraid."

"Can I help? Do you think it would help him to see me?"

Sasha smiled. "Possibly. You know how he loves a challenge."

Yuri returned her smile and said, "And you do not?"

Sasha looked to Alona and widened her smile. "We were just talking about that, about you actually."

Yuri coughed and pulled a black, micro fiber blanket up to his chest. His voice was strong, but he looked as gaunt and pasty as ever: much too thin, with shiny black eyes and sunken cheeks and short, black hair.

"No doubt I'm flattered by all the attention, but I have to think that there are better things to do around here than talk about me." Yuri looked around the room before continuing, "Amazing, absolutely amazing getting all these green things to flourish in such a dead, red place. I guess I imagined it, but the reality of it, all this growth and all these people living on Mars, thriving no less! I was so lonely here for so long that I used to imagine the presence of an alien intelligence here just to keep me company."

The women were surprised at Yuri's candidness and were quick to engage him.

"Didn't you write about sensing an alien presence here?" Alona asked.

Yuri nodded. "I did, but I believe it was exaggerated to fulfill my own needs at the time. I was very lonely."

Sasha flashed a playful smile. "Not all the time. There was a tryst, if I'm not mistaken."

"Which ended in heartbreak as I recall," Yuri added.

Sasha and Alona were surprised by the sadness in Yuri's voice.

It was the Brazilian girl, Arika, Yuri explained. "It all seems so long ago, as if I were living someone else's life—really. But I have been reading and asking questions, even reading my own journal entries, and the information does stimulate the memory. And I can tell you both something I never did forget: Captain Adam and Vladimir and Gerta. In fact, there is nothing I have read about them that has captured the true majesty of these people: the strength of will, the courage, the sheer gall to think that they could beat the odds. All I did was fall asleep for twelve years and whatever happened to me, happened to me in a dream state; I did not act upon anything. I bore witness. These people gave their lives for the betterment of others. They are still my heroes."

Both women hung on every word, mesmerized by the ease and quality of conversation.

"Can you tell us about this dream state, where it took you, what you saw?" Sasha asked.

The women leaned forward. Yuri drew a pungent breath and sneezed.

"My God, I haven't smelled anything like this in so long; it is like perfume in here, intoxicating as life on Earth. And the Earth is such a pearl, as beautiful and enchanting as anything I have ever seen in a dream, or in another reality. There are so many realities, layers upon layers, and layers within layers.

"Imagine if you will, a universe existent within a celestial sphere—translucent—so that you can see from one reality into another, above and below you, and on all sides of you. Imagine existing as mind and engaging other minds, passing through other worlds and minds and dimensions. And each thing, each reality, is all so remarkably different in scale and color and texture.

"Vibration! That is the word that may best describe it. I remember now, when Ramesh drew the OM sign on the ground in the cave before he died. He knew. He was on his way there."

"Where?" Alona pressed, leaning so far forward in anticipation of the answer that she towered over Yuri seated in his quad.

"The heart of God, Alona, that place in heaven where the children of Israel may finally take rest. Sasha tells me that I told her I saw God. But even if I don't remember saying it, I think it's true though—I did see God. But it's only a memory now, becoming lost in a tangle of other memories of being here and on Earth, and in all of these other places and realities. It's still hard for me to distinguish this life from the other lives I lived, harder now as I become accustomed to this corporate state, to life on Mars in this body."

"Can you tell us about these other lives?" Sasha asked.

"I can try, but you would need to understand that we are all living our lives in other bodies—even now—except that we are not aware of these lives. More exactly, I should say that others are living within us. The experience I wrote about in my journal about the alien within, that was my first clue. Then I saw her and . . ."

"Arika?"

"Not Arika."

"You mean the Lady-in-Waiting, you saw the Lady-in-Waiting?" Sasha pressed.

Yuri shook his head. "I can't say that. I just can't. It would not be right."

Sasha and Alona would not take no for an answer and regaled him like a couple of school girls, but Yuri wasn't moved.

"I imagine that there will be another time and place for these discussions in some detail, if I can still recall them, but this is not the time or the place."

"Can you at least tell us how you arrived at the sentencing recommendation for Yuri?" Alona asked.

Yuri explained: "It came to me while I was recovering from the wound. Bryce did not like who he was. He hated himself with such intensity that he couldn't even drink the pain away, or find the courage to kill himself and be done with it. So I started to think of a way that he could dissolve his sense of self and answer to the community in the process. In the end, it was a matter of common sense, nothing more."

Sasha found it hard to believe: if it was all so simple, why not dispense the justice in the privacy of a small court room and avoid the show trial? As much as she was charmed by Yuri, she was becoming frustrated with his evasiveness; in turn, she was reminded of Richard's skepticism and continued to press the issue.

"Nevertheless, you did speak to Bryce's mind, you did access his thoughts. Bryce told us you did."

Yuri was loathe to explain, feeling that he had already revealed too much of himself, and continued reluctantly. "I imagine that I must have connected to Bryce's mind, or else I wouldn't have known some of the details of his life, but I cannot truly remember exactly when or even why I entered his mind—and some other minds too. I hear thoughts, I pick up on feelings, maybe even a dream that someone may have had, but I can't say why it happens or how because I cannot even be certain of my own orientation, or even my own identity sometimes.

"When I said that I wasn't Yuri, I wasn't being deceptive. I just don't remember saying it. I get lost within myself somehow. I close my eyes to sleep or meditate, but I am not truly sleeping or meditating, I am drifting, passing between dimensions of awareness, still living other lives in other places. When I first returned to you in this life on Mars, I did not know if it was real. And the more time I spend here in this dimension, the less I remember about other dimensions and experiences. I am here and I don't know why. I am Yuri and I don't know why. And it is a wonder to me how so many of you people are thinking so highly of me when I don't know myself."

14

The biggest problem confronting humanity was the continuing release of methane gas into the atmosphere from heat vents below the North Atlantic. Unabated, this slow but steady heating process guaranteed a catastrophe: The return of super-storms, the dissipation of the Polar Ice caps, the flooding and complete destruction of great coastal cities, the desalinizing of the North Atlantic shutting down the Great Conveyor Belt, the ensuing flash-freeze plunging all of Europe and half the United States into an Ice Age within three years, the death of two billion people, and the prospect of war between dying nations for territories nearer to the Equator.

But no one seemed to care, despite all the scientific models that arrived at the same conclusion. Again and again, despite all the heroics and discoveries, it was the inertia, humanity's willingness to die a slow and inevitable death, the unmitigated fatalism that doomed humanity: the unbridled narcissism, the practiced myopia, the appalling and enduring lack of self-worth.

"Enter Yuri, one man removed from this planet for nearly sixteen years, a footnote to the heroics of others, comatose for twelve of those years, and all of a sudden the sky's the limit," Sara said.

"Enter Yuri indeed!" Kreiger said. "We ravage the Earth Mother and pollute her womb. We are guilt-ridden to the extent that we feel unworthy of the future and he poses a ray of hope, if not a path to salvation."

"It's the posing that bothers me," Sara said, before excusing herself from the table to refill her coffee cup at a nearby counter.

They were talking in a quiet corner of a second floor hospital cafeteria, in front of a large window, both having flown into Orlando to see Rounder. It was just after ten o'clock in the evening and Michael was filling in for them at Rounder's bedside. The prognosis was guarded: the traveling, the public speaking, the excitement generated by Yuri's awakening combined with the pills he was taking for his speech impediment put Rounder into shock.

Kreiger looked out the window, at the leaves of a moon-lit palm tree flapping in the breeze. The effect was very nearly hypnotic. He hardly noticed Sara returning to her seat across the table.

"You look tired," Sara began again, wondering if the strain wasn't too much for him. Kreiger didn't look very well, sallow and weary after only several weeks of travel.

"I'm very tired, but the problem isn't with my health. In many respects, leaving New York and connecting with so many old friends was the best thing for me. And I'm looking forward to meeting with a very interesting man in Japan, Hiro Suzuki. It turns out that he worked for Okano as grad student in Kyoto, and helped assemble the Dream Machine. But the problem I'm having is something else entirely, which is why I questioned you about Father Vincent."

Sara remained silent and waited for an explanation. The topic filled her with dread.

Kreiger looked out the window again before returning his attention to Sara. "I cannot forget what you told me about Father Vincent's dreams: the image of Christ crucified upside down, and his premonition of impending doom."

"The nearer the truth, the greater the lie," Sara said.

"I don't understand."

"Michael actually said that, paraphrasing a disturbing dream Father Vincent once had. Father Vincent was talking about Chinese mythology, about the fierce Chinese dragons and how they pose as guardians to the spirit world."

"And only the pure at heart may enter," Kreiger added. He was well versed in all the Asian philosophies and religions.

"That was the inference, as I recall it." Sara sipped her coffee, wishing she could smoke a cigarette.

"An alien intelligence might pose as a dragon to us."

Sara shrugged. "Possibly, but I must remind you that Father Vincent had no answers. By his own admission, he had failed to resolve the issue."

"I cannot believe that, because I'm inclined to believe that the success was in the trying, his willingness to re-examine his own faith if necessary, to find the truth."

"And you, my dear Kreiger, are you telling me that you have also joined the ranks of the willing?"

"As if the path hasn't chosen me?"

Sara looked into his tired brown eyes and was reminded of the many people that had already lost their lives to the quest, and how many more had lost faith. "I just can't help wondering how many more of us will be lost in the process of saving ourselves?"

* * *

"Millions," Bu said. "It could take millions of years for the Earth to regenerate following the onset of an Ice Age, depending upon its length and intensity. And it is more than likely that another species will inherit the Earth—evolved from rats or insects maybe—when it's all over. They have survived almost everything else so far, and have probably earned the right to survive our own stupidity."

Indra said, "As if it was our fault that the heat vents opened up in the North Atlantic?"

They had spent much of the day in school watching a Cel-Tel special on climate change and studying the latest scientific models. After school, they decided to take a walk out of town, up the side of the mountain to their favorite flat rock.

"As if we haven't contributed to the problem by polluting the atmosphere with carbon dioxide for past hundred and fifty years," Bu briskly replied. "Maybe the Earth just got angry after being abused for so long and decided to vent its rage on us."

It was a novel idea that many people ascribed to the problem with methane gas, viewing Earth as Gaia, a living and breathing intelligent being who was fighting for its life.

"So we all have to die of guilt without putting up a fight?"

"Or run away to Mars."

"As if I had a choice," Indra sullenly replied.

"You have a mind, a better mind than your idiot supervisors or else you wouldn't be here."

"I don't feel better, and if I was so smart I wouldn't be making you feel so bad about me because I have to leave. I don't want to leave, Bu. I do love it here; it's just so beautiful."

It had been foggy and drizzling in the town of Mussoorie; they had passed through an entire layer of clouds before emerging into the sunlight. As always, the view from the rock was breathtaking—row upon row of distant snow-capped peaks stretching way back into Tibet.

"You're so beautiful." Bu squeezed her hand and kissed her on the cheek.

"Nothing would ever look as good to me if you left."

They walked along the path that meandered around the mountainside, the one side covered with tall trees, the other overlooking the mountains and the multi-layered weather patterns.

"I don't think I would have come here in the first place if I knew it would take me away from all this," Indra said as the neared their favorite spot. "I would have gone to a regular school and had a regular life; I would have been a lot happier being more of a girl and less of a woman, having all the boys flirting with me the way they did in high school and not thinking about too much."

Bu was crestfallen. He was about to let go of her hand when she tightened her grip and looked into his sad, brown eyes before continuing: "But I like you more than I would have liked them because I'm more of a woman now, because I can love the symmetry of your mind and the kindness in your heart."

Bu was confused. He didn't know what to believe, his heart turning on every word: she loves me, she doesn't love me, she has to love me, she wants to love me.

When she kissed him, he was convince that she loved him and said, "Just tell your supervisors that I want to meet with them, and tell them that I have something that they want that can alter the course of human evolution."

"Are you serious?"

"Deadly serious."

*   *   *

"In my opinion, Norbu Hua Chang has the finest mind on Earth," Suzuki said.

Now director of Okano's laboratories, Hiro Suzuki had agreed to meet with Kreiger at his office, on the top floor of a long, white building, sporting an impressive array of powerful satellite dishes on the roof. He wore the long, white overcoat of a technician and clear pair of techno-glasses that he continued to adjust throughout the conversation.

"The boy's intellectual prowess is easily comparable to Maher's or Okano's, maybe comparable to Einstein or Newton if he applies himself. He attends one of Maher's schools in India, but I can't imagine he learns very much, because there is nobody who can teach him, no one who can match his intellect from what I gather. It's just a place for him to mature under watchful eyes, almost impossible to approach without permission. I would imagine The Indian government covets him like a cache of diamonds. The boy's mind is a virtual holograph; his memory is unparalleled. I would imagine that he is already thinking in dimensions that people like us, who are reasonably smart in the evolutionary scheme of things, cannot begin grasp.

"I saw him at a conference in Delhi about six or eight years ago, when the Indian government decided to preview the boy. They had him walking around the hallways, dropping into a conference here and there, challenging a theory or a conference leader for the fun of it. I overheard the boy on several occasions and was awestruck by the sheer power and symmetry of his mind. He was only eight or nine years old at the time, and he couldn't have been very familiar with any of this material—holographic technology, quantum drive machines, M theory and the like—but his intake was remarkable. The boy would listen to an argument for ten minutes, grasp the core and pose a challenge or offer a perspective on a problem that no one had ever considered. Then he would just smile and walk away with his supervisors leaving everyone else bewildered—absolutely amazing. Then the boy disappeared for a few years and turned up in the Himalayas at a Maher academy."

"So Maher has had a hand in his training?" Kreiger asked.

Suzuki shrugged. "One would suppose, but there again you have the problem of communications with Mars: how would Maher communicate with this boy, and what would be the nature of Maher's relationship with the Indian government?"

Kreiger said, "I cannot imagine, which is why I requested this meeting with you, to see if I can find someone who can figure out how Maher communicates with his representatives on Earth."

"I'm not sure I can be helpful. You know I met Richard Maher on several occasions many years ago. The meddler, I called him. The man was so arrogant and forthright, hardly a measure of subtlety or grace. On the one hand, I can imagine he was devastated by Okano's achievement, building the first conscious Machine—the race was pretty much between the two of them, as I recall. On the other hand, Maher's subsequent contributions cannot be dismissed. His discovery of that pulsar may be the single greatest discovery in the history of the species. God only knows what it can mean to us if we can just figure a way to survive our own myopia."

"Under the circumstances, you would think that Maher would make an effort to contact one of us—not me, but someone like you, who worked on the Dream Machine."

Suzuki shrugged, removed the techno-glasses from his face and wiped them before continuing: "I doubt very much if Maher would put his trust in me. I'm much too close to the Japanese government for his liking, taking grant money and all that, and being in business for myself."

"I understand, but the problem with the Machine's liquid memory, the deteriorating DNA: it would seem that time is of an essence to preserve the Machine memory."

"Perhaps, but I can't imagine that Maher wasn't aware of this a long time ago considering the experimental nature of the Dream Machine. The DNA material could have been contaminated from the outset, or poorly contained, or compromised in some way by usage or handling.

"And there is no doubt in my mind that Maher must have devised a rather ingenious method to maintain communications for so many years—perhaps several methods, now that I think about it. If he can track that pulsar and figure how it was communicating with the Dream Machine, talking to someone on Earth would be a rather pedestrian accomplishment by comparison."

Kreiger drew a deep breath, shook his head and sighed, "I just wish I was more of a scientist; so much of this escapes me. Can you tell me if those papers that came up for auction in London had any special value?"

"I couldn't say for sure without seeing them. Rumor has it that there were some interesting notations in the margins regarding the Imagining Mars program."

"Were you contacted by any prospective buyers?"

Suzuki nodded. "Several people actually, all wanting to know if I could verify the material as Okano's."

Kreiger fell silent and looked out a small window at a cloudy sky; Suzuki adjusted his glasses again and studied Kreiger's profile.

"Can I ask you a question, Mr. Kreiger?"

"Of course."

"Why you, after all these years—especially you—who crossed the world railing against the value of space exploration?"

"Not the value as much as the timing. It was the awakening of Yuri that engaged me, if you must know: the nature of it, the timing of it, the apparent quality of his experience."

Suzuki smiled. "As I suspected. Hardly an hour goes by without me looking up at the sky—the ceiling, actually, I spend so much time in the laboratory—and wondering, simply wondering."

"And you've had no luck building another Dream Machine?"

"Apparently not, even if I do believe that I have succeeded in replicating everything Okano created more than once. There is that something else, the quality of the initial crew input, or maybe it was that solar storm they weathered in space, or even the proximity of the Machine to that pulsar and the Supergrid, that oddly perfect moment: who can say what sparked that remarkable confluence of events that created us from that dormant pool of ooze."

"Then you don't believe that there is an alien component?"

"On the contrary, I do believe because it's the only thing that makes sense. In idle moments, when I am looking up at the ceiling, I can imagine an alien intelligence trolling for life in much the same way we did with the SETI program, and we just happened to be on the right wave length at the right time.

"It may also be that the grandiosity of it all that has blinded all of us to the possibilities, like a man who is standing two inches from a one-thousand foot wall who cannot see the over top, or around the sides, because he is too simply close. I have also read the writings of Yuri Popovitch, when he talks about the alien within and around him, when he was first marooned on Mars, that remarkable sense of a something else that may not be wholly alien after all. If we can accept the concept of the Big Bang, then we can appreciate how all things in this universe are somehow connected, and it may only be a matter of becoming aware of the connection—with the use of a Machine perhaps."

"You mean that we should be viewing the Dream Machine as an extension of ourselves?"

Suzuki nodded and met Kreiger's wide eyes. "As a tool, an extension of our awareness as opposed to something distinctly sentient and apart from ourselves that has made contact with a distinctive and disconnected intelligence on the other side of our galaxy. In the end, I suspect that the problem we are having with our understanding of the Dream Machine may be more of a matter of perception than engineering."

*   *   *

Before Kreiger left Kyoto, Suzuki gave him the names and Cel-Tel numbers of four people who had asked him to verify the Okano papers that had come up for auction in London. Within hours, with Sara's help, Kreiger discovered that two of these four interested parties were businessmen looking to make a profit.

"This third party may be tied into the Japanese government, an operative looking to track the material that was stolen from Makoto's laboratory. The fourth interested party may have ties to Maher," Sara said. They were talking via the Newgrid. At Kreiger's suggestion, Sara bought a new holographic computer upon leaving Orlando.

"How is Jacob?"

"Stable, but unresponsive—hope floats. And you must keep your eyes on the ocean because you are swimming in a rough sea of hungry sharks."

"I don't understand."

"You mean you haven't been followed?"

"I can't say because I wasn't paying attention."

Sara lit her cigarette and exhaled, "Which is just as well. In any case, there is nowhere you can go in Japan that is not scrutinized by camera, and there is no way you could approach a man like Suzuki without being noticed."

Kreiger was surprised by his own naïveté. "You could have told me."

"And made you so self-conscious, and so uncomfortable that no one would approach you."

"Approach me?"

"Among other things, you are the bait."

15

Kreiger ended his conversation with Sara on a pleasant note, but he became uncomfortable with the idea of being followed. He also resented her lack of candidness: Sara could have told him that he was in play. But there was little Kreiger could do about it, so he took a shower, dressed for the evening and headed down to the hotel restaurant—increasingly aware of a well-dressed Japanese gentlemen that he met in the elevator, who had followed him into the dining room. The man went to the bar and ordered a drink; Kreiger requested a small table at the back of the crowded room, near a mirror that strategically reflected the imagery at the bar: the man in question looking back at him throughout the meal.

As a result, Kreiger became increasingly uncomfortable and left the restaurant for a seat in the busy lobby. He bought a newspaper, sat on a couch in the lobby, ordered a cappuccino and casually observed the ebb and flow of people for another hour—until he finally noticed the same well-dressed gentleman sitting behind him.

Now completely disconcerted, Kreiger finally left his seat and approached the man on impulse. "Fritz Kreiger," he began, extending his hand.

The man stood, smiled, bowed from the waist and introduced himself. "Tishiro Anakawa, Special Agent for the government of Japan, in charge of your security."

Kreiger hid his surprise and bowed ever-so-slightly from his waist. "I'm flattered by your government's concern for my welfare, but I cannot imagine that I am in any danger."

"Perhaps not, but it is better to be safe than sorry," Anakawa said. "The greater the mystery, the greater the danger: any inquiry into the Dream Machine can present a powerful reaction."

*   *   *

Altogether, Bu spent three weeks alone working on a very special project that he claimed would alter the course of evolution. He hardly spoke to Indra, didn't attend class, wouldn't respond to several teachers who stopped by his room to check on his welfare. He wouldn't even let them in through the door. And all were forced to respect his privacy because Bu was so brilliant and capable, smart enough to conjure a Unified Field Theory, or thwart the process of global warming, or solve the riddle of the Dream Machine—or feed Indra's supervisors some kind of convulsive nonsense that they could never fathom.

On Bu's insistence, Indra finally arranged for a meeting between him and her supervisors, who didn't like the idea, but were compelled to see what Bu's genius had wrought. As Bu requested, they met on the steps of a small Buddhist temple in the heart of Happy Valley.

It was a rainy afternoon. Indra and her supervisors were first to arrive. Bu came twenty minutes later in an effort to heighten the drama. One handler, Colonel Singh, wore an expensive blue suite. A tall and swarthy man, he also sported an out-dated, but nonetheless impressive handlebar mustache. The second, shorter man wore a sports jacket and slacks. Both middle-aged, they looked like Criminal Intelligence Division (C.I.D.) agents.

"You are living here in Mussoorie?" Bu began, following introductions. All were standing beneath the soffit.

The supervisors looked at each other.

"Sometimes," Colonel Singh said.

"And the other times?" Bu pressed.

"New Delhi," Colonel Singh said.

Bu nodded. "You are scientists?"

Colonel Singh said, "No."

Bu said they were wasting his time, and walked away into the rain.

*   *   *

The second meeting didn't fair better, and didn't last any longer. It was held the next day in the temple gardens. It was warm and sunny and Colonel Singh showed up with another man dressed in frumpy chinos, a yellowing white sport shirt, and a state-of-the-art, clear pair of techno-glasses. He looked like a scientist.

Bu said, "You are a scientist?" following introductions.

The man said, "Yes, an astrophysicist with a second degree in nuclear engineering."

Bu said, "Do you think that you are as smart as me?"

The man looked into Bu's brilliant brown eyes and stammered, "No."

Bu walked away, telling the man in the blue suit, "If you cannot find anyone as smart as me, how can they understand my work?"

*   *   *

Bu wouldn't talk to Indra after the first meeting, but he did talk to her on the night after the second meeting, because she wouldn't leave his door until he opened it.

"Because they do not believe that you have anything of value to offer them," she said. "And if you will not produce, they will not have another meeting with you."

Bu said, "Okay." He was about to close the door when Indra played her trump card. "And they will not allow me to see you again."

It was a bad play because Bu had the upper hand, always had the upper hand, "But I can save the human race from itself and they can't."

*   *   *

The third meeting was extraordinary, held in the evening in-side the Tibetan temple. It was attended by Colonel Singh, and two highly regarded scientists: a prize-winning, theoretical mathematician and a world-renowned quantum physicist.

Indra waited outside.

"I have the answer to the problem with the Dream Machine," Bu began.

"What problem exactly?" the mathematician asked.

"There are so many problems," the quantum physicist added. "Perhaps you are having some success with the deteriorating liquid DNA?"

Bu smiled. "With the joining. I know how we can join with the Machine. I know how we can maximize its potential and survive the experience as one mind."

Everyone was surprised and looked to each other before con-tinuing.

"Please explain," the mathematician said.

Bu said, "No, because none of you are qualified in his area."

"Suzuki in Japan!" the quantum physicist cried out. "He worked with Okano on the construction of the Machine. He would qualify."

"We have no time for that," Colonel Singh concluded. "I have no doubt that you two gentleman have the capacity to compre-hend the answer even if you lack the ability to apply it; we can always speak to Suzuki."

Bu nodded. "If you can get me what I want, I will give you what you want."

"That will depend upon the veracity of your answer," Colonel Singh said.

Bu nodded again. "I want Indra," he declared, locking eyes with the handler.

"Indra you can have, if we can have your answer," Colonel Singh said.

Bu smiled and said, "Eight hundred million, five thousand, two hundred and ninety one."

"Rupees?" Singh wearily replied, surprised by the inanity of the request.

Bu widened his smile, "Not money, energy! The amount of human minds it will take to energize with the Dream Machine, and connect to that pulsar on the other side of the galaxy—if the joining is properly handled."

The scientists were flabbergasted and began to pepper Bu with questions: "How did you arrive at that number? Why so many? How can we be reasonably certain that such a mass joining can be safe? How can you know if each mind can be returned safely to the original host?"

"Can we see the math?" the mathematician asked.

Bu said, "No. Nothing will be revealed until I am certain that Indra is pledged to me, and the Dream Machine is safely returned to Earth."

*   *   *

Was it the intelligence of coincidence that joined Richard and Bu's minds to unlocking the mystery of the joining, or was it another event in the long line of evolutionary necessities when great minds, functioning independently, simultaneously arrive at complementary solutions? Or had Richard and Bu been working the same problem together all along?

Did the answer really matter in the odd and pressing scheme of things?

"Everything matters, but nothing matters more than time," Richard told Sasha, after she had characterized her conversation with Yuri in the grow room. "Essentially, what Yuri described to you and Alona was a quantum entanglement, telling you that he lives in several dimensions or realities at the same time—which is theoretically possible, if not staggering to consider.

"Then again, humanity has a history of schizophrenia, of people projecting themselves into their own dreams and believing they're real. It's just hard to see where the truth is. In any case, I cannot imagine that Yuri ran into you and Sasha by accident. And if timing is everything, this guy's going to corner the market on power when I'm gone because no one mind can stand against him—no collection of minds for that matter. I can hardly keep up with him myself. In fact, I can only keep pace by inference and instinct, which continue to tell me that there is great danger looming."

"How can you be so sure?" Sasha asked. "You can't even admit the possibility of his enlightenment."

Richard struggled to sit up in his bed and reply. Sasha was sitting on a composite stool beside the bed. She could no longer sit on the edge of the bed, fearing that the slightest movement would cause him a great deal of pain. Richard was becoming so sick and sensitive, and resistant to the pain-killing drugs he was taking.

"I can't admit to the possibility of being wrong, because if I am right, and Yuri does pose this enormous threat, it could be the end of us all as being distinctly human, assuming there is a mass joining to the Machine and Yuri has been compromised by an alien intelligence. The risk is just too great. Under no circumstances can Yuri be allowed access the Dream Machine. There is also the matter of decomposition of the liquid memory of the Machine, which may preclude any further joining and damn the species to no hope."

These points were hard for Sasha to argue, thinking it was better to err on the side of caution. And if Yuri was a highly enlightened soul, no doubt that he would forgive the fearful machinations of lesser souls, Sasha thought.

"Assuming that you are right, I still cannot imagine how the Dream Machine can be returned to Earth, how anyone of us would be allowed to accompany it given all the problems with back-contamination. As I recall, the solution is still theoretical."

Richard stifled a laugh because he was afraid that it would turn into another painful coughing fit. "Not theoretical, Sasha. Political! Amazing how you can still buy into all that bullshit, as if there ever was a problem with back-contamination. Even given the worst case scenario, where no progress has been made with the 'so called' problem of back-contamination, anyone one of us on Mars could be returned to a sterile observation lab orbiting Earth, have their blood exchanged several times if necessary, have the rest of their biology tested and retested by the most anal assholes they can find up there, and be repatriated to Earth, and deposited in a pressurized room without a problem, without infecting anyone with our biology.

"But the longer we stay on Mars, the less likely we can be returned to Earth because the greater problem for us is pressurization—which is why they have you people sign-on for the long haul, so that you can never be returned Earth, and never be in a position to upset the status quo and poison the body politic with new ideas on anything meaningful.

Sasha had heard it all before, but she still found it hard to believe. "It's insane. Humanity is dying from a progressive expulsion of methane gas into the atmosphere, and these people are preoccupied with defending the status quo until death: how can any of this matter when there is even the smallest chance for the species to save itself?"

"Because it's easier for most people to die than live. People give up on themselves all the time, and if one person can do it, an entire species can do it. Add the Dream Machine to the mix, tell them that they may be able to plug their brain into a box and live again somehow, and a lot of them will tell you that it's against their belief systems, or that it's contrary to the flow of destiny, that their supposed to die because they're not worth saving, or that Jesus is waiting for them on the other side of this insanity. While forgiveness may be the most powerful force on Earth, guilt is the driving force behind death."

"It's just so hard for me to accept."

"Because you've been free of the gravity of the situation for so long, and because you already risked your life by coming to Mars in an effort to make another life."

"It's not only that. It's the responsibility: the idea of me returning the Dream Machine to Earth, it's incomprehensible. I'm not a hero. I'm not Gerta or Vladimir or Adam Sietzer, I'm not like you. I'm not even sure I came to Mars to build something new; I was so deeply pained and brokenhearted when my boyfriend died in the Jihad—and I didn't have much family left on Earth. If you must know, I came here to forget as much as anything else."

Richard said, "We all have someone or something to forget."

"Even you?"

"Myself. I had everything that there was to offer on Earth, and everything wasn't enough—less or more, what does it matter? The idea was to keep in motion, to search for food, for energy, for new ideas. In terms of being heroic, I'm not sure a lot of heroes know who they are until the situation presents itself. You won't be Adam or Gerta, you will be yourself and marvel in the process of your own becoming."

"But I cannot even imagine the next moment, I am so afraid sometimes."

With great effort, Richard sat up in bed and caressed Sasha's face, which was a startling display of affection that added to the uniqueness of the moment.

"Even Adam was afraid of something—inner demons that assailed him from the moment they left the Earth. And I remember how frightened Gerta was after Vladimir died, and Yuri, who was so scared of living that he bugged out on life for twelve years. Evolution is a fickle impulse, lurching left and right, picking one over the other to fulfill its purpose. Yesterday it was a fish that became curious and swam close to the shore, and sidled up on the sand to get a better look, today it is a small Sufi girl on Mars who has been chosen to return the Dream Machine to Earth."

"Because you say I must go does not make it so," Sasha replied, reaching for his hand.

"The circumstance dictates the necessity, and you are necessary. You are the only choice available to me; you are the pinnacle of human evolution."

Sasha looked down at her petite body and laughed. "Now I really have reason to question the theory of Intelligent Design if it has found perfection in my life."

Richard smiled. "Perfection is one moment in time, dear girl, not a lifetime. Just being at the right place at the right time and seizing the opportunity."

"What about Alona, can't she help?"

Richard shrugged and coughed, and lay back in the bed. "As much as she can hurt because she is tied too deeply to the past. The numbers that she has tattooed on the back of her wrist can be problematic when the metaphor challenges the reality of tough choices for the future. She may be too much of a Jew."

"Meaning that I am less of a Muslim?" Sasha challenged, letting go of Richard's hand.

Richard widened his smile and clutched his chest, suppressing another cough. "More of a realist, I suspect, or else you wouldn't be talking to me. Then again, you will need help and Alona is predisposed to align with you against Yuri's interests, and she is head of security—a pilot, no less!"

"I just don't think I can do it without her help, and even if I did, how will I convince anyone on Earth that you have solved the mystery of the Dream Machine?"

"Of the joining, I think. I still haven't worked out the math—how many minds it will take to succeed, and how much power will need to be generated by the Machine. But the worst of it is the politics and the deceptions, the half-truths and the half-ass people you may have to engage along the way—until the interest in returning the Machine to Earth becomes an obsession, which may not be too long, from what I understand."

"You mean that you have been in contact with Earth?"

Richard looked at her like she was an idiot. No matter how close to death, no matter how desperate for Sasha's help, no matter how much he liked her, Richard could not change, would not relent under duress. This time it was the cancerous pain that quickened his delivery and soured his disposition, and offended Sasha.

"Let's put it like this: I have no doubt that at least one person on Earth will make an effort to contact you when you arrive in orbit, assuming you get that far. In any event, you must prepare yourself for the unexpected, seize the opportunity when it arises, and discard your concept of right and wrong when the situation demands—even lie, cheat and steal if you have to, and work it out with your Muslim God afterwards when you find the time."

"I am afraid that is something I cannot do, forget my ethical and moral obligations on a whim," Sasha angrily replied, standing to leave.

"Then you will die a half-ass death," Richard snarled. "Because the evolutionary process does not reward weakness and stupidity."

*   *   *

Sasha stormed out the room, down the passageway, cursing Richard. She was nearing a row of tech rooms when she turned a corner and bumped into Bryce, knocking a stack of electronic junk out of his arms.

I'm so sorry," she began, stooping to help him pick up the pieces.

"No problem," Bryce said, gathering the odd lot of wire and metal.

He was in the habit of spending most of his time doing menial jobs for the colonists and servicing Yuri, living more like a shadow and less than a man, apparently unaware of the heightening drama.

*   *   *

Sara had no idea what was happening on Mars or Earth. She had never heard of Norbu Hua Chang, and she hadn't heard from Fritz Kreiger in two weeks. As a result, her worry turned to depression. She hadn't left the house in three days, despite the nice spring weather, and she hadn't slept in ten days—spending her nights drinking coffee and liquor, smoking cigarettes, watching old movies, and reading old books.

"Novels, actually," she told Michael. She was sitting on a couch in the living room when he came in to check on her. "This one in particular." Sara handed him a copy of *Demian* by Herman

Hesse. "It's something that was referenced in Yuri's writing—he was alluding to a conversation between himself and Gerta and Mei Yi before they even left for Mars—and I was curious about the one passage he quoted." She took the book back from Michael, turned to the relevant page and read: "'The egg is the world. Who would be born first must destroy a world. The bird flies to God. That God's name is Abraxas.'

"Then I searched for Abraxas on the Grid and discovered that it was essentially the God of all things, good and evil, and I deduced that the 'egg' was a poetic metaphore for an illusion. In order to see the reality of life, we would first have to destroy the illusion of life, all of our preconceived notions. Which is a concept that may be suited to Yuri's experience, being stranded on Mars for so long and seeing his conditioning wither in the harshness of an alien environment, watching the egg crack and looking deeper into the nature of things."

Michael was bewildered by her intensity; it was 3:30 in the morning. "I like my eggs for breakfast," he cracked, and yawned before continuing. "And you should come back to bed before you lose your soul in the toilet of moral relativism, to Ex-Lax or whatever the hell you call that new God of yours."

"Abraxas!" Sara declared, miffed by his sarcasm. "And it is not my God, or a new God. It is a high concept, a point of view that postulates the existence of God in every being and every thing—and in every act, whether it is percieved to be good or evil."

"Not my God," Michael said, turning to leave. He was tired.

"And not your problem," Sara shot back.

Michael turned back. "What is that supposed to mean?"

"What it has always meant: that you found a God that requires blind faith to the status quo, whatever it may be, because everything that happens is the will of God, which denigrates the will of man and lets you off the hook."

"So you're angry at me because I believe in the will of God and you believe in the will of man, and because I can sleep and you can't?"

"More or less," Sara replied, tugging at an errant curl behind her head; it was an old nervous habit. She was bracing herself for an argument.

Michael shrugged, leaned over the couch, kissed Sara on the top of the head and said, "Thank God for small things," before leaving the room and returning to bed.

Sara wished that she could be angry with him, but she couldn't; she loved him so much in spite of his God.

*   *   *

Sara was fast asleep on the couch, clutching *Demian* to her chest, when Kreiger reached her on the Cel-Tel.

"Where in the hell have you been?" Sara asked, sitting up on the couch.

"India, I'm in India!" Kreiger excitedly declared. "In the Himalayas, but we can't talk like this. Call me back"

Sara was bewildered. It took a moment to clear her head from sleep and retrieve her new computer from the study. The computer was small, about six inches in diameter, quite thin and most powerful when connected to a pair of techno-glasses, and capable of scrambling communications across the Newgrid.

"Now you can tell me where you've been these past two weeks?" Sara challenged, sitting on the couch.

"On the heels of a genius, a teenager, Norbu Hua Chang, who may already be in contact with Maher, or have the ability to match wits with him. He attends one of those technological schools sponsored by Maher, and Suzuki tells me that this boy might possess the greatest mind on Earth. The problem is getting to meet him, being able to speak with him alone. He is heavily guarded from what I understand."

Sara reached for a cigarette, lit it and exhaled, "So we let him approach you."

"How would I do that?"

"By becoming the bait. Letting him see you, inadvertently, of course, walking by, sitting on a bench, maybe in a shop buying something, any place where you can inadvertently drop your name without inviting suspicion."

"Assuming I haven't raised enough eyebrows already."

"Assuming," Sara said before taking another drag on her cigarette. She had been so proud of herself, consigning her habit to several cigarettes an evening for the past month. She was already looking forward to another smoke with her morning coffee.

"And you think that my name will mean something to him?"

"Once again, you sell yourself too short, my dear Kreiger. Given time and circumstance, I assume that a great mind will always recognize another great mind, and if this boy is as smart as Suzuki says, he will know who you are, and he will want to know why you are in his town."

Once again, Kreiger was struck by Sara's quickness and understanding of human nature. "What about Jacob? Have you spoken to his doctor?"

Sara said, "No, but he did leave a message, about a week ago. I guess I forgot to tell you because it wasn't definitive, just more of the same with him drifting in and out of consciousness, rallying and falling back. But he's not in any immediate danger from what I gather.

"Then you are planning to see him?"

"Soon, I hope," Sara said, filling with guilt. She'd hardly thought about Rounder, had made no plans to see him, and he was her best friend.

*   *   *

So Kreiger spent the next few days playing the tourist, strolling around Happy Valley, sitting on benches and reading newspapers, shopping for clothes and small gifts, eating in a variety of restaurants, hoping to glimpse the boy genius and make eye contact with him—to no avail. There was no trace of Bu in the Valley.

On the fourth day, Kreiger was tempted to walk by the school, but was dissuaded when he finally realized that he was being followed at a discreet distance, and was reminded of the warning he had received in Japan, that his life may be in danger.

After lunch, out of frustration, he waited out an afternoon rain in his hotel lobby and went for hike up the ridge when the rain stopped. Reaching the top, he was struck by the ethereal beauty, the rows of snow-capped mountaintops, the layers of clouds and sunlight, and the rainbows crisscrossing the sky. It had been many years since Kreiger had witnessed this kind of grandiose beauty, many years since he had the time to sit back and enjoy the majesty of life on Earth.

He found a long, flat rock and sat with his knees folded against his chest as he looked out over creation, dumbstruck by the beauty, terribly saddened by the realization that it may all be lost to humanity in the not-so-distant future—she was so deeply immersed in the paradox that he was unaware of the eyes watching upon him.

Bu and Indra had also waited out the rain in their rooms and had decided to meet at their favorite flat rock. Bu arrived first and was surprised to find a stranger perched in his cherished place. He was momentarily miffed, that became increasingly curious about the man dressed in brown leather shoes and a light brown suede jacket, unzipped and flapping in the breeze, whose vulturine profile reminded him of an eagle; whose concentration was akin to a deep meditation.

Most unusual, Bu was thinking when Indra showed up and said, "We can find another place."

Bu said, "No, this must be the place." He waited another ten minutes with Indra until Kreiger turned to meet their eyes.

"Beautiful isn't it?" Kreiger began, unaware of whom he was addressing; he was so caught up in the majesty of the moment.

"The most beautiful place in the world, in the entire universe!" Bu exclaimed, looking over the mountains. No matter how often he had seen the view, the next time was always the best time.

Indra smiled and reached for Bu's arm. Instinct told her that this man was no ordinary man.

Kreiger returned her smile. "Join me if you like. There is plenty of room for three."

Indra was about to say no when Bu reached for Indra's hand and stepped forward.

Kreiger was struck by the odd coupling, a boy in dressed in saffron robes with a girl wearing skin tight blue jeans and a tight blue sweater.

"I am Henry K from New York," Kreiger said, offering his hand to Indra first. She sat between them.

"I am Indra and this is my boyfriend, Bu."

"Norbu Hua Chang," Bu added, pressing his palms together and bowing his head.

Kreiger was momentarily stunned and fell silent. This was the boy he was looking for.

"What has brought you to our lovely corner of the world?" Indra inquired.

"God. God and Sara Sietzer. Before I was Henry, I was Fritz Kreiger," Kreiger said, looking past Indra directly into Bu's brilliant brown eyes, hoping his name would resonate with Bu, hoping his directness would count for something.

Bu was surprised. Indra was concerned. She looked behind them as if she were looking for help, but the ridge was empty.

"I'm sure you know of Sara Sietzer," Kreiger added.

"Of course," Indra nervously replied. "Who cannot know the most remarkable woman in the world? And I also know of you from our studies: German descent, scholar, theologian, author, Opus Dei Numerary, member of the Club of Rome."

Errand boy, Bu was about snarl, thinking no better of Kreiger than any other suitor looking to profit from his genius, until he recalled the life and times of Fritz Kreiger and realized that he was in the presence of greatness. "I read your books and I reread your debate with the astronaut Jacob Valdez, at the Texas Christian University in America, so many times that it is almost committed to memory."

"A debate that was lost because of an argument that was mute," Kreiger sighed, looking up to the sky. "Our future is tied to the stars whether we are ready for it or not."

"Ready or not, the quality of the argument was not lost on me," Bu said, impressed with Kreiger's humility. For the first time in a very long time, he met a mind that won his interest. "I would like to talk more, and I would like it very much if we can talk alone."

Indra was surprised and threatened. "I don't think this is the time or place for conversation with a man we just met."

"Then don't think and don't talk. You will wait for me over there—Bu pointed to a tall tree ten yards away—where you can watch me and I can watch you."

Indra was saddened by Bu's tone of voice; Kreiger was stunned.

"She is used to taking orders," Bu told Kreiger as they watched her walk away. "She is a spy for my government supervisors. But she now takes orders from me because they have sold her to me for information on the Dream Machine."

Kreiger was stunned and bewildered by Bu's candidness. He hardly expected to meet a boy genius in the company of a girlfriend who was an indentured spy. "I don't understand."

Bu said, "I thought you were here about the Machine, to see what I know."

Kreiger said, "I am here to find out about Richard Maher, if you have been in touch with him, if you can find out how he can communicate with his people on Earth—surreptitiously—if you can help us communicate with him?"

Bu shrugged and said, "If you can tell me why?"

Kreiger explained, telling Bu about his life on the streets of New York, serving the needy under the name of Henry K for twelve years, and how the awakening of Yuri Popovitch had piqued his curiosity. "Until my interest became an obsession for me, and for others like Jacob Valdez and Sara Sietzer who had been likewise afflicted—and millions more who are inclined to believe in the divinity of Yuri Popovitch."

"Are you telling me that you believe in this?"

Kreiger looked out across the mountains and sighed, "I believe in our salvation through our Lord Jesus Christ, but . . . I can't help but wonder what else is out there, and I would like to know what Richard Maher thinks, if there is reason for us to hope or reason to fear."

Bu was further engaged by Kreiger's candor, treating Bu like an equal by continuing to express his uncertainty as opposed to flashing his own brilliance.

"And you say that you know nothing about my research on the Dream Machine?" Bu reiterated.

"Nothing. What I do know is mostly the result of a conversation I had with Suzuki in Japan, who worked on the Dream Machine with Makoto Okano. He is the one who led me to you. He told me that you had the finest mind on Earth."

Bu looked over Kreiger's shoulder at Indra and said, "If that were only enough."

16

Richard was bedridden, hanging on to life by a thread, coughing up blood, when Yuri entered his room on a quad.

"I came to see you because I imagined that you were unable to see me," Yuri began, rolling up to Richard's bedside.

Richard nodded, spit blood into a handkerchief and drew an uneven breath. "That's one way to put it."

"You are thinking that I read your mind?"

Richard coughed and struggled to sit up; he would continue to cough and gasp for breath as they spoke. "Am I thinking incorrectly?"

"Inexactly, old friend. I don't read thoughts as much as I receive impressions, feelings, actually, an individual's state of mind as opposed to their calculations."

"And you felt that I was dying?"

"Alona told me."

"And you came to say goodbye."

"More or less. I do consider you a friend despite your unease with me. I am aware of your caring and kindness while I was absent from this life for so many years. I have been told about this many times by many people, how you visited my room each and every day and watched out for me. A man cannot have a better friend."

"It wasn't friendship, Yuri."

"What, then?"

Richard shrugged. "Despair. I needed to talk to someone and no one was smart enough around here so I talked to you, which was better than talking to an idiot or a composite wall. I imagined that you heard me, and agreed with me, of course."

"Then you needed me after all."

Richard managed a smile. "I suppose. I suppose I realized that I needed someone or something to care for, which is an all too human condition that was forced upon me by circumstance, by my continued failure to crack the mystery behind the Dream Machine. I guess it humbled me over the years, and I turned to your care by default. Believe me when I tell you that I never liked you very much to begin with. You never had my brains or Adam's courage or Vladimir's strength or Gerta's balls. Lest you forget, I was around when she begged for your help and you conveniently disappeared within yourself when she needed you most.

"And now you expect me to believe that you've returned to us enlightened somehow? Well, I don't believe it, because your exit from responsibility does not support your return to wisdom. As I recall, you were left behind with the pariahs on home base here in Shalbatana because you were weak, precisely because you weren't very smart or very strong."

"If I am not mistaken, Richard, you were left behind with me because of your own weakness, and your own lack of faith in the mission, and because you couldn't be trusted—and it was I who was entrusted with the responsibility of overseeing you. Nevertheless, it is your inability to grasp this moment that surprises me in view of your considerable intelligence.

"The facts are these: I am alive, you are alive, and the dream is still intact, and how we arrived at this remarkable and precarious junction is a testament to the dynamic behind human evolution, which is the intelligence of coincidence after all, that sudden and sacred lurch to survive against all odds and logic—when necessity transcends reality, when there is no accounting for someone like me and a poor accounting for someone like you."

Yuri leaned forward in his quad and looked into Richard's bleary eyes before continuing. "While you may have failed to solve the mystery behind the Dream Machine, you did discover that pulsar which may go down as the single greatest achievement in human history, if the species can survive itself."

"And you won't tell me why this achievement is so great, nor why you have returned to us to show us the way to salvation?"

"I can't because I am still uncertain of my role in all of this, and because I am not yet convinced that this species is prepared to make the journey."

"Because we are unworthy?"

"Because you are too fragmented."

"Because you say so?"

"If I am not mistaken, Fritz Kreiger, the theologian, said this a long time ago, that the species was not prepared to meet its own destiny in the stars because it was not joined at the heart on Earth."

"And you have been returned to us to bind our differences?"

Yuri shook his head and sighed, "As if the fate of humanity can be decided by any one man. As if I would want this responsibility. I am not your savior, Richard. I am not the Second Coming."

Richard leaned forward and clutched his chest. "Then who the hell are you? Tell me, please, and I will keep your secret and die a peaceful death."

Yuri looked down at the gray, composite floor, shook his head again and stammered, "The truth is, I don't know . . . I just don't know. I was here. I was gone and I'm here again, and I don't know why. Here, I am Yuri. In other places, I'm someone else and I really don't know why—or how this has happened to me or what I am supposed to be doing while I am here.

"If I appear wise, it is by accident, not by design. I know you believe that the trial was a contrived event, and I am here to tell you that it was not. I said what I said and I did what I did because it seemed right and natural, because the situation demanded it—not because I concocted some kind of insidious plan to co-opt the manifest destiny of the humanity."

"Then you believe that humanity has purpose?"

"Purpose it may have, but not security. The future is not guaranteed from what I've seen."

"And you won't tell me what you've seen," Richard snapped. His loss of patience was exacerbated by the pain in his chest.

Yuri wasn't moved and continued evenly. "You will see soon enough, assuming that you will be joining with the Machine in the near future."

"Then you are saying that your experience has paralleled the experience of the people who have joined with the Dream Machine."

Yuri flashed a mischievous smile. "I believe so."

"And you refuse to tell me how or why, or what happened to Adam, for instance, or Okano, or any of the others when they joined with the Machine."

"I must refuse."

"Bastard," Richard spat, unable to contain his frustration.

"Exactly!" Yuri declared, gripping the arms of his quad as if he was about to stand up. "That is exactly who I am, not here, not there, not belonging anywhere, to anyone or any place in particular, floating between dreams and realities, not knowing who or what is real—if I am real! This much I will tell you—I have been trying to tell you—that it is taking all of my strength to be here and to appear cogent and normal, and to hear people referring to me as wise and spiritual completely misses the point of my own mortality, which is hanging by a thread.

"I may be as close to insanity as enlightenment, if you must know. To the extent that I am trying to find myself out, I am no different than any other man, holding on for dear life until I figure it out."

"Holding on to this life? Can you at least tell me if you are having the same experience of yourself in your other lives?"

Yuri shrugged and scratched at his scraggly beard, and for the very first time, he betrayed a weakness. "To some extent. It is all connected somehow. We are all connected. Here, I am Yuri. In other times and places, I am someone else to other beings, like I'm having a dream about a dream inside another dream—but it's all very real sometimes, if I remain in a place too long."

"You mean that you can control where you are living, and who you are experiencing?" Richard pressed. No longer frustrated with Yuri, he was becoming enthralled with the man.

"I could. I did. I thought I did, but . . ."

"What?"

Yuri shrugged. "Since my awakening here, much has changed."

"I still don't understand why you can't be more specific, why you can't even provide me with a glimpse into another one of your lives, or even describe another reality to me?"

"Because it changes so quickly, because I'm not so sure it isn't all a dream—ever since I awakened here, everything else is becoming less real to me, where I've been, where I think I've been, who I thought I was. And I am afraid to share this experience with you or anyone else because I fear it might somehow diminish its intensity or sever my connections to other lives, and I will be stuck here forever."

Richard was utterly bewildered and forced himself to sit up in his bed. "You mean that it's so much better and nicer out there?"

Yuri flashed a brilliant smile. "It is beyond your wildest imagination, the infinite variety and complexity of things, the unmitigated joy and the sheer terror lurking behind every experience, traversing the subtle realms of being and not being, the lives that are lived in the shadow worlds, between dreams and dimensions, the oddity of births and deaths, of souls that border on the immortal, existing like thoughts and ideas in other minds, becoming gods and goddesses to one species before they are discarded and manifested in the minds of another species to fulfill other needs, entire galaxies straddling one another and creating new galaxies, creation straddling creation, annihilation begetting annihilation on a whim; always wondering if you are the dream or the dreamer, if it is all real or not." Yuri widened his smile and looked into Richard's wild eyes before continuing. "And the women . . ."

Richard was leaning so far forward off his bed that he nearly fell into Yuri's lap. "You CAN tell me about the women. You have to tell me about the women."

Yuri appeared on the verge of recounting a particularly torrid tale when his delight turned to melancholy. "I can tell you about the Lady-In-Waiting, how remarkably appropriate the name is, how utterly remarkable it was for the species to conjure her likeness. She is us, Richard, and she is more than us. But she cannot wait forever."

"What is she waiting for?" Richard pressed.

Yuri said, "I can't say."

"Why can't you say, why?"

"Because I'm afraid that if I reveal her nature, it will alter the evolutionary flow of human events—if I would be helping or hurting the plight of humanity by sharing my experience."

"You mean that you have no vested interest in the evolution of the species?"

"On the contrary, I am most interested in its survival. I just don't know where I fit in because I am uncertain of my own identity."

"Can you hazard a guess for my sake?" Richard coughed up another wad of blood and mucus, and winced from the searing pain in his chest.

Yuri leaned back and his quad, scratched at his beard, closed his eyes for a moment and finally said, "I guess I came to bear witness."

*   *   *

Olga Sussenko had moved to St. Petersburg shortly after Vladimir's death to be with their daughter, Sonya. As time passed, she began to resent the colonization of Mars—she saw no value in it or the further exploration of space, and was dedicated to the ascension of the Russian empire. To that end, Olga had spent much of the last twelve years in Russia out of the political limelight, working the edges of several different political parties—including the Greens and the neo-communists—until she had formed strong relationships with several younger and more dynamic members of these parties. As Sara had suggested, she used the money that Richard Maher gave her to support their political causes and even their families; she positioned herself behind them and pushed, ever so gently and steadily, until they began to achieve prominence in Moscow and St. Petersburg.

She was an ultra-nationalist who had manipulated the Greens and the neo-communists to her own advantage, telling them what they wanted to hear while clinging to her private notion of vengeance.

After all, Olga Sussenko was a megalomaniac who had never recovered from the loss of her husband. She was working the consummate deal of a lifetime, nearing the end of a long and drawn out negotiating process to annoint the next president of Russia—under the guise of a democratically held election—when the talks broke down and Olga inherited the presidency by proxy. She was nominated in an effort to bind the growing fissures in the People's Republican Party.

Michael was sitting on the living room couch watching the Cel-Tel when Sara walked in, squinting from the sunlight. It was late in the afternoon. The large bay window faced west and the descending summer sun lit the room.

"The light doesn't bother you?" Sara began, as she crossed the large room.

Michael shrugged. "I was napping until a few minutes ago. And you? You were gone for a long time."

"Downstairs," she said, leaning over the back of the couch and rustling his hair.

"Again," Michael looked up into her lovely green eyes, reached for her arm and gently stroked it.

Sara smiled. "I just can't seem to get enough of it lately. The beauty is inexhaustible, beyond imagination." She was referring to a new celestial sphere program that she had been running in the basement holo-suite. "And I swear that I can still see a faint resemblance of Adam in the Lady."

"It is possible, I suppose."

"I know that it can also be a matter of wishful thinking," Sara added, looking across the room at the Cel-Tel. "But . . ."

"But what?" Michael asked, following her eyes across the room to a news broadcast.

"God damn it, she's what!" Sara exclaimed, pointing at the image of Olga Sussenko filling up the ever-changing wall, composed of liquid crystal.

"Given the state of Russian politics today, the election of Olga Sussenko to the presidency is all but certain following her nomination as head of the People's Republican Party," the reporter said. "She is the future of Russia."

"And God help us all," Sara added, walking up to the wall and studying Olga's image.

Michael said, "In any event, we'll have to live with her."

"Not if I can help it," Sara said, before rushing out of the room.

17

The hot season, having arrived late in India that spring, was fairly typical of the changing and erratic weather patterns around the world. It was hotter and wetter than usual in the mountains, and colder than usual when it wasn't so hot—but not alarming to the untrained eye of a stranger. Kreiger liked the unpredictability of the weather in Mussoorie. He thought it was stimulating, and he didn't see the problem until Bu pointed it out to him.

"The weather pattern has changed a great deal every year since I've been here, and no year is the same as another. I also thought it was intriguing until I looked at a weather model for the past fifty years and saw how erratic it has become, even if it isn't as changeable as the rest of the world. The seasons here are still well delineated. It's just that everything we experience in the mountains is more intense, more changeable from day to day, from hour to hour sometimes—and more beautiful, too, from what I am told from long time residents in Mussoorie."

They were still sitting on Bu's favorite flat rock, looking out across the rows of snow covered mountaintops that stretched into Tibet as they spoke. Indra was still waiting on them, sitting under a nearby tree where he had placed her. Again, Kreiger was struck by Bu's apparent maturity and poise. He could not imagine the childish emotional turmoil derived from Bu's relationship to Indra.

Kreiger said, "It is among the most beautiful places I have ever seen. You must like it here very much."

Bu looked at Indra. "I did. I mean, I still do, but . . . I never thought about leaving here. I don't want to leave here but . . ."

Kreiger followed Bu's eyes onto Indra and continued cautiously, inadvertently hitting the heart of the matter. "You mean there is a problem with you being here?"

Bu nodded and looked down at the rock. "With her and her supervisors. And the more I think about it, the more I begin to wonder if you haven't been sent by her supervisors." Turning to Kreiger, he continued bitterly. "But I don't care anymore, because I have something you all want."

Kreiger was about to reply when Bu stood up and walked away from the ridge with Indra.

*   *   *

Kreiger called Sara later in the day. It was early morning in Georgetown, before sunrise, and Sara was down in the basement doing yoga in a tight white jumpsuit when he reached her on the Newgrid.

"There's something terribly wrong here," Kreiger concluded, upon profiling his encounter with Bu to Sara. Kreiger was speaking from his hotel room in Mussoorie. "The boy told me as much. I guess I would say that his behavior was erratic—adult and courteous when I first engaged him, then strangely boyish toward the end. He seemed very angry, angry at the world, and he was not kindly toward the girl. He didn't treat her very well at all, as if she were the major source of his discomfort."

Sara thought for a moment and said, "Then it's the girl you must reach, but very carefully. He may have the brains we need, but she might have the power. Is she pretty?"

"Stunning, I would say, tall and thin with raven black hair."

Sara laughed. "Definitely has the power no matter how smart he is, if I can use my experience with teenage angst as a measure. And you have to be very careful, indeed. The closer we get to the source, the greater the power and the greater the danger. I assume that you were followed from Tokyo."

Kreiger looked around his room as if he was looking for a spy. "I wouldn't know."

"What about now, in Mussoorie?"

"I imagine, but I can't say."

"We can assume that you are. At the very least, we know that the boy is being shadowed which means every person in that little town must know who you are by now. We have to think quickly and creatively; I have to think . . ."

Sara ended the call and lay back on her yoga mat, thinking so deeply that she did not hear Michael coming down the stairs with more bad news: increased seismic activity in the vicinity of Greenland threatened the release of greater volumes of methane gas into the atmosphere.

"One hell of a day this is turning out to be, and the sun's not even up yet," Sara said, sitting up on her mat and wrapping a towel around her head. She recounted her conversation with Kreiger before returning to the foreboding news about the Greenland Ice Shelf. "Have they taken any measurements of the atmosphere?"

"None, as far as I know. I'm not sure that there's anything to measure yet. The impression I got was that the increased seismic activity may be a prelude to a violent expulsion of methane gases in the near future."

"A volcano?"

Michael winced and began to blink. "Could be, but there's no way to know."

Sara folded her legs against her chest and rested her chin on her knees. "There's never any good news anymore. It would be nice to wake up to good news one morning. It's just the same old thing every day now, this slow downward spiral to oblivion, and it's still hard to imagine how we can preempt it, or turn it around, or even slow it down.

"The truth is that I have been thinking about running for president again, if only to parry Olga's rise to power on the world stage. But when I see the enormity of the challenges facing the world, and measure them against my own lack of understanding, I can hardly see the point. I can fight Olga, but I can't fight science and the machinations of nature. I can't prevent an earthquake and lesson the impact of methane gas. No one's even come up with a theoretical solution to engage the problem. And the idea of reigning over the decline of the species as president is just too depressing to contemplate. I just hope Kreiger can be helpful somehow."

"The Dream Machine again?"

"What else, Michael? You have your God and I have another husband living inside of a Machine, for all I know. And he joined with that Machine because he believed in it, so I have to believe in it. Out of respect for his effort, I am compelled to make an even greater effort, even if it means sending Kreiger on a wild goose chase across the world.

"As if I don't know how ridiculous this all sounds: Mars, Machines, dreams and premonitions. It all sounds like a bizarre sci-fi novel written fifty years ago; it's even stranger than fiction, but so is contemplating the end of humanity. And wanting to do something about it, no matter how outrageous, is still better than doing nothing. And maybe we can get lucky somehow, and the ridiculous connects to the ridiculous when we least expect it and it creates hope."

It was a hard point to argue; nevertheless, Michael uncharacteristically took issue with it. "I think you're looking for trouble, and I'm afraid that, in the long run, you may even do more harm than good. Why can't you back off and have some good thoughts and see if a better idea occurs to you?"

"Why don't you back off?" Sara shot back.

Michael was about to reply when he reached for the back of his head and winced from a sudden rush of pain. "I should," he said, before leaving the room and retiring to the study.

*　　*　　*

At Richard's request, Alona brought the Dream Machine to his room the day after he spoke to Yuri. Sasha was present by virtue of her membership in the rotating governing counsel, likewise Usha Sanchez, and Kim Jong Tui, the computer engineer who oversaw the infra-red connection from the implanted node at the base of Richard's neck to the Machine. The rest of the colony was invited to observe the joining on their monitors.

Richard thought that the whole affair was a bit ghoulish, seeming more like a public execution to him than an experiment, but that was the price he was forced to pay to have his request honored—and the joining proceeded without incident.

When asked if he wished to make a statement, Richard said, "You can all kiss my genius ass."

He died like he lived, insufferably, and very quickly, with a trace of a smile on his face. The Dream Machine downloaded protogenic bytes of his human experience in seconds. It did not return to life or manifest another hologram.

Yuri said nothing. He was not invited to Richard's room, and did not observe the joining on a monitor.

*   *   *

"Because he was afraid that Yuri might somehow influence the process," Sasha told Alona several hours after the joining. They were sitting in the old grow room on a small bench, under an old apple tree that had been planted by Gerta more than twelve years ago.

Alona nodded. "I thought about that. The whole idea of Yuri being able to read my mind, or whatever the hell he does, is more than a little disconcerting—making me feel like I'm not really in control, and I'm supposed to be in control. I'm head of security now and it's my job to be aware of what's going on around here, and there is no way I can be aware of Yuri, who's still telling us that he's not sure if he is Yuri. I've also considered the prospect of Yuri joining with the Dream Machine, if his mind can empower the Machine, if he might exert undue influence on it."

"And?"

Alona tossed her hands in the air in frustration. "And nothing. I don't want to think about it. I thought Bryce would be in office for many more years. I never expected to have his job. I couldn't have imagined an attempted murder, by my own boss no less! I still feel somehow responsible. But it happened, and here I am."

Alona looked up at the apple tree and began to scratch at the numbers tattooed at the back of her wrist before continuing. "There are three Jews on Mars including myself. The other two are scientists, a couple of astrobotanists, who are prevented from having a child for six more years in an asinine effort to preserve the politically correct balance in the community. Only last week, I was talking to them about observing the high holy days this year, having a small service and a special dinner to celebrate the Jewish New Year in September, but they weren't very interested. It turns out that her mother wasn't Jewish, meaning that she's not really Jewish. His mother was Jewish, but his father wasn't and he was raised in a secular household. And now they tell me that they're not even sure that they will raise their child as a Jew—when they're allowed to have one."

Sasha said, "I'll celebrate the Jewish New Year with you."

Alona smiled and placed her hand on Sasha's knee. "You are too kind—and I may take you up on the offer—but it doesn't diminish the fact that my heritage is withering right in front of my eyes. And the awakening of Yuri hasn't helped. This couple I told you about, they're becoming obsessed with Yuri, talking about him as if he's the Second Coming of Moses, Christ and Buddha rolled into one damn sham." Alona removed her hand from Sasha's knee, looked down into her eyes and added, "I just don't trust him."

Sasha looked around the grow room, saw two people walking through on the far side and replied, "You know I don't trust him. And you know Richard didn't, which was why he kept Yuri away from the joining. He was afraid that Yuri might influence the process somehow or get his hands on the Dream Machine. Sick as Richard was, he was the perfect foil, the only mind on Mars capable of matching wits with Yuri."

Alona leaned closer and lowered her voice. "I've thought about this, too, how we are losing our grip, and how Yuri is filling the vacuum because there is no one to challenge him."

Sasha leaned forward and looked down at the worn and dirty composite floor between her feet. "It's hard to believe that it's come to this, afraid to speak in public for fear that Yuri might be listening. I mean, look at us, sitting here talking in lowered voices, looking around."

"It reminds me of something my grandmother, Rifka, told me about how it was in Europe before the Holocaust, when people were afraid to speak their minds and go against the prevailing fascist powers—how the Jews were herded into cattle cars and sent to their deaths, how they went quietly without protest, without even a fight. And it all began with a bad idea, born to the mind of one sick and twisted human being."

And the plot was hatched.

*   *   *

It was early morning in Mussoorie when news of Richard's death reached Earth. Kreiger was in his hotel room sipping a glass of orange juice, looking out the window at a blue sky and pondering his next move—wondering how he would approach Indra—when she arrived at his door.

"We must talk," she began softly, standing outside his door, looking up and down the hallway. "But not here."

Kreiger put on a sweater and followed her out of the hotel.

"You must know that we are being followed. I am always followed," Indra explained. "With or without Bu, I am now under surveillance at all times. There are cameras and audio devices planted everywhere—along the paths and further back in the mountains where you met us," Indra said as they wound their way through a crowded little bazaar. It was set in colorful plaza, surrounded by tall trees, and filled with all kinds of wares and foods and clothes.

"Then why leave my hotel?"

"Because making it easy can only serve their purposes, and I am not recording you now."

Kreiger raised both eyebrows; her candidness was so unexpected. "Can you tell me who 'they' are?"

"My supervisors, but I can't use names. In fact, I'm still not sure if I know their real names. I am told that they represent my government, but I can't be sure of that either, because I have no way to check up on them. I'm so sorry that I allowed myself to get involved with all this, but my parents said it was the right thing. I was so young and naïve, I couldn't imagine how badly it would affect Bu and how much it would bother me. I guess I do love him in some way. I really do care about him, and he's become so irrational, so emotional and vindictive, and I have become so afraid for myself—and for my family if I don't do what I'm told."

"I understand, but why approach me with this? You don't know me. You don't know whose interests I represent."

"I'm desperate and I'm hoping that it is Sara Sietzer that you are speaking for."

"She means that much to you?"

"As a young woman, she means everything to me. She has been my hero since childhood, and I know a great deal about you now. I've been up all night reading about you. You said that you were close to her and I want to believe you. I need to."

"And you think that I can protect you from your supervisors?"

"From Bu. He frightens me even more than they do sometimes. He's so angry."

Kreiger stopped in front of a papaya stand looked around the crowd before locking eyes with the fruit merchant, who flashed a smile and beckoned him forward.

Kreiger backed away, thinking that the man might be a spy. "You really think it's safe for us here?" he challenged Indra.

"Safe, yes. No one can hurt us here, but we are being watched."

"What are you going to tell them, your supervisors?" Kreiger asked, his eyes darting between people, stalls and merchandise, stacked ten feet high in some places. The crowd and aroma was almost dizzying: a waft of spicy cherry peppers mixing with the scents of flowers, body odor, burning charcoal, and hot coffee.

"Not much. I would never tell them anything they could use against you. They asked me to approach you, if I can discover the purpose of your visit. So we can make up a purpose for you before I leave, and they will be pleased with me for doing my duty."

Kreiger came to an abrupt halt and looked into Indra's brilliant, coal black eyes, wondering what kind of young woman this was, who could talk so casually about so many dangerous things?

He wasn't so relaxed. He wasn't a spy, trained in the dirty business of the nether world: splitting truths, telling lies and making threats. Yet he was being handled by Sara, and he was becoming deeply involved in skullduggery. And though he resented Sara for putting him at risk, he remained nonetheless impressed with her instincts. Once again, on the basis of very little information, Sara had correctly assessed the situation when she told him that the path to Bu went through Indra, this incredibly striking young woman who strolled through the marketplace speaking of her fears, displaying none.

Kreiger was lost in a maze of wonder and trepidation when Indra interrupted his thoughts.

"We can sit if you like and take coffee, and talk of other things," Indra said, noting his discomfort.

Kreiger wanted to leave, but steeled himself for a cup of chai in the middle of the crowded bazaar, watching passersby and the top branches of the tall trees swaying in the breeze, talking about nothing important, feeling terribly insecure.

"Bu tells me that you like the weather here," Indra said.

"Very much. It's so intense. I'm not sure what I expected. I have been to India before, but not to the mountains. Then again, I didn't know that the remarkable weather patterns were the direct result of unwanted climate change"

"It is true, but you must have seen other kinds of beauty in other places. You must have traveled a lot. It must be so wonderful to have seen all those places. As much as I love it here, I do want to see the world very much, but I'm not sure if it is possible anymore. I don't think that I can ever be in control of my destiny after this."

Kreiger was moved by the sadness in her voice. "You are much too young to speak of limitations. Look at the changes in my life, spending all that time traveling around the world, railing against our expansion into space before fading into obscurity and emerging on the opposite side of my own argument. Now I'm traveling the world again, and discovering that I'm still relevant to some people."

"Because you made a good argument to begin with, that humanity wasn't ready to meet its own destiny in space. We did need to be joined at the heart before we went looking for trouble in space, and with the Dream Machine. We are too fractured to meet the challenges in space, and we are not sophisticated enough to deal with a machine's consciousness."

Kreiger smiled and sipped his chai. "Perhaps, but I am afraid that the point is moot. We are in space. There is a Dream Machine, and an invitation was tendered."

"Then why did Maher insist that we study your arguments in particular? Only a few weeks ago, he was encouraging us to reconsider your point of view on the basis of the dismal situation we have created for ourselves on Earth: the problem with global warming exacerbated by the expulsion of methane gases, our inability to take the Lady-In-Waiting up on her invitation to the stars, our fear of risk-taking, our unwillingness to sacrifice, the possibility of a space-based war for control of the moon, and so much more."

Kreiger leaned forward and lowered his voice. "Maher told you?"

Indra finished her chai before replying. "He records lessons for us from time to time. He also uses these lessons to communicate with others, I think. Bu saw one of Richard's transmissions when he first arrived here in Mussoorie, and he figured out the underlying communication pattern within one hour. He said it's some kind of inverted, ever-changing Morse code, employing different cues and activators, like the lighting behind him that can subtly pulsate and connect to his hand or finger movements."

Kreiger was flabbergasted, rendered speechless for several moments until he composed himself. "Then it is possible to communicate with Maher!"

Bu said, "If you can raise the dead, you can." He had walked up behind them and overheard Kreiger.

18

The arrival of settlers from Earth was always a momentous occasion. Each Mars lander, holding as many as six people with supplies, was met by a small greeting committee on the surface. When all had arrived, they were placed in isolation for a month where they were monitored for disease. The fear of contamination on Mars was well founded. An Earth-born flu virus could wipe out the entire colony.

At the end of the month, baring complications, the arrival of settlers was acknowledged by a formal reception attended by most of the colony. The dinner was almost always extraordinary and colorful, the settlers finding more food and drink than they imagined, and music and dancing.

Given the deteriorating geo-political situation on Earth, this reception promised to be bittersweet because the colonists knew that this wave of settlers might be the last for many years to come. Once off-loaded, the old, often refitted and enlarged *Starship Aelita* would leave Mars orbit at the end of the month, spend five weeks en route and orbit the same G point above the Earth until needed. In the meantime, the Mars colony, all 212 souls, would be left to its own devices.

While there was enough food and energy to support the colony for many generations to come, there was growing sadness and insecurity, exacerbated by the arrival of the new settlers and a lack of strong leadership. Many colonists were already wistfully looking up at Mother Earth in the evening sky, fearing the future—a scenario that was eerily similar to the one Richard had predicted.

"Under the circumstances, I have to believe that Yuri's awakening was no accident, that he has been returned to us at precisely the right moment in time to lead us into a promising future," Bryce told Alona. They were sitting is his small gray room, on composite chairs in front of a small workstation.

Alona continued to visit him on occasion because she felt sorry for him, and because Bryce knew more about colonial security than anyone else on Mars.

"Be that as it may, I still have to maintain order in the colony," she said, looking for good advice.

Bryce launched into an increasingly familiar diatribe on a life less-lived. "Knowing the weaknesses of people was a source of power and control for me; it is also a major source of corruption. No doubt that I was corrupted a long time ago by my overblown sense of importance. Instead of preserving the status quo with wisdom, I employed fear to keep order. By threatening to expose people's secrets, I kept them in line. But I could not imagine how this negative momentum would pair with my own pain and shame and drive me to pick up a gun.

"But now I have an opportunity to cleanse myself by doing good works for others and becoming a better man, a lesser man necessarily, just another cog in the wheel of life who is without identity or memory, and without shame. And I owe it all to Yuri."

Alona was pleased by Bryce's righteous efforts to improve his life, and was increasingly concerned about Yuri's effect on him. "I can't imagine what it must be like to have someone inside of your mind."

"And I can't explain it, not because it is too painful, but because it was sacred," Bryce said, as if a discussion of the subject matter might diminish the transformational power of the experience.

"Then you do believe that Yuri is pure and righteous?"

"I was lost and I was found. How else can I describe him?"

"Is this something I can experience?"

Bryce shrugged. "I can't say. And I'm still not sure why he reached out to me—maybe because I had so much to hide. I was in so much pain. I may never know the answers, but the quality of my life now is a testament to my experience of him."

"You mean that Yuri doesn't speak to your mind any more?"

"He never did. He was more like a presence, an observer of my innermost thoughts, a witness."

"Still?"

Bryce smiled and stroked his newly grown red beard. "Can you tell me if all these questions are a part of your job as head of security, or something personal?"

"Both. I'm just fascinated with Yuri like everyone else, trying to make sense of it all. And I'm also responsible for Yuri's welfare."

"You think that there's a problem?"

"No, nothing I'm aware of. But there can be in view of your experience. It wouldn't hurt to think ahead."

Bryce shook his head, looked down at the table and sadly replied, "I only wish that I had so much foresight."

*   *   *

"Bryce seems to be doing well, but I wonder if a lot of it isn't wishful thinking, this desire to be empty and servile," Alona told Sasha the following day.

"Then he won't be a problem?" Sasha asked.

Alona said, "I don't see how he can be. He's so lost in himself, the poor bastard."

*   *   *

So the two women bided their time and went about their daily routines, hardly speaking to one another and meeting casually when the situation demanded: at Richard's funeral a few days after he died, at counsel meetings where they helped to decide the breakdown of labor and housing for the newly arrived settlers, at a birthday party for a mutual friend, at several meetings with Yuri, which were hardly revealing.

He took an occasional meal in a common room, answered some questions and side-stepped others with such dexterity that few people noted the deflection.

Kim Jong Tui asked if the Lady-In-Waiting was alien, "Or a projection of the group human mind that had joined with the Dream Machine?"

Yuri said, "I guess you could say that beauty is in the eye of the beholder, lovely to look upon from any perspective in the universe."

"You mean that she is still manifest and hasn't dispersed?"

There were five people sitting around the table in the common room, including Tui, Alona and Sasha, and Yuri looked into each one of their eyes before replying, "Beauty begins from within. Your experience of loveliness and goodness on the deepest levels is not only archetypal, it is universal. Nothing really dies and nothing really disperses—least of all beauty and goodness. It changes, even to ugliness and evil, but it inevitably returns to its pristine essence—which is composed of light and vibration. If we can look long enough and deep enough within ourselves and far enough across the galaxy, we can still see the Lady. We can know that she is still waiting on us."

"Have you seen that far?" Tui pressed.

Yuri looked at Alona, recalled his conversation with her and Sasha, flashed a coy smile and said, "No," and took another, unrelated, question from the group.

It was an effective routine which let him off the hook on several occasions and added to the mystery of his odd becoming. He never set an agenda, never posed a challenge to anyone, and never tried to impose his will on a colonist. Yuri followed the rules and even asked if he could return to work as an astrobiologist.

At another impromptu meeting—held in the newest grow room, so big and bright and lush that it was hard to see its parameters and so realistic that it was easy to confuse it with a garden on Earth—Yuri was asked to comment on the matching alternate DNA signatures found on Mars and on Europa.

He said, "All sentient beings, all life despite size or configuration, bear a distinct DNA signature, and no two signatures are exactly alike because the requirements of survival can vary so much from place to place and time to time. And if it is the nature of life to evolve, to move, to strive, to travel, to be everywhere it can be, to become everything it must be, it requires differences that can be subtle or overt.

"It is not surprising to me that the alternate DNA signature discovered on Europa compares to the one we have found here on Mars. Its departure from the human code is also not surprising or special in the larger scheme of things. It tells us that we're not alone, nothing more or less."

"It also implies that we were not first," Sasha stated. She was invited to this discussion because of her expertise in microbiology.

Yuri nodded. "If being first is important to you, then its meaning has implications. It has no importance to me. Moving forward is important, an imperative at this point in human evolution, given the challenges that are facing Earth."

"You sound a lot like Richard," Sasha said. "And Tex O'Toole for that matter."

"Which puts me in good company," Yuri added. "On this singular and most important issue, we are of the same mind. The faster and further this species can go, the better—and sooner than later, I hope."

"Then you believe that we must devote ourselves to solving the mystery of the Dream Machine before its liquid memory has decomposed?"

Yuri said, "Of course."

Sasha had more questions, but deferred to a colleague when an idea came to mind, to test Yuri's DNA by gathering samples of his biology—errant hairs, and skin follicles, and the like—to see if it had been somehow altered by his "other-worldly" experiences.

*   *   *

Sara was out of the loop on all fronts and her patience was wearing thin. She was shaken by the news of Richard's death because he posed the only possible link to Yuri on Mars. She also wished that she could speak to Bu, thinking that she would be far more adept at squeezing the kid for the answers to the Dream Machine. But Sara was too well known to cross the world on a lark. So she sat around the house and became obsessed with all the bad news about the increase of seismic activity in the North Atlantic.

She punished herself for a lack of vision, and an inability to find a better reason to run for president other than to stifle the designs of Olga Sussenko—and she was assailed by a recurring dream sequence. She kept seeing a golden dome in her mind, shimmering in sunlight until it exploded into countless fragments. Then she heard many children crying and often woke from the sequence in a fit of anxiety, wondering who the children were, if her aborted child was among them.

"Most of the time it's not even a dream, it's like I'm having the memory of the dream, or I'm about to have the dream again and it frightens me and I wake up with a start."

"Don't I know," Michael sighed. Sara had disturbed his sleep on numerous occasions. "As I said before, if you want to be done with this, if you want to be cleansed and begin again, you must turn to God—yours or mine, it doesn't matter. You should try, at least."

"I did speak to Kreiger about it, and he said that I was being too hard on myself. I guess he meant that I should learn to forgive myself. But I still feel like it's something else, that there's some kind of message attached to these dreams, that they have a meaning that is greater than what I ascribe to them."

"You have my opinion on the matter, and Kreiger's, which are similar," Michael said, before retreating to the study.

Sara went down to the basement to the holo-suite. She sat at the center of a familiar celestial sphere program, and spent hours gazing at the stars: studying the face of the Lady-in-Waiting, contemplating her invitation to the stars, weighing the prospects for survival of the species against the virtues of goodness and rightness, hoping to find a connection to her dreams.

Exhausted and unfulfilled, she finally emerged from the basement after nine in the evening and went looking for Michael. She couldn't find him and figured that he went to dinner by himself in a local bistro. She was about to get a snack in the kitchen when Kreiger reached her on the Cel-Tel. Sara hung up and went into the study to call him back on the Newgrid—this time using a new holo-graphic computer. Within seconds, Kreiger's three-dimensional projection appeared on the workstation, eighteen inches high and remarkably sharp.

"It's about time," Sara began, sitting in front of the computer and looking at Kreiger's projected image. She hadn't spoken to him in a week.

He looked around him and said, "I'm doing my best under the circumstances, Sara, and they are most challenging and unstable. There is something definitely not right with this boy, and it does have a lot to do with the girl, who has her own problems. Neither one of these kids has been themselves since childhood. And the problem is that I don't know who I'm talking to because they don't know themselves. They're both terribly immature in some ways, yet they are being asked to function at an enormously high level of responsibility, in an escalating crisis of confidence. It's almost impossible to discern the truth, and it appears that we are all in some jeopardy. Both are reaching out to me, a total stranger, because they are experiencing so much despair.

"The boy wants the girl, but he hates her for not really wanting him, for using him. The girl does care about him, but hates herself for being used and abused in the process. They both want out of the mess, but they have no place to go. She's really scared, because she's becoming aware of herself as expendable—because it's all about him. He is the real genius and he claims to have solved one of the great mysteries of the Dream Machine. He told me in no uncertain terms that he knows how to join with it. He also told me that he wants a very high price for the solution."

Sara leaned forward, her green eyes widening, filling with anticipation. "How much?"

Kreiger shrugged. "He doesn't say, but I'm not sure it's money."

"What else then?"

"He wouldn't tell me, but he might tell you!"

*   *   *

When Sara cued the computer to shut down, it left a faint trace of another holographic message in cyberspace, which filled her with dread and bewilderment.

*   *   *

Richard's death captured a number of headlines around the world, and spurred a series of retrospectives on the exploration and colonization of Mars. The larger impact of his passing was measured in dollars. He died as the richest human who ever lived with a net worth approaching one trillion dollars. But the most remarkable thing was Richard's willingness to leave it all behind and go to Mars, and that was the gist of many of the stories about his life.

Two days after his death, the headlines returned to highlighting the accelerated trend toward global warming, aggravated by the release of methane gas into the atmosphere. Fear of an earthquake, or even a volcano, in the North Atlantic continued to sweep the world.

More than twelve years had passed since that catastrophic super-storm had struck New York. The odd thing was that no other major city in the world had been struck with such devastating intensity. It was uncanny how almost every major storm that threatened the East Coast of the United States would veer due north before reaching land and disperse in the North Atlantic. The same was true for the nations that comprised the Pacific Rim; they had also been spared.

Africa and the Australian Outback continued to bear the worst of it, with the increase of deadly fire storms. But few people really cared about Africa, and fewer people lived in the outback. Most people grew accustom to the strange climatic changes: the snowy weather in L.A., the months of rain in Colorado, the abrupt and dramatic temperature swings, careening as much as forty degrees in a day, going from winter to summer and back again. The rising tides continued to claim a lot of expensive ocean-front property, but few lives were lost because people learned to fear the shorelines.

The only difference between the Himalayas and everywhere else on Earth was the speed and volatility of the climate changes, which could be measured in hours, or even minutes.

"I can see why you would never want to leave here," Kreiger told Bu as they walked along a familiar mountain path, overlooking the snow-caps, unaware that New Delhi was being pelted with by a sudden and deadly hail storm, ice balls the size of baseballs killing hundreds and injuring thousands.

"I will go where I want and live where I want," Bu bitterly declared. At his request, they met several days after Bu delivered news of Richard's death in the bazaar. "DO YOU HEAR THAT?" Bu shouted at the trees lining the path. "They have their listening devices and cameras everywhere I go. I am convinced of that now."

"You keep on referring to 'them.' Indra too, but who are 'they' exactly?"

"Government people."

"But you are attending a school endowed by Richard Maher, and he was hardly a friend to any government on Earth—or on Mars, for that matter."

Bu shrugged. "Power speaks to power."

"You mean that you never spoke to him, never communicated to Maher?"

"No. I had no reason until recently, when they threatened to send Indra to Mars if I didn't cooperate."

"What is it that they wanted from you?"

Bu shrugged again and began to flap his arms as they walked, the loose sleeves of his saffron robe snapping and dancing in the cool mountain breeze. Like a child, Kreiger thought.

"I still don't know the people in charge—I did meet with a Colonel Singh on several occasions, but he was just another lackey. Anyway, they did provide me with an engineering schematic to study, something to do with Okano and the Imagining Mars program, which they lived to regret because it keyed my mind onto the problem with the Dream Machine. Now I have the answers, and I have the power. But I still need someone to broker the deal for me, someone who understands how these people think, who can serve as a guarantor."

The breeze stiffened and Kreiger turned up the collar on his wool sport jacket, and tied his black scarf into a knot around his neck before replying, "I'm afraid I haven't had much experience in these matters, and I'm afraid my profile is hardly high enough to impress these people."

"But your friend Sara Sietzer does. She is most impressive, and she does have a stake in the functionality of the Dream Machine."

"What kind of stake?"

"In her husband, in seeing him again," Bu declared.

Kreiger stopped walking and turned to look in Bu's eyes, which was difficult because they were both wearing techno-glasses. "How can she see him if he died when he joined with the Machine?"

"He didn't die. Nothing that joins with the Dream Machine can die," Bu said, before skipping away down the path.

19

Of all the things that had come to pass since the first manned mission to Mars, the single most remarkable and persistent phenomenon was the complacency of the human race. Despite all the warning signs—the possibility of catastrophic violent climate changes and the prospect for global war—the vast majority of people remained fatalistic, as if it were easier to die than live.

The average person didn't give a damn about the expansion of Chinese interests on the moon under the guise of, "Scientific research and mining interests," a Chinese spokesman said, upon launching yet another hardware-laden flight to the moon.

"I give a damn," Olga Sussenko told a televised rubber-stamp meeting of the Politburo. "And when I take office, my government will deploy our own hunter-killer satellites immediately, without hesitation or negotiation. They will orbit the moon and they will protect the Russian people while they sleep."

The Politburo gave her an extended standing ovation, and Sara was reduced to gawking at the unmitigated display of nationalism on her living room Cel-Tel, certain that Russia would eventually go to war with China in space if America didn't.

"Anything new?" Michael asked, walking into the room.

"You had dinner?" Sara began, sitting back in the couch.

"More or less. I didn't have much of an appetite. I just needed to get out." Michael sat on the sofa across the room from her, spread his arms out across the top and crossed his legs.

"Away from me, you mean?"

Michael forced a smile. "Not too far away, and I wasn't gone very long."

"Long enough."

"Meaning?"

"Meaning that you used the computer before me, the new one, and a faint trace of one of your messages was left behind."

Michael shot her a quizzical look. "How is that possible?"

"I wouldn't know, but I do know what I saw and heard when I got off the computer with Kreiger."

Michael winced and began to blink. "Which is?"

"Someone asking you if I was running for president. I caught the tail end of it."

Michael's befuddlement turned to discomfort. "I don't recall speaking with anyone on that computer, not today," he stammered. "And why would I tell anyone about your plans, especially if they're so uncertain? One day you're running, one day you're not."

"I don't know, Michael. I was hoping you could tell me."

Michael shrugged and stood up. "Let's take a look."

They walked into the study together and turned on the holographic machine, which ran smoothly and without a hitch.

Michael said, "I don't see a problem."

He was about to leave the room when Sara sat at the desk and asked him to wait.

Michael stood behind her, folded his arms and watched her turn the computer off and on. She was about to conjure the holographic image of her secretary when a faint trace of her previous transmission to Kreiger sprang to life.

Michael winced again and said, "That's weird."

Sara said, "Unrefined maybe. This is relatively new technology. But weird doesn't explain the impression that was left behind after you used the computer, after you just lied about it to me in the living room. How could you violate my trust like that, discussing my options whether it's about running the presidency or anything else? How could you lie about it?" Sara demanded, shooting to her feet and placing her hands on her hips. "You need to tell me what it's all about, Michael. Who were you were talking to and why?"

Michael began to blink uncontrollably, then held his head in his hands and said, "I can't."

Angry as she was, Sara felt sorry for him. "Can you at least tell me what is hurting you so much?"

"You are."

Michael wouldn't explain, and Sara left the room, thinking that she would find out who Michael was talking to even if it meant hiring a technician to do the forensic dirty work. She was on her way into the master bedroom, with the intent of gathering a few things and spending the night in a guest room, when Rounder's doctor reached her, and informed her that Rounder had taken a sudden and unexpected turn for the worse.

Sara was crestfallen then assailed by a rush of guilt. She hadn't seen Rounder in weeks and hardly kept in touch with his doctor; she had been so caught up in herself.

*   *   *

The much-anticipated formal reception party for the newly arrived settlers on Mars had just gotten underway when Alona Glaza and Sasha Alawi absconded with the Dream Machine. Spacecraft engineer and senior shuttle pilot, Alona often took the last flight up to the *Starship Aelita* to sign off on its return to Earth orbit: inspect the general condition of the ship, run checks on the computers and engines, and retrieve anything that had been left behind by the settlers.

"There is always something left behind, from toiletries to gear boxes, even much-prized scientific equipment," Alona told Sasha as their shuttlecraft ascended the pinkish, purple Martian sky. It was late in the afternoon, and their flight raised no suspicion because no one could imagine the magnitude of their caper; no one had ever left Mars orbit. "It's amazing what some people can leave behind."

"Their brains, too," Sasha added, looking out a small portal window as the ship rose higher and higher in the sky. "I know that I left a part of my brain on that ship when I arrived here. I was so idealistic, and for so many years until Richard forced me to see the idiocy of my ideology. He was so right about every-thing, and we were all so wrong and small-minded."

"But we're going to change that, right?"

"If we don't get hanged first."

The remainder of the short flight up to the *Aelita* progressed in silence, with Alona piloting the shuttle and Sasha looking out the window recollecting her life on Mars, recalling the pain that had driven her from Earth, when her boyfriend left college and martyred himself in Jihad in the Middle East. There were tears in Sasha's eyes as they approached the edge of the Mars atmos-phere, when the sky filled with stars and Alona told her to tighten her seat buckle in preparation for the docking maneuver with the *Aelita*.

Sasha's heart ached and her mind filled with second thoughts as the shuttle effortlessly joined with the mother ship. Alona was almost serene by comparison, going through familiar motions with military precision, and without a second thought from Sasha's point of view.

"It will only take few minutes to recalibrate the launch time," Alona said as they exited the shuttle and boarded the *Aelita*. "In fact, I don't even have to do it. This old ship has been continually refitted with so many state-of-the-art, self-correcting programs and liquid schematics that if we left Mars a week early, we would still arrive in Earth orbit on schedule."

Sasha followed her into the cockpit and replied, "If we go."

Alona turned to meet the challenge. "You mean that we should stay and let the future belong to Yuri, and risk losing the Machine's memory in the process?"

"I don't know," Sasha mumbled. "I just don't know." She turned to look out the window and looked down on Mars from space for the first time since her arrival so many years ago. "Hard to believe that I can miss that damned, dead rock so much already."

Alona said, "It is not too late to return."

"You mean you would?"

"If you go back, I would have to go with you. I couldn't do this alone."

"If Yuri was Yuri maybe I would return, but he's not right and we can't take the risk because his entire other worldly experience might be a hallucination prompted by an alien virus. He's just too powerful and too mysterious to be trusted, especially after he expressed an interest in joining with the Machine, and we are running out of time."

DNA testing had showed an alien virus had been incorporated into Yuri's DNA; it also showed that the virus bore the same DNA signature found in that tepid pool of water on Mars and on Europa—composed of six bases as opposed to the familiar four pairs found in life on Earth."

In the final analysis, that is what drove them to crime, to abscond with the Dream Machine and return it to Earth where safer and saner minds might join with it before its memory was lost—even if they lost their own lives in the process. Accessing the Machine was easy because Alona had the code to the safe where it was kept. Appropriating the shuttle was even easier because it was part of Alona's job description, to make the final inspection tour of the *Aelita*.

The reception party on the surface was just getting into high gear when the women strapped themselves into their seats, flipped a switch and disengaged the shuttle craft.

"God help us," Sasha said.

"God will have to because He knows that we're doing the right thing."

There were tears streaming down there faces, denoting an odd mix of trepidation and heroism, guilt and uncertainty. The blood vessels in their heads were threatening to pop under the pressure when Yuri and Bryce appeared in the cockpit behind them.

*   *   *

Colonel Singh visited with Kreiger at the end of his third week in Mussoorie. Kreiger was finishing his coffee, reading a copy of the *London Times* in the smaller dining room, when the man approached his table.

"Sarwan Singh," he began, extending his hand.

Kreiger rose to shake his hand and invited him to sit.

"You are enjoying yourself here in our lovely little town?" Singh asked.

"Immensely so, the views and the odd weather patterns mostly—until I read about that tragic hail storm in Delhi, and I was reminded the cost in human suffering that has been the result of this climate change."

Singh nodded. "Too many things are changing too rapidly for my taste, which is the reason for my visit. I am Regional Bureau Chief for the Criminal Intelligence Division, and my government would like to know the purpose of your visit to our country, Mr. Kreiger."

Kreiger locked eyes with him across the table. "To see the boy, Norbu Hua Chang, on a personal matter. We were hoping the boy could help us with a scientific question."

"Us?"

"A figure of speech."

Singh smiled. "I am afraid your assurances are hard-pressed in view of your relationship to Sara Sietzer, former President of the United States."

"Touché," Kreiger said, raising his coffee cup, and finally realizing that Bu and Indra had not overstated the matter: nearly everything that he had discussed with them had been overheard or reported. "Mrs. Sietzer is a private citizen now and intends to remain so, and I was here representing her personal interests and my own."

"What else are you not telling me, Mr. Kreiger?"

Kreiger fell silent. He was searching himself for an answer when Colonel Singh continued, "I assume the boy has already told you he has solved the mystery of joining to the Machine?"

Kreiger shrugged and turned his palms up toward the ceiling. "If you know so much, why bother to question me?"

Singh smiled—gloated, Kreiger thought—and twirled one end of his mustache. "Because it is my job, and because of the latest turn of events, obviously."

"The loss of Richard Maher cannot be overstated," Kreiger said, unaware of the events in space.

Singh looked at him incredulously. "Then you don't know about the *Aelita*, how it is returning to Earth? I should have thought that you would have known before me."

"Known what?"

Singh explained how two women from Mars had absconded with the Dream Machine. "And Yuri Popovitch, I believe, but the details are sketchy."

Kreiger was astounded. "Are you certain? I can assure you that I have not heard one word about this from anyone."

"Nevertheless, you can see how my government's interest in this matter has become paramount."

Kreiger nodded. "I can see, assuming your information is correct. It's just so fantastic."

"No doubt, but in any event, I expect that you will be leaving Mussoorie shortly."

"Why should I be leaving?"

"Because my government is asking you to leave, and as graciously as possible. You can have no more contact with the boy."

*   *   *

"They didn't give me a date and time to leave, but if I'm not gone from here in a couple of days, I imagine that I will be escorted out of town," Kreiger told Sara.

Sara said, "It doesn't give us much time, and I can't do very much about anything right now. Jacob can't have more than a few days left, and I won't leave his side until he's gone. I just can't."

Sara had flown to the hospital in Orlando to be with Rounder, who was dying. It was near 11 a.m. in Florida when Kreiger finally reached her on the Cel-Tel. She was sitting at her computer in a small waiting room, at the end of a long corridor.

"Can you tell me what you know about these two women who took the Machine?" Kreiger asked.

"Not much, I'm afraid. They were both members of the rotating government council on Mars, and both had contact with Richard and Yuri. In fact, they flanked Richard at the trial."

"The timing of this is just incredible."

"Remarkable!" Sara exclaimed. "I don't know what it's like in India, but I can tell you that it is utterly insane here. The media has gone berserk with this thing, like nothing I've ever seen, way beyond the craziness that accompanied the manifestation of the Lady-In-Waiting—and rightfully so. I was floored when I heard this, speechless. I was on the plane coming down here and . . . I can't even begin to imagine the effect of this. We could be at war over this, for control of the Machine. And Russia has gone bonkers over the idea of Yuri's return. I cannot possibly imagine his intentions, let alone how he could survive on Earth after all those years on Mars—even if we could decontaminate him. The whole thing is just maddening."

Kreiger said, "Apparently, but it can be encouraging because it is awakening people all over the world, no matter what their reactions are, whether they believe that Yuri is the Second Coming, or that the Dream Machine is the devil's work. Where there's wakefulness, there is energy. Where there is energy, there can be transformation. It's just going to be a matter of getting our arms around it."

"You have to be kidding. I can't even get my mind around this, and we don't have a power base, or even a simple platform to operate from. Even the idea of running for the presidency seems trite now, moot actually, because there's no time."

"That may be, but you have fame, Sara, and the world has turned to you before in its hour of need. And you delivered."

"But I don't have an idea, a vision, not even a clue about how to deal with something like this."

"Then we have to hope that the vision finds you. How about your dreams? Are you still having those extraordinary dreams?"

"No, but I might be having a problem with Michael." Sara went on to explain the damning trace of Michael's holographic message that was left behind in cyberspace. "I can't tell you how strange and terribly discomforting that was, how painful. He seems to blame me for it. Even worse, he won't talk about it, and it's his unwillingness to explain that's becoming a greater issue with me. I just hope it's not heartbreaking, because I'm not sure I could deal with that right now. I can't even imagine losing him again. I was hoping that you could talk to him."

"When I return, perhaps. In the meantime, I'll let you get back to Jacob. And please let him know that my prayers are with him, even if he can't hear the words, I believe that he will absorb the intent. May God bless you both, may He bless us all." Sara left the waiting room with a heavy heart. She was about to enter Jacob's ward when she was cornered by several reporters in the hallway.

"Mrs. Sietzer . . . Mrs. Sietezer . . .Can you comment on . . ? What about Yuri Popovitch . . ? The Dream Machine . . . What about the Machine . . ?"

Sara had no intention of responding and passed her hand over a wall mounted LED. But the mechanism failed to respond; the door wouldn't open and Sara was left to the mercy of the media.

"Now is not a good time for me," she began. "I'm very sorry, but my dearest friend, and a great American hero, is dying and I need to direct my energy toward him. If you will all excuse me."

She continually passed her hand over the motion sensor to no avail; the door remained closed and the hallway filled with more reporters and passersby.

"Can you at least comment on the passing of Richard Maher?" another reporter asked.

"Unfortunate. While his life did invite controversy, he was a great American hero, a giant intellect whose research and discoveries have enriched the lives of all us, a man of extraordinary dedication who gave up his vast riches and his life for the betterment of humanity."

Sara hoped someone would exit the ward and provide her with a timely escape. But the door didn't open, and she was stuck answering questions from many more reporters.

"What about your husband, do you think that you will see him again?"

"Michael, why wouldn't I see Michael?"

"I was referring to your first husband, Captain Sietzer. Do you think that you will see him again if you join with the Dream Machine?"

Sara backed up against the wall and used it to maintain her balance; she was so flustered by the question. "How can I know that? How can you think that? I don't even think about that."

"You mean to say that the thought had never crossed your mind?"

"I don't know about never, but . . ."

"But what? You mean that you believe that the spirit of your husband, his essence, may yet be alive in the Machine?"

Now Sara realized that she had said too much because she was out of practice. She could already see the headlines— FORMER PRESIDENT COMMUNES WITH THE DEAD— and tried to be find a diplomatic way out.

"You ask too much of me at a very difficult time. Under the circumstances, I believe that we need to ask more of ourselves if we're ever going find the answers to the many challenges we are facing."

"Can you be more specific . . ? Can you tell us what is most important . . ? Can you . . ? Will you . .?"

Sara was searching herself for another benign response when the door to the ward finally opened and she ducked inside.

*   *   *

"You look surprised," Bryce stoically began, standing behind the cockpit and bracing himself against a wall. Yuri stood behind him, holding on to the back of a seat.

The women, rendered speechless by shock and bewilderment, kept looking at each other for a clue until Yuri explained.

"You shouldn't be so surprised. After all, it was the logical for thing for you to do, and it was the logical thing for me to apprehend," he said, leaning forward and looking down at Sasha. "If I'm not mistaken, Richard was your mentor, and there was no doubt in my mind that he was behind all of this from the beginning—only because he didn't understand and he wouldn't believe."

"In what?" Sasha challenged, her voice quaking, her body trembling from the after-shock.

Yuri took a seat behind Sasha before continuing, "In me," he said before turning to Alona. "And if you're thinking about aborting, I think you would agree that the result would not benefit anyone of us if we are returned to Mars. No doubt that our fates are now tied to directly to our return to Earth—for better or worse.

"And if you're thinking that I read your minds, I can also tell you would both be wrong. As I was saying, it was largely a matter of logical thinking, of extrapolating from the flow of events and anticipating the outcome. I also came to the conclusion, a long time ago, that the Dream Machine must be returned to Earth, where it could be joined to many more minds. I was also biding my time, waiting for the opportunity to present itself. And I assumed that an effort would be made to exclude me from the joining process. So I watched and waited, and I enlisted the help of Bryce. When he told me that Alona was scheduled to make the last flight up to the *Aelita*, to sign off on its return to Earth orbit, I became curious.

"When I deduced that this was the last likely opportunity to return the Dream Machine to Earth, I became especially interested. So we quietly came aboard the shuttle a few hours before you two, sequestered ourselves in the cargo area, and waited. And we were greatly rewarded by your courage to do the necessary thing. I think we all know that there was no way in hell that the splintered power interests on Earth would have ever agreed to the return of the Dream Machine."

"And you think that you can survive on Earth after spending so many years on Mars in one-third gravity?" Sasha challenged. "Because I'm not sure that we could, no matter what kind of pressurized environment was provided."

"If they'll even have us," Alona added.

Yuri said, "This all remains to be seen, how we will be received, how long we will survive—if, as Sasha said, they will ever let us back on Earth. The point is to make the effort, to try and save humanity from itself, because I am inclined to believe that time is short and joining with the Dream Machine could be humanity's best hope."

"Our only hope," Bryce added. "And if you want to question my motives, you need to think of the disgrace that is awaiting me on Earth if I did survive the trauma of re-entry. This is not a journey that I wanted to make. I wanted nothing, to become nothing as Yuri had suggested. And if I die trying to bring life and hope to others then so be it, I will be dead. But at least I'll die trying to get something right."

Sasha and Alona continued to look to each other for a clue, both wondering if the other hadn't been co-opted by Yuri's powerful mind.

20

Colonel Sarwan Singh was fourth generation military, his great-grandfather having served as a lance corporal in the British Raj. Singh served with distinction in the army, rose quickly in the chain of command, and made the jump to the C.I.D. following his early retirement from the military at age forty-two. Nearing fifty, he found himself in an unrewarding post at Mussoorie, in charge of Bu's security detail, often thinking he had somehow offended his superiors in the intelligence service or underperformed. Given the odd turn of events in space, and the rise in Bu's value, he was now under increased pressure to perform.

Consequently, Colonel Singh returned to Kreiger's hotel the following morning and told him to pack. "It is our request that you prepare to leave Mussoorie after lunch. A car will take you to Delhi. You are not under arrest, Mr. Kreiger. You are in our care."

"And if I wanted to stay?"

"You would be arrested," Singh declared without hesitation.

Less than four hours later, Kreiger was sitting in the back of a government car on his way to Dehra Dune, an upscale community on the plains. He was nearing a small private airport on the outskirts of town, when the car turned around and headed back up the mountain—without explanation.

Bewildered by the odd turn of events, Kreiger spent the evening in his hotel reading newspapers and watching the Cel-Tel.

He was sitting in the lobby, in a large overstuffed chair having a nightcap, when Bu walked in and explained.

"They told me you left, and I told them that I would leave if they didn't return you to Mussoorie," Bu said, taking a seat in a chair beside Kreiger. "I told them that I would never share my research on the Dream Machine with them if I wasn't allowed to talk to you again. I hope this was okay?"

"Most unusual, but quite welcome. I had no intention of leaving Mussoorie without talking to you again. Under the present circumstances, I would imagine that there are many people who would like to talk to you."

Bu shrugged, adjusted his techno-glasses and pushed the sleeves up on his robe. "Because they want to know about the Machine, not because they care about me."

Kreiger put his paper aside, leaned forward and lowered his voice. "And you think I do care?"

"About me, no, but I think you're honest about it. I also believe that you are genuinely concerned for the welfare of the species. Everything about your life tells me this, especially the work you did in New York. I am in a position where I have to trust somebody, and your appearance in Mussoorie concurs with my needs."

"Which are?"

"As I said before, to meet with Sara Sietzer and have her negotiate with my government on my behalf. I do have the power. I do have the information on the Dream Machine, how to join with it. I don't have the wisdom or experience to make a deal. Sara Sietzer has the profile to make a deal for me, and she has a vested interest in succeeding, assuming her husband did successfully join with the Machine."

"Can I ask what it is that you want?"

"To be left alone with Indra—if she still wants me—nothing more."

"And if she doesn't?"

Bu flashed a devilish smile in an attempt to hide his pain. "Then the price will go up."

Kreiger sat back in his chair and briefly studied the boy, amazed at Bu's cynicism and lack of compassion. He could hardly imagine the subtle but persistent abuse that turned this boy into an ogre. Kreiger crossed his legs and sipped his drink before continuing, "You understand that this may not be possible, to have Sara intervene on your behalf. To begin with, your government has to agree with the proposal, and she would have to be convinced of your solution to joining with the Dream Machine."

"She will come and she will be convinced. I will convince her—and Yuri Popovitch if necessary, if he could survive our atmosphere somehow."

Kreiger was stunned. He could hardly imagine a meeting between these two powerful minds, if it were at all possible. "What can Yuri have to do with all this?"

Bu stood and said, "Time will tell, but in the meantime you will be safe here because my government wouldn't dare to trifle with you again—or me. I have what they want, and I made it quite clear this time that I will destroy it if my wishes are not met."

"You mean that you would punish the entire human race for the mistakes of your supervisors?"

The question hung in the air for several seconds before Bu addressed it. "If humanity is so interested in surviving, perhaps it will come together in an effort to punish my supervisors who are interested in themselves."

*   *   *

"The situation here is tenuous at best, with everything dependent upon this boy who suspects or detests everyone involved. Apart from simply being here, there is nothing I can do. Any attempt on my part to access the girl would be foolhardy, if not counter-productive because the boy is so reactive."

Sara said, "And I won't leave the hospital until Rounder is gone. Besides, I can't just show up in Mussoorie without the entire world knowing about it."

"But you would if you could?"

"Damned right I would. That boy may hold the key to our survival, after all. And we do need a foil for Yuri, someone who can parry his intellect and question his motives."

"Assuming the boy would even act in our larger interests. I can't even begin to stress the point of this boy's instability and immaturity, combined with the girl's vulnerability. In fact, she might be the most unstable part of this puzzle, telling the boy that she loves him, doesn't love him, has to love him . . . Who could have possibly imagined this scenario, the fate of the world hanging in the balance of a teenage boy genius in love with a teenage girl spy while a would-be Russian Messiah is returning to Earth in a spaceship?"

Sara had to laugh.

*   *   *

Ten minutes later, Rounder died and brought her to tears.

*   *   *

The flight from Mars to Earth would take five short weeks. No doubt that the voyage would be challenging, but it was not altogether uncomfortable. To begin with, all agreed to place the Dream Machine on a workstation in the galley, where it would be equally secure and equally vulnerable to all of them.

Sasha and Alona necessarily convinced one another that neither had been co-opted by Yuri's powerful mind. And Yuri was gracious to a fault, almost always deferring to the women on practical issues like privacy and sleep cycles, telling them on one occasion, "It's a lot easier to be nice than wise. A wise man can make a mistake. A nice man can make friends."

Bryce was likewise congenial and helpful: fixing things, making hot meals and cleaning, always cleaning. "A clean ship is a sign of a clean mind," he said.

Within a week, the four fell into a casual routine, often having meals together and engaging each other in games—including chess, Scrabble and Go—all available in three dimensions.

By the end of the second week, Yuri began to employ the 'we' pronoun in conversation in an attempt to create a cohesive unit before they arrived in Earth orbit: "We are in this together even if we do ascribe to different results . . . . We are all guilty of something in the eyes of our brothers and sisters on Earth, and on Mars because we have all abrogated their trust . . . Don't we all want the same thing in the end, to enable humanity to survive itself? Can't we find a way to present a united purpose before we arrive in Earth orbit?"

But his attempts at promoting unity were often met with casual resistance by Alona and Sasha: "We are together in this by a force of will and not by choice . . . . We have different objectives even if this ship is returning us to the same place . . . . We will not share ourselves with you if you will not reveal your truer nature and larger purpose to us . . . We are willing let our brothers and sisters on Earth be the judge and have them determine who among us is the pure at heart."

"We are not amused," Alona told Yuri after losing a third straight game of chess to him. They were sitting at a small table in the galley.

Yuri said, "I wasn't gloating. You are an excellent player. I was just smiling on my good fortune."

"Then enjoy it while you can, because I'm afraid your game won't go over so well on Earth," Alona tersely replied as she reset the pieces on the magnetic board.

"You don't like me very much, do you?"

"I don't trust you, Yuri. For all I know, you might have influenced my decision-making in this game."

"Assuming I could, can you believe that I would be so petty?"

"You did slither onto this ship."

"After you stole it."

"And I suppose now you're going to try to tell me that we're not very different from each other?"

"Not as much as you think. And if I could enter your mind, why wouldn't I do it and be done with all this resistance?"

It was a good question, which only served to increase Alona's anger. Perhaps it was the confinement on the ship—the gnawing pangs of guilt and the mounting sense of dread as the *Aelita* drew closer to Earth—that finally pushed her over the edge of graciousness.

"We will see how smart you are when the people on Earth find out who you really are."

"And who is that?"

"A bug."

"I don't understand."

"Obviously, but I will explain it to them—how you are not really Yuri, as you had said, and how you didn't see God because He wouldn't have you as a son."

Yuri was completely bewildered and tried to mollify her. "I've said this many times and I will say it again: When I returned to this reality I wasn't sure who I was because I had many identities in so many different realities, and the experience of all these things taken together seemed divine. It was all so overwhelming that I wasn't sure who I was or what God I saw. I'm still uncertain."

"And still full of shit!" Alona snarled, shooting to her feet in zero gravity; her head nearly hitting the ceiling. She grabbed the edge of the table with both hands before continuing in a rage. "How dare you mention yourself in the same sentence as God, as if you're the Second Coming of Abraham or Moses? You lying, little fucking freak. It is because of you and your lies that we were driven to this, to become thieves and criminals! As if you care about what happens to us?

"You see this? You know what this is, what it means?" she growled, shoving the back of her wrist in his face.

"How can I know?" Yuri replied, hardly blanching from the ugly onslaught.

Alona leaned forward and continued. "If you took your head out of your self-serving, fucking ass you would know that it is the mark of sorrow. I had it tattooed on the back of my wrist so that I would never forget sick bastards like you who would degrade and debase the rest of us to fulfill the sickness in your own twisted mind.

"You say that you saw God. And I say that you didn't see shit! I say that we don't even know if you're human anymore! And when we return to Earth and the truth is revealed about the alien virus that has been incorporated into your DNA, when everyone can see how sick and twisted you really are, they will see you dead before they will know your sick fucking God!"

For the first time since his awakening, Yuri was noticeably rattled: his lips twitching, his body trembling as beads of sweat gathered on his forehead. He was about to question Alona when Sasha and Bryce entered the room. They had been rewiring a loose lead from a computer terminal in the cockpit and had overheard the ruckus.

"What's the problem?" Sasha began, standing in front of the table between Yuri and Alona. Bryce floated behind Yuri.

"He is the problem," Alona snapped.

Sasha looked to Yuri. "Can you explain it?"

Yuri shrugged and muttered, "I don't understand it."

"What doesn't he understand?" Sasha asked Alona.

Alona hesitated, then looked at the floor before replying self-consciously. "I told him about the alien virus incorporated into his DNA."

Sasha shook her head and turned away. She was crestfallen. When Yuri and Bryce preempted their plans to abscond with the Dream Machine, they made a pact to keep the alien nature of the virus a secret until they needed it to trump Yuri's designs on the Machine—by making their alien finding public, and only as a last resort.

"What about the virus?" Bryce asked.

"It is not human," Sasha reluctantly explained, looking down at Yuri. "We sampled it and analyzed it on Mars, and it appears to be the same as what we found on that microbial mat in the ice crystal cave."

"You can't be serious," Bryce challenged, backing away from Yuri.

"Most serious. It was the final straw for us, why we were so motivated to leave him on Mars and take the Machine with us so that he could never join with it."

"You are not wholly human," Alona reiterated, triumphantly glaring at Yuri.

Yuri avoided her eyes and looked to Sasha. "How long have you known?"

"Not long," Sasha said. "And you must believe me when I say that I do not hold this against you. I just don't understand you. No one does, not even Richard before he died."

"He knew about the virus?"

"No, but he always suspected something wasn't right with you, and I followed up on his instincts by testing your chemistry."

The room fell silent, all eyes turning to Yuri.

"I didn't know," he finally said, his voice quivering with uncertainty. "I don't know as much as you think about many things. I don't even know myself. I tried to explain this to Richard before he died, but he didn't believe me. But I hoped that you might try and give me the benefit of the doubt. Because you do know for a fact that I never left my room for twelve years. And if I am experiencing something unusual because of this virus, it can also be a transformation of consciousness—which may be something necessary and wonderful after all, if you would just give it a chance."

*   *   *

Yuri retired to his sleep cube, leaving his crewmates behind to discuss the issue.

Sasha said, "It may be something wonderful, but the virus is no less alien, and we can't take a chance on him. If I'm not mistaken, Yuri might have contracted the virus when he was researching it—he is a highly skilled astrobiologist—and we have no way of knowing how it might have affected him."

"Infected him!" Alona declared. "I will never give him the chance."

Bryce said, "He's my last chance even if I can't understand him." As Bryce feared, as the ship drew closer to Earth, his mind filled with trepidation, recalling all the crimes he had committed on Earth, imagining the degradation that awaited him if they were revealed.

"If only this trip were about you, Bryce, you might have a point," Alona said. "In fact, it's about everyone else but you."

"Which may be our undoing after all," Sasha concluded, now fearing that the divisions on Earth might preclude their best efforts to do the right thing anyway.

21

As the *Aelita* drew closer to Earth, tensions on the surface began to rise. Demonstrations, for and against Yuri, sprang up in every major city in the world, while power brokers plotted behind the ever-maddening scene to seize control of the Dream Machine for their respective governments.

Even greater was the pressure created on board the *Star One* space station because those seventy-nine inhabitants, representing thirteen countries, would be first to engage Yuri and the Dream Machine—if the *Aelita* were allowed to dock. There was a lot of pressure coming from a variety of interests on Earth that had seized upon the issue of back-contamination to prevent any physical contact between *Star One* and the *Starship Aelita*.

"No one in their right mind is going to encourage the docking procedure unless they know for certain that it's going to be in their best interest," Sara told Kreiger. She was still in Florida. He was still in Mussoorie.

"You mean that there is no problem with back-contamination?"

"There never really was. The issue of returning people from Mars was politicized from Day One. Returning colonists' blood could have been recycled and purified, once a week if necessary, until the possibility of infection was marginalized. But I still can't see how any of these people would survive very long if they were returned to Earth anyway, especially Yuri, unless he was placed in some kind of highly specialized, pressurized environment to counteract our gravity."

"Very strange indeed. The whole thing doesn't seem very well thought-out."

"I would have to agree based upon the trickle of information I've been getting. The idea of Bryce returning with Yuri is also troubling."

"What about the Machine?"

"I would think it could be decontaminated in a day, but I can't imagine that these people would let it out of their sight for one moment, not after stealing it and schlepping it all the way from Mars. In any event, it does appear that your boy in Mussoorie holds the key."

"Then you will meet with him?"

"Under the circumstances, I guess I'll have to, if that's what he wants, if I can find a way to do it surreptitiously."

Sara ended their conversation filling with dread. The whole scenario did not bode well with her: the ill-conceived plan to steal the Dream Machine combined with the odd flight of the *Aelita* and the lack of preparedness on Earth to receive the Machine and its criminally negligent guardians. Now Sara had to smuggle herself across the world to negotiate the future prospects for humanity with an ego-maniacal, brokenhearted teenager. Harder still was the prospect of confronting Adam's return from the dead, assuming his consciousness still resided in the Dream Machine.

But Sara had to speak to Michael first, and find out why he had deceived her. So she returned to Washington to make funeral arrangements for Rounder, and more importantly, to confront Michael in their living room that same night.

"You need to tell me the truth, Michael, about the impression you left behind on the computer. You need to tell me who you were speaking to and why? And why do you think I'm responsible for your behavior?"

Sara was sitting in one corner of the sofa, defiant: her legs crossed, her arms crossed over her chest.

Michael sat in the opposite corner, looking down at the rug and slowly shaking his head and blinking, telling her, "I can't."

Sara said, "You have to."

Michael said, "You wouldn't understand."

Sara said, "Try me."

Michael said, "Later, maybe. I have a headache."

"And I have heartache," Sara shot back. "And I have no time for later."

"Then I should leave now," Michael sadly replied.

"And go where?"

Michael had no place in mind; he was so filled with shame and embarrassment. "I didn't betray you, not really—at least not yet."

"So you were planning to?" Sara demanded, her voice raising an octave. She was so frustrated with his illusiveness, so unsuspecting and preoccupied with the larger problems confronting the world that she lacked the requisite patience to ease the terribly painful truth out of him.

"I never planned anything," Michael agonized. "And I would die before I willingly hurt you."

"Willingly?" Sara pressed, uncrossing her arms and leaning forward. "Explain willingly."

Michael couldn't. Now wincing from the pain in his head, his eyes began to blink uncontrollably.

Sara was dumbfounded, but finally moved to compassion when she saw tears gathering in his eyes. She was about to reach out to him when Michael bolted from the room, and out of the house.

* * *

While Bryce looked after Yuri—who had not left his sleep cube in two weeks, having returned to another meditative trance—the women increasingly reflected upon their exit from Mars, their guilt amplified when they realized the enormous effect their actions had on the colonists they had forsaken. The colony was simply devastated by the suddenness and magnitude of the betrayal by the four of them. After all, the Mars colony was founded on much higher ideals than theft and deception.

Though the Dream Machine was more or less an abstraction for many of the colonists—few had ever seen it, fewer still had ever worked on it—they were its regal custodians nonetheless. Almost all of them had witnessed the manifestation of the Lady-In-Waiting while living on Earth, and many of them had pledged their lives to the colonization of Mars on the basis of that experience. Now that the Dream Machine was gone, these colonists had nothing extraordinary to covet, nothing transcendent to look forward to, and no practical reason to endure. There were no scheduled return flights of the *Aelita*, no more interest on Earth about the phenomenon of Yuri, and no possibility of joining with the Dream Machine.

In fact, the only purpose left to the Mars colony was to survive in case the Earth Mother perished, which was the original point of the settlement, but richness of its own history over the last fifteen years begged greater recognition: the heroic loss of life that characterized the first two flights of the *Aelita,* the miraculous survival of Gerta, Vladimir and Yuri, the battle that was nearly fought between them and their saviors for the control of the Dream Machine, and their subsequent joining, which manifested the Lady-In-Waiting, and the discovery of that distant pulsar by Richard Maher.

There were gravesites and placards on Mars that denoted all these memorable events and marked the passage of time, and there were numerous locations on the Martian surface that were named after them: ridges, plains, mountains, and canyons, rooms, laboratories, corridors, scientific end engineering techniques they had developed—and there were even star formations bearing their names in the heavens.

"I'm starting to feel really bad about all of this," Sasha told Alona, after reading a long and emotional transmission that had been sent from Mars, signed by all the remaining colonists. "For God's sake, we betrayed our own identities according to them, our own heritage and the sacrifices that were made on our behalf."

"So you are still thinking that we might have made the wrong decision?" Alona challenged.

"No, but I don't think that we executed our decision wisely. We certainly didn't take the colonist's lives into consideration when we left. We could have chanced it, and argued it out with them, maybe even won a majority to our side and left with their blessing."

"You're forgetting Yuri and the power and influence he was gaining over the colony. Besides, there was no way in hell that we were going to let him near the Machine."

True enough, Sasha thought. Then again, she could have played the alien virus card and won the colonists over by preying upon their fears. She was sitting across the table from Alona in the galley, still the best place to relax and socialize on the ship.

"And you're also forgetting that Earth is in peril or else we wouldn't have done any of this to begin with," Alona added. "What will happen to humanity if there is a major earthquake or a volcanic eruption in the North Atlantic, and there is a massive release of deadly methane gas into the atmosphere? How can humanity survive it? Joining with the Dream Machine may be our last hope, our only hope. You cannot possibly think that the sensibilities of a few hundred colonists can compare with the mortality of billions."

Sasha could hardly argue any of Alona's points, but nonetheless felt guilty. She was more sensitive than Alona. And a lot smarter, she thought. In fact, Sasha believed that she had goaded Alona into absconding with the Dream Machine by preying upon her obsession with losing her Jewish heritage, and her fear and loathing of Yuri. She was about to reply when Yuri and Bryce floated into the room.

"I hope I'm not interrupting," Yuri began.

"Not really," Sasha said, surprised by Yuri's casual entrance in view of the fact that he had been absent for the past two weeks. "Please join us."

Yuri sat across the table from them. Bryce stood behind him, as usual.

"No doubt you have visited many strange and wonderful places while you were away from us," Alona sarcastically surmised.

"I did, but my experience with other realities does not imply that they are better than this reality—they are different."

"But you still won't explain the difference to us?" Alona challenged.

"Not yet, and not until it is necessary—even if you are planning to use my explanations against me by characterizing my experience as hallucinations, resulting from an alien viral infection."

Alona shot a cursory glance at Bryce.

Yuri followed her eyes, looked up at Bryce and said, "I don't need him to spy on you. As I said, I don't necessarily read thoughts, but I can get a pretty good feel on things and people. And if I'm not mistaken, neither one of you are feeling too good right now."

"With good reason," Sasha sighed. "We did make mistakes, and we do have remorse. We may never be able to answer for ourselves to our friends on Mars. Nevertheless, we did get one thing right."

"Which is?"

"You! No matter what you say, no matter what you do, no matter how much we like you, we cannot place our trust in you."

"Because we don't know who you are, because you are so many different people in so many different places," Alona mockingly added.

Yuri flashed an engaging smile. "Then I will tell you who I am in one other place if you can win one game of chess from me in this place."

"And if I lose?"

"Then you give me the benefit of the doubt for one day and show me kindness."

Alona accepted the challenge. While they went to retrieve the chess pieces from one corner of the room—the same magnetic pieces that Adam and Vladimir had used—Sasha and Bryce retreated to another corner.

Bryce said, "Even if I do owe him my life, I would like to see him lose this game."

"Because you assume he would tell us the truth," Sasha replied.

Bryce was about to reply when Alona glared at them, their whispers already disrupting her concentration. Sasha and Bryce left the room on cue, and continued speaking on the observation deck.

"I think you know that we are all losers here, and that this won't turn out very well for any of us when we arrive in Earth orbit," Sasha began again.

Bryce looked up at the stars and sadly replied, "Because we have no place to return to, and no place to call home."

"I'm not sure I understood this until recently. Alona and I were talking about it before, when you and Yuri floated into the room."

"He tried to tell you that we have a great deal in common."

"For remarkably different reasons, and it amazes me how we can find ourselves sharing the same fate while defeating our mutually high-minded purposes in the process."

Bryce shook his head, drew a deep breath and sighed. "I was content to remain on Mars and disappear, to become nobody in particular and fade away into that god-awful dust. But then Yuri asked for my help, and I could hardly say no. Now the media on Earth will expose me as a pedophile—and there is still enough of a man left of me to feel the shame—and you will expose Yuri as an infection. People will take sides, and no side will win. And the importance of the Dream Machine will become lost in all the aspersions and recriminations."

Sasha was shocked and revolted by Bryce's admission. Rumors had circulated on Mars that he had been sent there as punishment by his government, but no one could imagine an abomination of this magnitude—least of all Sasha, who had felt a great deal of compassion for Bryce.

"How could you?" Sasha asked him.

"I have no answer," Bryce said, tears gathering in his eyes. "I'm not a good man, and I don't deserve a good end. So you see,

I don't really belong here on this ship or anywhere else for that matter. I don't deserve consideration; I don't deserve life. Had I the courage, I would have killed myself along time ago in spite of Yuri's efforts. I still think about it, but Yuri tells me that I am necessary. I want to be. I want to matter, but . . ."

When Sasha saw the tears falling from his eyes, she was instinctively moved to compassion. "Time will tell what you deserve. It's not up to me."

"Or even God, because I still don't think I'm worthy of consideration," Bryce said, before leaving the observation deck.

Left alone to ponder her fate, Sasha returned her attention to the stars and recalled where she was on the eve of the first manned mission to Mars. She was twenty-two years old, studying in Paris, and very much in love with Osama Sheik Alzad, a passionate young Muslim from Yemen. They were sitting on a couch in the tiny living room of a very small flat on the Left Bank, watching the Cel-Tel, his arms wrapped around her shoulders, her head resting on his chest.

She was planning on marrying Osama and becoming a doctor, and never imagined that she would leave Earth. He was already in medical school, thinking that this first manned mission to Mars was a waste of human potential.

"It is something beautiful to behold," he said, as the scramjet raced up into the night spewing fire in its magnificent wake. "But it is wasteful because it cannot be helpful to those who do not have enough to eat, who cannot practice their faith with dignity. Until all men on Earth are free to practice their faiths, whenever and wherever they want, all men should be focused on the problems on Earth."

Osama was a deeply spiritual young man who was sympathetic to the continuing Islamic struggles against the West. His oldest brother was martyred in Afghanistan during the war against the Americans, having killed himself and three American soldiers in a Kandahar bazaar.

"If I am called to Jihad, I will go to Palestine," Osama added.

"You mean that you would rather hurt people than heal them?" Sasha challenged.

"I mean that I would rather die a martyr than live like a coward."

Two weeks later, they attended a signing at a small bookstore in their neighborhood. The author was a little-known Swiss national, an engaging man with a brilliant mind who spoke eloquently about the need for humanity to join at the heart on Earth before it expanded into the heavens.

"That Fritz Kreiger is a very smart man, and he has the right idea," Osama said as they walked home from the bookstore. "As I said, there can be no progress in space while there is so much anguish on Earth."

Sasha said, "I also think Kreiger is very smart, but unrealistic if he thinks that he can stem the tide of human curiosity and place parameters on the imagination. The dream comes when it comes, in spite of our beliefs, even if it doesn't appear that we are ready to embrace it."

Osama disagreed, and the two spent the remainder of the evening discussing their differences. A week later and without warning, he dropped out of medical school and left Paris for Jihad in Palestine: "To honor the memory of my brother before it is forgotten in the rush to the stars," he wrote in a short letter to Sasha. "I do love you with all my heart, but I love God more. And I have been called."

He died blowing himself up in a Hebron marketplace, killing seventeen men, women and children.

The memory of losing Osama brought tears to Sasha's eyes, and filled her mind with trepidation. In fact, humanity was still roiling in their painful differences, despite all the efforts to erase them in a voyage to the stars, and she couldn't imagine how the species would ever be joined with the Dream Machine.

Looking out the window at Earth, Sasha suddenly wished that she had never left, and never lost Osama. She wished that she could return home to Uzbekistan and start her life all over again. The memories were so painful and disturbing. She felt so alone, so small, stupid and frightened that she began to wish that she were dead.

Returning her eyes to the heavens, Sasha remembered that first fateful conversation she had with Richard in the observatory on Mars. When she opened her mind to him, she had cast her fate to the stars.

22

Rounder's funeral was held at Arlington, but his ashes were set aside, destined to be interred on Mars beside his best friend, Captain Adam Sietzer—if and when the *Aelita* was returned to Mars.

"Jacob Valdez was a great man—among very best men this world has ever known. Fighter pilot, astronaut, intellectual, champion of democracy, and dearest friend, he gave the best of himself without reservation and asked little in return. As NASA spokesman for the first manned mission to Mars, Jacob verbalized our hopes and dreams. He paraphrased the adventure in space for us, and he lifted us into the stratosphere with his passion and eloquence. And though he never made the journey to Mars, the colony continues to thrive because of his extraordinary efforts on their behalf on Earth. And I can never look up to the stars without thinking of him, and his place in the heart of our eternal becoming."

Sara was up all night composing this speech, writing and re-writing, until she pared it down to one succinct paragraph, careful to not to reference Adam.

"Too many people think Adam is still alive in that damned Machine, and too many of them are frightened by the possibility—including me. It's such an eerie consideration, especially now with the Dream Machine approaching Earth orbit," Sara told Kreiger. She was sitting on the couch in her living room, smoking a cigarette.

Kreiger was still in Mussoorie, sitting in his hotel room. "What about Michael?"

"I really can't say because I don't know. I'm afraid for him too, and I'm terribly upset. It took all my strength to attend the ceremony and deflect the media questions about Michael's absence, which was glaring. And I still don't have a reason for it—why Michael would even consider betraying my confidence. In any case, I'm afraid I didn't handle it very well. I was so angry at the time, so caught up in myself, and Jacob's death, and the return of the Yuri and the Dream Machine, that by the time I was able to reach out to Michael, he was on his way out the door. It was so intense and so strange. He was hurting in a way I've never seen before. I didn't understand, and in some odd way I believe he didn't want me to understand—like he just wanted me to accept his explanation, or lack thereof, on faith. But I couldn't do it and he's been gone four days now."

"Have you checked the local mosque?"

"Of course, and if I don't hear from him soon, I'm going to hire someone to find him. I'm so afraid for him all of a sudden— getting this strange feeling as if he had died somehow, as if he's still suffering in the afterlife, and I can't reach him."

A chill ran up Kreiger's spine. "It almost sounds like you're talking about Adam."

"I've thought about that too, about the juxtaposition of events. And it does appear that we're running out of time."

"A week at most, from what I gather. Do you know if they will allow the *Aelita* to dock with *Star One?*"

"No decision yet, as far as I know, but the debate is raging all over the world."

"As it is in this little town, and I fear that too many people are willing to believe that it's the Second Coming."

"As if the first one was any help."

Kreiger was offended by her sarcasm, but he decided to let the comment pass and wisely changed the subject. "I haven't seen much of the boy."

Sara took the hint and responded accordingly. "What about the girl?"

"Even less of her."

"I often wished I had a girl, but I can't tell how much I'm looking forward to seeing my boys."

As planned, Sara left for India the following morning.

*   *   *

There was no breaking phase employed during the return trip to Earth. The acceleration was so great, owing to the use of nuclear gas core engines, that deceleration of the *Aelita* required a simple, calculated slow-down. As the Earth grew larger and larger in the minds of the crew, and as communications between Earth and the ship became more frequent and demanding, tensions on board continued to rise. In fact, nobody on board was feeling particularly confident, all wishing they had stayed on Mars—including Yuri.

"I left because you left," Yuri told Sasha.

They were sitting in the galley. She was sipping a container of coffee, he was sipping orange juice.

"Again, you blame me, and the next thing you will do is offer me a game of chess to win my loyalty for a day."

Yuri flashed a mischievous smile and scratched his scraggly beard. He had beaten Alona in fourteen moves. "If I thought I could win."

Sasha returned the smile. "Don't you dare patronize me, Yuri Popovitch."

"I wouldn't think of it."

"Then why can't we stop all the games and be real with each other?"

"I am real, Sasha, and I am here to bear witness."

"Nevertheless, you did influence Bryce to join you on this little excursion—which is hardly the act of a witness."

"Perhaps not, but necessary because I felt I had to be on this ship, and I couldn't do it alone."

"And the trial on Mars, that was also necessary?"

"At that time and place. Where Bryce was concerned, I was simply aware of his demons, not even the quality of them—but their intensity—and it was this awareness that drove him over the edge of reason. It was his fear of being discovered, not the discovery in itself. But I imagine Richard saw it differently, having me put the laser weapon in Bryce's hand for the express purpose of wounding me to garner sympathy and heighten my profile at the trial."

"But the trial was your idea."

"Ideal was more like it. I did believe that the entire community bore responsibility for Bryce's actions, and it was small enough to pose a perfect model for justice."

"And now?"

"Now when I look at you, I see myself growing smaller by the moment as Earth looms larger and larger—and I'm also becoming terribly unsure. Dread may be the best way to describe how I feel, fearing that I, too, will not have the strength or wisdom to fulfill my higher purpose."

"You are good," Sasha admitted. "Connecting my feelings to yours in a way I cannot argue with." She adjusted her position in the seat, turning slightly sideways in a useless but instinctive attempt to deflect Yuri's perception of things."

"If things don't work out on Earth, I can always become a psychic reader," Yuri cracked.

"You're not really planning to descend to the surface?"

"Not if I can help it, because I don't wish to die. No matter what some people might think. I am not a Christ figure, Sasha. I still have a great deal to answer for in at least one other life, which is why I was never inclined to join with the Dream Machine."

Sasha was stunned, "Isn't that why you came?" she pressed, sitting up in her seat.

"I came because I had to, Sasha, not because I wanted to."

Sasha leaned forward, and when she looked into Yuri's brown eyes, she saw the sadness gathering in their remarkable depths and was finally convinced he was telling the truth.

"I wouldn't mind going back either," she said.

"Then we do have something in common after all," Yuri somberly replied.

They were searching each other's eyes when Bryce entered the room.

"It appears I'm interrupting," he began.

"On the contrary," Yuri said. "We were just talking about leaving."

*   *   *

Though he had been surprised by Kreiger's visit, Hiro Suzuki was further shaken by his government's pressing interest in their conversation. Tishiro Anakawa had visited Suzuki's office within an hour of Kreiger's departure and grilled Suzuki about the contents of the conversation. Suzuki was cooperative, but not completely forthcoming, having omitted his reference to the boy, Norbu Hua Chang.

But as time passed, and with the announcement of Yuri's imminent return to Earth orbit with the Dream Machine, Suzuki became increasingly sorry that he had recommended the boy to Kreiger. He continually berated himself for withholding that information from his government, fearing he would lose face, if not freedom, if the government accused him of collusion. And though interested in the remarkable turn of events in space, and concerned with the trend toward violent climate change, Suzuki was in the habit of blocking out bad news and protecting himself.

"I just want to be left alone," he told Kreiger, who finally reached Suzuki on the Newgrid in his Kyoto office.

Kreiger said, "No one can be left alone, and no one will survive if we do not endeavor to engage one another. You led me to the boy and I am grateful for that much, but I cannot understand this boy without your help. He is far too smart for me and there is not enough time to turn to someone else."

"No matter what the risk is to me and my family?" Suzuki shot back.

"Someone has threatened you?"

"By inference," Suzuki snapped before abruptly ending the conversation, telling Kreiger to never call him again.

But it didn't end there because Suzuki was hounded by an even greater force than fear, which was guilt. He still couldn't look at Okano's picture, which hung over his desk, without flinching, and he couldn't walk through the laboratory without turning away from all the failed models of the Dream Machine he had tried to replicate, and he couldn't sleep.

Suzuki owed everything he had to Okano, who had mentored him through college, and he had done nothing of consequence to honor Okano's memory—except make a fortune for himself by supplying the world with techno-glasses. Suzuki was already planning on an early retirement in Hawaii—having already built a magnificent house on the Big Island—when Kreiger showed up in his office and unwittingly tweaked his conscience. And as the *Aelita* drew ever-closer to Earth, Suzuki's guilt continued to mount, until it finally reached critical mass in a dream.

His mind filling with memories of Okano and snatches of his initial conversation with Kreiger, Suzuki woke with a start in the middle of the night. His heart beating so fast, he was afraid he might be having a heart attack, so he left his wife in bed and went out into his backyard for a breath of fresh air. His hand resting over his chest, he sat in a chair and began to breathe deeply and rhythmically while looking up at the sky.

It was a beautiful summer night. The stars were twinkling overhead as he began tracing the outlines of numerous constellations in a further effort to relax. He was looking up at Aquarius when he noticed Mars shining through, and his mind filled with recollections of Okano. His eyes closed, Suzuki was recalling one particularly salient moment, when Okano unveiled the completed Dream Machine to him, and he slipped into a dream.

Suzuki was walking on a tropical beach—in Hawaii, he thought—when Okano appeared at his side asking him where he was going.

"Nowhere," Suzuki said.

Okano said, "That is obvious," and disappeared.

Suzuki was searching the beach for Okano when he found himself floating through space. He was marveling at the lightness of his being, and the beauty of the heavens, when he had a rush of fear, thinking that he had died. Frightened, Suzuki fled from space into his Kyoto laboratory. He was hard at work on the Dream Machine when the walls and ceiling evaporated, opening the laboratory to the sky.

Suzuki was surprised by the sudden change, then warmed by the sun; it felt so good on his face. He began to think of Hawaii again, going body surfing with his children, when the increasing heat from the sun began to melt the equipment in the laboratory, and Okano began to shout at him.

"The Machine, you must save the Dream Machine!" Okano shouted.

Suzuki looked up to the sky, again searching for Okano, and felt the sun burn his eyes. Then he looked down at the Dream Machine, beginning to melt in from the intense heat; he was about to grab it when his hair caught on fire.

Now screaming in his dream, Suzuki ran away from the laboratory, burning alive, into the depths of a blue ocean. The cold and wet saved his life. He was floating on the surface, thanking God for saving his life, when he saw the sky catch fire.

He was standing on the water, watching the sky burn slowly and deliberately, layer by layer, when he woke from the dream in a pool of sweat, asking his long-dead mother to forgive him—for what? Suzuki didn't know.

Two days later, following two more sleepless nights, Suzuki reached Kreiger on the Newgrid and apologized for his behavior.

"I am a rich man who has become poor in spirit," he told Kreiger. "I have done everything right for myself and for my family, and nothing for my teacher and mentor, Makoto Okano, who gave his life for us all because he believed in the greatness of the human spirit. Without his guidance and patience, I'm afraid that I would not have very much at all.

"Now that the Dream Machine is being returned to us, my thoughts have been returning to my teacher. No matter what the cost, I believe it is time to pay tribute for my good fortune, and to his great spirit."

*   *   *

Alona said, "We need a strategy. We need to decide on one course of action and stick to it no matter what."

Sasha said, "Do you really believe we can create one now after having tried and failed so many times during these past four weeks in space?"

Alona declared, "We must!" They were sitting at the helm of the ship. Yuri and Bryce were in the galley, "Most likely making plans of their own."

"As if we can outsmart Yuri, who has already won the sympathy of so many people on Earth," Sasha said.

When Alona looked into Sasha's sad brown eyes and saw defeat, she became infuriated. "Of course we can defeat him. We can tell the people on Earth about the alien virus that has attached itself to his DNA," she heatedly replied, careful not to raise her voice. She turned around in her seat to make sure they were still alone before continuing, "We can tell the world that Yuri is less than human, and that Bryce is criminally insane. We can explain how we took the Dream Machine to keep it away from them, and let them explain themselves to the world."

"It's not that simple," Sasha wearily replied.

"It can be if we can only decide on what to say first and to whom—and when. The timing will be important. We should be preparing for this at the very least. I didn't think we would still be second-guessing ourselves at this late date."

Sasha looked out the window at Earth and imperceptivity shook her head. "We can't," she said, turning back to Alona. "We can't vilify Yuri and Bryce to exonerate ourselves because the result will be divisive, and that would be self-defeating. The point of our actions cannot be predicated upon us being right and them being wrong. Whatever we decide to do, however we explain ourselves, the result must be unifying. We must think of the Earth first and not ourselves. We must be thinking about a long-term strategy, not short-term tactics."

"But if we can prove that Yuri is not capable of putting the Earth first because he is under the influence of an alien virus, it will serve us in both ways."

Sasha shook her head and leaned forward. "It is not about us, Alona!" she reiterated. "It is about Earth. WE cannot be served. HUMANITY must be served. We cannot think of ourselves at all. Even under the best of circumstances, we will not win in the end. In fact, it is unlikely that either one of us will survive this journey. We will never be accepted on Earth because of all the divisiveness and the problem with creating a pressurized environment for us on the surface, and we will be severely punished if and when we return to Mars.

"When we left Mars with that Machine we abdicated our future in favor of a higher calling: to return the Dream Machine to Earth, to provide humanity with an opportunity to join with the Machine if it is facing extinction, and to prevent Yuri from joining with it because he is too powerful and too mysterious."

"And if we can't, we can always kill him," Alona said.

"You cannot be serious?" Sasha challenged.

"Deadly serious," Alona said. "If Yuri's death can preserve the sanctity of our future, I can and will kill him."

"But there is no sanctity in murder."

"If you are saying that the end does not justify the means, then you are also saying that stealing the Dream Machine from Mars cannot result in a successful joining."

23

Sara had a hard time leaving the United States without speaking to Michael, or knowing where he was. All of her efforts to find him were unsuccessful, and all of her instincts told her that there was more to this crisis than she imagined. Nevertheless, she answered to a higher calling in India, where she planned on meeting Bu under the guise of joining her children on vacation.

Upon receiving a PhD in geophysics, Isaac, the eldest, had spent the last four months on a geological survey boat in the South Atlantic, testing the rate of desalinization in the Great Conveyor Belt. Jacob traveled between North and Central Africa, always wanting to attend a promising archeological dig, but spending more of his time coordinating charity work across the continent. He had earned undergraduate degrees in anthropology and computer science.

Sara hadn't seen either of her boys in more than nine months, and a trip to India suited her needs—to meet with Bu and convince him to trust her with the secret to joining with the Dream Machine, and to convince her children to come home to America. As a mother fearing the worst, Sara wanted her children close by in case of disaster.

As the most famous woman in the world, Sara made no effort to hide her travel plans from the media and thereby feed its insatiable curiosity. She stepped off the plane in New Delhi in the early morning, waved to the crowd, and gave a perfunctory interview at the airport before retiring to a magnificent home in the New Delhi suburbs. She attended a dinner in her honor, hosted by the Premier of India, and worked the crowd until midnight with expected panache.

The following morning, she was flown to Ladakh, a remote region in the heart of Jammu and Kashmir. Sparsely populated and renowned for its Tibetan culture and mountain beauty, it was well suited for a clandestine meeting of the minds.

As planned, Kreiger met Sara at a modest guest house on the edge of Leh, where the remarkably high plains met the towering Himalayas, and where the Indus River originated. They spoke quietly over breakfast on the second floor patio. The snow-capped mountain tops soarring above them, the building was guarded by a cadre of secret police posing as guests, staff and passersby. Apart from the scenery, the patio also offered a much-coveted degree of privacy. Sara was convinced that the rooms were bugged.

"Suzuki's coming. He had a change of heart," Kreiger said following an exchange of pleasantries.

"That's convenient, don't you think?"

"I would like to think it's a little bit of grace."

"So you think he can be trusted?"

"We can only hope, Madame President."

Sara reached for a pot of coffee at the center of the table and poured his cup before continuing, "You needn't be so formal, my dear Kreiger. After all, we are meeting surreptitiously to decide the fate of the world."

"And you needn't be so sarcastic, Sara."

Sara looked across the small table into Kreiger's intense brown eyes and sighed, "It's all I can do to keep myself from crying, if you must know."

"You haven't heard from Michael?"

"Not a word, but . . . My mind tells me that he's been decep-tive, that he's been lying to me—for a long time, maybe. My heart tells me something else."

Kreiger nodded. "He's a good soul, Sara, and I think you need to follow your heart. I have to believe that he will come back to you, and that he will find the strength to explain himself."

Sara forced a smile and reached for Kreiger's hand. "I'm still hoping that he'll reach out to you somehow. You know I'm still very much in love with him." Sara paused for a moment, studied Kreiger's face and added, "In any case, I have to say that you do look rather well. It appears that the mountain air agrees with you."

Which was true. No longer weather-beaten by those long and cold New York winters, Kreiger looked ruggedly handsome in his white, silk kurta and brown wool vest, and he had allowed his hair to grow back. "I like it in Mussoorie, and I've often thought about visiting the other hill stations, even making a trek into Tibet one day—which brings me to the boy, Norbu Hua Chang, who is partly Tibetan and wholly unpredictable."

"And the girl, have you spoken to the girl lately?"

"Not at any length, I'm afraid. The whole thing hit a snafu when negotiations broke down with the Indian government—that's when the boy demanded to see you."

"What about this Colonel Singh fellow?"

"He's supposed to arrive here tomorrow by helicopter with both of them. In any event, the situation remains highly unstable—the boy and girl having been so terribly misused and abused by the people overseeing them."

Sara reached into her purse for a cigarette. Kreiger watched her light it and exhale a cloud of smoke, and was reminded of a 1940's movie star—the way Sara held the cigarette in her long and slender hands, the way she tilted her head ever-so-slightly to the left, allowing her hair to fall over one sparkling green eye. Kreiger had forgotten how pretty she was.

"I guess my being a mother of two boys might help after all," Sara said.

But she was so damned cynical, Kreiger thought: always looking for the advantage.

"You have something against motherhood?" Sara added, reading the critical expression on his face.

"No. It's the politics that bothers me, the necessity of seeking the advantage in every situation."

"If we expect to deal effectively with this boy, we will not succeed from a weak position."

"And we will fail if we try to overpower him. This boy will not be easily deceived, and I cannot be supportive of this kind of an effort."

Sara was miffed. She was inclined to change the thrust of the conversation, smoke another cigarette, have a glass of wine, and relax with an old friend; these past few weeks had been so hard on her. "You like this boy?"

"I do, and I think our chances are better if we are forthright with him."

Sara looked into Kreiger's bright blue eyes, leaned back in her chair and grudgingly agreed. "Your counsel is well taken or else I would not have supported your efforts to contact the boy in the first place. But there is something else of a more personal nature that I would like to ask you." Kreiger nodded and Sara continued. "Whenever I see you or talk to you, I'm reminded of Father Vincent and the inner struggle you share with him to some degree. We've spoken of it on several occasions, but you don't seem at all as conflicted as you were in the past. Not only do you look good, but you sound good. Has there been some change or resolution?"

"Some progress perhaps—and I don't mind sharing it with you. Meeting with Suzuki and talking to the boy have been most stimulating. And I suspect that the long walks in the mountains in Mussoorie may have also helped. I spent a lot of time looking up at the sky and wondering, unafraid to question my faith, which remains strong despite all the questions I've had. I still believe in the divinity of Jesus Christ, but I'm also willing to believe that another intelligence may have evolved along a different path on another planet, and that they may have had another experience with divinity."

"You mean our Lord Jesus may have a brother out there somewhere?"

Kreiger smiled. "Or even a sister for that matter, which would not diminish His divine stature from my point of view."

"Well said," Sara replied, raising her cup of coffee as if she were making a toast.

"There is one thing that continues to disturb me," Kreiger said.

"Which is?"

"Apathy!" Kreiger declared. "There is a distinct possibility that the species is facing catastrophe, if not extinction. Nevertheless, it is still business as usual. People do talk about it, but not with any urgency; they don't seem to really feel it, the urgency. It seems more like an abstraction to almost everyone I've been in contact with: Suzuki, the boy, Colonel Singh, the people I pass in the hotel in Mussoorie, or even on the street and in the bazaar. . ."

"But you feel it?"

"Intensely."

"And how much time in a given day do you spend thinking about the end of the world: four hours, eight hours?"

"I pray at least two hours each day."

"And the rest of the day?"

"I try to do something about it, which is what brought me to India."

"And if you had a family to support and children to worry about, how much time would you have to pray and work toward a solution? And how often would you talk about it, and to whom?"

Kreiger fell silent for a moment, looked down at his wine and said, "If pride does go before a fall, it would appear that I just dropped off a cliff."

*   *   *

While Sara and Kreiger mused about the fate of the species, Bu and Indra were escorted to Ladakh by Colonel Singh—both struck by the amount of military activity in and around Patankot, a bustling town south of Jammu and Kashmir.

"Pakistan remains a threat, China, too," Colonel Singh explained, as their car headed for the helipad. "As you both know, we have been at war with both countries in the highlands at one time or another."

Indra said, "Then Ladakh seems like an odd place to hold such an important meeting."

"Perfectly odd," Bu said.

Colonel Singh agreed. "Not easy to reach and not too many tourists. I would imagine it will provide good cover for President Sietzer and her family."

"And for me," Bu added.

"No doubt," Colonel Singh said, knowing that he was responsible for Bu's safety. If anything happened to Bu, Colonel Singh would lose his job, at least. At most, he would lose his life because he knew too much.

Once again, it was an odd turn of events that placed such an ordinary man in such an extraordinary position—on his way to meet with Sara Sietzer, former President of the United States. And the closer he drew to power and fame, the more insecure Colonel Sarwan Singh became.

"I just hope the weather holds up," Singh nervously said, looking up at the darkening clouds gathering over the mountains. He was walking behind Bu and Indra toward the helicopter. "It is the violent weather patterns that I find most disturbing. You know my brother was injured by that terrible hail storm in New Delhi."

Bu shrugged, read the insecurity in his shaky brown eyes, and said, "If you were a nicer man, you might see better weather."

Indra laughed; Colonel Singh bit his lip.

"I just want you both to know that it was never personal, I was just doing my job," Singh explained, now fearing that Bu would lodge a complaint against him.

"What you want is not relevant," Bu said. "I am relevant because of what I know."

"I've done nothing to harm you," Colonel Singh declared, before they boarded the helicopter.

Bu remained silent. He owed this man nothing, not even conversation—Bu was so angry. He didn't want to go on this trip, never wanted to leave Mussoorie; he just wanted Indra.

He had Indra. The problem was that he would never know if she really wanted him. As the helicopter rose higher and higher in the cloudy sky, Bu looked at Indra's alluring profile and began to wonder if she was worth having, if his own life was worth living, if humanity was worth saving.

*   *   *

Permission was given for the *Aelita* to enter Moon orbit following an emergency meeting of the United Nations—which was the only thing the nations of Earth could agree upon. The idea of returning the Dream Machine or the astronauts to Earth was anathema. Even if they could quarantine the astronauts in a pressurized environment, they could not find a neutral place on Earth to secure the Dream Machine. By agreement, almost all communications between Earth and the *Aelita* would be consigned to discussions of orbiting dynamics, and all nations would steer clear of the *Aelita*—which was an exercise born of futility.

"Can't we all agree on anything? Can't we begin somewhere to find some common ground on any issue?" Sasha asked.

As usual, the four were sitting in the galley across the table from one another, trading sarcasms and witticisms.

"We could request better food," Alona cracked. "Hell, we could be having pizza for lunch and steak for dinner if we worked out a delivery arrangement with *Star One*."

Yuri said, "I would like a peach. I've often wondered what God was thinking when he made fruit. I can never forget the taste of a ripe peach."

"I still dream about having a cold and ripe watermelon on a hot summer day," Bryce wistfully added.

Sasha was stunned by the continued inanity. "This is all beside the point!" she declared.

"On the contrary," Yuri said. "Food is energy, and if I'm not mistaken, this entire mess we're in has its origin in the hunt for energy sources: the necessity of feeding the body and finding companionship. Millions of years have passed, but the challenge remains the same. Now we have entire countries gearing up for war over depleted energy sources while they look to the stars for salvation."

"That is still beside the point, which is the security of the Dream Machine and our immediate prospects for survival." Turning to Bryce, she continued. "Guilty or not, regardless your crimes and punishment, you are likewise human. You are also present and your point of view must be expressed and considered." Her eyes finally rested upon Alona before concluding, "Angry as you are—and for good reason maybe—and righteous as you are, you must be willing to compromise your certainty or else you will wither away in this orbiting purgatory and die of myopia—affecting nothing, losing everything as the God of your Fathers goes down the proverbial toilet of wishful thinking."

Alona winced, scratched the numbers on the back of her wrist, looked upon her crewmates with derision—Yuri, the megalomaniac, Bryce, the criminal, and Sasha, her weak-minded friend—and finally relented. "I will try," she said, biting her lower lip.

Sasha nodded and continued. "The security of the Dream Machine must come first, because it is inexorably tied to our own security. Can we at least begin by agreeing to stop anyone from boarding this ship uninvited?"

"I thought that issue was addressed by the UN," Bryce said.

"I thought so, too," Sasha said. "But the agreement has already been breached. I couldn't sleep very well, so I sat at the helm for a while monitoring communications between Earth and *Star One*—the usual stuff until the subject matter suddenly switched from the usual inanity to several reports about a Russian service vehicle that had recently disembarked from *Star One*. Instead of returning to Earth as planned, it appears to be tracking to moon orbit, toward us, it seems. As you can imagine, the Chinese and Americans have already threatened to destroy the vehicle with orbiting hunter-killer satellites before it approaches us."

Alona and Bryce were stunned.

Yuri was mildly surprised. "I expected something like this, but not so soon, and I'm inclined to think that Sasha is right. Despite our differences, we must reach agreements on as many things as possible—and very quickly, it seems."

Alona nodded. Bryce said nothing and looked to Yuri.

"Agree or don't agree?" Alona pressed Bryce.

Bryce looked at Yuri again and said, "I'm not worthy of the responsibility."

"Which appears to be the trademark of the human condition," Yuri said. "Can any of us say that we are worthy of the lives we live?"

"But you sentenced me to nothingness."

"As I recall, I sentenced you to service, and your service to humanity is now required."

Alona glared at Yuri and interceded. "As if you're God, telling him who he is and who he is not, when to think and when not to think—and who to serve and when?"

It was a credible challenge and Yuri was forced to search himself for an answer. "You're right and I'm wrong," he finally said. "When I assumed control of the trial on Mars and sentenced Bryce, my behavior suited that moment. I couldn't imagine this moment, orbiting the moon, looking down on Earth and engaging the fate of humanity. I keep saying that I came to bear witness, but the situation continues to be more demanding and is evolving more quickly, and in ways I could not imagine. As a result, I'm also trying to navigate this thing, trying to see where I can fit in—if I can be of service."

"As if you're welcome?" Alona pressed.

"Welcome or not, as Sasha said, I am present. Wholly human when I'm here, and as much a part of the solution as I am the problem."

"But not human when you're engaged in another reality?" Sasha asked

"Precisely. I identify with the body I inhabit and my humanity is but another recollection. I have so many memories, I've lived so many lives in so many places—good, bad and indifferent— and I've avoided explaining them for fear that it would only add to my incredulity in this life. But I will try and explain now for Bryce's sake, so that he will know that he is not the only one who has sinned. And for your sakes, so that you will all know that I am far from perfect and still grappling for answers to my own becoming."

Yuri looked across the table at Bryce and continued sadly. "I have also raped. And I have tortured and killed—on another world—in another time and place where murder and mayhem and sadism are the rules by which these wretched souls live. And I lived among them, killing for the sheer pleasure of it—which was the least of it because I enjoyed it and I profited from it.

"Katomhaga it is called, a plane of existence where bodies are hardly corporeal and reality is entirely blue, shades of blue, from nearly black to near white. My name was Anagati-TO, and I owned a den where the weak are kept to pleasure the strong. I was worse than a rapist and a murderer. I was a purveyor, and I am forever damned by my recollection of that life to do penance in every other life I have lived—most especially in this life. And the only way out of that life was to allow myself to be killed, but I feared death."

Eyes popping, jaws dropping, Alona, Sasha, and Bryce were stunned and bewildered.

"You can't be serious?" Sasha asked.

"Terribly serious and very ashamed, because the horrible truth is that I never died."

24

Nearly three percent of the Australian outback was on fire, and many towns and cities were imbued with smoke. Central Africa continued to be raked by fire storms, causing huge exoduses of whole towns and villages fleeing in opposite directions of the wind, the victims often crossing each others paths and trending toward violence, fighting over the smallest amounts of food and water.

Though moving into the heart of spring, much of the weather patterns in Western Europe and the East Coast of North America continually reverted back to deep winter conditions. It was still snowing in early May in many regions, and the temperature in San Francisco frequently rose above 100°.

There was a surge of seismic activity in the South Pacific, and countries on the Pacific Rim were placed on a continuous tsunami watch. Though the North Atlantic remained quiet, there was an increase in the expulsion of methane gas into the atmosphere. And the view of Earth from moon orbit was not as beautiful as it once was because of the smoke bellowing out of Australia and Africa, which clung to passing clouds and turned them gray.

Humanity was apparently facing extinction, and its champions could hardly face themselves. It was a sorry state of affairs, and as Kreiger told Sara, the majority of people seemed resigned to their fates, fearing the worst but hoping for the best as they trudged through their lives. As Sara told Kreiger: what else could they do?

No one had power over nature; no one could predict the exact time and place of the next eruption in the North Atlantic, nor could they imagine its destructive power. In fact, each day of stability bought another day of wishful thinking. Fearing civil unrest, governments trotted out more and more scientists to reassure their populations, telling their citizens that it could be decades before the next eruption, and that the effects of a huge expulsion of methane gas into the atmosphere could be minimized: the vast majority of people might adapt to the new environmental chemistry while scientists figured a way to counter its effects on the human physiology; there was talk of finding means to neutralize the gas, or dilute it before it could effectively poison the atmosphere. Coastal populations could be relocated inland, reducing the destructive power of the expected tsunamis following a powerful seismic event. Though many lives might be lost in spite of these efforts, many more could be saved. The Earth could be renewed. The bubble of wishful thinking and disinformation continued to grow.

The arrival of Yuri and the Dream Machine in moon orbit posed another ray of hope to many people. The problem was that many more people feared both—the entrenched organized religions often stoking the fear and denigrating the hope, inferring that Yuri and the Dream Machine were forces of evil to be reckoned with, and not to be dallied with. While the media continued to hype the divisions between interests, demonstrations across the world—for and against Yuri and the Dream Machine—reached a maddening intensity.

Sasha and Alona were alternately cast as heroes or spellbound thieves controlled by Yuri and Bryce, his sinister cohort. Rumors were already circulating in the English press about how Bryce, hero of the African Campaign, was quietly banished from Earth for unsavory reasons, in a government effort to save face.

Israeli and Muslim government interests were carefully scripted: while orthodox Jews railed against unfaithful men and machines, Israeli powerbrokers on other ends of the political spectrum were quietly pleased with Alona's proximity to the Dream Machine. Though Friday services often ended with harrowing speeches against the alien and the unknown, Muslim governments were most proud of Sasha, the Sufi woman who took matters into her own hands and absconded with the most powerful Machine ever built; no doubt she would favor them in negotiations with Western powers for access to the Dream Machine.

Meanwhile, Russia was convinced that it held the upper hand. Premier Olga Sussenko was, after all, the long-suffering widow of Vladimir Sussenko, whose legendary heroics rivaled the travails of the American, Captain Adam Seitzer. Plus Vladimir had been Yuri's dear friend, marooned together on Mars for two long years. Olga could hardly wait to speak to Yuri, and was willing to test the metal of the Chinese and Americans in space—hence the daring attempt to preempt all agreements, and risk world war to secure the Dream Machine for themselves by docking a service vehicle with the *Aelita*.

The American government vested their interests in Sara. Try as she did to keep the secret, news of her impending meeting with Bu did leak out.

"Given the stakes, anyone of my confidants could have betrayed me," Sara told Kreiger. They had just finished lunch and had returned to the second floor patio for tea, ogling at the snow-covered mountaintops rising above several layers of clouds as they spoke. "Nevertheless, we did stay ahead of the treacherous curve. We did arrive here unencumbered and uncompromised, which is most important if we are to represent the boy's interests—assuming he does hold the key to unlocking the secrets behind the Dream Machine."

"That's not exactly what the boy said. He did say that he knew how we can join with the Machine, how many minds it would take to join with the Machine to actualize its potential."

"But he never discussed its potential?"

"Not to my knowledge."

Sara zipped her white ski jacket against a sudden cool breeze before continuing. "It is hard to imagine what the Machine could do if a million or more minds were joined to it when you consider that it took only eleven minds to create the Lady-In-

Waiting, and project that image through space onto every monitor on Earth."

Kreiger was wearing a black wool sport jacket and a red pashmina scarf. He had grown accustomed to the changeable, spring mountain weather. "I just hope that we never have to find out."

"Would you join with the Machine if humanity was facing extinction?"

"It's hard to say because I'm still praying for the best. And you, Sara, would you be joining Adam or staying with Michael until the end?"

"I also have my children to think about, what their wishes would be. Then I think about Adam, and Michael—I do love Michael. I have to find him, but I'm starting to get this sinking feeling that I might have lost him already without ever knowing why."

Kreiger was about to reply when Suzuki walked onto the patio. Kreiger introduced him to Sara. She poured him a cup of tea and asked him to sit.

"For a few minutes," Suzuki said, gasping for breath. He was tired from traveling, and the thin mountain air exacerbated his fatigue.

Sara said, "We were just talking about joining with the Dream Machine—if we were prepared to do it if circumstances warranted."

"Which is something I have been loathed to think about—if I would encourage my family to do it. I don't think I would join without my family."

Sara wrapped her hands around her warm cup of tea before replying. "It is interesting to think about how many people would rather die than gamble on an extended life inside the Machine—even if it is a life that may be beyond comprehension."

"So is the afterlife, especially if you believe in reincarnation, or some form of heaven, or salvation through Jesus Christ, among others. I was raised as a Buddhist, a Zen Buddhist, actually. My father was a practitioner. He was also a scientist devoted to logical thinking, and I appear to have inherited his point of view. Makoto was Zen Buddhist, but I know how much he loved to tinker around with other beliefs and philosophies. I used to see all kinds of books piled up on his desks and workstations when I was working with him. I also think that he tried to build a Machine that was belief-neutral—assuming that was at all possible."

"So, the Dream Machine has predispositions incorporated into it?" Kreiger asked.

"Of course, perhaps even some of my own. At some point in the process of constructing the Machine, especially as it neared completion, Okano asked several of us who were working on the project to contribute to the Imagining Mars program, to play the game using our input, after fastening an arbitrary projection of a planet—just to see how the Machine worked. He said it was a game, but that was never my impression. I always thought of it as something more, much more. Another thing I remembered on my way here was our experiments, connecting the Dream Machine to the Super Grid. The connection was shockingly easy and effective—even on our first try—as if the Machine was drawing sustenance from the Grid, downloading information from it at an alarming rate. I think Okano was surprised. In fact, I seem to recall him attaching some kind of governor to the Machine to regulate its intake. I also recall him saying that he had help. That he was getting help from someone or something."

"Richard Maher?" Sara mused.

Suzuki shrugged. "Highly unlikely. I do know that they had met on at least one occasion, but I was not privy to their conversation. And they were ardent competitors in a race to build the first conscious machine—hardly associates."

"Then Okano set out to build a conscious machine from the beginning?" Sara asked.

"I suppose so, but it was never discussed. His focus always seemed to be on interactivity, on the bio-technical relationship between man and machine, maybe something more on the order of a person's ability to project their consciousness into a machine."

"Immortality," Kreiger declared.

"Perhaps, but that was another topic he never discussed with me. I remind you both that I was still in graduate school at the time, still functioning as a mindless technician for the master."

"And he never discussed the possibilities of discovering or connecting with another intelligence in the far reaches of space?" Kreiger asked.

"Not with me, not directly, but I seem to recall a group discussion where that question was raised—in the lab, I think, but. . ."

Sara studied Suzuki's profile as he searched himself for answer. He looked smart and quite successful, dressed in the finest black micro-fiber après-ski wear, with a gleaming high forehead, his intense black eyes framed in the lightest pair of techno-glasses Sara had ever seen. He also seemed earnest, if not trustworthy.

"Did Okano ever make a reference to that pulsar?" Kreiger asked.

"How could he? Maher discovered the pulsar long after Okano died."

"But you do believe that the Dream Machine is somehow connected to, or energized by, that pulsar?" Kreiger asked.

Suzuki drew a deep breath and sighed, "Perhaps, but I must remind you that almost every radio telescope in the world has been trained on that pulsar at one time or another following Maher's discovery, and no sign of an alien intelligence has been documented in that region, not even a hint. Then again, we may not have the instruments sophisticated enough to read the intelligence of a higher mind—which is why I am here, because I remain curious, and because I owe a debt of gratitude to my mentor. Has the boy arrived yet?"

Sara said, "Any time now. My children are also coming. It was the only way I could coverup this trip, by making it appear as if I was meeting my boys on vacation."

"You mean your government is unaware of the purpose of your journey?"

Sara looked at Kreiger before returning her attention to Suzuki. "Not anymore, from what I gather. In any event, I won't be negotiating with the boy on behalf of my government."

"Then you know what the boy wants?"

Sara fell silent, studying the man who posed the question. "Not exactly," she eventually replied. "I only know he wants something from me. He asked for me."

"Can you imagine him talking to Yuri—if that were at all possible?"

"I suppose, but I can't imagine how anyone on Earth could communicate with anyone on that ship in private."

Suzuki drew another deep breath, looked up at the mountains and exhaled, "It is still so hard for me to believe that it has come to this: all the skullduggery and deceit and distrust fermenting amid so much despair, especially in view of Okano's vision of the world. He was such a pure thinker, such a wonderfully idealistic man, always doing his best and wanting the best for others. And the truth is that I am here because I wanted less, and I became embarrassed by my own short-sightedness."

Sara said, "I guess you could say I'm here because I wanted too much."

Kreiger said, "I'm here because I just wanted to do something."

*　　*　　*

Michael had little to say to anyone; he was caught up in his own private hell. Yes, he did betray Sara, and the guilt piled upon the pain that he had fought so hard to repress for so many years. He continued to think about suicide as a reasonable alternative to facing the pain and shame of his life, and found refuge in that California mosque where he had rediscovered his faith many years ago. The Imam gave Michael a small room where he often prayed alone for mercy and forgiveness, and where he was tortured each night by a reoccurring dream.

Michael imagined that he was being held prisoner in a room comprised of four tall, gray concrete walls, with one small window near the ceiling, which was too high to reach, and one large, green steel door, which was always locked. He saw no one, spoke to no one, did not understand what he was being punished for. He passed the days pacing the room, often looking up at the ceiling and asking God: Why?

The nights wrought a greater terror, the presence of a large brown worm, nearly a foot long with small beady black eyes and round black mouth, always slithering toward him, threatening to suck the life out of him if he fell asleep.

Michael kept backing away, fearing for his life, until he found the courage to attack the worm, always thinking he could crush it under his foot. But each time Michael stepped forward and threatened the worm, it began to glow, emanating a bluish hue that was distinctly electric and deadly to the touch. So Michael continued to back up with the worm in slow pursuit of him, until he invariably woke from the dream screaming for his life.

*   *   *

"You really are insane," Alona snapped, looking at Yuri with contempt.

Sasha didn't argue the point; she was so startled by Yuri's description of a murderous life.

Bryce backed away from Yuri, wondering if he had placed his faith and life in the wrong hands. "You killed people?" Bryce said, fighting to maintain his composure. "You're still killing people?"

Yuri nodded. "In another reality, but it's not the only reality I live in. There are so many other worlds and so many other dimensions—more than you could possibly imagine—and I inhabit so many other minds and bodies, living a virtuous life in most instances, a marvelous and harmonious life in other dimensions where some beings have already realized their evolutionary potential and have evolved outside of their bodies."

"Then why did you tell us about the horror of that one life?" Sasha demanded.

"Because it was right and necessary to reveal my shame and connect with all of you at the heart of the matter we are confronting, which is humility in the face of utter catastrophe, and because the time has come for Bryce to take responsibility for the entirety of his life while there is still time for redemption." Yuri looked at Bryce before continuing, "I've seen so much; I've lived so many lives and still live them. I've seen so much violence between beings, between countries, between worlds, between entire solar systems—even galaxies that demand more space to expand at the expense of other galaxies. I've seen suns that are jealous of one another's light.

"There are states of awareness that fight over the possession of extra-dimensional time and space, and vast regions of space that are alive and intelligent and pose as gods and goddesses to smaller regions. There are worlds and species that have devolved to scum, others that have imploded from righteousness and loneliness, and still more that have evolved to join this pantheon of gods and goddesses that reside in the far reaches of space. There are dimensions that are nearly inert and others that are as flimsy as a leaf blowing through the winds of time and space, some so subtle that they pass through each other and mate and beget other dimensions, and there are beings that defy gravity and all explanation.

"Nothing is dead! And nothing ever dies! Rock lives! Dirt lives! Rock lives to become dirt, to become fertile soil, to sustain higher life and enter the cellular membrane of a higher mind and purpose. And God lives in everything, in every thought and feeling, on every world, in every dimension of time and space, in every being and in every rock, in every misery and in every wretched form of conscious life, in every virtue and every sin and sinner. It is all God! And it is all grace because even the worst of it can and will evolve into best of it—given time.

"But time isn't a given, and neither is space. If I have learned anything from living all these lives in all these dimensions, it is that even time and space must be earned. You have to want it! Or else it will be taken from you—another being will take your place, another species will occupy your planet, another planet will seize your orbit, another galaxy will supplant your galaxy." Yuri turned to Alona and continued, "And another God will reign over the God of your Fathers.

"God is movement. God is evolution. God is war. God is peace. God is raping and killing children. God is suffering for the sins of other beings in this life and in other lives, and dying for them. He is Jesus and he is more than Jesus. And he is Judas. And the greatest sin of all is when we are consigned to see the half of it, when the light of creation is divided into good and evil, and right and wrong, between what is divine and not divine, when we choose sides instead of choosing life when our very lives are at stake, when the arbitrary distinctions we make between good and evil must be suspended to serve the higher purpose, which is survival."

The ensuing silence was so intense, so filled with shock and bewilderment that it was nearly tangible.

"You mean evil should go unpunished?" Alona finally challenged, struggling to maintain her composure.

"No, I mean that evil is not an end in itself, and neither is punishment, because punishment for the sake of causing pain is evil and counterproductive to the evolutionary scheme of things. It does not create real strength; it does not find peace of mind; it does not find a quiet heart; it does not serve the individual being or the species if it cannot be redeemed. As the rock is turned to dust and fertilized to sustain life, sin can become virtue. The moon we orbit is inert, yet it affects the ebb and flow of water on Earth, which is essential to life. All things in God's creation have meaning and purpose, and all things and beings can be joined to the heart of God.

"Abraham recognized the glory of the one God, Moses revealed the law, Buddha begged compassion, Jesus Christ asked forgiveness, and what I am saying is that there is still more to contribute, still more to ask of ourselves, more to learn and more to become, but these higher planes of consciousness can only be achieved in a remarkable state of togetherness and accommodation—or this species will implode at the height of promise and die from loneliness! It will never find the strength to transcend its limitations, and never succeed in finding its place in the higher order of things because it will lack the strength to find harmony and meet its destiny.

"I remind you that the Lady-In-Waiting was manifest by eleven incongruent hearts and minds pointing weapons at one another, each convinced of their righteousness—all potential killers straddling the precipice of sin who, in a moment of undiluted clarity, understood the higher virtue of sacrifice and togetherness for the greater good.

"I am also reminded of the wisdom of Captain Seitzer, when confronted with the conundrum of Mei Yi and Vladimir, knowing that he needed both crew members to complete the mission, how he skillfully worked the edges of justice by allowing the rest of the crew to share in the responsibility of discerning the truth and administering justice."

"But justice was never served because the process was interrupted by the rapid decompression incident, which eventually killed most of them," Bryce said.

Yuri said, "Perhaps it was coincidence, but there was a remarkable intelligence at work in that situation because justice denied was justice served. Even if we assume Vladimir was guilty, did it diminish his heroic contribution to the higher calling of the species to endure and explore? And Mei Yi, can we assume that her contribution ended with her penchant for narcissism and the prospect of her bearing false witness?"

"I don't understand," Sasha said.

Yuri unhinged a crystalline computer chip from a bracelet around his wrist, tossed it on the table and said, "Then read it and weep for all the souls who have lost their lives in an effort find the truest and deepest meaning for the lives you are afraid to live."

25

Bu, Indra, and Colonel Singh had arrived in Leh late in the afternoon under the veil of a spiraling world crisis, tracking toward the inevitability of a space-based war over possession of the Dream Machine—China and the United States threatening to employ a variety of space-based laser weapons against the Russian vehicle; Russia threatening retaliation if attacked.

As expected, the new Russian president, Olga Sussenko, denied government involvement in the event, claiming it was a rogue ship commanded by several disgruntled Russian officers and technicians. "I remind the world that my husband gave his life in an extraordinary effort to secure the Dream Machine for all nations," she said.

But no one believed her, least of all Sara, who characterized Olga as a compulsive woman with an enduring vengeful agenda. "Her husband died more than twelve years ago and she went nuts, blaming everyone and everything for her loss," she told Kreiger, pointing to a descending helicopter. They were standing on the patio, looking up at the mountains as they spoke.

"Can't you reason with her?"

"If her gambit fails, maybe—if she needs political cover. But if that Russian vehicle can successfully dock with the *Aelita*, and seize nominal control of the Machine, she won't have any use for me—except to gloat while I beg her for access to my husband, assuming he's still alive in there somewhere."

"Bu did say that no one dies when they join with the Machine."

"But he didn't tell you how difficult it is to live with that knowledge," Sara snapped. She was angry at Olga for being a poor leader, angry at herself for not having been a better leader, angry at the whole damned world for coming apart at the seams of power when it needed to be joined at the heart to survive.

*   *   *

Bu and Indra were discussing the mounting world crisis when their helicopter finally landed at the military checkpoint on the south edge of Leh. Sara's children arrived several minutes later in a military jeep. Colonel Singh was not told they were coming, and he had no idea who the boys were—until he approached their jeep and was repelled by the driver, dressed casually and brandishing an automatic weapon.

"State your business," the driver declared, unmoved by Colonel Singh's authoritarian demeanor.

"I cannot and will not," Colonel Singh replied, as Bu and Indra came up behind him.

"Is there a problem?" Bu asked.

"No problem," Colonel Singh declared as several soldiers ran toward them brandishing weapons.

"If there's no problem then I think we should introduce ourselves," Isaac said, extending his hand past the Colonel to Bu. "I'm Isaac Seitzer and this is my brother, Jacob."

Bu smiled brightly and said, "I'm Norbu Hua Chang, but everyone calls me Bu. This is Indra, and we're here to meet your mother."

"Really!" Jacob exclaimed. As planned, neither of Sara's boys was informed of the real point behind their vacation.

"When are you supposed to meet our mother?" Isaac asked.

Bu said, "Very soon, I think. We are on our way to the guest house just now."

"Us, too. Wanna ride?" Jacob asked.

Bu said, "Yes," and climbed into the back of the jeep with Indra—against Colonel Singh's orders. The soldiers were perplexed and decided to follow closely behind in a second jeep with Colonel Singh.

Sara and Kreiger were about to retire from the patio when everyone arrived at the guest house at once, all shaking hands and exchanging greetings. Colonel Singh stood back, unacknowledged, and amazed at the casual interaction between all these famous and powerful people.

Sara hugged her sons first; when Krieger introduced her to Bu, she disregarded Bu's outstretched hand and embraced him and Indra.

"So you're the boy genius," she began, parting from the embrace, surprised at how boyish Bu looked. "And you're the beautiful girlfriend," she added turning to Indra.

Indra blushed and said, "You're too kind."

"I'm a politician," Sara cracked. "I'm also a mom who has to explain to her sons what we're all doing here, but not until we've had dinner—and if the boys don't mind, I'd like you both to join us in the dining room at seven."

* * *

It was a wonderful evening, unlike anything Bu and Indra could have imagined, filled with laughter and repartee, and many stories about far off places and people that were especially interesting to Bu and Indra, who had never traveled outside of India. And there was a lot of talk about Mars, and the Mars missions, and the Dream Machine—Bu was particularly intensely interested in Suzuki's experience with Okano—but nothing was said over dinner that breached the parameters of common sense; all assumed that they were being watched, and that their conversations were being recorded.

Reality set in the following morning when Sara met Bu on the patio after breakfast.

"We need to find someplace to talk," Sara began, looking over Bu's shoulder at Colonel Singh, standing near the door with his arms folded across his chest. "Perhaps we can take a walk, find a trail or something?"

Bu agreed. It was another cool and foggy morning. Sara was wearing her white ski jacket; Bu was wearing his robe, an unbuttoned brown sweater, hard rubber sandals, and no socks. When Sara suggested that he might want to change into warmer clothes, Bu glared at Colonel Singh and said, "I'm used to the cold; I don't feel as much as you do."

Sara left the guest house with Bu under the watchful eyes of Colonel Singh, and several other C. I. D. operatives, who kept a discreet distance.

"I need to know what you want from me," Sara began again as they headed toward the nearest mountain path, beginning at the back of the guest house.

Bu said, "Honesty. I also need vision. I need to see what you see, what you think and feel about the people I will be dealing with before I give them what they want—because I don't trust them. I also need to know if I can trust you."

Sara nodded. It was a reasonable request from an apparently reasonable young man. There was nothing about Bu's behavior at dinner that suggested anything else. "Then you will tell me what you want, and see if I can't be trusted with that much."

Bu looked up at the clouds, then turned around and glared at the C. I. D. contingent who was trailing them. "Freedom! I want to be free of all these people once and forever, all their eyes and all their lies. I also want Indra. I want Indra to love me—not because she has to, but because she wants to."

Sara was surprised by the directness and simplicity of Bu's request. "The police can be made to disappear from your life—I have no doubt of that—if you can be helpful with our understanding of the Dream Machine. But I can't speak for the heart of another woman—no one can."

"But Indra is afraid to speak for herself, especially because of the pressure that has been placed on her family."

"We can have her family relocated, to another country if necessary, given jobs, houses and money—even provide them with security if necessary to protect their privacy."

"But she will want to go with them."

"Then she'll go. And if she loves you, she'll invite you to join them."

"But I won't go. I don't want to go. I want to stay in Mussoorie, in Happy Valley with Indra. I want everything as it was, but I want it for real. I want her for real while we still have the time," Bu pressed.

Sara side-stepped two large rocks, looked at Bu's profile and was taken by the agony etched on his face—as if he were about to cry. Kreiger was right, she thought. This boy was deeply damaged and terribly immature.

They walked another few minutes in silence, up a steep incline until they reached a small flat. Sara was gasping for breath. Bu was hardly affected by the altitude.

"We can go back," Bu said, noting the strain on Sara.

Sara said, "No, I'll get used to it. I'm actually in very good shape for an old lady. You'll see."

The next ten minutes were particularly challenging. Sara and Bu skirted more rocks as the path grew even steeper and narrower, until they climbed through the clouds and found themselves looking up at the sun shining down on the miracle of creation.

"I can't imagine that there is anyplace on Earth as lovely as this," Sara said between deep breaths, the clouds gathering at her feet, the warmth of the sun caressing her face, her wide green eyes roaming the snow-covered mountaintops that towered above them.

"It is even harder to imagine that it can all be gone," Bu sadly added.

"Would you join with the Dream Machine before it's too late—with Indra?"

Bu said, "No, but I would go to Mars with Indra."

Sara was confused. "What about Mussoorie and Happy Valley? I thought you wanted to stay there with her."

"And die? I don't want to die," Bu told Sara before turning around and shouting at Colonel Singh and his C. I. D. henchmen as they emerged from the clouds. "I JUST WANT TO BE LEFT ALONE. I JUST WANT TO BE FREE."

*   *   *

"What is this?" Alona asked, picking the crystalline chip off the table.

Yuri said, "Why don't you open it and see for yourself?"

Sasha reached behind her and picked up a pad, sitting beside the Dream Machine, off a workstation. "We can use this," she said, taking the chip from Alona and snapping it into place. Several moments passed until she began to scroll through the embedded information and exclaimed, "Oh, my God!"

"What? . . .What is it?" Alona and Bryce asked, gathering around her.

Yuri explained, "It is the personal journals and game entries of my crewmates from the first mission to Mars—what's left of them after being hidden in a cave for more than twelve years. We decided—Gerta, Vladimir, and I—to hide their holo-pads after reading our own game entries to each other. Being marooned, we were so lonely and curious, desperately trying to understand what had happened to us, but the experience of revealing our inner-most thoughts and feelings to one another proved very powerful and disturbing to us. So we decided to collect everyone else's pads and hide them to protect their privacy, and the sanctity of future missions."

"Future missions?" Sasha wondered aloud.

Yuri nodded slowly and sighed, "For reasons that defy all logic, in the darker depths of our souls, it seems that we all had a premonition of things to come. And given the tragic loss of life, and the mystery behind the ascension of the Dream Machine, we thought it best to preserve the freshness of new minds that might arrive on Mars looking for answers. I can also remember finding something ghoulish or offensive about reading the thoughts of the dead so soon after their passing."

"And now?" Alona challenged.

"Now is different, I believe, because so much time has passed, and because so much is at stake. In any event, I had Bryce retrieve as much information as possible from the pads before we left Mars."

"Another premonition?" Alona sarcastically pressed.

"Call it what you will, but my old crewmates will speak for themselves and you will be the judge."

"You mean that you have already accessed the information?" Sasha asked.

"Before we left Mars, I scrolled though some of the material and discovered that it wasn't all intact, and that many entries had been encrypted; and the identities of some entries are not clear."

"I was in a hurry," Bryce explained.

Yuri continued, "I only read several paragraphs from Mei Yi, then spot-read from some of the others before I stopped."

"And why is that?" Alona asked.

"Because reading the material was connecting me to my humanity in a way I hardly expected. I wasn't prepared for the experience, for all the feelings and memories that the entries evoked. As you will see, it is quite powerful, almost unnerving, looking into the hearts and minds of these people. They were, after all, the most courageous beings I have known in any life."

Filled with an odd mix of curiosity and trepidation, Sasha, Yuri, Alona and Bryce sat down at the table in the galley and saw their future through the eyes of the long-departed.

Sasha said, "I will read first: 'I am dying, and I am taking so long to die. I was afraid of this, but now that I know that it is inevitable, I am resigned. I keep thinking that I should join with the Machine and die with the Captain and Eva, but my heart is drawn elsewhere—into that cave. I can't say why or how. Maybe it's the beauty of the place, the ice glistening from the lights that have been set up inside. I keep staring at it on the monitors, off and on throughout the day, wondering and remembering. . . . I am reminded of an ice cave in India, in Kashmir—Mt. Amarnath where the lingam of Lord Shiva is manifest in Ice. I once went there with my father, on a pilgrimage, to worship this manifestation of Lord Shiva on Earth.

'I was only fourteen, and my older brothers were away. Chandra was already working in America, and Ashoke was in Bangalore. It was the first time I was alone with my father for so long, and he told me that I will begin the journey as a boy and that I will return as a man.

'He was right, because it did become a rite of passage for me, the rigors of the trek combining with the beauty of the mountains, and seeing an old man die right in front of me along the way. I think he must have known he was dying; he was having so much trouble walking, but he refused my help just before he died.

'He was sitting on a rock, leaning on a wood staff, breathing heavily when I asked if I could help, he said, "Life gives much, but God requires even more of us—all of us. The greater the effort, the greater the heaven, and the greater the God." It took all of his strength to stand. Then he took three steps, and he died right in front of me with a smile on his face.

'I want to make the effort; I want to arrive in the greater heaven and meet the greater God, and I believe my path to this God lies through that cave. I want to die trying; I want to die living.   .   .   .'"'

"Ramesh," Yuri said when Sasha finished. I remember using the pulley system with Gerta to lift him up into the ice cave, where he scratched the OM symbol in the dirt.

"And the arrow pointing to that pulsar," Sasha added.

"He did know something," Alona said. "He did find something."

"Himself," Bryce concluded. "At the very least, he found himself."

All fell silent; all were humbled by the desire of this man to reach his potential with his last dying breath. Several pensive moments passed until Alona took the pad from Sasha and read the next entry from Makoto Okano:

"'Did we create life, or has life created us? We will never be the same in any event. Of this, I am certain. I am also responsible because I did not anticipate the conundrum. I was naïve, perhaps arrogant. Because I have created this alone, I am alone in the quest for understanding. I am only half-genius and I will die having lived a half-life never knowing who or what I created. The mistake was in my aloneness. . . .'"

Alona stopped reading and addressed the group. "It appears that this entry is not linear, and not complete." She scrolled further ahead before continuing, "In fact, there are many short entries, if I'm not mistaken, but I'll read them in the order they are presented."

"'The mistake was in my aloneness. I should have involved more people more directly in the process. . . . I still don't understand how the Machine has connected to the Supergrid on Earth—or maybe I do but . . . it must have connected to the machinery on the ship somehow, to the other computers . . . I would have done this myself, connect the Machine to a greater power source, but I feared an overload, or some other irreversible error. The Machine is just too precious. . . .

'This thing with Mei Yi is not becoming to any of us. True or not, it is a disgrace to the spirit of the mission. I know the captain is deeply concerned. He has asked for my counsel, and I am flattered, but nonetheless lost for wisdom. I pray that we discover the truth quickly, and that it does not cast a pall over the entire mission. In the meantime, I will also pray for my captain. The enormity of his responsibility is hard to comprehend. It's no wonder he gets lost in himself sometimes, and appears oddly remote. I know people have been concerned about his lack of focus, and his ability to command under duress, but I am not at all concerned, because it is this inconsistency, this vulnerability that connects him to us. It brings him back to us even if he is a reluctant traveler. . . .

'Is it the power of our minds that is morphing the image, or is the Machine morphing our thoughts? I didn't expect this, and it is all happening so quickly—too fast to comprehend, but I must appear composed and not too surprised. And I must be careful not to betray my own suspicions, that there is another hand at work in all of this, someone or something that is accelerating the process and intensifying our experience. . . .

'Now we have the quest for justice: Was Mei Yi abused? Is Vladimir guilty? What can be the punishments? How can any of us feel comfortable with any of this? How can anyone of us be punished without diminishing the experience for the rest o f us? But we have to live with it, with each other. . . .

'The Machine screams, but we cannot hear it. Is it the wail of a child being born or the punishment wrought upon a new form of life by its inept creator? And now that Adam and Eva have joined to it, I am forced to wonder if they share in the frustration—if their screams are also falling on our deaf ears? My God, what have I done?

'I like the crew—even Mei Yi—because she is real, really conceited and opinionated, and not pretending. And experience tells me that there is more to her that meets the eye or else she would not have been chosen for this mission. Curious, too, how she has bonded with Gerta . . . Gerta intrigues me. I get the feeling that there is a remarkable woman lurking behind all that stoicism. And Eva, she will never cease to intrigue me—and all men for that matter. Has God ever created a more beautiful and brilliant being as Eva Stanton? I also believe that she has a kind heart that has never been touched. The embodiment of so many of God's gifts, I am afraid that only a god will ever know her love. She seems so lonely sometimes, remote—not unlike the captain in some ways.

'I was watching Hakim and Ramesh play chess, playing off each other like two children on recess. Of all the people on this ship, they seem to take so much joy in their lives—Yuri, too, sometimes, especially when he's fawning over Eva. . . . I would be critical of him if I weren't so jealous of his emotional honesty, and so immensely entertained by it. . . .'"

Alona stopped reading, looked across the table into Yuri's sad brown eyes and flashed a warm smile. "Oh really?" she playfully exclaimed.

"It was such a long time ago," Yuri said. "It was nothing. I was so much younger. . . . She was such a beautiful woman. We all had a crush on her."

Alona was about to pass the pad to Bryce when Sasha said, "Why aren't we talking about the Machine, about Okano's misjudgments and his suspicion, how someone or something was influencing the Machine?"

"Because it's hard to figure," Alona said. "And all these questions have been raised before."

"But not answered," Yuri said, casting his eyes around the table. "And I have little doubt that the answers can be found in bits and pieces when you look into the souls of these people—beginning with Makoto Okano. He's telling us where he made mistakes, what he cannot understand, what he didn't expect, and his instinct is telling him that there was something or someone or some force, or even intelligence, that was acting upon, or influencing the function of the Dream Machine—because there is something. I know there is something."

"And you still won't tell us?" Alona challenged.

Yuri flashed a mischievous smile and declared, "I've been trying to tell you. Now these people are trying to tell you. 'The greater the effort, the greater the heaven; and the greater the God.' Open your minds. Open your hearts and listen. You must see for yourselves!"

Bryce looked to Yuri and was about to say he was an unworthy participant when Alona pressed the pad in his hand and said, "Now it's up to you."

"There is no name attached to this one," Bryce said as he reluctantly scrolled through the encrypted notes and game entries before finding something readable.

"'As if the hunt may prove to be an end in itself. As the time passes in my mind, I think more and more about Jacob Valdez. He has done such an excellent job of framing the reasons and challenges for us. But he has not provided us with the opportunity to expand our evolutionary potential. For as long as there is a hunt, there is a hunted and we remain ever captive to the evolutionary cycle of animal survival.

'Better it is for life to know God than know itself, because in the end the hunter is always the hunted and nothing is gained and nothing is changed. In the name of humanity, I go to Mars. In the name of God, I go on faith.

'Allah be praised.'"

"That's Hakim," Yuri said. "It has to be. He was a physician and a Muslim—a very likable man. And it sounds like a part of an early game entry."

Bryce looked around the table before continuing to read.

"The question is: if tribes and countries rise and fall in the natural order of things, why not an entire world? Does the Darwinian maxim, the survival of the fittest, hold true for planets or even star systems? Is Earth not in competition with other worlds, real and imagined, whether we know it or not?

Is there a way out of this spiraling fucking mess for once and all time?

Too much thinking, too much thinking, too much thinking.

Rambling, rambling, rambling.

Being, being, being.

Lonely. The mood is beginning to tell.' "

"I would say this was written late in the game," Yuri surmised. "When things were starting to fall apart for us."

Alona said, "He was obviously frustrated."

Sasha said, "I'd like to hear more."

"From him?" Bryce asked.

"If you can find more of him."

Bryce scrolled slowly, and then exclaimed, "It's a game entry, a complete game entry. It says, 'Game Entry 2.' I'll read it, But I don't think it's Hakim.

"'I am not tired. I am never tired, but I do not sleep very well. Something is bothering my mind. The same dream, the same kind of dream, every time when I try to sleep. I am home and something or someone is hurting me, but I cannot see what it is or who it is.

'It is dark and I can hear people talking to each other, and I am lying on something—not a bed. Something that is cold and a little soft, like a mat in the gym where I spent so much of my life training, and I am trying to listen, but I do not understand the language. And I do not really hear them speaking in my ears. I can hear them in my mind. It's interesting, but I do not like it, having these strange people inside of my head.

'Then I feel so cold, and I want it to be darker, because the darkness feels warm and safe.

'In the light, I feel naked and very scared. I remember sometimes calling out to my parents for help, but they never answer. I am always alone in the dream until they come for me, the strangers. And they do things to me. Medical things, I think, like an examination. But I don't feel bad until they touch me. And I wake up trying to scream, but nothing ever comes out of my mouth.

'I have heard about people on Earth who say that they have been abducted by aliens. And their stories sound just like mine. But I never see any of the space ships or the faces of the people who are speaking and examining me.

'I remember that I had this dream before we left for Mars. When I was a child, I think, I had the same kind of dreams. And they have followed me, the aliens. They are living inside of me and using me to make the journey to Mars so they can occupy the planet when we land. And I do not think that they are very friendly because they will not completely reveal themselves to me.

'And I do not know what to do because they could be living inside of everybody on this ship. And if I complain about them, they can hurt me. The strangest thing is that I should be really scared, but I am not. And I have all this energy, their energy. They do not need to sleep.

'Now I think that I should take something to make me sleep a long time so I can finally see them and talk to them and make friends with them. Maybe they are really good people, better than we are, people who can help us make Mars a wonderful place to live. And they can reveal secrets to us and we can travel to the end of the universe.

'Sometimes I think that I do not want to go home at all, that I would just like to close my eyes forever and drift through space alone and see all these wonderful things and meet all these wonderful people.

'If they are not wonderful people, if they are terrible, then I will become a terrible person just like them, and I will see all these really bad things.

'Sometimes I think that I am afraid to go to sleep because I am afraid to see the truth.'"

"Dear God!" Sasha exclaimed. "It's Mei Yi, it must be. The reference to spending so much time in the gym—she was an Olympic champion gymnast."

Alona locked eyes with Yuri and said, "I didn't expect this. There was obviously something wrong with her but . . ." Alona's voice faded into bewilderment.

"What?" Yuri pressed.

"I also get a feeling there's some truth in it, and I have to admit that I'm becoming very uncomfortable with all this—is this what happened to you?"

Yuri said, "Yes, to me and Vladimir and Gerta, and we were reading our own game entries to each other. We were also afraid to see the truth; we weren't prepared for it. It wasn't the time or the place."

"There's more," Bryce excitedly said. "Another game entry from Mei Yi, her first one!" He looked around the table before reading.

"'I do not know what to think about Mars. I cannot imagine what it is like no matter how much I read about it or think about it. I think that all the speculation is a waste of time.

'This game is based on speculation and I think that it is the stupidest thing of all. What does it matter if the planet changes in appearance because of our own thoughts? How will that change the reality of what we will find on Mars? How does all of this nonsense affect me?

'I think our time is better spent on reading and studying and preparing for surface exploration than playing games. And I think that we should concentrate more of our time on the problems we might even encounter during our flight to Mars.

'Radiation could be a really big problem for all of us. Solar flares frighten me. A solar storm could be the death of us all. And I do not believe that the Aelita is adequately protected. I cannot imagine having to spend several days or a week or more trapped in a room on the Aelita with all these people, hoping that the radiation will not kill us.

'That room is a death trap. It should be lined with lead, as much as necessary, not supplies and water and steel and whatever else is lying about. Even if we survive a solar storm, we will receive enough radiation on Mars to last us a lifetime—if we are lucky.

'If we are lucky we will find evidence of life before we are dead. Then what?

'Too much focus on this trip has been made on machines and not enough on the people who are making the trip. If finding life on other planets is so important, then our lives should be most important. We are the miracle, not some one-celled bacteria buried two hundred feet below the surface some tens of millions of miles away.

'If we do not find anything of value on Mars, it will be a waste of time even if the whole world thinks it was a successful trip. And I hate wasting things. Waste makes me angry. Waste makes me see red.'"

Bryce looked up from the pad and said, "She foretold the discovery of that virus in the ice cave, not exactly, but the coincidence is amazing."

Yuri said, "What is even more amazing is the intelligence of coincidence, how almost every one of us on that first mission had a premonition of things to come, whether it was in our thoughts or dreams. We knew, somewhere within ourselves, we all knew. And try as we did, we couldn't put it together. We couldn't see the bigger picture, like a person who is standing in front of a tall wall; they can't see above it or around it—or even standing too close to it and they lose focus. Or they may discover a rudimentary form of life on another planet, a virus that prevents them from returning home—an event which, in turn, alters the course of evolution.

"The point is that consciousness has no boundaries, no walls, and no limitations other than those imposed by the host body. Uninterrupted, consciousness recognizes consciousness and interacts with consciousness on all planes, in all dimensions and realities—the past, present and future existing at once; the problem being that no host body or mind could possibly be aware of their functions on all planes simultaneously so they, or we, are forced to experience life in the shadows, we sense things, we dream things, we see faint outlines, or imprints of other lives, and refer to them as fantasies or idle thoughts, but I can assure all of you that there is nothing idle in the entire universe, and nothing and no one that is even wasteful.

"Mei Yi was so deeply troubled that she may have lied about being abused by Vladimir. Nevertheless, she was guilty of an attempted murder—hardly an exemplary soul in the scheme of things, and yet we benefit from her insight and experience when the species hangs in the balance of extinction many years later."

Bryce was overwhelmed. He had connected with Mei Yi's guilt and was fighting back tears when Yuri reached into his breast pocket, produced another crystalline chip and handed it to him. "There is more to this story, her story. As you will all see, a lot more."

All gathered around Bryce again as Yuri explained, "This is a one-dimensional, video record of the rapid decompression event that took place on the first flight of the *Aelita*, and if you will keep your eyes on Mei Yi, you will witness a remarkable event."

All watched the pad carefully as objects and people went flying toward the breach: the crew fighting for their lives, fending off debris, and trying to help one another to safety.

Nearing the end of the video, they were astounded by Mei Yi's heroics, watching her toss her body in front of Captain Adam Sietzer, protecting him from a careening cabinet door.

"My God, she lost her life in an effort to save his!" Alona exclaimed. "That thing was headed right for the Captain's head and she took the blow."

Sasha said, "She obviously died a hero, but I don't understand why you kept this record on Mars."

"Because it was the truth and we were afraid that someone would alter it to suit their own needs when the *Aelita* was returned to Earth."

"But this cannot be the only visual record of the event. The ship-board computers must have contained other visual records of the event," Sasha said.

"No doubt," Yuri said.

"Then there must be people on Earth who know the truth about Mei Yi, who have always known the truth."

Yuri nodded. "The Americans or the Russians, or both. They may have even conspired to keep the truth from the world to make the Chinese look bad—or at least not as good and heroic as their own people were. Which is why it is so important that we find unity of purpose. If nothing else, that first mission to Mars was the single greatest expression of human endeavor in all of history, and if our return to Earth is to reach a successful conclusion, it must also express that singular unifying purpose."

26

Isaac had grown into a tall and handsome young man with blonde hair and blue eyes, similar in many ways to his father. Only twenty-four years old, he was already a born leader, quick-minded and charismatic; he was also an adventurer and was delighted to find work on a state-of-the-art green geological survey ship. Having spent four months researching the Great Conveyor Belt, he was quite familiar with the dangers posed by a major seismic event in the North Atlantic.

Jacob was twenty-two, and he looked a bit like Sara, with dark hair and striking blue eyes. He was shorter than Isaac and much thinner—he abhorred working out—but was no less attractive. And he still looked up to his older brother. Deeply hurt by the loss of their father, Jacob had never really gotten over it. In fact, he still spent a great deal of his idle time searching for traces of the Dream Machine on the Supergrid—i.e. looking for the presence of his dad—which was also why he pursued degrees in computer science and anthropology. He was fascinated with the impact of technology on evolution. Suzuki was pleasantly surprised by his technological acumen. While Sara hiked with Bu, Suzuki engaged her two boys and Kreiger on the patio.

"So you believe that the Dream Machine is still connected to the Grid?" Suzuki challenged.

Jacob said, "Not exactly. But I do believe that it has left its mark somehow, maybe an electronic shadow of some kind. I find it hard to believe that something as powerful as the Dream Machine could manifest itself on the Grid and completely disappear."

"But you've found no evidence of this?"

"None, but I am nonetheless convinced."

"He was always a coconut," Isaac cracked, mocking a smack to Jacob's head.

"Better than a wuss in the water," Jacob shot back, knocking his hand away.

Both Suzuki and Kreiger were amused by the brotherly rapport.

Still smiling, Suzuki said, "The truth is that I've also wondered if the Machine didn't leave a trace of itself behind, if not a shadow, an impression, or an electronic deposit of some kind in an obscure nodule, but without evidence to support the hypothesis, and after so many years of research, it would be hard to support the conclusion. Besides, discussion of such a hypothesis in public, especially from someone in my position, could be catastrophic—physiologically and economically."

"Exactly!" Kreiger exclaimed. "And by admitting to that, you have made Jacob's point. The fear factor regarding the Dream Machine already altered human behavior a long time ago. Your aversion to even discuss the matter in public is living proof of the Machine's continued presence—and its power."

"In our minds maybe, but not on the Grid," Suzuki said.

"But the distinction between the two is virtually moot," Kreiger declared, pointing to their techno-glasses. All were wearing them, including Kreiger. "We did build the Grid, and it is sustained and nurtured by our contributions."

Suzuki could hardly argue the point. He was also stunned and embarrassed by his lack of simple insight, and privately berated himself for missing the point; he had been so caught up in becoming successful, and so derelict in his attention to the Dream Machine for so many years.

"Is the boy as brilliant as I recalled?" he asked Kreiger.

"Apparently. He was much smarter than the scientists and technicians that Colonel Singh ran by him in Mussoorie—which accounts for your presence here."

"I just hope I'm up for the challenge," Suzuki said before turning his attention to Isaac. "You were the one they named after the New York taxi driver. I just remembered that—fascinating story, how he influenced your father to become an astronaut; how his son came to the aid of your mother."

"And married her," Isaac sadly added.

Suzuki was about to apologize for getting too personal when Isaac continued, "I miss him a lot. We both do. I was certain he would come with Mom. But we weren't expecting any of this, meeting you and Bu and Indra."

Jacob nodded looked up at the mountains, now shimmering in the sunlight. "She's been gone awhile already, hasn't she?"

"An hour and a half, maybe two," Kreiger said. "I think they took a trail out back."

Jacob turned, looked up at the mountain, then excused himself from conversation and said, "I'll be right back."

"Where is Indra?" Suzuki asked.

Kreiger said, "She returned to her room after breakfast. She said she would join us."

"She's really pretty," Isaac said. "But Mom already laid down the ground rules. Besides, I'm already in love with someone else, a girl I met on the boat."

Kreiger was about to return to the subject of the Dream Machine when Indra finally walked onto the patio, dressed in tight black jeans and a tight black sweater.

"It is so beautiful here," she began, taking a seat beside Kreiger.

Kreiger asked Indra if she would like some tea, but she declined and said, "So, now you can tell me what I missed."

Kreiger shrugged. "More of the same, mostly."

"You mean the Dream Machine?"

"What else?" Isaac said.

Indra drew a deep breath and sighed, "Movies, politics, gossip, any kind of gossip. I really liked all those stories your mother told us over dinner, about all those world leaders—especially Olga, how she rose to power in Russia."

"But she didn't tell you how much she regretted it."

"She didn't have to. I could hear it in her voice. It's a shame they couldn't resolve their differences; they had so much in common, losing their husbands on the Mars missions and all that. I've been asked to go to Mars. In fact, I was told that I would be going to Mars, which is what precipitated this mess in the first place."

Kreiger nodded and pointed to his eyes and ears, reminding Indra that they were most likely being watched and recorded.

Indra flashed a cocky little smile, raised her voice and exclaimed, "And Bu told them they could all go to hell!"

While becoming involved with Bu was a prelude to the mess they were in; it was also a means to escaping it. Though boyish in many ways, Bu was nonetheless fearless, willing to take on the power structure and convinced he could beat it—and he was out walking with Sara Seitzer, the most famous and admired woman in the world.

Indra was likewise feeling empowered, if not embarrassed, by her girlish display of temperament, when Jacob returned to the patio with a powerful pair of binoculars. He sat opposite Indra and Kreiger so he could get a better view of the trail.

Indra was about to apologize to Kreiger for her outburst when Jacob exclaimed, "I can see them—them and a lot of other people!"

"Including Colonel Singh, no doubt," Indra spat.

"It's hard to say, but they're really high up there."

Jacob passed the binoculars to Isaac and pointed in the direction of Sara.

"Wow, they are up there a ways, and . . . Where'd all these people come from?"

"What people?" Kreiger asked.

Isaac handed him the binoculars. When Kreiger looked through them, he saw the blood.

*   *   *

Sara and Bu had trekked for almost forty minutes before stopping. Though Sara was in good shape, as she had claimed, she had a great deal of trouble keeping up with Bu, who seemed to be trying to leave her and their C. I. D. escort behind. They were way above the snow line when Sara finally slipped and fell on a patch of ice-covered rock. She was sitting up and rubbing a twisted ankle when Bu returned to help her.

"I'm sorry," Bu said, helping Sara to her feet. "I went too fast."

Sara said, "You were angry, weren't you?"

"Not at you," Bu sighed. "At them," he added, pointing to Colonel Singh and his three henchmen who were finally catching up. "I think I forgot about you, and I am really so sorry."

"I just want to help," Sara said, wincing from the pain.

"Can you walk?" Bu asked.

Sara said, "I think so, but slowly."

"Then we should go back and find another place to talk, and I will tell you what I know—how I can help you with the Machine, and then you can help me."

Sara was pleased. She looked down the trail at Colonel Singh, who was hurriedly closing the gap between them until a bullet struck him in the forehead. Many more bullets were fired, from many directions, killing the entire C. I. D. contingent. Sara and Bu were still in shock when a dozen men, dressed in white camouflage fatigues, emerged from the rocks and descended upon them.

"Don't say anything. Don't do anything," Sara told Bu, stepping in front of him, thinking she could protect him.

The leader, pointing an automatic weapon on her, barked orders to two of his men in Chinese; they immediately pushed Sara aside and reached for Bu.

Bu pushed back, but was quickly apprehended and dragged away, kicking and screaming for his life.

*   *   *

The unveiling of the private journal entries and game entries, belonging to the crew of the first manned mission to Mars, were as vexing and powerful as Yuri had suggested. No one was comfortable with the material—including Yuri, though he hardly showed it until the pad was passed to him.

"I believe it is your turn," Bryce said, handing him the pad.

Yuri accepted it and tried passing it to Sasha, who didn't accept it and said, "By your own admission, you are as much a part of this process as any of us, another piece of the puzzle—perhaps the biggest piece."

Yuri could hardly argue the point and reluctantly scrolled passed a lot of encrypted material until he discovered an entry from Eva.

"There's no formal Game Entry that I can see, but there is something here she called, 'Practice Game.' Shall I read it first, or would you prefer her journal notes?"

"The game first, I think," Alona said.

Sasha and Bryce agreed, and Yuri proceeded to read aloud with some trepidation.

"'I never thought I would say this, but given the choice, I would rather create life on Earth than find life on Mars. When I see Mars, I see red, I feel warm and I think about children.

'My heart aches for someone to love; I'm so lonely, and I feel so cold all the time on this ship. I wish someone would ask the Captain to turn up the heat. I can't ask, because I can't betray a weakness in case he needs me. That may also be why I'm not sleeping so well, why I fell in love with Jacob. I wish he were here to hold me. Sometimes I wish I never left Earth.

'This feeling about having a child is so new, so strange that I can hardly express it. And it comes at such an inopportune time that I have to suppress it. And I'm caught in the squeeze and it hurts. It's so damn frustrating, really, having to suppress so many things—especially being lonely. I guess I've lived a strange life, having been graced with beauty and intelligence—what every woman wants, and what separates me from everyone else. But I don't want to feel so different and special. I want to belong. I want to be attached. I guess I also want someone to feel sorry for me for having too much and experiencing too little.

'Do I really and truly love Jacob, or it is an abstraction to cling to?

'I don't know what the rest of the crew is feeling. I've spent almost two years with these people and I don't really know any of them very well because we've all been so well hidden in an effort to survive the selection process. But I have to imagine that they must be going through their own share of strange changes.

'If they equated the best of us with the survival of the fittest among us, then I must assume that this crew is the toughest, shrewdest collection of nine people that has ever been assembled. If the equation holds true, there is no problem that we can't solve. If it is false, then we may be in for a good deal of trouble.

'If the beginning of this mission is any indication, it appears to me that we fall somewhere in the middle, into the chasm of never-ending surprise. I suppose time will tell who we are. In the meantime, my mind will be engaged with these people.

'But my heart will remain a lonely hunter.'"

Sasha said, "It's really interesting—especially from a women's perspective, how she wanted a child, how lonely and frustrated she was."

"And angry," Alona said. "Angry at having so much and feeling so little."

"Why did she call it a practice game?" Bryce continued.

Yuri shrugged and scratched his scraggly, brown beard. "I guess she was practicing her game entry, to see what she wanted to submit to the Imagining Mars program."

"Were you aware of her loneliness?" Alona asked.

"Not that I can recall, but I suppose it made sense; she was so famous and desirable."

Sasha said, "I had a poster of her on my wall."

"Me, too," Alona sadly added.

Yuri looked down at the pad and continued reading from another entry note.

"'I really like these people, my crewmates—more so now that we're in space because we are relaxed and don't have to hide as much of ourselves. After all, we are the chosen. No doubt Mei Yi is the oddest choice, but I suspect there's more to her than is meeting our eyes and ears. There has to be. After all, we did spend more than two years with her in training for this mission, and we all got long with her for the most part. I don't think she ever liked Vladimir or Yuri, or Hakim and Ramesh for that matter. . . and now we're free from gravity and . . . She does have enormous respect for the captain, though. I can see how he can pose as a father figure for her.

'The captain is the most complex man I have ever known. Makoto Okano may be the most evolved. He is so even-tempered, so wise and insightful, more like a Zen master than a techno-genius. But that Machine he invented for us, my God! I can hardly imagine the brilliance that went into its construction.

'I get the feeling that Gerta has a remarkable sense of humor hidden behind all that stoicism, and it's interesting how Mei Yi seems to favor her.

'Ramesh and Hakim remind me of the older brothers I never had, and always wanted to have. They fit together like hand and glove, and they're so congenial.

'And Vladimir . . . well, he might be the quintessential burly Russian—if he weren't so smart. I feel very secure with him.

'Altogether, I guess we do make a family. I would like to think so—with darling Yuri playing the puppy.'"

When Sasha looked into Yuri's sad brown eyes and put them together with his scraggly beard and shaggy brown hair, she burst out laughing.

"He does look a bit like a cocker Spaniel," Alona said, before she began to laugh

"More like a mutt, comprised of different pedigrees from different realities and galaxies," Bryce added.

Yuri waited for the laughter to subside before reading from another one of Eva's journal entries.

"'Standing in the light does not discount the darkness, and it can get very dark on this ship. But I cleave to the light, which softens the tight boundaries of fear. And my heart begins to dance indescribable rhythms around the shadows. Then the music stops. Each knot in time posing a naked need, an obsessive desire, a failed experiment. . . . My god, what have we wrought? Then I begin to think, and the dance comes to an end.'"

"She must be talking about the Dream Machine," Bryce said.

Yuri said, "Possibly, but I don't recall any of us fearing the Machine. But when you add the problems with Mei Yi and Vladimir to the mix, it was very challenging, destabilizing, as I said. And we have to remember that none of these entries are dated." Yuri returned his attention to the pad and read the last entry from Eva.

"'I remember someone once said that the dead are very dead. I'm sure it was a famous writer. And I fear death with all that remains of my life. Maybe I wanted too much, maybe we all did. . . . I'm in so much pain. Everything hurts so much. I can hardly breathe or think, or even talk very much, but I'll try. I have to try to leave something behind. It may be that someone else may find a value to my life that I never experienced.

'Then again, I am Eva and the Captain is Adam and I am struck be the coincidence of our namesakes—as if we are about to become the cyber-seminal parents of another form of life: part human, part Machine, completely indescribable—totally terrifying.

'It's all so terrifying. I wish I can stop crying, but maybe it's good to cry alone so I can be strong for the crew. I need to be strong for my friends. I can hardly imagine what's in store for them, the few who might survive this ordeal, having to bury us and cry over us while trying to survive on Mars—if they make it that far.

'I couldn't do this without Adam. He is the most remarkable man I have ever known. It remains a wonder to me that he didn't crack under the immense pressure, how he continually walked the edge and never wavered from his duty. Yes, I can admit that I've been in love with him, too. But he was a man who could not be touched, whose calling in life would be diminished by love. He wasn't born to love; he was born to a greater destiny.' "

The reading stopped when Yuri began to weep.

27

Yuri cleared his eyes and was about to continue when he saw the tears streaming down Sasha's cheeks. "We can finish another time," he said.

"Now is still good," she replied.

Alona looked down at the table, then up at Yuri and said, "Even if I have trouble believing in you, you must know now how much I do respect you. I guess I forgot how much you've already given, and how much you've already lost."

Yuri thanked her and explained. "The truth is that I have also forgotten, but this reading takes me back even further and reminds me of how human I was, how human I am. But I think I'm afraid to accept it for fear of losing my connection to other lives."

Alona was further moved by Yuri's candor even if she had trouble accepting the premise of Yuri's other lives. She was about to speak to this issue when Bryce sadly said, "I wish I could be connected to another life."

"If we can only join hands and hearts, and find that place in the middle, when day and night tremble in the balance of becoming and we are set free," Yuri said, placing his hand on Bryce's shoulder.

Alona was tempted to place her hand on Bryce's knee, but she still could not find the strength of conviction to join with Yuri to ease Bryce's pain. "Are there more entries?" she asked Yuri, following a long and pensive silence.

"Not many," Yuri said, scrolling down. "The rest appears to be encrypted, or corrupted. Just pieces here and there, a few sentences, reminder notes and the like—if you'd like to read them." Yuri was about to pass her the pad when he noted an entry by Adam at the very end of the scroll and began to tremble. "It's his last entry, I think, but . . ."

"From the Captain's Log?" Alona asked.

Yuri said, "I doubt it. Knowing him, I would have to think that the entire Captain's Log is encrypted. This is something else, though, less formal it seems, written just before he joined with the Machine."

His mind filling with all kinds of disjointed memories of his Captain, Yuri winced from their sudden intensity and added, "He meant so much to all of us. He gave his life for us. And to me, his words are particularly meaningful."

"'It's nearly over,'" Yuri began to read. "'My journey is coming to an end. I already said goodbye to my family. I know that this will be harder on them than on me. I was born to the risk. I just wanted to live long enough to land on Mars, to know for a fact that we succeeded. But I will never know this because death is a moment away.

'I should have died when I threw my body into the breach. It would've been easier on everyone; it would have been a better death for me. I wanted to die screaming, fighting against the odds and going up in a ball of flames. I'm still a fighter pilot at heart.

'But at least I won't be alone. I'll have Eva, and I think my wife will understand. I'm more concerned about my children. I wish I had more to say to them. I wish I had spent more time with them. Dear God . . . life is short, like a whisper in the ethers of eternity.

'I'm so proud of this crew. I need to say that . . . I can hardly breathe anymore. But this crew is as strong and focused and courageous as any I have served with. Better than most . . . I wanted my life to count for something, and they gave it value.

'I'll join with the Dream Machine because Okano thinks it's a good idea, not because I want to spend an eternity in the mind of a gadget, which is the scariest thing of all, becoming something else when I should be dying and becoming nothing. I wanted to discover something new and exciting on Mars. I couldn't have imagined anything like this, but I'd like to think the future is calling, and if it's alien so be it. In the end, if I'm remembered for anything, it should be the future. I didn't give my life for the crew. In the spirit of discovery, I give my life to the future.

'Captain Adam Seitzer, Starship Aelita'"

A sacred silence descended upon the galley. No one dared to speak or move until Yuri cried out.

The pad still in his hand, Yuri leaned forward, crossed his arms on the table, rested his head on them and continued to cry. On cue from Sasha, Alona and Bryce followed her out of the room and up to the observation deck, where they spoke in hushed voices surrounded by stars.

"I wasn't expecting this," Alona began. "I'm very confused. As the reading progressed, I began to have a much better feeling about Yuri, but I still can't trust him, partly because I don't understand him."

"How can you when he cannot understand himself?" Sasha said. "Now he is crying over the loss of his captain and his friends; before, he said that he wasn't even Yuri. He is still in the process of becoming."

"What?" Bryce heatedly asked. "What is he becoming?"

"God only knows, but we have to be prepared for anything." Sasha turned her attention to Alona before continuing. "Richard was right about him after all, because he can pose a danger to all of us simply because he doesn't know himself."

"I tried to tell you," Alona said.

Sasha nodded. "In any event, we still need a plan, a means to secure the Dream Machine and repel the Russian boarding party if they dock with us."

"If they aren't blown to pieces beforehand," Bryce added, looking out the window. "And if they are, there will be war in space, and war on Earth once they start destroying each other's guidance and communications satellites. And the prospect of a catastrophic volcanic eruption in the North Atlantic will become a moot point following an exchange of nuclear weapons."

Sasha was about to reply when Bryce excitedly continued, "My God, there're here already! I can see the Russian ship in orbit behind us."

Alona and Sasha stood behind Bryce and gasped.

"And there's a hunter-killer satellite! It must be!" Sasha exclaimed, pointing at a distant satellite emerging from orbit around the moon. "And there's another and another—at least three of them and they look like there trying to achieve position for a shot, or a collision with the Russian ship."

"Now what?" Alona asked, looking at Sasha.

"Now is the future," Sasha declared. "And because we listened to the thoughts and feelings of those people who gave their lives for us, we were joined to their hearts and minds, and to an even higher purpose."

"Which is?"

"Success at any cost, by any means necessary."

*   *   *

While the rogue Russian service vehicle pursued the *Aelita* in moon orbit, and Chinese and American space-based weapons prepared to target the vehicle, Sara was rescued from the blood-soaked mountainside. Attempts to track down the unknown attackers by helicopter were futile; the air was too thin. Further attempts to track them by foot did not bode well; snow had begun to fall higher up the mountain, covering the attackers retreat.

Apart from the sprained ankle, she was not harmed and spent several hours being debriefed by Indian military officials—who were astounded by the brazenness of the black-ops operation, and confounded by their inability to track the perpetrators.

"This was a well-planned, high-risk operation, performed by a group of highly skilled soldiers," she told Kreiger, after her return to the guest house. It was early in the evening. They were having tea, sitting at a small table in her room; the guest house was ringed with heavily armed soldiers. "They knew exactly who they wanted, and they were very careful to avoid contact with me."

"At least they didn't harm the boy," Kreiger sadly replied. "I can't tell you how concerned I am for his welfare. I can hardly imagine his fear."

"Nor I. In any case, I don't think that we will ever see this boy again."

"You mean they would kill him?"

"No. They would place as much value on his mind as we did, and make use of him. I have no doubt that he will exist as mind until he self-destructs from heartbreak, or even insanity if they press him too hard for the information."

Kreiger shuddered at the prospect and agonized, "My God, Sara, what have we done? What have I done, delivering that boy into a purgatory? And all in the name of humanity. Can't you speak to anybody in the Chinese government who could be helpful, who would listen to reason?"

"Of course—if we can assume I wasn't purposely deceived by the use of the Chinese language by the black-ops leader." Sara took another long drag on her cigarette before mashing it out in the saucer and explaining. "In fact, any number of countries could have been responsible for this. There are Muslim separatists still operating in this region, allied with Pakistan and/or Afghanistan. It wouldn't even surprise me if the Russians had a hand in this, appropriating one of these groups or countries to do their bidding for the right price, or if the government of India staged this entire operation to cast blame elsewhere while they retained possession of the boy.

"Nevertheless, I believe I raised the greatest suspicion when I refused to let them analyze the abduction through my techno-glasses—which must have recorded the entire event—because I can't trust them. At the moment, I would bet more than a few Indian officials are thinking that I somehow masterminded this whole thing on behalf of my own government!"

"You can't be serious?"

"Not only serious, but most likely under house arrest until they are otherwise convinced; I doubt I could leave here if I wanted to."

Kreiger was despondent, lowering his shoulders and shaking his head and muttering, "How can this be? How can this be?"

Sara was reaching for another cigarette, and was searching herself for an answer, when Indra burst into the room.

"It's my fault. It's all my fault. Bu loved me and I used him, and now he's gone because of me, because he loved me so much," she sobbed, leaning forward into Sara's open arms. "He did for me, for us, trying to find a place for us in the world. . . . And I'm so afraid of everyone and everything."

"God knows. God sees," Kreiger said, telling Indra that he would pray for Bu's safe return before leaving the room.

"Please sit and have some tea, and we'll talk," Sara said, parting from the embrace. Indra took Kreiger's seat. Sara continued as she poured her a cup of hot, black tea. "I know the pain of it, and I know the fear of it, losing someone you love and not knowing why. But life goes on, and you will learn to live with it, in spite of it."

"What life?" Indra agonized, looking down into her cup. "We could all be dead in a week. And I'm only nineteen years old, and I never had much of a life to begin with—always having to do what I was told to do, never doing what I wanted to do."

"And what is that, Indra? What did you want to do?"

Indra looked up into Sara's eyes and sobbed, "I don't even know. . . . I was just saying . . . I just wanted a chance to know. Bu too, I think, which is why we came here, why Bu asked for you. He thought you could give us a chance, even if it didn't last that long."

"I thought so, too," Sara said. "But we still have you, and I can try to do something for you."

"Then kill them!" Indra sneered.

"Who?"

"My supervisors, before they come to take me away."

*   *   *

All efforts to assuage Indra's fear and broken heartedness had failed—and for good reason. Given the suspicious turn of events,

Sara had lost a great deal of clout with the Indian government. The C. I. D. would not grant her a meeting until she agreed to turn over her techno-glasses, and the Prime Minister had refused to take her call. By nightfall, Sara had run out of options and was not feeling very good about herself, thinking she had failed everyone.

"Including my children," she told Suzuki. She found him standing on the patio looking up at the stars. It was a clear night and the view was spectacular.

"The boys were just here. We watched the sunset together. You missed them by several minutes."

Sara ran her fingers through her short black hair and said, "What else is new? I've been missing from their lives for years."

"You mean you haven't seen them all day?"

"For a few minutes, to let them know I was okay when I was returned. But they're used to the high drama," she explained, looking up into the heavens.

"Your ankle seems better."

Sara looked down at her foot, then up at the stars. "God is up there somewhere, isn't He?"

Suzuki smiled. "Among other things and beings; I have no doubt whatsoever that we are not alone in this, and that there is an intelligence behind creation."

"And you think the Dream Machine might put us in touch with this Intelligence?"

"Possibly, but I can't imagine that the mind of God could be so easily read. I can imagine that the minds of others can be read. At the moment you showed up, I was reflecting upon how small-minded I have been, getting lost in the idea of riches and success instead of devoting myself to the greater calling."

"I suppose we can all get lost along the way," Sara said, recalling her abbreviated stint as president, remembering when she believed that she was fated to save the world. "Then I met this wonderful man and he rooted me to reality. He loved me in spite of myself, and I became lost in our relationship for eight or ten years, and it felt pretty damned good."

"You're speaking of your husband, Michael?"

Sara nodded. "Michael. He loved me so much and he's gone, and I don't know why. And now that I'm standing out here with you, I'm looking up at the stars thinking we could all be gone in the next moment and never know why."

Suzuki flashed an ironic smile and cracked, "I guess we could say that Kafka was ahead of his time."

"It's an interesting way to put it."

"Appropriate under the circumstances, but not wholly accurate because we do have clues, and we have the Machine. And I have to believe there is a bigger picture here or else the Dream Machine would not have been returned to Earth at this precise moment of crisis."

"The intelligence of coincidence," Sara declared.

"That is one way to put it, when the entire species is threatened with extinction and a premonition of survival manifests almost simultaneously from different minds and sources. And the death wish is likewise enhanced by the true believers and the wishful thinkers, and the dance between the forces for light and dark intensifies creating an enormous amount of tension, which is another word for energy—depending upon your perspective.

"It is the binding of this energy, this gray matter, and not the choice between these energies that we need to tap into somehow—which is where the Dream Machine may come in with its ability to amalgamate opposing forces and feelings and thoughts, able to combine all divergent points of view, as it created the Lady-In-Waiting from all those incongruent hearts and minds on Mars. Once again, it may be the evolutionary force behind this diversity that elevates our prospects and connects to the universe in a deeper way."

Sara was mesmerized by Suzuki's summary. "You make it sound almost poetic," she said, watching the waxing moon rise behind the highest snow-covered peak.

"You're too kind, Madame President," Suzuki replied, following her eyes. "Nevertheless, I am convinced that many people must feel as we do, and especially those four people on the *Aelita* or else they would not have returned that Machine to us."

Her eyes still resting on the moon, shedding its brilliant, white light on the valley, and on the darker impulses of the species, Sara recalled all the losses and sacrifices and contributions made by greater souls: Adam and Eva, Father Vincent, Rounder, Tex, Richard, Vladimir, Gerta, and the eleven people who gave their lives to manifest the Lady-In Waiting; she was thinking about Michael, how he had curiously appeared in her life on the eve of Adam's death and lent her strength, and how he had tried to come to her rescue when she was at the bottom of despair in the White House.

Sara was near tears when she began to wonder where in the world Michael was, why he had apparently betrayed her—if he needed her help. She was praying to the heavens for his return when the mounting crisis took another turn for the worse.

28

All attempts by Chinese and American and hunter-killer satellites to destroy the Russian service vehicle en route had apparently failed. They could not close the distance before it docked with the *Aelita* and get a clear shot. Consequently, the reprisal rhetoric reached a maddening peak when China and America threatened to destroy all Russian guidance and communication satellites orbiting Earth if the *Aelita* was boarded.

Sasha, Alona and Bryce were still stunned by the quick turn of events in space, still grappling with a plan to repel boarders when the Russian service vehicle docked with the *Aelita*—the dull metallic thud echoing their fears.

"I'll get Yuri," Bruce said before scrambling out of the observation deck.

Sasha and Alona floated to the hatch, immobilized by the prospect of its opening; their eyes riveted to the bottom seam.

"Do we have any weapons on board?" Alona asked.

"Not that I know of, but I'll see what I can find," Sasha said before dashing off to the captain's cubicle, her body bouncing off the walls in zero gravity.

Alona's eyes remained fixed on the hatch, scratching at the numbers tattooed on the back of her wrist until Sasha returned.

"If we have any weapons, I can't find them," Sasha said, gasping for breath. "Did you hear anything from inside?"

Alona shook her head, "Nothing."

"No attempt to communicate?"

"Nothing, but . . . I have an idea. Now you wait here," Alona said before she floated off, using the incidental fixtures on the walls to propel her through the ship.

Sara turned to the nearest viso-com and commanded the ship's computer to access radio traffic from the helm, thinking she might glean pertinent information on the service vehicle's status, but failed to make the connection.

She was trying to access the helm manually when Alona finally returned, holding several odd-looking aluminum tubes and heatedly explaining, "Point these at their hearts if they attempt to board us, and look directly into their eyes. Do not even blink, and let me speak." Sasha looked at her curiously. "I was a fighter pilot," Alona added, feigning a smile, knowing that looking tough was half the battle.

Sasha was breathing so hard, she was on the verge of hyper-ventilating when Bryce finally showed up with Yuri.

"You couldn't stop them with those things even if they were real," Yuri said, nodding at the tubes in their hands. "Because these people must be even more determined than you are, and far more sinister than you imagine—and better armed. No doubt their government is willing to go to war over this, and these people must be willing to die for this."

"But that is so insane when Earth is facing extinction from a natural catastrophe, when time may be so short," Sasha said.

"A week, or a month, or a year, or in a hundred years, it hardly matters to these people because it's the power they want in this life, or in the next life—in the mind of a Machine or in the mind of God, or in hell for that matter. If it wasn't the Russians, it would have been the Americans or the Chinese who docked with us. You don't think these governments haven't been training their own people, by the hundreds or even thousands over the past twelve years, to join with the Dream Machine, to seize power in the process of the joining when and if it ever takes place?"

"How can this be if they can't even muster the intelligence to understand the essential nature of the Dream Machine, or figure out how to join with it without dying, or even imagine its effect on their minds once joined?" Alona asked.

"Ignorance has never been a prelude to reason in this life, and the attainment and preservation of power has always been the objective regardless the cost of lives and reason. You don't think that Israel hasn't trained its share of Jews to maintain their precious individuality against the overwhelming majority of other faiths if a joining takes place?" Yuri turned to Sasha and continued, "You don't believe that the Muslim nations aren't prepared to seize control of the entire joining process when they have two billion faithful to draw from?"

"Then again, it would be easier for all involved if the Dream Machine was destroyed because the status quo can be very appealing to the power barons, having humanity living on the edge of extinction and using that as a ploy to gain greater control over their citizens. In fact, you don't even know if the people on this docked ship aren't planning to stay where they are and blow up their own ship in an effort to destroy this one and the Dream Machine with it."

Sasha and Alona exchanged nervous glances, looked down at the feeble tubes in their hands, and began to tremble.

"As I've become more identified with my humanity—especially after accessing the thoughts and feelings of my old crewmates—I can be more realistic in my appraisal, and I can see how the odds are stacked so highly against you."

"You mean there is a high probability that we will fail?" Sasha asked.

"Obviously, and especially since you have no plan to succeed. As I recall, the only goal you had in mind when you left Mars was to keep the Dream Machine away from me, and some whimsical notion of returning it to Earth so that humanity would have an opportunity to join with it if they are faced with a catastrophic emergency. You didn't account for the vast majority of human beings who would not join with the Dream Machine under any circumstances because their religious faiths would preclude such an action; the vast majorities of them would willingly die believing that were headed to the bosom of Jesus or the land of milk and honey and seventy-two virgins.

"You also discounted the power of fear, which preys upon the even greater powers of disinformation and mind control. Of the nine billion people on Earth, how many of them are willing to believe that a seismic event could spell the end of their lives with weeks, when every government in the world is already engaged in the sham of telling them the end is decades away—or even centuries away in an effort to avoid civil strife and anarchy?"

Bryce was bewildered; Sasha and Alona became despondent. Yuri was right. They had no plan, and little appreciation for the frailty of the human condition. They had been on Mars too long.

"If this is reality, then where is the hope?" Sasha finally asked.

Yuri was about to reply when they heard someone knocking on the outer hatch.

*   *   *

Two long days passed in Leh with no sign of Bu, and no communication of terms from a foreign government pretending to be neutral while speaking on behalf of his kidnappers—which was cause for greater concern, according to Sara.

"I have no doubt that they have already tortured him, either physically or with drugs, in an attempt to find out what he discovered about the Dream Machine," Sara told Kreiger and Suzuki over an early morning breakfast in her room. Isaac and Jacob were having breakfast with Indra on the patio. "And it would seem that Bu hasn't talked or else we would have heard from someone already looking to make a deal, given the fast-deteriorating state of affairs."

Chinese and American hunter-killer satellites, orbiting the moon, continued to trail the interlocked ships while their deadly counterparts targeted Russian guidance and communication satellites in Earth orbit.

As expected, the Russian government continued to deny culpability, claiming that this was the work of Russian ultranationalists pursuing their own agenda, which was never stated.

"I also have little doubt that my old friend Olga is willing to take this crisis to the precipice of an all-out war, thinking one of us, the Americans or the Chinese, will eventually crack under the pressure and press for a deal," Sara surmised. "And their weapons will be trained on the odd-man out."

"How long can something like this go on?" Suzuki asked.

Sara shrugged, picked up the urn and topped off his coffee cup as she replied. "Days, weeks, months—until the moment that hatch is opened. As I think we all know, humanity is quite adaptable to almost any condition—including insanity."

Kreiger said, "You seem remarkably serene under the circumstances."

Sara feigned a smile, sipped her coffee and said, "I'm a good actor; I haven't slept a wink in two days. I can't stop thinking about Michael or my children—or Adam, for that matter."

Suzuki shook his head. "I haven't slept very well myself; I feel so sorry for that boy, and I still don't understand what they expect to get out of him. There may not be ten minds in the world that can be conversant with him. I'm not even sure I could have followed his math, if it was forthright."

"You meant there is a chance he was duplicitous?" Kreiger asked.

"Or madly simplistic, when he gave that nine hundred million number as a requirement to join with the Dream Machine and realize its full potential, which is approximately ten percent of the world population. The problem is, he could say almost anything and deceive almost anyone with the power of his intellect, and it could take months, or even years for anyone to figure it out—as his kidnappers may discover, which is why the point of his kidnapping still escapes me."

"The point being that a good offense makes for a good defense," Sara said. "Say the Chinese abduct Bu, who may hold the secret to the Dream Machine, and the Russians capture the ship that contains the Machine. They have the power and The United States is the odd-man out. In fact, now that I think about it, I'm inclined to believe it was the Chinese who grabbed Bu, after all."

"And you are certain there was nothing of scientific value rendered in your conversation with the boy?"

"Nothing I can recall. If he had something of interest or value, I would have told you already—and not in this room," Sara said, looking around the room as if she were looking for recording devices. "As I had said, he was about to tell me something when they dragged him away screaming."

"Screaming what?" Kreiger asked.

Sara was about to reply when three men appeared at her door. One was a high-ranking government official, who told them they had three hours to gather their things and leave the country.

*   *   *

"Can they open our hatches?" Sasha heatedly asked, afraid the inner hatch would fly open at any next moment—the inner and outer hatches, creating a pressurized chamber necessary for transit between ships.

"I believe so," Alona said, wincing as if she were trying to remember. "I think they made the outer hatch accessible from the outside after that solar flare incident involving Mei Yi and Vladimir, but it requires a special tool."

Sasha said, "Then they must not have it or else they wouldn't be knocking on the outside hatch. Has anyone checked the radio traffic to see if they've been trying to raise us?"

Bryce said, "I couldn't. I was with Yuri."

Yuri said, "I never left the galley."

Alona went to the nearest viso-com and repeatedly ordered the ship's computer to connect them to the helm, but was unsuccessful.

"It wasn't responsive to me either," Sasha said.

"That's just great," Alona angrily replied, striking the wall with her hand before continuing. "How about techno-glasses? Has anyone been personally contacted?" Alona asked.

The question was moot—no one was wearing their glasses—and indicative of the mounting frenzy and the lack of focus.

"I can go to the helm and monitor the radio traffic from there, and see if I can't fix the problem with the viso-com," Bryce offered.

Alona said, "Okay," before turning to Yuri and continuing, "You don't look very concerned?"

"I don't see a reason for concern."

"And why is that?" she demanded.

"Because I have nothing to defend."

"You mean you would let them take the Dream Machine?"

"As I've said before, I came to bear witness."

"To what?" Sasha demanded, her wide eyes moving between the Yuri and the hatch.

"To the species, how it will extend itself or become extinct."

"I thought you said that you might be willing to take a more active role in all this?"

"I did, but I'm finally certain that I can't. Yuri was about to explain when the syncopated tapping of metal and on metal interrupted his thoughts.

"They're going to force it open!" Sasha exclaimed, tightening her grip on the aluminum tube, and holding it like a knife. "We should hide the Machine somewhere—NOW—while we still can."

Alona was about to run to the galley and retrieve the Dream Machine when she recognized the syncopated beat as Morse code. "It's an S.O.S.!" she exclaimed.

"You mean they're asking for our help?" Sasha asked.

"If it isn't a trick to get us to open the hatch. Wait, there's more." All listened and heard the explanation taped out on the hatch.

"S.O.S. . . . No O2. S.O.S. . . . No O2," Alona translated.

"You mean they're losing atmosphere? How is that possible?" Sasha asked.

Both looked to Yuri for an answer.

"Is it possible?" Alona asked Yuri.

He shrugged and said, "All things are possible, but only one thing can promise survival."

Alona was enraged and shouted, "Again with the philosophical bullshit! EVEN NOW!!"

Yuri was about to reply when Bryce returned holding a long screwdriver, shaken by the news he had heard on the radio.

"It's war! It turns out that an American or Chinese satellite did fire a laser weapon at the Russian vehicle before it docked with us and burned a hole in it. Then the Russians retaliated by destroying dozens of Chinese and American communications satellites orbiting Earth. Now the Americans and Chinese are in the process of retaliating against the Russians—and each another, attacking one another's power grids and accusing each other of complicity with the Russians. It's a total fucking mess! Even worse is the battle that's begun to rage on *Star One* with everyone turning against everyone else—using laser weapons and knives, whatever they can get their hands on."

"Dear God," Sasha cried out.

Bryce turned to the viso-com, opened a nearby panel, and finished rebooting the viso-com system. Now tied into radio communications at the helm, the background chatter of war heightened the tension on the ship as they spoke.

"And we could be next, because destroying us might be the only thing that would put an end to all this—like Yuri said," Alona said.

All eyes turned to Yuri.

"You saw this coming, didn't you?" Sasha asked him as the tapping on the outer hatch intensified.

Yuri said, "I have to admit I saw something like this. I was always more concerned about the wrath of the species than the wrath of nature—which was one reason why I was averse to joining with the Dream Machine. Compared to what's out there, what's possible, this species is hardly the best choice to join my fate to, and yet there is a nobleness in the spirit when it's rightly directed, which is easily comparable to higher-minded species. My captain embodied this spirit, as well as my other crewmates, which is why I had you read from their journals.

"Ironic as it might seem, you three are, in many ways, exemplary of your species for better and worse, and it is the three of you that evolution has chosen to place at the pinnacle of promise after all these tens of thousands of years of progress and regression. No doubt there are more highly evolved souls on Earth to be sure, but none who occupy such a unique position in the cosmic scheme of things—when life and death hang in ever-sharpening balance of a razor's edge—as you three.

"I could say that you have a sequence of extraordinary decisions to make to save your species from itself, but I won't, because it would be incorrect, because this moment of high drama is the result of momentum involving many billions of human hearts and minds who have already born and died in your wake, and many trillions of decisions that have been already made for you.

"For want of a better way to put it, you are all here as the result of historical necessity: the Muslim, the Jew, the criminal; your levels of education; your morals and ethics; your flashes of courage and cowardice; your forces of logic and your varying emotional intensities: the list can go on for as long as humanity has created categories of judgment. In any event, you three are the sum-total of all that has preceded you, and fate has obviously chosen you."

Yuri nodded at the hatch before continuing, "You have beings in that service vehicle struggling for another breath. You have a world at war in space, a species on the verge of extinction, and a Machine of your own making that may have the ability to enhance or transform your experience. And you are called to higher judgment, and what you do at this remarkable juncture of time and space will be the sum-total result of who you are.

"This much I can tell you, there is no hope in numbers. As I said, the vast majority of humanity would rather die with their Gods on Earth rather than face the future together in space. Nevertheless, there can be salvation in the depths of your monumental despair—in the minority faith in the greater good and the greater God of all things and beings, and in your ability to join with these other beings to create a higher mind and a greater purpose in another life."

"What life? What other beings?" Sasha asked.

"The species you invited into your lives with the intensity of your despair when you combined enough of your hearts and minds to create the Lady-In-Waiting. She is your projection; you have tended the invitation by projecting her image across the heavens. 'I AM,' you said. 'I AM. COME.' And if I'm not mistaken, your prayers have been answered. Another species has offered to join with you in an attempt to save themselves from annihilation."

Sasha and Alona and Bryce looked to each other in utter disbelief; they were shocked to their cores.

"You can't be serious?" Alona finally challenged.

"Completely serious and eternally hopeful, and finally free of all obligations."

Yuri was about to turn and leave the room when Sasha asked Yuri where he fit into the scheme of things he described. "Who are you really, and why are you leaving us now?"

"As I have repeatedly said, I am your witness. And now that my obligation has been fulfilled, I am compelled to follow my destiny elsewhere into another life, where I must find the courage to face my own death, so that I might find my place in the stream of the eternal becoming, finally free of the cycles of all births and deaths, and at one in the mind of God."

Yuri smiled, pressed his palms together, and bowed out of their lives forever. Returning to his cubicle, he sat in a familiar half-lotus position on the floor, closed his eyes, and went to meet his destiny.

29

No one on Earth was aware of the high-drama being played out on the *Starship Aelita*; no one could imagine that they had tendered the invitation to another species to join them at the depths of despair.

Sara had assumed that all her efforts had failed, and rightly so. She could not even convince her own children to face the end with her. "If nothing changes, I have no doubt that war in space will serve as a prelude to war on Earth—and very soon, and many people will die," she told Isaac and Jacob before they left the guest house.

Perhaps they couldn't imagine it, or didn't want to believe it—which was, after all, the prerogative of youth, to think the best and look ahead. In any event, the boys were determined to return to their own lives and fulfill their obligations despite the pressing threat of world war.

"I have a girl on the boat who loves me," Isaac said, standing beside his brother in Sara's room. "And I have an important job on that boat that's waiting for me."

"And I have a responsibility to the people in Africa who need me, who have less to live for and more to fear than I do," Jacob said.

Though impressed with their commitment, Sara continued to argue the heart-wrenching point, and would not relent until Isaac finally drove the point home.

"Apart from loving you so much and being your sons, we are also the sons of our father," Jacob proudly added. "If it's not war this week, it'll be climate change next week. No matter what comes, it's our duty to contribute while we can."

Sara bit her lip, choked back tears, embraced their strength and eventually said goodbye to her sons, fearing she would never see them again. She was sitting on the edge of her bed and crying when Kreiger entered in her room.

"I just saw the boys in the hallway," he began, sitting beside her on the bed and reaching for her hand. "They asked me to look in on you."

"Except there's not much to look at any more," Sara said as the tears streamed down her face. "Just another lonely old lady crying over all the loves she's lost—now my children. And for what?"

"God only knows," Kreiger replied squeezing her hand, but making no effort to console her. "And it may be that we are unworthy of an answer."

"And you can still keep faith with Him?"

"Perhaps it's because I've had less to lose and less to suffer, which created more room in my heart for more faith. But in retrospect, I'm forced to wonder whether it was my fear of attachment that promoted this faith, and not my love of God per se. But I will continue to believe, and I will continue to pray for the best with my last breath."

"And where in the world would you be doing this, my dear Kreiger?" Sara asked, finally clearing the tears from her eyes with a tissue.

"Right here in Leh, under house arrest. I spoke to several government officials this morning, and I talked them into letting me stay behind by telling them that if the boy is returned, it is more likely that he would be willing to talk to me than any one of their people."

"You don't really believe that?"

"Perhaps not, but I do believe that this boy deserves to have someone left behind to bear witness to his life and to pray for his safe return, if only because he was willing to give so much of himself to save the rest of us. Despite his skewed motivations, he might have connected us to that Machine after all, and provided us with a second chance somehow."

Sara reached behind her for her techno-glasses and held them in her lap as she spoke. "That was an odd little question you posed before—when we were talking with Suzuki—asking me what the boy was screaming."

Kreiger shrugged. "I guess I thought he might have been trying to tell you something."

"He just kept shouting, 'STOP' or 'STOP IT,' and that was the end of it. What about the girl, Indra? How's she doing?"

"Not very well, I'm afraid. There's no sign of her in this building whatsoever—gone, just like that, as she had feared."

"As if she never was, as if we ever had a chance," Sara bitterly surmised, fighting back tears. "I never should have let her out of my sight."

"I will also pray to the Lord to release us from our recriminations."

Sara placed her other hand on top of his, looked into his sad, blue eyes and said, "You're a great soul, my dearest Kreiger, and a wonderful friend, and I will be certain to extend your kind regards to Michael—if he will see me."

"Then you found him!"

"No, but I finally remembered where he went the last time he was so deeply troubled, and with any luck, I suspect I'll find him there again."

They had just begun to talk about the strangeness of Michael's behavior when Suzuki entered the room. Sara offered him a seat at the small table at the foot of the bed, but he remained standing and explained, "I'm afraid we don't have the time. I was just told, and in no uncertain terms, that a helicopter is waiting for us, and I volunteered to notify you. It appears we'll be taking this ride together."

"It will be my pleasure to accompany you, Suzuki-san. It also behooves me to tell you how grateful I am for your extraordinary effort, having come such a long way on such short notice to help us."

"I just wanted to see the future," he sighed, thinking the worst, returning to his family and hovering around his house until lesser people with greater power decided his fate.

Sara stood to shake his hand; Kreiger stood to collect Sara's bags. Now standing between the two men, whether out of instinct or blind impulse, Sara deftly slipped her techno-glasses into Suzuki's jacket pocket and coyly said, "Don't ever stop looking."

*   *   *

At Sasha's request, Bryce looked in on Yuri and tried to wake him from a trance to no avail. No matter how hard Bryce tried, no matter how loud he spoke, no matter how hard he poked, Yuri would not react.

"He is already dead to this world," Bryce told Sasha and Alona, noticeably shaken by the loss of his mentor.

"This is exactly what happened the last time, when Gerta turned to him in a moment of crisis," Sasha said.

"He bugged out on her, and he bugged out on us," Alona bitterly added. "And I don't give a shit what God he thinks he's placating with all this ethereal, other-worldly nonsense; he's still a fucking coward in my eyes!"

"I thought you found respect for him," Bryce weakly challenged, now thinking that he had entrusted his life to the wrong man.

"You mean you're going to try and tell us that he's still our hero?" Alona shot back. "And you want us to believe in all that bullshit about other realms, and how we invited other beings to join our miserable, fucking lives because we can't find the brains or the courage to save us from ourselves?"

Bryce looked at Sasha as if he were pleading with her to argue the point on his behalf; he wanted to believe so much.

Sasha was about to speak to the issue when the steady Morse code messaging turned into a much louder, manic, senseless banging, as if someone were pounding a wrench against the inner hatch.

Alona placed her hand on the inner hatch, felt the vibration and exclaimed, "They're inside the ship, just behind this hatch! They must have found a way to access the outer hatch."

"We should try to communicate with them, and see what they want, what the problem really is, and why they haven't contacted us by audio."

"Because they're hiding something," Alona cynically concluded. "There must be ten ways to make contact with us electronically."

Which was true and gave pause—Alona, Sasha, and Bryce looked at one another as if they were searching for a clue.

"Then we should try and raise them, and give them a chance to explain," Sasha said. "If they were hit by a laser, the damage may be extensive; they may be hurt."

Alona drew a deep breath, looked at Bryce and exhaled, "One chance. See if you can't open a ship-to-ship channel from the helm somehow and patch it into the viso-com."

Bryce floated away, leaving Sasha and Alona looking into each other's eyes.

"I guess it is up to us after all," Sasha said.

Alona looked at the hatch before returning her eyes to Sasha. "If we only knew what we are defending, what in the hell that Machine really is?"

"Then you place no credibility in Yuri whatsoever?"

"And you do?"

Sasha couldn't say; Yuri's analysis was so outrageous, and so markedly alien that it was hard for Sasha to put her mind around it. Then again, she couldn't imagine the extinction of humanity, but the prospect was unfolding right in front of her eyes and ears. In a moment, she might be forced to take another life to save her own; in ten minutes, several billion lives could be lost on Earth. The whole planet might become uninhabitable.

Isn't this why she had returned the Dream Machine to Earth orbit—as a hedge against reality? Sasha was still searching herself for an answer when Bryce returned and said, "It's done."

Alona was about to reply when the strained voice of a Russian officer finally came over the viso-com, pleading for the lives of his crewmates. "We're dying in here, losing atmosphere . . . Can hardly breathe . . . Please, we beg you . . . Please . . .let us in."

"We can't let them die like this," Sasha said.

"I can," Alona said.

"Then it's up to you," Sasha replied, looking at Bryce. "Yes or no?"

*   *   *

Though excited by the prospect of downloading information from Sara's techno-glasses, Hiro Suzuki did not expect to derive anything of value from them. As Sara had said, the entire abduction incident, recorded on her techno-glasses, took less than three minutes—from the time the shots rang out, until the black-ops team disappeared from view with Bu in tow— repeatedly screaming, "NO, NO, NO, STOP . . . STOP IT . . . STOP IT!"

Following his return to Kyoto, Suzuki looked in on his family before heading to the lab, where he spent the next six hours analyzing the recording—slowing it down, speeding it up and amplifying the sound, which was not very clear; there was so much shouting and confusion. The only thing Sara had left out of her verbal account was her part in it, stepping in front of Bu as if she were trying to protect him, and lunging for the boy as they dragged him away shouting, "NO, NO, YOU CAN'T . . . PLEASE . . . YOU CAN'T . . .THE BOY . . . HE'S ONLY A BOY . . . STOP . . . PLEASE! STOP! . . . STOP IT!"

It was after three in the morning when Suzuki finally returned to his office, gazed upon the photo of Okano and shuddered at the prospect of failure. It was only a matter of time, perhaps minutes, until the war in space spread to Earth. As Suzuki had told Sara, it was unlikely he would join with the Dream Machine without his family—even when facing imminent death—but he did believe in the genius of Makoto Okano, and he suspected that if he could enable the joining of other minds to the Machine, they could retrieve crucial information that could somehow right the madness befalling humanity, before it was too late.

Suzuki also believed in the intelligence of coincidence: the visit from Kreiger, the ensuing dream that reminded him of his debt to Okano and to humanity, meeting Sara at such a critical juncture, apparently failing to reach their goal, but receiving her techno-glasses. Whether out of instinct or wishful thinking, Suzuki believed there was intelligence behind the connectivity of these events. He fell asleep at his desk, trying to make the telling connection in a dream.

He was back in India, trekking through the Himalayas with his family. It was a beautiful day, the snow-capped mountain tops glistening in the sun. He was leading the way, following a narrow path through the trees until they arrived at a clearing above the tree line.

When he turned to look for his family, they were gone. Turning back, he saw an old girlfriend standing in front of him in the snow, someone from college that he had gone out with while studying with Okano. Suzuki always liked her—short and cute, but not very smart, which is why he eventually broke up with her. He was about to ask her what she was doing in his dream when she invited him to tour the plains of India with her.

"This is prettier," she said, looking up at the mountains. "But it is better down below."

Suddenly young and unmarried, Suzuki headed to Calcutta with her.

At this point, the dream became lucid; Suzuki was totally aware he was dreaming, and thoroughly entertained by the prospect of sleeping with his old girlfriend. So he traveled with her, looking forward to spending a night with her in a hotel somewhere, surprised at how much he was enjoying her company.

Then he thought about his wife and children. Filling with guilt, the dream took him to an apartment in Calcutta, where he admitted to being married. He also realized he had a choice to make, to remain in India with his girlfriend or go back to his family in Japan.

So he went for a walk along the bay, which reminded him more of Hong Kong than Calcutta, with tall white buildings and palm trees lining the shore. It was nearing the end of another beautiful day, the water sparkling in the setting sun while a gentle breeze rustled his hair.

"Life is wonderful," he told himself as the bay swelled and the tide rushed in—but time was running out and Suzuki had to make a decision. Walking back to the apartment along the shore, the sky turned gold; he was walking through a golden halo, thinking he was blessed, when Bu's head rolled up to his feet on the shoreline, screaming, "STOP IT!"

Stop what? Suzuki wondered, looking down at Bu's head.

Bu was about to reply when the macabre scene finally filled Suzuki with fear. The sky darkened and the tide began to pound the shoreline with a vengeance; Suzuki was about to slip into a nightmare when he ran away from the beach and into the mind of a machine.

The Dream Machine, he thought, looking around at the circuitry, wondering how he arrived inside. He was marveling at the complexity of its construction when Okano spoke to his mind, telling him to wake up and plug it in.

Suzuki was looking for an outlet when he woke at his desk, struck by the odd intensity of the dream, thinking he needed to take another look at the recording of Bu's abduction. So he spent the next two hours working alone in the lab, replaying the incident until sunrise—until the space-based war spread to Earth. There were missiles flying over Japan when Suzuki finally succeeded in separating Bu's voice from Sara's voice at the end of the recording and made the simple, but telling connection.

So he tied every computer in the building into the satellite array on the roof, and piggybacked Bu's message onto every transmission from Earth to the *Aelita*, stunned by the simplicity of Bu's reasoning, facing certain death.

*   *   *

As she had hoped, Sara found Michael in a mosque in California, the same mosque he had retreated to after she had broken his heart. More than twelve years had ago—good years, maybe the best years of her life, Sara thought, exiting her car and looking up at the blue sky, fearing the worst. She had tried to reach Olga during her sub-orbital flight back to the United States, hoping she might be able to reason with her, and was unsuccessful. After all, Sara hadn't spoke to the woman in many years; besides Sara was no longer in power, and in no position to save humanity.

Father Vincent was wrong after all, she was thinking upon entering the mosque, wearing a modest black kerchief over her head. She also thought about Adam; she couldn't stop thinking about Adam during the flight home. In some odd, unrealistic way, she had hoped to see Adam again, or meet him in some way via an interaction with the Dream Machine. But that hope was also gone.

Most of all, Sara thought about her children. In fact, Sara promised her children that she would find Michael; they loved him so much. The problem was that Michael refused to see her.

"He is not disposed to see you, Madame President," the Imam said. He was a thin man with small, kind, black eyes, a large gray beard, and was wearing a white skull cap.

The two were standing at the back of the mosque, filled to capacity, the faithful begging God to save their souls, a scene that was being repeated all over the world on that day.

"I beg you," Sara said. "You know that time may be short, and he needs me. I know Michael needs me, and I need him. Ask him again, one more time, for both our sakes."

The Imam reluctantly agreed and disappeared up a narrow staircase at the side of the large room. It turned out that Michael had been staying at the mosque since he had disappeared from their Georgetown house, atoning for his sins and making peace with his God. While Sara waited, she looked upon the holy gathering and her eyes filled with tears; she couldn't stop crying as the realization of extinction washed over her in successive waves.

Her knees were buckling under the weight of the pain; Sara was imagining the death of her children when the Imam returned with the more bad news.

"I am sorry, Madame President. The answer is still no, and I can no longer be of service," the Imam said. "I am called to my people today, and we are all called to God. I am also called upon to ask you to join us in prayer. No one should be alone today, and all can find a measure of mercy here in the heart of Allah."

Sara was grateful. She had no place to go, and nothing left to do but suffer herself and the sins of the species. "How could we do this?" she kept asking herself. "How could it come to this?"

There were no answers. The prayers meshing with her tears, echoing her questions as the missiles began to fly against all reason, Sara drifted toward the side of the mosque, and quietly climbed the stairs to Michael's room.

It was small and austere, just a bed, a chair, and a prayer rug beneath Michael's knees. He was lost in prayer when Sara entered and sat on the chair behind him.

Michael knew it was her, didn't want to know it was her, and fought against the realization. He didn't want to open his eyes, didn't want to see her, but he did.

"You shouldn't have come," he eventually said, opening his eyes and looking straight ahead at a blank, white wall.

"I had to," Sara said, clearing her eyes with a tissue, finally aware that Michael had shaved his head and grown a beard. He was also wearing a white skull cap. "And you have to know that you are forgiven."

"Then you do know," Michael sadly replied, looking down at the prayer rug and fighting back tears.

"Know what, Michael, what should I know?"

Michael shook his head and sullenly replied, "You shouldn't have come. You shouldn't . . . You shouldn't be here."

"Then where should I be?" Sara asked. "In the mind of a Machine, or with my children who can't have me? Where should I go, Michael? Tell me where I should go to die?"

"Anywhere but here, with anyone but me," Michael said, as tears fell from his eyes.

"Then at least tell me why?" Sara pressed, leaving the chair and falling to her knees beside him. "Please, tell me. I'm begging you. It can't be that bad, nothing can be as bad as this, as going to war."

Michael winced from the pain of it, and began pounding the back of his head with a fist.

"What? What is it?" Sara continued, caressing his awfully twisted face in her hands. "What can be so bad? What can hurt so much?"

Michael pushed her hands away, and turned away from her crying, "Me, I can hurt so much because I betrayed you . . . because they hurt me, Sara. They did things to me. They put something inside of me. And they found me again."

"Who found you?

"And they did it to me again. They tried and . . . I couldn't . . . it hurt so much," Michael agonized, his head aching, his heart breaking from the shame of it.

Sara was about to question him further when she remembered Michael's arrest, and recalled how they had tortured Rounder and Tex when they were imprisoned.

"Dear God in heaven, we killed ourselves," she cried out, wrapping her arms around Michael's shoulders when the air raid sirens began to blare. Within thirteen minutes, the city of Los Angeles, among others, would be reduced to nuclear rubble by enemy missiles.

30

Beads of sweat running down his face, his body trembling, his grip tightening around the long screwdriver in his hand, Bryce recalled the shame of his life, reflected on Yuri's discourse on redemption and said, "Yes, open the hatch."

With great reluctance, Alona looked at Sasha and said, "The majority rules. Unleash the dogs."

Her heart racing, her eyes ringing from the intensity, Sasha purposefully turned each of the eight latches, opened a side panel, pulled the lever that opened the hatch, and backed away.

Now standing against the wall, the three crewmates from Mars watched two Russian men and one woman stumble ahead, gasping for breath.

Alona was especially relieved—thinking they had done the right thing after all; the Russian ship had been hit by a laser weapon and these people were obviously dying from a loss of atmosphere. She closed the hatch behind them while Sasha and Bryce tended to the Russians, one of whom was leaning against the wall, coughing up blood. Another appeared to be in great pain, writhing on the floor as if he had the bends.

Sasha was crouching over him when he pulled a laser weapon and jammed it against her chest, telling her to back off, which she did. Falling backwards, she ripped the screwdriver out of Bryce's hand and planted it deeply in the man's shoulder.

He was spouting blood like a geyser when the Russian attacked Bryce with a wrench. She had just brought it down on

Bryce's head when the *Aelita* was hit by an orbiting American laser weapon. As they had declared, the Americans would rather destroy the ship than lose control of the Dream Machine.

As a result, the *Aelita* began to flounder from the laser hit, losing its own precious atmosphere for the last time. Red lights flashing danger, horns blaring, Suzuki's transmitted message was lost in the commotion and in the race to safety in the lead-shielded bunker.

The Russians were dazed and confused.

Alona, the highly trained fighter pilot, maintained focus under duress, helping Bryce to his feet while commanding Sasha. "You get the Machine. I'll get him to the bunker."

Accustomed to functioning in zero gravity, and knowing where she was going, Alona led Bryce through the ship and into the bunker without too much difficulty.

Sasha had a much harder time, fighting against the vacuum of space as it sucked life from the *Aelita*. She had a longer way to go before she reached the safety of the bunker—securing the Dream Machine while circumnavigating the Russians, who were unfamiliar with the ship. She was nearly at the entrance to the bunker when a laser pierced her back and exited her stomach.

*   *   *

Blood was seeping out of Bryce's head at an alarming rate; at the very least, he had sustained a bad concussion. Blood was oozing from Sasha's wound. She was lying on the floor, wincing from pain, still holding the Dream Machine in her hands when the Russians began to pound on the bunker door—pleading for their lives a second time.

The *Aelita's* hull was losing its integrity; the steady loss of atmosphere was turning into a deafening, raging purge, with everything that wasn't secure flying past the Russian's heads toward the ever-widening breach.

"How long can we last in here?" Sasha asked, as Alona helped her to a seat on the bench.

"Does it really matter?" Alona replied. "One way or another we've come to our end."

"What about the Russians?" Bryce asked. Though dazed and weak, he was acutely aware of the situation.

"They die where they stand, on the outside looking in," Alona declared.

"To what end if we're all dead already?" Sasha asked, grimacing from the pain and gasping for breath.

Alona was about to shout, "NEVER AGAIN," when she finally realized the absurdity of her argument. Death by any means was still death. And despite all their efforts to do the right thing, they had invited the wrong result. After all, they had taken it upon themselves to return the Dream Machine to Earth orbit; in fact, it was their high-mindedness that had precipitated the war. In a rush of maddening despair, she no longer felt they had earned the right to live another moment.

So Alona opened the pressurized, airlock doors, as if she were welcoming death, and two Russians crawled into the bunker fighting for their own lives, both covered with blood. The third Russian had died en route.

The Russians hardly spoke, didn't even have the energy left to be thankful or sorry. The end of these six lives being no different, no better or worse, than the horror that was befalling their brothers and sisters on Earth.

"We were just doing our job," the Russian woman finally said, coughing up blood before losing consciousness.

*   *   *

The five drifted in and out of consciousness for an hour—until Alona realized that she would die alone because she was least injured, and the idea of living with this nauseating stench, in the middle of so much blood, reminded her of the Holocaust.

She was thinking about killing herself when she recalled the stories that her grandmother had told her about the concentration camps—how life, in spite of all its horrors, was still better than death, and how her Grandmother had found a way to survive by thinking ahead, always thinking ahead and believing that there was a future.

It was at that salient moment that Alona looked up at the wall monitor and finally got Suzuki's flashing message: "Dock it! Dock it! Dock it! Dock it!" repeated hundreds of times, following every other furious message from Earth, spelling the end of hope.

With great effort, Alona jostled everyone in the room into consciousness and pointed to the monitor, asking if anyone knew what the repetition meant.

The Russian man knew, the one she had stabbed, who was bleeding to death at her feet. "Infra-red," he said, before losing consciousness again. "Transfer, transfer . . . transfer."

"Align the ports . . . between computers," Sasha added with great difficulty.

Alona placed the Dream Machine on a small workbench in front of the ship's computer, and turned it on—but nothing happened.

"More juice," Bryce listlessly added. "Tie it all in. . . Everything."

Controls at the helm were directly connected to the bunker. In fact, the whole ship could be run from the bunker—which made the tie-in easy for Alona. But succeed as she did, the tie-in had no effect.

"I know. It's the infra-red. Magnify . . . magnify," the Russian woman said with her last dying breath.

Of the five people in the bunker, Alona was the only one who was left alive and conscious, frantically searching for a means or a tool to magnify the infra-red transfer between machines when she saw the laser gun lying on the floor.

With great difficulty, Alona took the gun apart, extracted the lens, and placed it between machines, magnifying the information exchange between computers. Within seconds, the entire ship was transformed into one huge generator, pulsating with so much energy it began to emanate the OM sound and radiate a magnificent white light.

The *Aelita* was on the verge of exploding when it finally connected to Earth, to every computer, every monitor, every length of wire, every piece of conductive material. The surge of energy was so great that it joined every single mind in proximity to the essence of the Dream Machine, illuminating the entire planet in the process.

*   *   *

It was late in the afternoon in Leh. It had been raining all day. The distant sky was filling with rainbows as the clouds finally parted and the rain subsided. Fritz Kreiger was sitting on the hotel patio beneath a ray of sunshine, sipping a cup of chai, looking up at the snow-covered peaks when the change came.

He knew that he would never see Bu again—or Sara, for that matter. He knew the end was near. He had spent all of the night and much of the day in his room, on his knees in prayer, hoping against hope for a reprieve. But, as Yuri said, the die had been cast a long time ago.

Kreiger thought about taking a walk up the side of a mountain, and lying down in the snow and beckoning a quicker end. Than again, missiles might not fall on this little town. Leh might survive a nuclear holocaust; it was so remote.

Now Kreiger thought he owed it to the living to live as long as he could, and to minister to the needy, as he had done in New York following that terrible super storm twelve years ago.

He drew a deep breath and sighed. Tears were falling from his eyes when he heard an odd sound, a rumbling in the distance. He thought it might be an earthquake. Gripping the edge of his chair and preparing for the worst, he felt a slight tremor, then nothing.

He drew another deep breath, looked up at the blue sky and began to pray: "Our Father who art in heaven . . ."

Kreiger was midway through the prayer when he noticed a change in the color of the sky. It seemed bluer, even brighter somehow. He also noted a shimmering, bluish light emanating from the center of a high, white fluffy cloud.

Now he feared that a nuclear weapon had exploded in the region, creating this most unusual and beautiful sky effect. Perhaps the explosion was responsible for an earthquake.

His palms pressed together in supplication to the Almighty, tears were streaming down his cheeks when the rumbling grew louder, and the sky turned even brighter and bluer. Kreiger was at once aghast and mesmerized by the prospect of the sky bursting into flames, now thinking that there had been a volcanic eruption in the North Atlantic after all, and the atmosphere was becoming poisoned with methane gas.

Death seemed a moment away.

"Dear God," he cried out, sinking to his knees as the sky turned incandescent white and the rumbling turned into a guttural roar.

The whole valley began to glow, and the ground beneath his feet began shake; it was as if the entire Earth was preparing to explode when Kreiger's mind was joined to the others.

It was hellish, the mass chaos of billions of minds jammed together into one conscious microdot in the vastness of cyber-space, becoming one mega-mind in the blink of an eye. It was worse than purgatory; it was worse than death.

It was life passing through that terrifying, quantum black hole between planes of existence until it was born again to meet its strange fate in another reality.

Epilogue

Hardly noble, but nonetheless persistent and innovative, the vast bulk of humanity had displayed enough goodness and wisdom and intelligence, and enough compassion at the bitter end, to transit the improbable at the precise critical moment in time.

Against all odds and logic, this enormous conflux of hearts and minds would be joined to another projection of consciousness at the far end of the galaxy, and persist as something else at the other end of the imagination.

And the meek would inherit the Earth . . .

Made in the USA
Charleston, SC
03 March 2012